Who hasn't thought Pride and Prejudice could use more dragons?

Praise for Maria Grace

"This lady does know how to tell a story and how to invent an incredible new world ." **From Pemerley to Milton**

"Maria Grace did a wonderful job spinning a tale that's enjoyable for Austen lovers who do and who don't typically delve into the fantasy genre because she does a great job balancing the dragon world she has created alongside Austen's characters." **Just Jane 1813**

"It's a brilliant world Maria Grace has dreamed up and researched meticulously... based on dragon lore of Britain, Scotland, Ireland, and northern Europe.." **Medative Meanderings**

"I was ... surprised by how well this concept worked. Maria Grace makes the introduction of dragons into Regency life seem seamless, ... It's by turns clandestine and tense, and playfully silly, and I found myself weirdly invested." **The Boot Rat**

Dragons
BEYOND THE PALE

Maria Grace

White Soup Press

Published by: White Soup Press

For information, address
author.MariaGrace@gmail.com

ISBN-13: **978-0-9997984-4-7** (White Soup Press)

Author's Website: RandomBitsofFaascination.com
Email address: Author.MariaGrace@gmail.com

Dedication

For my husband and sons.
You have always believed in me.

1
Chapter

"What will you do?"

Elizabeth shrugged. "The same thing I usually do—think like a dragon and act accordingly.

January 10, 1815, Darcy House, London

"ELIZABETH, ELIZABETH!"

No, please, just a little more sleep.

A heavy, warm hand weighed on her shoulder, shaking her firmly enough to dislodge the fading dream from her head. Botheration! That one seemed worth remembering.

Where was she?

She rubbed her eyes with the back of her hand.

Vaguely warm, rosy streaks of morning sunlight slipped past the drawn burgundy velvet curtains to play across the plush dark leather squabs as the coach rocked and bounced over the road in time with the horses' clip-clop.

Oh, yes, the carriage. They had left the inn at dawn—it must be at least nine o'clock, now. So, they should be in London.

At last.

Darcy had insisted they not push through last night, but rather turn in early and get a solid night's rest before arriving in town. At least as solid a night's rest as one got whilst traveling with an infant, who still was not apt to sleep through the night. And a very young tatzelwurm, who had only recently conquered her extended hatching hunger.

Thank heavens for Nanny, whose need for uninterrupted sleep was far less than her own. Even so, after the last several months in Bath, the dear drake might yet decide to hibernate for six months to catch up on her rest. No one would blame her.

Elizabeth pushed herself upright. Everything smelt of Darcy's sandalwood soap and shaving oil. Of course it did. She had been lying—quite comfortably—with her head in his lap. "How long?"

"Almost since the moment we left." He helped her sit straight.

Stiff neck, shoulders, back, everything, despite the excellent springs and generous squabs. Precisely why Papa detested travel even when his health had permitted it.

Darcy slid the curtains open several inches. She blinked against the morning brightness and shivered.

Even with the sun through the side glass, the coach was a touch cold, especially after having been cuddled up close to him.

The white ironwork fairy dragon 'cage,' mostly covered by its blue quilted cozy, swung gently on the hook opposite the door. April balanced on the swing, twittering. "Perhaps you will now believe us when we insist you have been working too hard." She fluttered out and perched on Elizabeth's knees, scratchy toes piercing the grey-blue wool of her pelisse.

A sunbeam caught the tiny fairy dragon's blue feather-scales just so. She sparkled like a little gem as she presented her chin for a scratch. Her soft hide was still vaguely warm from her hot-brick-heated 'cage.'

"I seem to remember you singing a great deal. Perhaps that might have had something to do with my excessive slumber." Elizabeth yawned into her hands.

"You slept, he did not." April pointed her wing at Darcy. "What does that tell you?"

"She is right," Darcy murmured, stroking April's back with his fingertip.

"There was a very great deal to be done, what with Twelfth Night and trying to take leave of Bath."

"Every dragon there must have called upon you, twice." Darcy's lips pressed into that hard, straight line that was not a frown but might as well be.

"Cornwall did not." All told, that was probably a very good thing.

"Cornwall is quite the exception to the rule. He will always resent the part you played in denying him the gold that Kellynch purloined from the Merchant Royal."

"Thankfully, the rest of the Blue Order Council and even the Brenin himself are satisfied with the outcome of the court proceedings. Cornwall was in violation of so many laws, it could have gone very badly against him." She stretched to dissipate a shudder that would have disturbed April.

Just how narrowly had they averted disaster at that special court? Best not dwell on it just now.

"Not to minimize your outstanding success, my dear, but I hope our stay in London is not nearly so interesting." Darcy shook his head a bit, his dark hair falling just a bit into his face. Now they were back in town, he would need to see his favorite barber soon. The man he saw in Bath had hardly deserved the title of barber.

"On that we shall agree. I hope to apply myself to sleeping late, eating biscuits, and attending teas and parties with the other ladies of my rank."

"There are no other ladies of your rank," April murmured under her breath as she cleaned between her long toes.

While that was only true in part, the isolation it suggested was not pleasant to consider.

"Has there been any word from Nanny's coach?" Elizabeth pulled the curtains fully open and peered through the side glass, catching a glimpse of the black carriage, curtains tightly drawn, following close behind them.

"Not a one."

"Your hatchling seems very happy to travel with the little wyrmling. It is as though her purr is as soporific as my song."

"Junior keeper, if you please." Darcy cleared his

throat and covered his ears lest April's ear nip catch him unawares. He had acquired that habit very soon after coming into April's acquaintance. "I confess, I find it odd that our daughter, not even walking yet, travels with not one, but two companion dragons. You must grant it is very unconventional."

"I am convinced children would come into their hearing sooner if exposed to dragons at an earlier age." Elizabeth harrumphed, her hackles rising. Had they not settled this matter months ago?

"The Order might have a point, though. Children do pose a great risk of exposing the Order, especially if one is not certain whether they can hear or not."

"The Gardiner children have been well-versed in the dangers of exposing the secrets of dragonkind."

"But they are considerably older than Anne, and were identified as hearing before they were regularly exposed to dragons. Rustle avoided their company until it had been established."

Stubborn, vexing man! "Are you suggesting that Anne cannot—"

"I do not question your decisions regarding our daughter. There is no doubt she is as exceptional as her mother. But I fear the ladies of the Order might not be as open to such ideas." He ran his fist along the edge of his jaw.

"They will just have to harden themselves to the idea that they do not know everything—"

"Lady Matlock questions your methods."

Why did he have to bring her up? She was nearly as exasperating as her husband's sister, the honorable Lady Catherine de Bourgh! That name, that family still left her clenching her teeth and biting her tongue. "And what do I care for her opinions? She is not an officer of the Order."

"Some courtesy is required, as her husband is Chancellor of the Order, to whom even you have to answer. Not to mention Cownt Matlock is, technically, her Dragon Mate. And he has done us a great favor by walking Pemberley back to London for us."

"Probably as a means to get out of traveling with the good lady."

"Elizabeth?" His tone stopped just short of rebuke.

Botheration! He was right. Mama had taught her better manners than to even permit such untoward thoughts.

"Forgive me. I am a bit out of temper this morning. Perhaps I am in need of a bit of rest." She closed her eyes and leaned back into the soft squabs. A touch of a headache pulsed just behind her eyes.

So many hours spent reading and writing late into the night. So many dragons to meet. So many questions from Keeper and dragon and Friend alike, all needing answers. Even at the inns they stayed in, all run by members of the Order, minor dragons and their Friends had all but lined up to greet them and seek her advice.

Most of the questions had been simple, even banal: advice for talon rot, bad teeth and scale mites; the management of pucks' hoards; territorial disputes between fairy dragon harems; hunting rights, rights of way. But there were just so many of them.

All the more reason to get those monographs written and distributed into the hands of Dragon Friends as soon as possible.

"You are working again." Darcy tapped her knee

with his fingertips, his voice low and thoughtful.

"Not working, but thinking about all that needs to be done."

"Have you considered my suggestion? Apply to the Order for a secretary to assist you. I know there are several apprentice scribes, human and drake, that Lady Astrid has deemed ready to become journey-men."

"I just prefer to do things myself." She leaned back and sighed. "I suppose I now know why Father fought so long against such help."

April twittered something disagreeable and Darcy muttered a dissenting sound. He knew better than to actually form words—those she could always hear.

"But I shall learn from Papa's stubbornness. After we have recovered from this journey, I will speak to our esteemed Scribe myself."

He offered a warm nod of approval that ended well short of gloating at his success. At least he was not insufferable when he was right.

The coach stopped in the mews behind the Darcy House, near the little walled garden just beyond the terrace house's back door. Shadows still covered near-ly all of the mews' space—the sun only reached there after noon. Still, the private stillness of the familiar carriage house and small courtyard welcomed her.

The driver let down the steps with an echoing, me-tallic clank and opened the door. Crisp air flooded in, carrying with it all the unique London scents: coal smoke, the Thames, a particular mix of dragon musk different to that in the country. In a few days it would all fade into the background, but for now, each breeze would remind her they were in the city now.

Darcy exited first. He preferred to hand her down

himself. Such a dear man.

A dark blur launched from the driver's box toward the roof. Walker.

He would be conducting a sweep of the area, checking for anything that did not meet with his approval. How protective he had become towards Elizabeth, Anne, April and even little Pemberley, and even more so since May had hatched. He and the wyrmling were inexplicably close—an odd pair to be certain, but May adored her curmudgeonly cockatrice uncle. And he tolerated familiarities from her that none other would dare. Who else would dare lick his feather-scales, attempting to groom him?

Such an unusual, and very dear, draconic family they had formed.

She stretched, careful not to dislodge April from her shoulder, adjusting to the intrusive, even overwhelming, sounds of the city. Even so early, how noisy it was. Carriages with horses on the street beyond the mews; peddlers calling out about their wares; a tatzelwurm chasing a rat—and catching it; a puck arguing with it over the catch. Not entirely unlike Bath.

It was home, though, and that made all the difference.

Knee-high minor drakes, Slate and Amber, the Darcy family livery badge emblazoned on green baize vests buttoned across their chests, bounded out to meet them, with toothy draconic smiles. No doubt the housekeeper had fashioned those to help keep them warm in the chill weather. There was a reason Elizabeth liked the woman.

April warbled a greeting, which the drakes returned in kind.

"Lady Sage, Vicontes Pemberley arrived a few hours ago. She is sleeping in her nest in the cellar. I expect she might sleep for a day or more." Amber's deep yellow-orange eyes glittered in the sun; her well-oiled dark-green hide spoke of the excellent care the staff dragons enjoyed. It was good to see that continued without their presence in the house.

"I am not surprised. It is such a long walk for a little dragon."

"Cownt Matlock suggested he might sleep for a week," Slate added with an almost mischievous grin.

Nanny approached from the second carriage. More blue than green in the morning light, Nanny walked on hind feet with Anne cradled in her front legs. She moved like a tall, slender schoolmistress, posture perfect, each step purposeful and sure. May, the little black tatzelwurmling with tufted ears too big for her face, spring-hopped to keep up with Nanny's long strides.

"Mrrrow?" May skidded to a stop, staring at Slate and Amber with startled, wide, golden eyes. They were not the first drakes she had ever seen. Perhaps she had forgotten Elizabeth's reminder they would be present.

Elizabeth stepped close to May, crouching to stroke the back of her neck. "Slate, Amber, may I present our new Friend, May."

The lithe wyrmling stretched out her front paws and touched her chin to the ground. Slate and Amber licked the top of her head with their very long tongues. May looked up at them and licked their cheeks. Not the greeting she had been taught, but it worked. The drakes made a happy little warble in the back of their throats.

Elizabeth stood, knees still stiff and sore. "Show May around the house, then make up a warm basket for her in the nursery."

"The nursery, Lady Sage?" Amber cocked her long head so far it was almost upside down.

"Yes, she is to stay with Junior Keeper as much as possible. Slate, attend Nanny and help her with whatever she needs."

"Yes, Sage." They dipped in a small bow—or was it more of a curtsey?—and hurried off after Nanny.

Darcy followed Nanny into the house with his gaze. "Cats are generally not allowed in nurseries. Do you think…"

"Absolutely. Surely you have noticed, Anne sleeps so much better when May is with her. That alone should convince you! Besides, true cats do not harm babies, much less tatzelwurms–who have far more sense than the typical cat. If that is not sufficient, Nanny will be there watching over them all. I know you trust her."

Yes, there had been an impatient note in her voice, and no, he probably did not deserve it. She kneaded the back of her neck. Would it be wrong to go directly to bed now?

Walker swooped down from the roof and backwinged as his feet touched the ground. "The Matlocks approach."

"So soon? We have been here less than an hour," Darcy all but stammered.

"You cannot imagine your arrival has gone unnoticed. I expect the call is not purely social." Walker raked his talons against the cobblestones. What was he worried about?

Darcy pinched the bridge of his nose and wrinkled his forehead as though hoping to stave off a headache. "Lovely, just lovely."

"And it seems Lady Matlock is with him."

April squawked a discordant note. Elizabeth winced before she could stop herself.

"Do you wish to be home to her?" Darcy muttered through clenched teeth. His Aunt Matlock was too much like his Aunt Catherine for anyone's liking.

"Much as I would defer the honor of her presence, it seems that pleasure would come at a high price. Perhaps we can manage a cup of tea before they arrive?" Elizabeth dragged herself toward the door and certain vexation, April twittering a soft, soothing trill in her ear.

A quarter of an hour later, the housekeeper brought the tea service into the morning room, a lovely, snug room with dark furniture, a round table that could seat six, and bright white walls hung with drawings done by Lady Anne Darcy. The sort of place one wanted to linger and breathe in the fragrance of peace and rest.

Five minutes later, before the tea was even poured, the butler announced the Matlocks' arrival. The earl and his wife swept into the room, wearing their rank like court robes.

He was tall and looked like nothing so much as an older version of his son Richard, though his nose was a mite sharper, more aquiline, and his hazel eyes narrower. She was short and plump and proud; her double chin lifted a mite too high, so her beady dark eyes seemed to be staring down at everyone.

Elizabeth and Darcy rose. April hovered between them.

"Uncle, Aunt, a pleasure to see you this morning." The way Darcy emphasized the final word reminded all that it was too early for a polite morning call.

"Lord Matlock, Lady Matlock." Elizabeth curtsied despite her knees' protest.

"Darcy, Lady Elizabeth. Oh yes, and April, too." Matlock looked straight at Darcy. It did not seem an insult so much as preoccupation. That probably was not a good sign.

Lady Matlock grimaced just a little. She did not approve of Elizabeth having a title in her own right, or so the fairy dragon gossip suggested. A title so newly created would never have the weight of one properly inherited so was hardly worth having at all.

"Pray forgive our call on the heels of your arrival, but there are matters that just cannot wait. I would see you in your study, Darcy." Lord Matlock turned for the doorway.

April squawked softly as Elizabeth bit her tongue. No point in reminding either of them that it might be wise to include her. Whatever the issue, if it concerned her, she would find out, likely straight from the dragon's mouth, as it were. Why was it so difficult to convince the men of the Council that things often went better when she was brought into a concern earlier rather than later?

Vexing, hidebound dominance seekers.

A large, cold void filled the morning room, growing larger by the moment.

"Would you care for some tea, Lady Matlock?" Elizabeth gestured Lady Matlock to a place at the table.

"What kind is it?" April hopped across the table and landed on the edge of a dainty china saucer covered with tiny yellow roses, one intentionally set for her, which looked lovely against her bright turquoise feather-scales.

"Earl Grey." Elizabeth suppressed her smile. April had just recently developed a decided preference for the bergamot-infused beverage. She had refused to try it until she learned it was flavored with a fruit, then suddenly she was quite enamored with it.

"I would like some, with honey." April hopped from one foot to the other. It was entirely possible the tea was simply an excuse to drink honey.

"And you, Lady Matlock?"

Lady Matlock stared at April. Not pleasantly, but in the way one glared at a disobedient child or a clumsy servant. Of course. Dragons at the breakfast table were not covered in etiquette manuals, not even ones published by the Blue Order.

One more monograph she would have to write.

"Ah, well, yes, please." Her face said she was only taking the tea to humor Elizabeth, but at least she was attempting to be polite.

Elizabeth poured the tea, sweetened April's with a shocking amount of honey, and sat down.

Lady Matlock looked at her expectantly. What was she waiting for?

"How is Cownt Matlock after his journey? It was very kind of him to walk Pemberley back to London for us." If she wanted small talk, then it would be about dragons.

"In little humor for conversation. He had no idea how much young creatures talked nor how many questions they asked." Lady Matlock's features softened just a little.

"I had wondered if that would be the case. I did try to warn him, but little Pemberley gets so ill in a cart or carriage, he insisted it would be an indignity for her to be forced into such a conveyance. We are very grateful for his help." At least she could say that with genuine enthusiasm.

"He did say you and Darcy have done well by her. She is showing signs of being an excellent young dragon, which must be considered a good thing, all told. Will you be presenting her at the Dragon Keepers' Cotillion next month?" Lady Matlock sipped her tea, staring over the edge of the cup with an odd look of expectation.

"I think she is still full young for that. She has learned many of the proper greetings and displays when introduced to other dragons. But I do not think she is quite ready for so many people and so many dragons in company at once. Despite all she has learned, she is still a baby. It is one thing to have been forced together with many other dragons in court. It is quite another to try to manage all the trappings of a formal engagement as extensive as the Cotillion. I see no harm in waiting a year, or even two."

"Well, that is some relief."

"I am not sure I take your meaning."

"Perhaps you should see the list of presentations this year." Lady Matlock opened her reticule and pulled out a neatly penned card. "In particular, you may want to note the ladies you are sponsoring for presentation at the ball."

"I am sponsoring? You must be mistaken."

"I think not. This is the official Record and has been sent to all Keepers and other invitees." She tapped a spot at the top of the list. "See here: Dragon Sage, Lady Elizabeth Darcy."

"Mrs. Mary Collins, Keeper to Longbourn, and her husband? Mr. Collins will be presented to the Order? When was this decided?" And why now—but perhaps this was not the company for that question.

"You will have to ask our Historian." Lady Matlock's lip curled just a bit.

"Why is Father not sponsoring them? He is an officer of the Order, even if he has retired as a Keeper."

"He is without title, Lady Elizabeth." Lady Matlock stared directly into her eyes.

"So, he is using that as an excuse to get out of his duties now?" Elizabeth dragged her hand down her face and peered at the list again. "Miss Lydia Bennet? No one has consulted me. Have Auntie and her schoolmistress approved?"

"Another point to discuss with your father."

"Miss Georgiana Darcy? Should not you and Lord Matlock—"

"One would think so." Lady Matlock lifted her eyebrow.

"But why? It makes no sense."

"Pray, may I be frank with you?" Frank? A Lady of the *ton* wanted to be frank? What was one to make of that?

"Pray do."

"I understand you had nothing to do with the dragons' decision to create you as Sage or as Lady Elizabeth; and that there were no machinations on your part when you became betrothed to Darcy in front of the Conclave; and that your relationship with dragons, your knowledge of them is all hard won and comes at a cost. There are many who do not see things that way. Many who are jealous of your rather, ah, as it is called 'fairy tale' story."

"That is absurd. What does that have to do with the Cotillion and sponsoring all my sisters at once?"

"Not just your sisters, but Lady Wentworth as well. She and her husband are to be presented as Keepers to Kellynch."

"This is ridiculous! Impossible! How am I to possibly manage four presentations? Arrange for the dresses, teach them the protocols? There is so much other work to be done. The monographs alone that I need to write will require several months of effort." She clutched the edge of the table.

Lady Matlock leaned forward on her elbows, her eyes sharp and severe. "Work that can wait until after the cotillion. You have been so busy managing dragons, I think you have forgotten there are people in the Order as well."

"They do not require a Sage in order to be understood."

"But they do require a sage to help them to understand how to take their place in Blue Order dragon society. And I do not mean only the debutantes. Perhaps you have not noticed, but not many of the Order have your ease with dragons, and it causes problems. So, if I may be so bold, Lady Sage, pause your salons and your manuscripts and attend to the rest of the Order's members, the human ones, with as much fervor as you have the dragons. I expect your future influence depends on it."

Darcy led the way to his study at the front of the house. That Uncle stalked behind him, not speaking, spoke volumes: the matter was serious, not frivolous; and the information not to be casually trusted to the servants, human and dragon alike.

Simply put, this was bad.

Darcy paused at the study door to savor the image, just for a moment. His father's impressive mahogany desk, flanked by matching bookcases near the door, a pair of leather wingback chairs, dark brown and well-worn, near the fireplace, even the scent of wood smoke and old books, felt like home.

It seemed as though nothing had been touched since he left, just the way he preferred. The blue leatherbound journal on the desk had been left open to the page he had intentionally left it on, the books beside it bore a light film of dust. No doubt the housekeeper hated that, but it was exactly what he preferred. A man's study should not be interfered with.

Uncle Matlock closed the study door firmly, the sound like a throat-clearing introduction to an unpleasant conversation. "Walker should be privy to this discussion." He headed toward the servants' door, opened it and checked the passage.

Things were not simply bad. Apparently, they were very bad.

Darcy opened the window and blew the brass whistle on the watch fob Walker himself had given him so many years ago, the one he could hear from miles away.

"Before I forget," Matlock sat in one of the wing-back chairs near the room's ancient, iron dragon perch. "My wife is talking to yours about the Cotillion. Best you know now. Elizabeth has been assigned to present your sister, both of hers, and Lady Wentworth at the affair."

"Nonsense! Who could have planned such a thing?" Darcy slapped the top edge of the chair. "She is already overburdened. Someone else will have to handle the matter. Aunt can present Georgiana, and her father—"

"I attempted to argue the same thing. But it seems there are those who would be happy to take the Sage down a peg or two by allowing her to falter in her social duties."

"How could you have permitted such a thing? After the affairs of Bath—you know how hard she has worked. How could you sanction—"

"The invitations have been sent. To alter the arrangement now would only be to her detriment. The matters were established whilst I was in Bath, and there was little I could do once we returned. Besides, these affairs are overseen by the Cotillion Board, not the Council. I could hardly interfere."

"So, you support this ill-conceived attempt at—"

Uncle shrugged and flipped his hand, the same way he had dismissed Darcy when he was a boy. "Frankly, there are much more significant matters that require my attention right now. The details of a ball are the least of my worries."

Walker swooped in and landed gracefully on the

wrought-iron perch. He pointed at the empty chair with his wing and squawked.

Darcy obeyed, though he did not relax into the chair.

"Thank you for attending us Walker. It is only right that you understand the full breadth of what is happening."

"Pendragon's Bones! What is going on?" Darcy glanced at Walker.

"What indeed?" Walker hissed, focusing his piercing predator's gaze on Uncle Matlock.

"What I am about to tell you has not even been officially shared with the Council yet. I will be meeting with them directly after I leave here. Best close the window, now that I think of it. We do not need help from the local fairy dragons." Matlock marched to the window, closing it himself.

He did not call for Darcy to do it.

Very, very bad.

Why did he not just come out with it?

Back in his seat, Matlock rubbed his hands along his thighs. "On the basis of bits and pieces of fairy dragon gossip that have been picked up here and there, I took a circuitous route home from Bath, visiting a number of less appealing establishments, and some rather dissolute dragon Friends along the way."

"Associates of William Elliot and Jet by any chance?" Darcy asked.

"He was quite forthcoming with suggestions of those we might be interested in. No honor among that sort, to be sure."

Walker snorted.

"His information led us to several interesting," he cleared his throat to punctuate the word, "places and a few associates of your friend Mr. Wickham." Matlock allowed the name to hang in the air. He had never approved of Wickham and still held a grudge against Father for having favored him.

Walker hissed and flapped. Even after all these years, that sound still raised chill-bumps on the back of Darcy's neck.

"Dragon hearers mostly, but there were a few dragon-deaf amongst them who had been let in on the world of the Order. All are in secure custody now, of course. Some are quite ready to talk in hopes of not being eaten, or worse."

And who could blame them? "What has been learned?"

"We are still sorting that out. I am afraid it may be some time before we can piece it all together. All we are certain of right now is there is indeed an active band of smugglers dedicated to the traffic of dragons, their eggs, and," Uncle gulped, "even their bodies and parts."

"Dragon's fire!" Darcy leapt to his feet and began to pace the length of the narrow room. Anything to shed the electric energy coursing through his limbs.

"I have already sent word to Richard. He and Earl—fine young cockatrice, by the way, Walker, worthy of your line—will be working their way down from the north, looking into the matter. Several others with espionage backgrounds have also been similarly deployed. In the meantime, we must wait."

Walker growled.

"And watch, of course." Matlock nodded at Walker. "It is not a stretch to see how little Pemberley, now that she is far better known than a baby firedrake might otherwise be, thanks to Elizabeth's insistence she be part of every Blue Order activity possible—"

Darcy clenched his fists.

"Save your offense and your arguments. I am not going to fall into a debate of whether or not such risk is warranted. The point is that we know there are those connected to the smugglers who are aware of Pemberley and see her as an attractive target for their efforts."

"Then we should return—"

"Cownt Matlock and I have considered that possibility, but we agree, Darcy House in London is much more defensible than Pemberley, where the extensive grounds are much more difficult to keep watch over."

That seemed more than a suggestion.

"He is right." Walker muttered as he paced sideways along his perch.

"On the Cownt's orders, there will be a cockatrice guard stationed on your roof. They will report directly to Walker. Several of our larger minor drakes will be assigned to your house staff for security inside. I will leave it to you to explain their presence to your wife and staff. Without revealing the true nature of our concerns."

Walker growled. That should have caught Matlock's attention, but he seemed to ignore it.

"I cannot keep secrets from Elizabeth."

"I am not giving you a choice." Matlock leaned forward, elbows on knees and glared. "She has proven herself impulsive and unpredictable—"

"And generally correct—"

"In critical dragon matters, yet. But the situation right now requires a delicate diplomatic hand. That is not her long suit."

"You do not understand. One does not keep secrets from her. She will find out; the dragons will tell her everything. I know you will order them not to, but you do not understand the power my wife has with them. They will tell her. Nothing I say or do will make a difference."

"The Order's members will obey my commands. You will obey me. Both of you."

Walker shrieked softly, enough to raise the hairs on the back of Uncle's neck if the way he rubbed at it was any indication. "Darcy is right. No dragon bent on her protection will fail to inform her of the truth. We are forthright creatures by nature, not deceptive ones. It is not our nature to conceal. Something she knows, and you do not appear to understand." The statement ended with an angry hiss.

Had Walker really just told the Chancellor of the Order that he was refusing a command?

Uncle muttered and grumbled under his breath. "Then it is on your heads to see that she does not interfere with our operations in any way. I did not want to mention this, but we have concerns for baby Anne as well. Apparently, she is as well-known as Pemberley and an equally attractive target—"

"And you did not think it essential to inform her mother of that?"

Matlock avoided Darcy's gaze. "—it is critical that she not leave Darcy House for any reason. We need a better understanding of what we are facing. Nanny will, of course, need to be brought in on our concerns and security measures. An additional drake and cockatrice will be assigned to their protection at all times. And I suggest you avoid admitting any persons into your home who are not vetted members of the Order."

And all this he thought should be accomplished without informing Elizabeth? How had Matlock's judgment become so impaired? "I will inform the butler. The Cotillion then? Will that not be cancelled?"

"No, we cannot afford to do that and give away our hand."

"But the security risk of so many traveling to London?"

"I have taken the liberty of assigning cockatrice patrols to discreetly watch over Georgiana, Mrs. Collins and Miss Bennet's travels here. They are not nearly so well known, nor likely to be of great interest to smugglers. But just in case."

"And Elizabeth?"

Uncle rolled his eyes, closed them and shook his head, sighing. "If you cannot keep her to Darcy House, she should travel via the dragon tunnels at all times, with a guard, never, never alone."

2
Chapter

January 11, 1815, Kellynch-by-the-Sea

THE SUN HUNG midway between dawn and noon, steadfastly refusing to deliver enough warmth to vanquish the prevailing chill. Anne rubbed her gloved hands over the arms of her navy-blue wool pelisse and pulled the heavy basket closer to her chest.

Would she ever become accustomed to the near-constant sea breeze buffeting her every time she visited Kellynch's lair? Probably no sooner than she became accustomed to being addressed as Lady Wentworth—it was still difficult not to look for some dowager lurking in the shadows when she heard the name.

Perhaps Kellynch was right; using the dragon tunnels from the house to the lair would be more comfortable. If only they did not remind her of the dark alley behind the Bath Assembly rooms—and Mr. Elliot.

Thankfully, Wentworth understood and did not insist.

She sucked in cold, salt-tinged air as she looked over her shoulder and across the open—empty—meadow. Mr. Elliot and his cockatrice Friend Jet were safely ensconced in a Blue Order prison. Even if they managed to escape, Kellynch would not tolerate them anywhere near Lyme. With as many friends as Kellynch had made among the local minor dragons, and one other major dragon in the vicinity, Mr. Elliot could not possibly conceal himself anywhere near Lyme.

She smoothed the prickled hair on the back of her neck. An assault to one's person was not easily dismissed, even when one had been rescued by the man she loved. Yes, that was the part of the story she should dwell upon.

"Kellynch? Kellynch?" She stepped into the dim stony lair, dank and smelling of dragon musk. How much warmer it seemed now out of the wind.

"Come in." The space filled with the sound of scales scraping stone. "Have you brought their majesties, my wyrmlings?"

"Of course I have. They would not miss a chance to visit with you." She set the basket on the floor. Corn, the black and white tatzelwurmling with white tufty ears and blue eyes, and Wall with the black nose and green eyes, tumbled onto the dusty limestone floor. They bounded down the tunnel, chirruping with glee as Kellynch's long, toothy grey-green head came into view.

He rumbled something almost like a great purr,

which she felt in her chest more than heard. The wyrmlings pounced on him, licking his face and climbing onto the ridges above his eyes. Not the way one was supposed to greet their laird, but as long as they were all happy with it, what harm could it do?

Who would have ever thought Kellynch could be a happy, easy-going dragon?

"When will you allow them to visit me on their own? I do not get to see them often enough." Kellynch muttered, slithering closer, careful not to dislodge Corn and Wall.

She crouched to scratch the itchy spot between his eyes, just able to make out his pout in the meager light. "They are still small enough to be carried away by the local predatory birds. When they are big enough to no longer be prey, then they can visit whenever you and they wish."

"They could use the tunnels."

"Not until I am certain they will not lose their way. They are still very silly little babies and have occasionally lost their way in the house." She ruffled Corn's ears. Wall nudged her hands with his nose and demanded the same.

Kellynch sighed and snorted.

"Besides, you visit with them in the cellar nearly every day. You cannot be that lonely."

"It is not the same as having them in my lair with me. I have been alone so long—"

She sat tailor-style on the floor beside him, her hand on his scaly snout. "I know you have. In fact, that is what I need to talk to you about. Are you certain about us traveling to London, and you remaining here, alone?"

Kellynch grumbled, his lips working in little waves that rippled along his jaw. "Not really."

Finally, he confessed to the obvious truth. "Then we will inform the Order that we will take the house that boasts a lair with tunnel access to the Thames. That way you will be able to join us easily."

One brow ridge rose. "Wentworth says the house is not as pleasant as the other you were considering."

"It is a little enough thing to part with in the interest of your comfort." She scratched the ridges along his snout as he snuffled appreciative sounds.

"Is it true that I might attend the Cotillion whilst in London? I have never been to the primary Blue Order office."

"Indeed. The official invitation includes dragons with new Keepers. The three of us are expected to be presented at the Cotillion."

Presented by the Dragon Sage. She swallowed hard. Was it a privilege or a punishment to have such a prestigious sponsor? Certainly, the expectations of society upon her would be higher because of it. Father would approve, if he were not banned from all Blue Order society events.

Was Lady Elizabeth trying to mitigate the repercussions of Father's ignominy by her show of support? If only she and not Lady Matlock had written to her to tell her of it, it would be easier to judge what to make of it all.

If only Father had seen fit to have her come out to the Order when she began to hear and allowed her to attend a Keepers' Cotillion as a young woman. At least she would know firsthand what to expect now. If only he had not fallen from Blue Order society in disgrace, she would not be establishing herself while trying to overcome the huge hurdle he had raised before her. Yet more ways in which she was still paying for Father's failures.

Kellynch nudged her with his snout and trained a piercing look upon her. Could he tell what she was thinking or only how she felt about it? Who would have guessed he was such a perceptive creature?

"I should like to see such an event, if it would not be burdensome on you." How polite he was trying to be even though his longing to attend shone clear. He would love the attention and notoriety it would bring him. So like a true Elliot he was.

"I will consider it an honor for you to be there with us."

Kellynch rumbled happily. Corn and Wall purred along with him, though they had little understanding of why. His pleasure was enough to make them happy.

"You will bring their majesties?" He crossed his eyes trying to focus on the wyrmlings perched on his nose.

"Of course, they cannot be left alone."

"Good, good. I shall go out and have a good feed now so I need not worry about fishing rights whilst I am there."

How much had Kellynch changed since that day in court? He seemed like an utterly different dragon to the angry, hibernating, threatening sea serpent he had been.

"That seems a sound plan. I am sure Wentworth will agree. I will take their majesties back to the house now and get them ready for traveling in the morning." She called Corn and Wall back to their basket.

Though they lingered in their goodbyes to Kellynch, they did as they were bid. Someday, when they were grown, they would—hopefully—have the good sense of their sire, Laconia. But for now, they were silly, shatter-brained—if very dear — little creatures.

Despite the wind, she took the long way home. Kellynch-by-the-Sea was so different to Kellynch where she had grown up. How could she not miss the spreading old trees, the farmlands, the fields of sheep? The coast was not without its beauties—and it made Kellynch and Wentworth so very happy—but sometimes it still caught her off guard not to see her mother's gardens, or Lady Russell's.

A dozen, no there were more than that, small and moderate-sized white rent cottages lined the main road from the manor to Lyme Regis. Several more were set back from the road with small lanes or footpaths leading to them. So many people looked to her as the mistress of Kellynch-by-the-Sea. It could be daunting some days, more so than at Kellynch where she was only standing in for the mistress of the manor.

On the whole, the tenants were pleasant and good-humored, many of them dragon Friends who were quite astonished that Kellynch enjoyed the company of the minor dragons on his estate.

Despite all the new friends, Kellynch did not neglect Uppercross. Dragon tunnels linked the two estates, and they exchanged regular visits. Uppercross was developing a taste for fish, which Sister Mary definitely did not approve of—it left his breath quite frightful!

According to Lady Elizabeth's last letter, their whole relationship was very unusual among land dragons. But perhaps not so among marine creatures? She still hoped to visit them soon and learn more about England's only marine wyrm.

"Mrrrrow."

When had Laconia come upon her?

He bumped up against her leg, all three stones worth of fluffy, black tatzelwurm jolting her from her reverie. "Wentworth wonders where you have gotten to."

"I told him I would be checking on Kellynch. Is he very worried?" She glanced past Laconia as a gust of chill air raced down the neat line of cottages.

"He is accustomed to having all his sailors at an easy distance." Laconia glanced over his shoulder and backed up two steps, a very odd movement for a tatzelwurm.

"And I am out of range of his spyglass, I suppose?"

"Come back to the house with me." An odd note of concern tinged his voice as he turned for the manor.

She followed. "Is there something wrong?"

"It is difficult to say. A cockatrice messenger from the Order arrived not very long ago."

Merciful heavens!

Anne increased her pace to a near run; Laconia spring-hopped to keep up.

Anne stopped in the study's doorway and stared at an unfamiliar hawk-sized cockatrice, red-brown and a bit weather-beaten, wearing a small pack embossed with the signet of the Order strapped to his back. He stood on Wentworth's desk, shifting his weight from one foot to the other.

Wentworth did the same as he stood, a mite awkwardly, at the far side of the desk.

He still had not got the room quite arranged to his liking. Long and narrow, he complained there was both too much room and not enough at the same time. Too big to be compact and efficient like the accommodations on his ship, but not spacious enough for the desk that had been shoehorned in and the three leather-covered chairs that seemed to take up the remaining floor space. A bookcase lined the long wall, opposite the windows, lacking both enough books to look scholarly and sufficient bric-a-brac to appear well traveled.

He declared the entire affair felt a bit like a midshipman's effort. At least he judged the desk chair comfortable and that sufficient sunlight streamed through the windows so reading was possible most of the day. That was something.

Someday she would have enough saved to commission a proper suite of office furniture for him. An extravagance he would never purchase himself.

Laconia chirruped and pawed at the doorframe.

Wentworth glanced up and caught Anne's eye with a brief nod. "There now." He opened the messenger's pack and removed a letter bearing the Blue Order Seal.

The cockatrice shook out his compacted featherscales and scratched behind his tiny ear with his talons, leaning back on his dusty serpentine tail for balance.

"Laconia, show our guest to the kitchen for a solid meal whilst I read this and pen a reply. The wyrmlings may accompany you as well." That was not a suggestion, but an order.

Anne placed the basket on the floor. Corn and Wall tumbled out and led the way to the kitchen, spring-hopping with speed only the possibility of a snack could induce. The Blue Order messenger flew low behind them.

Wentworth beckoned her in, and she shut the door behind her. He closed the window that the messenger had probably entered.

"Would it be too optimistic to hope it is merely an announcement of time changes to the Cotillion?" She bit her lip and dodged around the clumsy chairs to join him near the desk.

He cracked the seal. "Considering this is written in cipher, I imagine something less mundane." He yanked open the top drawer and removed a small red leatherbound notebook no larger than the palm of his hand. "The specific cipher was pressed into the wax seal—one that is reserved for only select operatives of the Order."

"So definitely not good news." She perched in the nearest chair, stiff and smelling of leather polish.

He fell into his chair. It groaned, long-suffering. "It will take me some time to sort the message out. Tell me of your visit to Kellynch whilst I work on it."

"I still wonder that he is the same creature who threatened me in the sea cave. Though I suppose I should not be, considering what Lady Elizabeth has told me about dragons who have been wronged. They certainly take their offenses seriously."

"Indeed they do, large and small."

"Dragons or offenses?"

"Both." He snickered softly though his brow drew

low over his eyes.

"If he had his druthers, I think he would take up residence in the cellar under the house. At least he would if only it were a little larger and had a proper soaking pool for him, like his lair does—apparently after all the decades without water, he is unwilling to do without again. But still, he truly hates to be alone. Can you imagine? He complained he had not seen Corn and Wall recently enough. Who would have thought he would be so fond of them? At times I wonder whether they are our Friends or his."

"According to Laconia, they talk of Kellynch constantly, honored by the attention of a true wyrm. Shatter-brained little creatures! I half expect that the Sage will ask you to write a monograph on their relationship." He glanced up from his work.

Oh, the way he looked at her! It would never grow old.

The crests of her cheeks heated.

"I imagine you are going to tell me he has decided to accompany us to London, no?"

"He was rather considerate about it, though. He seemed concerned that the house with the lair might not be as pleasing as the other we had inquired after."

He set down his pencil and fixed her gaze with his own. "And you are all right with the change? You are being presented into Dragon Keeping society by the Sage herself, after all. I expect we will be required to do a great deal of entertaining."

She swallowed hard, her eyes burning just a bit. He was so considerate. "I cannot imagine a house with a dragon lair being any mean accommodation. As to it being unable to accommodate a large party—I think that is rather a good thing. Hosting small events, for now, suits me very well indeed."

"A baronet and his lady need not be seen living as a baronet and his lady?" The corners of his lips turned up just a mite.

"I think being seen as honoring one's dragon is living as a baronet and his family should, do you not?"

"I could not say it better myself." He chuckled, picked up his pencil and began scratching away again.

Perhaps on the journey to London they could talk about what entertaining Blue Order society during the Cotillion season would look like. Wentworth had no experience with such things.

Would he chafe amidst the expectations of "good" society? Would he be accepted among them, or simply viewed a novelty—a Dragon Keeping naval officer who had to be tolerated and humored whilst behind his back talk would fly? How hard did he expect, or even want, to work to be accepted? How important was it to him?

How important was it to her?

His expression slowly crumpled into a deep frown. "It seems the plans you made with Kellynch are fortuitous. Lord Matlock himself requests that Kellynch remain with his Keepers in light of current events."

A cold chill snaked down her spine. "Does he say what current events?"

He scribbled down a few more words. "Apparently, Mr. William Elliot finds his accommodations in prison rather uncomfortable—not gentleman's lodgings, it seems. He has attempted to trade information for some favors toward himself."

She clutched the edge of the desk. "They are not going to release him, are they?"

"No, that would be far too dangerous—for him. Kellynch will never forgive the assault on his Keeper. Not to mention Elliot is far from paying his debts to the Order. I am sure he has only bought himself a softer bed or better rations. In any case, the information suggests there are those, dragon hearers and some dragon-deaf, maybe even some members of the Order itself, who are hostile toward dragons. There are hints of schemes to profit off trading in dragons and—" he gulped, "—their body parts."

"Gracious heavens!" The dragon scale lotion she made from the scales Uppercross happily gave her was one thing, but this? The edges of her vision fuzzed and the room spun slightly. She clutched the arms of the chair.

"At this point, there is no way of knowing the accuracy of Elliot's information. It could have been merely a fiction traded for comfort. But then again, it might not. Matlock insists—and I agree—it must be thoroughly investigated."

"Of course, of course it must. The possibility is too awful to take lightly!" Anne stood, knees shaking almost too hard to hold her up.

"Lord Matlock asks that we alter our travel plans. He has arranged for post horses so we do not need to stop and rest ours. He wants us to visit a list of persons and places of interest along the way to London. If we travel day and night, it will delay our arrival by a day, at most two."

"That does not seem so bad. I am sure it will be hardly noticeable."

"It will be uncomfortable. At best. There will be no sleeping at inns, we will take meals in the carriage, not at proper tables. It is a form of travel to which you are not accustomed."

"I am hardly accustomed to any sort of travel at all. I will make do."

He skirted around the desk and took her hands firmly. "Are you sure?"

"This is what we decided upon when we wed. I admit, I had not expected Order business to come up so soon, or to be so serious, but I will not back down from our commitment." Hopefully he did not notice her fingers trembling.

"Then I will write to him straight away." He pressed her hands to his cheek.

"I will adjust our packing in light of our new plans. Corn and Wall will need plenty of snacks and a few extra bones for teething."

With a soft kiss on his cheek, Anne left to attend to those details she was so very good at arranging. Wentworth sighed and turned to the response he must pen for the Order. Did she have any idea what a wonder she was at —well, anything or anyone she put her mind to manage?

Several hours later, the housekeeper came to the study to announce a visitor—one heretofore unknown to Wentworth. That notwithstanding, the stranger insisted he had been sent to see Sir Frederick. It was still strange to think of himself that way.

All things considered, Wentworth would have sent him away if the man had not insisted on waiting outside, with his two, according to the dragon-hearing housekeeper, rather large Friends.

A man with dragons was probably important. Especially today.

Laconia accompanied him to the gravel drive at the front of the pale brick manor house. Amidst neatly manicured shrubs, a rather imposing man, wearing a dusty greatcoat with two capes across his shoulders, waited beside a large travel coach, making no attempt to be unobtrusive.

The vehicle alone made that impossible. Despite a fresh coat of black paint and the lack of any crest or identifying markings, there was no mistaking the quality of the carriage. Far more than Wentworth could have afforded.

Beneath the man's battered hat, grey-streaked brown hair hung limp past his jaw—no effort to style it at all. Bushy eyebrows shaded his deep-set dark eyes, sharp and glittering like a raven's. He could have used the help of a good valet—at least a week's worth of stubble dusted his jowls.

Two muscular drakes, standing waist high at their shoulders, sat on their haunches to either side of him. Their hides, well cared for under a coating of road dust, were dark brindle, their taloned feet broad, and their fangs imposing. They wore collars of Order-blue with embossed brass Order signets dangling beneath their jaws.

"Sir Frederick Wentworth?" The man asked, doffing his hat and bowing a bit dramatically. He wore a battered brass Order signet on his small finger. Probably real. Few would fake that much wear.

"I am."

Laconia pressed against his leg, fur pouffed and eyes wide, but no amount of display would make him more formidable than the two drakes, who carefully watched the stranger.

"Me name is Alister Salt. The Order sent me and me Friends." He reached into his worn, grey coat and pulled out a surprisingly neat, folded paper bearing the Order's blue wax seal.

"I have not been informed—"

"The arrangements have only just been made." He pointed at the paper.

Wentworth opened the missive. How many letters had he seen in this handwriting since taking Kellynch-by-the-Sea? Regional Undersecretary Peter Wynn—always such a joy to hear from. Best not roll his eyes in front of these strangers.

Thank you for your decision to let this travel coach and hire this driver and his hounds for your journey. My associates and I are sure you will enjoy the increased measure of comfort and safety they provide on your travels.
PW

Interesting.

Unexpected.

Telling. Or perhaps suspicious.

"Will you introduce your Friends?" Wentworth asked.

Alister Salt grinned widely—only missing two teeth— as he looked at the two drakes and scratched behind their pointed ears. "Most people see them as German Boarhounds, don't ya know. May I present Kingsley and Sergeant."

The two drakes, easily twelve or fourteen stones apiece, bowed, dropping their elbows to the ground.

Wentworth held his breath. Dragon introductions

were always tricky, even for minor dragons.

Laconia slither-stepped to the two drakes and sniffed their faces, jaw half-open and long forked tongue flicking. They dropped their hind ends to the ground, allowing him to smell them nose to tail. Twice. When he finished, he stood between them, the rich black fur between his shoulders standing on end, serpentine tail extended full length.

The drakes circled him, moving as a coordinated team, sniffing him nose to tail. They stared at each other over Laconia's head for a moment, conversing in facial expressions and low guttural sounds. Finally, they nodded at each other and dropped their chins to the ground whereupon Laconia licked the tops of their heads.

Odd.

As the larger dragons, they should be showing dominance over Laconia.

Did they recognize Wentworth's rank and impute that to Laconia? Either way, dragons did not relinquish dominance easily. That they conceded to the much smaller Laconia was significant.

Very significant. On the other hand …

No. Dragons, especially the often-communal minor drakes, were not, by their nature, deceptive creatures.

"They will do. The situation is … acceptable." Laconia strode up to Wentworth, proud and puffed as large as he could be. "They smell … their scent is tolerable."

Wentworth exhaled hard. "I am pleased to make your acquaintance, Kingsley and Sergeant." He offered his hand, fingers curled toward himself, for a smell.

The drakes took him at his word, sniffing his hand, his boots, and as much of the rest of his person as they could reach without standing up on hind legs. Rather personal, but not unusual for dragons.

"He will do," the slightly larger, darker Kingsley said in a deep, growly voice typical of drakes.

"We will guard him." Sergeant's tail tip flicked rather like a dog's.

Guard. Not travel with, but guard.

Was that Wynn's plan or Matlock's?

"We are not traveling alone. My wife and two wyrmlings sired by Laconia will be our companions."

"Mr. Wynn warned me of that." Alister Salt muttered, sliding his hands along the brim of his hat, his voice as gruff as either of the drakes'. "Be there some way you can dissuade your missus from going with? It won't be no easy journey as I been told it."

If only he could. "She needs must be in London soon. I expect this was arranged for her comfort."

"Thought as much, but it don't hurt to ask, you know." Alister Salt shrugged. "It be difficult to make a long, fast journey comfortable for ladies, you know."

"Yes, yes I do." Nothing like having one's own sentiments held up before him.

"You should meet the final member of our merry band, then." Salt beckoned him to the well-appointed travel carriage and rapped on the box, just below the driver's seat.

A panel popped open, and a younger, cleaner version of Alister Salt rolled out. He bounced to his feet and bowed. "Good day, sir, me name's Leander Salt."

"My son, relief driver, and all-around right hand.

With him about, you will always have a fresh driver." Alister snugged his hat back on his head as though that settled the matter.

Kingsley and Sergeant pressed in on either side of Leander and leaned into him hard.

"Aye, you brutes. You'll crush me with your antics!" He scratched behind their ears. Both tails wagged hard enough to knock a man off his feet.

"Stop your complainin'. You like it, and you know it." Sergeant pressed in a little harder, grinning toothily.

"You see how you like it when I sit upon you some day!" He pushed the drake back and crouched, laughing. "I 'erd you be Laconia?" He extended his hand to Laconia.

Laconia sniffed his fingers and shrugged. "He will do."

"I'll do, you 'erd that, dad? I'll do!" Leander stood and the drakes laughed with him.

"An astute tatzelwurm if ever I met one." Kingsley seemed amused, letting out a sound neither a bark, a growl nor a chuckle, but a little of each.

The drakes treated Leander like one of their own. What better testament of character could there be?

"Seriously, sir, for all their antics, I got the best damn team to get you here to there and to do it safe as can be done. With them two running beside the carriage, few have ever considered bothering me, and those that did, well, they ain't around to regret it none now." Something in Alister's voice made it clear he was not exaggerating.

For all the dust and scruff that rendered them easy to overlook, this seemed like exactly the sort of crew he wanted on deck beside him.

Perhaps there was more to the adage "The Order cares for its own" than he first believed.

"Excellent. We will leave at dawn tomorrow."

3
Chapter

January 12, 1815 Cheapside, London

Elizabeth's call on the Blue Order Matrons had been an astonishing waste of time. Short-sighted, unreasonable, dominance-seeking women! Easier to face down an angry firedrake with just her cloak and a table to stand on than deal with the likes of them.

A squadron of cockatrix—preening and squabbling and squawking—and even less reasonable!

How surprising it was that the Dragon Sage did not feel up to the task of sponsoring young ladies for the presentation. They each had several young women under their wings. Even Lady Astrid, an officer of the order herself, performed the service without complaint. It might be possible to find another sponsor at this late date, if that is what the Lady Sage truly wanted…

That final statement came with an unspoken threat. One she could not ignore.

Lady Matlock had been right. Ouch.

Elizabeth adjusted the torch in her hand to peer down the dark, damp, and dirty dragon tunnels leading from the Blue Order offices to Cheapside. How considerate of the tunnels to accurately reflect her mood.

Those matrons of the Blue Order reveled in their transparent plot to see her fail in her social duties. Horrible creatures.

But this would not be the first time she had dominated a cockatrix on her own territory. They would not best her. She shook out the folds of her blue cloak, extending them slightly. There was something satisfying about looking 'big.'

No wonder minor dragons were so apt to do it.

If she could manage to mollify quarreling dragons, a gaggle of society matrons would not best her. She kicked a small rock out of her way, its sounds muffled by the soft mud that coated the tunnel floor, which smelled vaguely of the Thames.

Brutus, an imposing minor drake guard who trotted alongside, stopped and looked up at her. He wore a harness with a brass Blue Order signet and an intimidating spiked collar to assist in passing as a large black guard dog. Sharp claws and a frightening bark helped the persuasion tremendously. His record as a personal guard for important personages was unmatched. He had even guarded Princess Charlotte—a major achievement of his career. It was an honor to have him assigned as a guard.

One the matrons did not miss. Or appreciate.

For such an imposing figure, he really was quite

personable, happy to chat about —well, nearly anything that came to mind given the opportunity. The
questions he asked! Was it possible he asked more
questions than Pemberley?

At least he had agreed not to tell Pemberley any
more stories—liberally embellished—of his work for
the Blue Order. She shuddered. No youngster, human
or dragon, should be hearing those.

"Just a little farther, Lady Sage." Brutus paused at
an intersection to look and smell in all directions.

It would not be polite to remark that she knew
precisely where they were and exactly how far she was
from yet another conversation she dreaded.

Papa.

Dear, frail, stubborn, unsympathetic, exasperating
Papa. Heavens, he was very much like the Blue Order
Matrons.

What an unpleasant thought.

He had refused to attend her at Darcy House lest
Mama find he had been there without her. Mama
longed to visit Darcy House, he said, and wondered
loudly when an invitation might be issued and how
she intended to call there if Elizabeth would simply
send around a card noting her 'at home' days.

A task she would tackle as soon as she could be at
home long enough to decide when she would be 'at
home.' Not the sort of thing either Papa or Mama
could understand.

Elizabeth had offered to call at Middle Set House,
as Mama called the townhouse the Order had provided her, Papa, and Kitty to live in since Mary and Mr.
Collins had taken over Longbourn. Situated in the
middle of the street, she thought it a very clever
name.

But Papa refused. He worried she might somehow disrupt the careful balance of his household. While he never came out and said it, he implied that she wreaked chaos with the dragons at any place she visited.

Hidebound, inflexible curmudgeon.

Thankfully, the Gardiners offered their parlor as a sort of neutral ground. They were truly the best sort of warm-bloods.

Warm-bloods? Heavens! Perhaps she had been listening to a few too many dragons recently.

"And here we are. Pray let me through the door first and ensure the way is safe for you." Brutus trotted to the heavy iron-strapped oak door, unlocked it, and shoved it open with his shoulder. Iron hinges groaned like a wounded beast.

She extinguished her torch in a bucket of sand near the door.

"Come, come, Lady Sage, all is well." Brutus ushered her through and up several steps to the street level, walking so close that his side brushed her skirts. He locked the door behind them.

She blinked hard, the sunlight burning her eyes as the alleyway beside Gardiner's warehouse came into focus. Such a shame that the tunnels did not extend all the way to Uncle Gardiner's house, but the expense to dig the additional tunnels was not warranted even by her position.

Brutus pressed against her side and encouraged her to take hold of the handle on his harness. Just for show and utterly unable to restrain Brutus should he need to move suddenly, it served as costuming to assist in the persuasion that he was really just a large, and possibly formidable, dog in the company of his mistress. Other pedestrians gave them a wide berth as they briskly made their way to the mews behind the Gardiner house.

Yes, it was more proper to enter through the front door. But going by way of the mews was far less likely to draw notice—or at least that was Brutus' reasoning.

With carriage houses at the end of the mews and four-story town homes to either side, the effect was snug and shadowed, a little like a dragon lair, with a stripe of sunlight running down the middle.

Children's shrieks and giggles filtered through the narrow way. Was that little Daniel Gardiner's voice among them? Aunt had not mentioned he was still home on school holidays.

"Lizzy! Lizzy!" Children's voices echoed off cobblestone and brick.

Brutus bared his teeth, a soft growl rumbling in his throat.

"Those are the Gardiner children I told you about. There is no need for concern." She laid her hand on Brutus' tense, muscled shoulder.

Her cousins bounded up, full of energy and mischief. Anna and Samuel, the littlest, had lost their babyish faces since their last visit. Joshua, the next, must have grown a full handspan and Daniel, the eldest, looked so like his father now! How could he have become a young man so quickly?

Aunt Gardiner followed, not far behind. She had not changed at all—why was that such a relief? A few curls escaped her stylish mobcap, but that was the only homage she seemed to pay to the energy and activity of her lively family. A fashionable green gown with matching velvet pelisse accented her trim figure and lively steps.

Rustle, the Gardiners' Friend cockatrice, cawed from the rooftop. Like Walker, he was keeping watch over the family. Apparently being related to the Dragon Sage was, at least at present, something of a hazard to one's safety.

Brutus called back to him in something that sounded much like a bark, but was really a form of dragon tongue that, to date, no warm-blood could decipher. One day she would sort that out, too. Eventually.

The children stopped a polite distance from Brutus. Good, they remembered at least something of the proper protocols for meeting minor dragons.

"Aunt Gardiner, children, may I present Brutus. He works for the Blue Order. Brutus, these are my Aunt Gardiner and her children, Daniel, Anna, Joshua with Phoenix on his shoulder, and Samuel."

Brutus bent his front legs in a bow. Aunt and the children bowed and curtsied.

"You work for the Order?" Daniel's eyes grew wide. He was still too young to readily contain his sensibilities. "Would you, can you, tell us about it?"

Brutus looked at Elizabeth and Aunt Gardiner, head cocked, eye ridges inched high on his scaly forehead.

Denying Brutus the opportunity to do what he loved best seemed cruel, and denying the children another dragon acquaintance equally so. "With their mother's permission, you may tell them stories I would deem appropriate for Vicontes Pemberley."

Aunt nodded slowly. "I think they would enjoy that very much. Daniel, take your brothers and sister up to the nursery. Brutus may join you there. I will send up a tray with some nuncheon for all of you."

Elizabeth pressed her lip. It might not be the right time to note that, apparently, she was not the only one who enabled dragon tea parties.

Joshua hung back from the others, Phoenix still on his shoulder. How much the little fairy dragon had grown. Some of his first adult feather-scales were coming in, giving him a ragged adolescent look. "Lizzy?"

"What, dear?"

He scuffed his toes along the cobblestones. "Phoenix has a new trick we want to show you before you go—please?"

Aunt Gardiner sighed as though this was not the first time she had heard this request. "Joshua, you should not bother—"

"I do not mind. Truly. I am never too busy for my cousins and their Friend fairy dragon."

"I knew you would say yes! Nobody likes fairy dragons as well as you!" Joshua's dark eyes twinkled with excitement and mischief. What could he have possibly taught stubborn little Phoenix?

"Go along with Brutus. I will be in shortly." Aunt Gardiner took Elizabeth's arm and headed toward the house.

"Is he very much of a scamp?"

"Joshua or Phoenix?" Aunt Gardiner chuckled as she guided Elizabeth inside through a pair of French doors.

"Both, I suppose."

They stepped into the main parlor that smelt of dried roses with a hint of lavender. Finished in dark wood paneling and sporting older dark oak furniture, upholstered in varying shades of burgundy, all faded with age, it welcomed Elizabeth with a warm embrace. Just as it always did, and hopefully always would. Blocks and tin soldiers lay piled in one corner and an unfinished board game took up most of the small table near the windows.

Aunt paused to straighten the striped pillows on the couch. "For all his attachment to me, Joshua and Phoenix have become as thick as thieves these last few months. Especially since Daniel left for school. You know, it was a week complete before Phoenix would speak to Daniel again after he returned from the autumn term."

"Fairy dragons certainly can hold a large grudge, especially for ones so small."

"Indeed. Phoenix still has not forgiven your father for his attitude toward the species as a whole."

Elizabeth shook her head and rolled her eyes. Precisely why April had not accompanied her on this journey. Her ear-nipping would not assist a difficult conversation. "I am not at all surprised. Papa appreciates them when they are useful to his purposes, which sadly is typically not the case. He is not the only one to hold such a prejudice against them."

"Quite the shame, really. Living with Phoenix has shown us all a very different side to fairy dragons. When you are ready, your father is waiting for you in the study."

"His mood?"

"Not terrible, although he did arrive by sedan chair, which you know leaves him rather out of sorts."

"Has his condition become worse?" That would be the sort of thing he would fail to mention in his very sparse correspondence.

"I would not necessarily say worse so much as he is far more aware of his limitations now than when living at Longbourn."

That hardly boded well.

Aunt gestured toward the doorway, and they proceeded to Uncle's study.

"Thomas! Look who has arrived." Aunt Gardiner swept into the study, a smiling ray of sunshine.

Unlike Papa's study, Uncle's was tidy, sunny and dust-free. Neat books—including all the monographs that Elizabeth had written!—lined the bookcase behind the desk. The family-heirloom, carved dragon perch sat exactly where it always had, near the window and the door to the little closet which was Rustle's own private dragon space.

"Good morning, Lizzy." Papa sat in an overstuffed dark brown chair placed in a sunbeam near Uncle's desk. He did not stand.

That was not surprising, all things considered. Sitting in the sun was usually a sign he felt particularly poorly. His face seemed a little more drawn, and his shoulders more stooped than the last time they met. How long had it been now?

"Good morning, Papa."

Aunt Gardiner backed out and shut the door.

Papa stared at her in that particular way, which had always made her feel judged and found wanting. "I have been meaning to speak to you about that cockatrix Viola."

What had Viola to do with anything? "I see, but—"

"I was not granted enough time with her. I was unable to take down a complete history. Why did you—"

"Her itinerary was entirely under the control of Mrs. Fortin."

"Well, she insisted on rushing back to that sanctuary of hers before I was finished. I am most put out."

Of course, he was. How tempting it was to stand and flare out her cloak, her newest design, particularly well adapted to flaring out and holding that position. But that would hardly impress him. "What do you wish me to do about it?"

"Order her—"

"I do not have that sort of authority! She does not answer to me but to the Blue Order Lord Physician. He is responsible for all Sanctuaries and their caretakers. Speak with him if you want to interview her or her charges. He might even be able to arrange transport for you."

"I have no desire to travel." He shifted uncomfortably in his chair. "Besides, your mother and Kitty should not be left to their own devices."

"That is new, is it not?" New and not good.

Muttering under his breath, he turned his face aside. "The distractions of London are very much to their liking. Her quest to see Kitty well married means a steady presence of strangers at my table and in my drawing room. For reasons I cannot understand, your mother seems drawn to dragon-hearing families. Families whose members cannot seem to recall that half my family are dragon-deaf!"

Perhaps Mama had some residual ability to hear dragons. It would make sense, considering …

"I dare not allow your mother in company unsupervised lest something untoward is said."

"Is not your secretary employed to assist with such things?" A very persuasive minor drake had been assigned to Papa.

"Yes, yes, Drew is helpful, essential even. But I prefer to avoid relying upon him more than necessary."

"So, Mary and Lydia—"

Papa slapped the arms of the chairs hard enough that he winced. "They cannot stay with us. Absolutely not! And do not even suggest I should sponsor them for the Cotillion. It was difficult enough to manage your own Blue Order come out without drawing your mother's attention to it. I cannot be expected to do more than that."

"They are your daughters, as an officer of the Order—"

"They are your sisters. I warned you there would be repercussions to your —choices. This is one of them."

Having sisters had never been her choice! "I have an infant and responsibilities—"

"All in a household of dragon hearers. Even your servants hear dragons." He spat the words as though it were a bad thing.

"As do yours—all provided by the Blue Order. It is your responsibility to —"

"No, absolutely not." He stood, slowly, painfully, and looked down at her. "I am sorry you find it inconvenient."

She rose—when had she become taller than he? "We were months in Bath managing—"

"Perhaps you should have considered that before you accepted your office. What did you think it meant to work for the Order?"

"Why do you think you can push off your responsibilities on me like you always have?"

He edged a step back, brows drawing low over his eyes, and clutched the corner of the desk as if for support. "Very well. If you refuse to sponsor your sisters, then they will simply wait until such a time as I can be certain your mother and Kitty can be sent to stay with Jane and Bingley."

"As they could have already been? I know they were invited to visit the Bingleys for Twelfth Night. You could have easily extended the visit to accommodate the Cotillion."

"I will not have you questioning the way I manage my family, Lizzy." His face turned red as he ground his teeth. "It is your choice. Will you sponsor them or shall I send them back from whence they came?"

No doubt he would do it, too. "And you will offer me no assistance?"

"What do you expect?"

"Nothing. Never mind." She turned on her heel hard and stormed away, allowing the door to slam behind her.

Three steps into the corridor, she stopped and leaned against the wall between two Gardiner ancestor portraits that had hung in those spots since she was a little girl.

Yes, she had been short-tempered and impatient. No, she should not have expected him to understand her situation or to be willing to go out of his way to help her.

But she had hoped, just a little, that he might.

Had he always been this way? Had there not been a time when things between them had been close and warm and happy? It seemed like there had been. And she missed it.

Oh, how she missed it!

Oh, Papa, why could things not be that way again?

"Elizabeth?" Aunt Gardiner peered at her.

When had she arrived?

"I think you know why things can never again be the way they were." Aunt tucked her hand in the crook of Elizabeth's arm and urged her to walk toward the stairs.

Had she spoken those words aloud?

The steps creaked softly under their feet.

"I know it is hard to be reminded of his flaws and foibles. But, for what it is worth, he is not exaggerating about your mother. Come sit with me, and I will tell you." Aunt led Elizabeth to her personal sitting room.

Delicate flowers abounded throughout the small room, in the walls' paper hangings, the upholstery, the curtains. Tiny and tasteful enough not to overwhelm, but enough to give the sense of sitting in a quiet, private garden. Just what she needed.

Elizabeth sat in an overstuffed bergère and pressed a plump green-striped pillow with little tassels on the corners to her chest. "I thought moving to London was going to make things easier for them, with people and events to keep Mama entertained."

"One might say she is too well entertained." Aunt sighed as she eased herself into the corner of the pastel floral couch. "Marrying off Kitty is her prime occupation now. More so than any of us would have imagined. She is frustrated neither you nor your father have used your connections to see Kitty well established in society. You are, after all, 'Lady Elizabeth Darcy' now."

Elizabeth scrubbed her face with her palms. "You suggest I am too hard on Papa?"

"I am in no position to judge that. I only mean to suggest that there may be something quite substantial behind his complaints."

"Did he even try to send Mama and Kitty to the Bingleys'?"

"I do not know, but I think if he did, and they refused him, he would not be apt to own it. Most people do not like to admit to their failures."

"But why would Jane not—"

"How much have you corresponded with Jane since you became the Dragon Sage?" Aunt's eyebrow arched in an expression she often used with the children.

"Not as much as I would have expected. But she has a home of her own to manage, so I expect she is busy."

"Probably, but she is also jealous."

Elizabeth sat a little straighter. "Excuse me? Jane? That cannot be."

"She might not be prone to excessive displays of her feelings, but even I could detect those sentiments in her letters."

"Why? She has a wealthy husband and home of her own. I am sure she will have a child soon enough—"

"Not your daughter, Lizzy, your title. Your mother talks of it constantly, brags on it and extols the excellency of your situation, though she understands nothing of the truth of it. She does it to your father, too. Hints constantly that he, like Sir William Lucas of Meryton, should have been titled as well. I have even heard her suggest it might be because he was too lazy to pursue such things."

"That is brazen even for Mama." Elizabeth

squeezed her eyes shut and pressed the heels of her hands to her eyes.

"I know he is proud of you, do not doubt that. But it is difficult for a man when his offspring—"

"You mean his daughter. He would have had no qualms about a son moving into such a role."

"I wish I could disagree with you. But it does not serve to dwell on such things. Though the dragons, and with them the Blue Order, might have very different notions about the female, I expect it will be quite some time before the rest of human society sees things the same way. Either way, it is difficult for him."

"What am I to do with him?"

Aunt leaned close and laid her hand on Elizabeth's elbow. Warm, strong and soothing. "You could start by forgiving your father for being what and who he is. I know he is maddening and stubborn, but I cannot imagine he will ever change. Holding on to your resentment will not improve matters."

"It would be so much easier if he did not continue to give me new things to resent."

"I know sponsoring both your sisters is a great deal—"

"It is not just them, but Georgiana and Lady Wentworth as well!"

"Surely the Matlocks—"

"Apparently the Dragon Keepers' Cotillion is managed by a cadre of female despots much like Almack's! Somehow they have decreed I should sponsor Georgiana because she is Darcy's sister and Lady Wentworth because she was never properly presented to the Order and her rank demands a titled sponsor."

Aunt frowned and chewed her upper lip. "It seems

you have not made friends among the ladies of the Order."

"Me? What have I done?"

"I imagine being given a title and an office in the Order is among their complaints."

"But Lady Astrid has as well, and I do not see the matrons conspiring against her." Elizabeth shifted in her seat. "They seem to approve of her."

"Have you noticed how she goes out of her way to socialize with those despots, as you call them?"

"I am the Dragon Sage, not the 'Ladies with nothing better to do than manage society' Sage."

Aunt snickered. Thank heavens she still had a sense of humor. "I understand your frustration, truly I do. There are days I find Phoenix's and Rustle's squabbling far easier to manage than the machinations of the local matriarchs. Perhaps we can talk more about navigating those waters once we have survived the Cotillion. With your Uncle's position as an Honored Friend to the Order, we have been invited to attend. Perhaps there is some way in which I might help."

"Yes!" Elizabeth gulped a breath of cool air, her eyes burning just a bit. "Yes please, and thank you. Perhaps, do you think that you might be able to help me manage their gowns—"

"Would it help you to know that in anticipation of the event, your Uncle's warehouse has a ready supply of Order-blue silks and muslins and satin? With ribbons and lace to match. We also have a number of gowns already made up, just in need of tailoring."

"Gowns already made? Truly?"

"Gardiner's warehouse has served the Order in this way for some time. Naturally, I only learned of it rather recently. But it seems your uncle worked with an Order-affiliated modiste on these designs. It is perhaps unconventional, but the nature of the Order Cotillion often makes it difficult for young ladies to arrange for their gowns before they come into town for the event. Order-blue is not a color easily obtained in the countryside. They often hope to have gowns made very quickly. While pre-made gowns do have their limitations, more often than not the debutantes are very pleased."

"Are you certain that is not asking too much of you?"

"Mama! Lizzy!" Joshua burst, breathless, into the parlor, banging the door against the wall behind. "Come, you must see."

"See what? Are your sister and brothers all right?" Aunt Gardiner jumped to her feet.

"Phoenix is ready! He says we must come to the kitchen immediately so that he can show you his trick."

"Him and his trick! When will he give this up?" Aunt Gardiner rolled her eyes.

"What trick?" Elizabeth stood and followed him to the stairs.

"Do not tell her; he wants it to be a surprise." Joshua trotted downstairs.

"He has yet to succeed, despite many attempts. I hope, if he fails in front of you that you will be able to convince him to give up this ridiculous effort," Aunt Gardiner whispered.

Gracious, what was Phoenix up to?

Joshua led them to the tidy kitchen, dominated by a large fireplace. Aunt's cook chopped vegetables at a table near the window overlooking the mews and a scullery maid washed pots in the far corner. That scent, almost too faint to notice? Was there a pigeon pie baking for dinner?

Phoenix hopped on the warm hearth of the fireplace. A low cooking fire glowed within.

"I brought them, just as I promised." Joshua pulled a small, wooden stool up to the fireplace and patted it, glancing at Elizabeth.

Phoenix hopped and fluttered. "You came! You came! I know I can do it this time!"

"Do what?" Elizabeth perched on the stool.

"I can breathe fire!"

The scullery maid snorted.

Elizabeth blinked hard and glanced up at Aunt. "I am sure I misheard you. Breathe fire?"

Aunt Gardiner nodded, none too happily.

Phoenix hopped and flapped hard. "I can! I promise you. I can do it. Pemberley will be so impressed."

"I think this is not a good idea. You should not be so near the fire lest you get burned." Elizabeth reached toward him. There was a knack to swiping up a fairy dragon who did not want to be caught.

"I can do this! Watch!" Phoenix hopped closer to the fire and held his wings wide. His throat expanded like a bright red balloon as he belched far more loudly than a creature his size should have been able to. Turning toward the flames, he hissed through his beak and a jet of flame appeared.

Pendragon's bones! It could not be!

Joshua clapped and laughed. "He did it! He did it! I told you he could!"

"Merciful heavens!" Aunt Gardiner gasped.

Did they really just see—

Brutus dashed through the kitchen and out the

back door, barking and growling, all fangs and fury.

"I fear Brutus is scaring off a delivery boy, excuse me!" Aunt Gardiner ran after him.

"See, see what I have done!" Phoenix trumpeted a funny sound.

Elizabeth held her hand out for Phoenix and lifted him to see eye to eye.

"No other fairy dragon has ever breathed fire! But I can! Just like Pemberley." His chest puffed, and he strutted across her palm.

No, not at all like Pemberley, but now was not the time to mention that. "How did you learn how to do this?"

"About a month ago we were in the carriage house, and he watched the horses eating straw." Joshua stood very close and scratched under Phoenix' chin.

"Foul, nasty stuff." Phoenix clapped his beaky jaws and spat.

"You tried eating straw? That is not for fairy dragons!"

"I know. I told him, too. Made him all sorts of ill and bringing up wind." Joshua giggled.

"Of course it did, fairy dragons are not meant to eat it—I am not sure any dragons are."

"But my wind, it makes fire!" Phoenix clung to her finger and leaned toward the fireplace. "I blew it out near a candle—"

"And nearly singed his face!" Joshua said.

"I discovered I have a part of my mouth that I can close up over my throat. I can hold my wind in—at least a little—until I want to spew it out! I did that today! I can make it work!"

"Clever little fellow! My Friend is the only fire-breathing fairy dragon in the world, Lizzy! I can't believe it." Joshua placed Phoenix on his shoulder.

Dragon's fire, literal dragon's fire! Only those two—

"Neither can I." She dragged her hand across her chin. "You do understand how dangerous this could be, do you not? Fire is not something to be handled lightly. Promise me, both of you, you will not do this trick again apart from your parents or Darcy or me watching over it. You could hurt yourselves badly, or even burn down the house."

"But I need to perfect my technique." Phoenix hiccupped.

"Yes, I know you do. We will figure out a way for you to learn how to do it safely, I promise you. No one will take this from you." Not that anyone could, regardless of what a good idea it would be. "We just cannot have you hurting yourself, or others, with this trick of yours."

"But, Lizzy!" Joshua pouted.

Aunt Gardiner returned. "Brutus is a most effective guard, I must say. I never did manage to catch that delivery boy. I wonder what order we will be missing."

"I am sorry, Brutus is rather single-minded in his assignment." Elizabeth dropped her chin to her chest and sighed. "After what we have seen here, I think, perhaps, Joshua and Phoenix should stay with Darcy and me, under Nanny's supervision, at least until we learn more about this little trick and how to manage it safely."

"No, certainly not. That is far too much trouble with what you have to manage already. I am sure—"

Joshua smiled at Aunt and blinked in a way he

must have thought looked innocent.

"Oh, Joshua." Aunt sighed, shaking her head. "I suppose with all the dragons in residence at Darcy House, he could be kept under better watch there. I will have the housekeeper pack your things."

4
Chapter

January 14, 1815 Darcy House, London

DARCY ENTERED THE attic nursery. Between Nanny, little Anne, May, and now Phoenix and Joshua, the plain, formerly sparse room had sprung to life. Children's furniture and toys—some he remembered from his boyhood— had been freed from storage, dusted and polished until they looked new. The faded striped blue carpet from his nursery days still warmed the wood floor. Fresh white curtains dressed the windows and a child-sized table held books and games. A pair of soft chairs had been purloined from another room to give Nanny and Elizabeth comfortable places to cuddle with Anne and May. It was not the nursery of his childhood. Not that it had been bad, but in all ways the room was better now.

The fireplace adjacent to the windows held a

cheery, crackling fire. Petite, black, and fuzzy, May curled in her generous blanket-lined basket near the fireplace, purring, whilst Phoenix in all his red scale-feathered glory perched on the edge, his wings spread in the warmth, twittering. Darcy yawned. The pair together were truly soporific.

That was probably why Anne did not awaken when he entered. A baby with preternatural hearing was a challenge indeed.

In the far corner, Nanny shared a large chair with Joshua. It should not startle him so to see a drake sitting in a chair like a lady, posture upright and perfect, but it did. She read from *Tales of English Dragons: A Young Dragon's Primer to the Pendragon Accords.* The same book she had been reading to Anne since she was born.

It would probably have been better if May and Phoenix seemed to be listening as well, but no doubt Nanny would ensure they would have their lessons, too. She was nothing if not particularly suited to her unusual mix of charges.

He probably should not be so proud Pemberley had already mastered that volume and was now being tutored by Barwines Chudleigh. The elegant amphithere, her maternal nature in full bloom with her own snakeling in residence, seemed delighted to take Pemberley under her wings, figuratively and literally. The two young dragons had become fast friends.

Pemberley was a very good little dragon.

Thanks to Elizabeth.

She had made all the difference in their lives and had given him the things he treasured most today.

And he would serve the Order faithfully to do whatever it took to protect them.

Joshua pushed away from Nanny and ran to him. "Are we really going to the Blue Order today? Do they really want to see Phoenix?"

"Do you recall what I told you?" Nanny strode up behind him as Phoenix landed on Joshua's shoulder.

Darcy cringed. Did every child-minder sound like his grouchy, old nursery maid?

"You told us many things." Joshua dragged his foot on the carpet.

"Forgive me, Mr. Darcy," Nanny laid her paw on Joshua's unoccupied shoulder. "I am not sure this is a good idea. Both of them are full young for an audience with a major dragon, even one as even-tempered as Castordale."

She was, of course, entirely correct. "The Order has insisted they come. Even the Dragon Sage herself has not the authority to countermand that request."

Joshua swallowed hard.

Good, he had not missed the implication of Darcy's tone.

"You must do your best to greet him properly and demonstrate proper decorum whilst you are there." Nanny squeezed Joshua's shoulder hard enough to make him squeak.

"Yes, Nanny," Joshua and Phoenix chanted, though their sincerity seemed questionable.

Ah, the arrogance of children.

"Come along now." Darcy ushered them out of the nursery.

Thankfully, all of their other guests were still occupied in the morning room. They made it to Darcy's office undisturbed.

Joshua peered up at him as they entered the bright, tidy chamber. Hopefully this very formal, very grown-up room would set the tone for their conversation.

"Sit down. We need to talk." Darcy closed the door behind them.

Phoenix perched on a neat stack of books on the desk while Joshua climbed into the large leather wing chair nearby, his feet not close to reaching the floor. "It will be good to get away from all the silly girls." Forced lightness raised his boyish voice an octave. "Cousin Lydia is still very silly no matter what Auntie says, and Cousin Mary—"

"Stop right now." Darcy slapped the desktop as he sat heavily, his desk chair groaning in protest.

Phoenix hopped backward, off the edge of the books. His wings beat furiously as he tried to regain his footing and his dignity.

"Miss Lydia has used her time with Auntie at the Blue Order school to her advantage. She has become a competent Dragon Friend and a more accomplished young lady." Words Darcy had never thought he would hear himself saying, especially when Lydia still seemed so gay and frivolous. "And Mrs. Collins has risen to the challenge of Dragon Keeping under very unusual circumstances. Elizabeth and I are very proud of her. And as for Georgiana—"

"I like her, she is pretty, and she doesn't chatter and giggle."

He was right, and her Friend Pax was certainly the most well-behaved fairy dragon of Darcy's acquaintance. "You will not criticize those who are more accomplished than yourself. Particularly when there is so much at risk."

"At risk? I do not understand. Phoenix has learned a lovely trick that no fairy dragon has ever done before—even Lizzy and Uncle Bennet say that. He is very special, and I am proud of him." Joshua stroked the back of Phoenix's head as the fairy dragon thrust out his chest and lifted his beaky snout.

"You were not told at first because you are a child—no, do not get that look on your face. You are most certainly not a young man. Your attitudes and behavior brand you nothing more than a child."

Joshua huffed and glowered. Phoenix tried to do the same, but only managed to look silly.

"You may stop posturing now. It only tells me I am correct." If Darcy had ever taken that attitude with Father or Uncle Matlock, he would have been quickly acquainted with Father's cane. "Nonetheless, serious matters are afoot, and I believe it is better for you to be aware of them before we arrive at the Order."

Phoenix cheeped and bobbed from one leg to the other. "What? What? You think they will tell me I cannot show my new ability? I will not be stayed. Think how many I can gather to my harem this way."

It would be years before Phoenix was ready for a harem. Foolish adolescent. "And therein lies the problem."

"I do not understand. What is wrong with a dragon doing what he can do?" Phoenix pouffed his feather-scales and spread his wings. Trying to be big. Silly little flutter-tuft.

"All of us must live under the rule of the Blue Order." Darcy trained his gaze on Joshua. "Your little Friend just declared he would not abide by their decisions. What do you say to that?"

"Other dragons are allowed to use their abilities. Even little Pemberley has breathed fire. It would not be fair to make Phoenix stop."

"You realize, that makes both of you dangerous to the Order. Very dangerous."

Joshua's face lost a little color. "But he is a fairy dragon, and I—according to you—am only a child!"

Phoenix hopped toward Darcy.

One should not laugh at the instinctive games of dominance, even from a fairy dragon.

"I am much stronger than you believe. It is right for the Blue Order to take me—and all fairy dragons—seriously!"

Darcy gritted his teeth and counted to five. Then ten. "Phoenix, you are correct. All dragons should be taken seriously. You must realize, fire is very, very dangerous. To man and to dragons. It is not a parlor trick or a means of attracting mates. It is a very dangerous ability, a weapon even, that in the wrong hands—talons—can cause a very great deal of harm. Cownt Matlock himself has taught Pemberley both how to use her flame and the very strict rules as to when—the very few times—it can be brought to bear."

"But I will only use it—"

Darcy grimaced. These were children, he was trying to reason with children. "Even if you can be trusted to do so, which is still highly questionable, there is the matter of other fairy dragons. If it becomes known that this is possible, how many others—wild fairy dragons, even—will seek to learn how to do it, too? If even a small percentage succeed, how much damage can be wrought? Remember, there is a reason that fairy dragons are not known for their wisdom or discretion."

Phoenix pouffed even larger and chittered, hissing and flapping. Even if cute, anger was still the worst possible response.

"What will the Order do?" Joshua's eyes were very serious.

At least that was a good sign.

Darcy laced his hand together and rested them on the desk. "I do not know. We will begin with a visit to Sir Edward Dressler, the Lord Physician of Dragons, and Keeper of Castordale. They will make an initial determination of whether Phoenix is unique in this ability, or it is something most or at least many other fairy dragons can do."

"What could they possibly do to us?" Phoenix snorted and tossed his head.

And this was why Bennet truly and completely disliked fairy dragons.

"They could order you away to a Blue Order school, like Miss Lydia, with a dragon watcher assigned. Unable to leave or return home without their approval."

"That doesn't sound so bad." Joshua's lip quivered just a little.

"They also have the authority to sever your Friendship and send Phoenix to a Sanctuary for bird-type dragons who need careful management."

"I could go to prison?" Phoenix squawked, eyes huge and afraid. "I will not go. I will not leave my Friends."

"I appreciate your attachment to them, but the Blue Order does have the final say in these matters. Remember, whether or not you like it or approve of it, you are subject to their rules ... and their discipline."

"Castordale will not eat Phoenix, will he?" Joshua's face went completely white, and all of Phoenix's dominance shows deflated.

"No, of that I am certain."

Joshua heaved a sigh of relief as he brought Phoenix in close to his chest.

"That sort of punishment requires a full judicial action, even for a fairy dragon. I am certain you both can be trusted to behave properly so that such an action can be avoided."

"Yes, sir." Both youngsters seemed suitably subdued. Hopefully that would last.

Hopefully.

A blue-liveried footman, tall, somber and silent, greeted them in the front hall of the Blue Order offices. Joshua stared at him, his eyes finally fixing on the Blue Order signet the footman wore on the small finger of his left hand. Joshua glanced back at Darcy's hand, then rubbed his own, probably wishing for as much importance as full members of the Order had. Someday, he would have it, but not today.

The footman—no doubt chaperoning them for Joshua's benefit—guided them up the long marble stairs. Portraits of past Blue Order officers, human and dragon, each with a brass nameplate, lined the staircase, reminding all who passed of the legacy that they had sworn to uphold. Thankfully Joshua and Phoenix showed the appropriate amount of awe and reverence, trying to look everywhere at once as though trying not to miss any detail. Had Elizabeth been as they when she visited the Offices for the first time?

Probably. At ten or was it twelve years old, she had been at odds with the Order over a fairy dragon as well. Pray this misadventure end as well as hers did.

They turned off the staircase at a broad landing that led into a hall wide enough for two men to walk abreast. The windows at either end of the corridor were frosted, allowing in light but not prying eyes. Strategically placed mirrors helped brighten the hallway enough to make out the faint claw marks on the worn limestone tile floors.

They stopped at an ornately carved office door.

"What is that?" Joshua pointed at what looked more like a Pa Snake than an actual snake, curled around a tall rod, carved deep into the door, intricate and finely detailed. The orange agate dragon eyes glistened in the morning sun.

"That is a depiction of the Rod of Asclepius, the staff belonging to Asclepius, the Greek god of healing. It is usually rendered with a regular snake instead of a dragon. Done this way, it is the symbol of the Blue Order Lord Physician of Dragons."

"A surgeon for dragons?"

"No, he is a physician. He oversees the doctors, surgeons, and apothecaries who tend to dragons."

Joshua whistled under this breath. "I never knew there were such men."

"Most of England has no idea of their existence. Secrecy is paramount in the Order." That was a critical lesson—if Joshua and Phoenix did not learn—well, no need to borrow trouble for now.

The footman nodded somberly, opened the door, and announced their arrival.

Sir Edward Dressler stood from behind his desk. Tall and thin, almost gaunt, the top of his head was entirely bald except for a little wisp of hair in the center that swept to the left and blended into the sparse fringe, which ran from one ear to the other. Thick wire-rimmed glasses perched low on his nose—he stared over them as often as not. Every one of his motions was calm and purposeful with an air that there was no crisis he could not manage. The sort of thing man and dragon wanted in a physician.

The room around him reflected the same calm precision. Large frosted windows poured their light into the room, reflected by mirrors on the opposite wall. Books in the three separate bookcases, all in order; Elizabeth's monographs had their own special section. Hopefully, he could keep his pride over that display under good regulation. Two large curiosity cabinets between the bookcases held carefully organized items and artifacts, which Sir Edward could lay hands on at a moment's notice.

The sound of many marching feet echoed from a large opening in the wall behind Sir Edward's large oak desk.

Joshua jumped and looked around. Phoenix hovered near, scanning the room, perhaps checking for an escape route as fairy dragons often did.

"Do not fear, young man, it is only Castordale." Sir Edward walked toward them in precise measured strides.

"I believe Nanny told you to expect that sound." Darcy grumbled and glowered.

Joshua hung his head. Perhaps he was feeling out of his depth. That would be a good thing. A humbling thing. A very needed thing.

A very large, very blue Pa Snake slithered through the opening into the filtered light. Such a remarkable color, almost never found in nature. So blue it was almost unnatural.

Castordale stopped near Sir Edward and reared up

to be the same height as his Keeper. Darcy's arms would not have been able to span around him, had such a gesture not been entirely too intimate an action. At least ten feet of Castordale's tail remained on the ground, making him no less than sixteen feet long. Fangs as long as Darcy's hand protruded from his very snake-like head. They would have been frightening but for the curious and rather sympathetic expression in his glittering, jet-bead eyes.

He tasted the air with his long, forked tongue. Phoenix ducked behind Joshua, who stared slack-jawed. Darcy bowed deeply, from the waist, almost parallel with the floor and held that posture until Castordale flicked his collar with his tongue. Thankfully, he did not keep Darcy waiting.

"I understand this fairy dragon hassss appeared to breathe fire." Castordale's slithery-snakey voice hung heavy in the room.

"That is correct." Phoenix peeked around Joshua's ear.

"Pray, permit me to introduce the Sage's cousin, Master Joshua Gardiner, and his Friend, Phoenix." Darcy signaled the boy to bow. Phoenix landed on his shoulder and covered his head with his wings. Not perfect, but good enough.

"He does not really breathe fire, though." Joshua worried his hands together. "Not like a true firedrake. It is just a trick. He is no danger—"

"We will be the ones to decide if he is a danger or not, son." Sir Edward stared over his glasses and crossed his arms. "Tell me how he came to learn this trick."

"We went to the circus with my parents, you see."

"They brought a young fairy dragon with them to

such a dangeroussss place?"

"Oh no, they did not know he was with us. He hid in the collar of my coat like April in Cousin Lizzy's hood."

"Do not implicate anyone else in your disobedience. You both knew you were going against your parents' wishes." Darcy barely restrained the urge to swat him.

Joshua jumped as though Darcy had. "Yes, sir. At the circus, we saw the fire eaters and watched them breathe fire like dragons!"

"And if a mere warm-blood could manage the feat, I was certain I, a proper dragon, might as well." Phoenix puffed up.

"But we could not figure out what the fire eaters breathed out that burned, so we gave up." Joshua turned to glare at the fairy dragon on his shoulder.

"You might have, but I did not."

"You must believe me. I did not encourage him." Joshua pumped his fists at his side.

"You did dare me to eat straw." Phoenix nipped his ear.

"Not because I thought it would make you belch fire."

"But you still—"

Sir Edward cleared his throat and they all looked at him. "So, am I to understand you ate straw, young Phoenix?"

Castordale wrinkled his nose.

"He dared me to after we watched the horses do it."

"So naturally you did it, too." Castordale snuffed. "Fairy dragons."

Joshua rocked from heel to toe and back. "The hay

gave him a lot of wind. All afternoon and evening. After dinner that night, he breathed wind near a candle, and it caught flame! It was not as though we were trying to make it happen. Truly."

Phoenix hopped into the air and hovered just in front of Joshua. "I have been working on the feat ever since."

"With your encouragement, I imagine?" Sir Edward caught Darcy's gaze and rolled his eyes, frowning.

"Um, ah, well, you see, sir, once a fairy dragon gets an idea in his mind—"

"Who do you think brought me the straw?" Phoenix dove for Joshua's ear, but he covered it too quickly.

Sir Edward clapped his hands and both youngsters focused on him. "And the straw, it is what enables this act? Without it you cannot accomplish it?"

"No. Nothing else I eat makes me bring up wind that burns. I have tried with so many other things." Phoenix landed on Sir Edward's outstretched hand.

"I should like to examine you."

"I do not—"

"It will be in your best interest." Castordale leaned close to Phoenix, his heavy breath almost enough to knock him from his perch. "And I should like to interview the boy privately, while you —" he looked at Darcy, "—go speak with Matlock. He asked that you report to him immediately."

It would have been nice to know that sooner.

"We will send for you when we need you again." Castordale pointed toward the door with his flicking tongue.

Darcy hesitated a moment, bowed from his shoulders and let himself out.

Was this how Bennet had felt when Elizabeth was examined by the Blue Order for membership? Probably not, who could know what that man actually felt? But it was how he would feel when it was Anne's turn.

Assuming this whole affair did not utterly poison the Order for admitting youngsters into their ranks.

Despite Elizabeth's insistence it was a good idea, Joshua Gardiner was the epitome of why it might not be suitable for young people to be introduced to dragons. He was a good lad, to be sure, but headstrong and arrogant as children were. Not old enough to have much sense about him and for that reason easy to manipulate. The wrong influences around him could lead to disaster. Hopefully this whole affair would help Elizabeth to see that before something truly tragic occurred.

Darcy rapped at the Chancellor's door, inlaid with an intricate replica of the Order's crest. The primary officers of the Order needed no name placards at their doors.

The man himself flung it open and urged him inside. The door all but slammed behind him. On the ground floor, on the opposite side of the building from the Lord Physician's office, the dimly lit, large room smelled of limestone and candle tallow. Lined with cabinets and bookshelves, it lacked all the warmth of a proper library. More like a dungeon. The Lord Chancellor's presence seemed to fill the space with an ominous authority, a suffocating presence.

"It is about time, Darcy. I was told you arrived here nearly an hour ago." Matlock settled into his large desk chair behind his imposing desk bearing a painted seal of the Chancellor of the Order on the front. A pair of pewter candlesticks lit a small circle around them. "Is it true about the fairy dragon?"

Darcy pulled a large blue leather wing chair closer to the desk and sat down. "After a fashion."

Matlock raked his hair back. "Lovely. The Order does not need to be distracted by such things when there are far more important issues at hand."

"There has been news?"

"We have reason to believe the suspected trade in dragons is in fact quite real."

"Pendragon's Bones!" Darcy swallowed back the rising bile.

"You will like this even better. It appears there may be some Dragon Friends and previously un-known deaf-speakers involved."

Darcy opened his mouth to speak.

Matlock lifted an open hand. "Moreover, it seems your friend Wickham was squarely in the middle of it all."

"But he was after a dragon to get a land grant to make him a gentleman." Not that such a thing was less repugnant—well, no, it was less awful than trad-ing in dragons themselves.

"No doubt he was, but like many of his ilk, he had connections, and possibly intentions, in many places. There is no telling what else he might have stooped to."

"How many dragons know?" And how could they prevent more from knowing?

"Obviously, the Council knows and those con-nected to our investigations. Beyond that, we are not sure. Richard should arrive shortly with further news from the north and Wentworth from Lyme. Expect that we will be calling upon the Knights of the Order soon, including you and the Sage."

"Why her? This is a human matter. Elizabeth is already in danger—"

"The gossip will be out amongst the dragons as soon as the first fairy dragon or garden wyrm catches word of these matters, if the process has not already begun. You know that as well as I. The Dragon Sage will be necessary in calming agitated dragons and keeping them from taking matters into their own fangs and talons. We need her expertise to keep the major dragons from feeling men are a significant threat, lest they overthrow the Accords and plunge us back into the days of dragon war."

5
Chapter

January 15, 1815 Thames House, London

ANNE GROANED AND stretched most indelicately in a
sliver of evening sun that fell in a single bright stripe
along the center of the mews behind Thames House,
their temporary London home. Save a few very brief
stops to change horses and attend to essentials, this
was the first time she had stopped moving in four
days—or maybe five. It was difficult to tell anymore.

At least she thought that she had stopped moving.
Closing her eyes, odd sensations in her limbs and
head made her question whether it was true. She
opened her eyes and stretched again.

Yes, it was good to no longer be in motion.

The traveling coach, with Kingsley and Sergeant
trotting beside, trundled down to the neat little carriage house at the end of the mews. As delightful as

the plush coach had been, leaving it was far better.

Wentworth had not exaggerated the trials of their journey. Especially regarding visits to some less than savory environs. Thankfully, Kingsley's and Sergeant's special talents had not been required, though in more than one village, she had been glad for their presence.

Whether those stops provided what he had hoped for, he did not say—speaking of such matters where they could be overheard was both foolish and dangerous. Hopefully they could find a measure of privacy soon—away from gossipy fairy dragons and wyrms, where they might discuss oh-so-many things.

Among them, why did the Order find it necessary for Mr. Salt and his crew to continue on with them now they were in London? The convenience of a coach and driver was certainly pleasing, but such a highly trained team and luxurious conveyance seemed an unnecessary expense on the Order. At least the carriage house was included in the lease of the town house, so it would not be a hardship on the Wentworth budget.

Perhaps she watched over that a little too closely. But after living with Father, it was difficult not to. Wentworth, though, did not complain, and it put Kellynch at ease to know the privations of his past were no longer a concern. So perhaps it was not a bad thing.

She turned toward the house. Four stories tall and connected to the dragon tunnels, it resembled Camden Place in many ways, though a mite less pretentious. If it was as pleasing inside as it was outside, Thames House would suit them very well indeed.

A rather large, efficient-looking woman, probably

the housekeeper, hired by the Blue Order, peeked out, flung open the back door, and headed toward them, brisk purpose in her steps.

And so it would begin, Anne's tenure as mistress of yet another house, and her unofficial entrance into proper Dragon Keeping society. How strange and pleasing and busy it all was. Was it wrong to admit she looked forward to mingle in society that she might have something important in common with?

A great number of tasks awaited her: Kellynch's lair to be fitted up to his satisfaction, the house to be set in order, essential entertaining to be planned, and an invitation from the Sage to be prepared for. Best begin immediately.

January 16, 1815 Thames House, London

Anne poured chocolate from an utterly remarkable chocolate pot. Blue, red and green Eastern Dragons encircled the white china vessel with a matching cup held in its delicate trembleuse saucer. No doubt anything consumed from such a piece of art would taste remarkable.

"Are you sure you are up to this, Anne? We only arrived yesterday. You are barely unpacked." Wentworth glanced at her over his newspaper.

The little morning room, painted a friendly pale green and overlooking the street, brimmed with the aromas of hot coffee, chocolate, and fresh Bath buns. A neat sideboard tucked into an awkward corner near the window, leaving just enough room for a round table that might seat six, if none were much larger than Anne. It seemed to suffer from the common morning room malady of being undersized and over-furnished. But somehow that just made it feel homey.

"I hardly think you would refuse an invitation from Lord Matlock because it was inconvenient." She sat next to Wentworth and sipped her chocolate.

Heavenly, simply heavenly. Was that nutmeg and vanilla in the chocolate? And no chile, different to how she was accustomed to it, but so delightful. Hopefully the housekeeper would not insist on keeping the receipt a secret of some sort.

Oh, it was good.

Wentworth, easy in his favorite marine-blue banyan, snorted. "It is an invitation to discuss our presentation, not a summons from the Order."

Anne set her cup down very carefully. "The Dragon Sage will be presenting us at the Dragon Keepers' Cotillion!"

"It is only a ball."

"No, it is not!" She rose and gripped the edge of the table. "It is our formal introduction into Dragon Keeping Society. It is incumbent upon us to remember many in that society outrank us both, and yet will be asked to see us as desirable connections and ignore the very ... unusual ... circumstances of our family. Lady Elizabeth's demonstration of support, approval, and connection to us will smooth the way with other Keepers and allow us to move in Blue Order society." Why did her voice have to break just now? "In the Navy, your rank and connections were sufficient, but that is not the way society—particularly Dragon Keeping society—works. We need this connection and the introductions she can make for us."

Wentworth set aside his paper and laced his still-calloused long fingers in hers, his expression somber.

"I am sorry to be so insensitive."

Dear man. The look in his eyes made it clear, the apology was sincere, but he did not really understand what she was about. He had not been raised in a baronet's house. There was much he had no reason to understand. But he was trying.

What more could she ask? "You will see to Kellynch's request while I am gone?"

He rolled his eyes and chuckled. "I am sure there is some connection to the Order who can be hired to clean out the tunnels between the Thames and the lair below the cellar. I cannot blame him for insisting that he should fit comfortably through the passage and not damage his scales. I took it on good faith when the solicitor said the tunnels were in good repair."

Kellynch had lost a substantial patch of scales and several whiskers attempting to traverse those tunnels last night. "Laconia has been a dear, tending to Kellynch's wounds and keeping him company until he can get to his lair. We must see that your Friend has his fill of cream and cod when Kellynch no longer needs his attentions. At least Kellynch did not take offense and throw a fit. That is an improvement, is it not?"

"He is in remarkable good humor, all things considered. Are you sure you want to bring Corn and Wall with you? They are such silly wyrmlings. Kellynch always appreciates their presence even more than Laconia's."

"They were included in the Sage's invitation."

"Why?"

"I have no idea. But she is the Sage, so I see no point in arguing."

Kingsley trotted beside the coach on the way to Darcy House, all the other traffic giving them a wide berth. Sergeant rode inside with her. The street, they said, was not wide enough for both drakes to run alongside the coach.

Corn and Wall, who had tumbled free of their basket almost as soon as the coach door was shut, found him fascinating, sniffing him nose to tail and crawling all over him, purring and mewling. Patient, patient drake. For all his fierce looks, he seemed amused by them, though all the while never allowing his gaze to leave the side glass.

The coach stopped in front of an elegant town home in the middle of the street: Darcy House. So much grander than Thames House.

Good. She would not be expected to emulate the Darcys' level of entertaining in her much more modest home. Strange relief that was.

She gathered the wyrmlings into their large basket. Alister Salt handed her down and helped her settle the weighty basket on her arm. Sergeant accompanied her to knock on the door with the brass drake's-head knocker whilst Kingsley stood on the street, near the coach.

A somber butler greeted her, but hesitated when he saw Sergeant.

"Been ordered to see the Lady Wentworth is not left unprotected." Sergeant stretched out his front legs in a sort of bow.

"Pray, wait a moment." The door closed.

Odd, a bit insulting even. It was not as though she

were showing up for a morning call and the lady of the house needed to decide if she were "in" or not. She had been invited by Lady Elizabeth.

Then again maybe not. If there were dragons in the house—not if, this was the Dragon Sage's home, of course there were dragons—territory, dominance and proper greeting protocols would all be significant. It would not do to have unfamiliar dragons encountering one another unexpectedly.

That was the sort of thing Anne needed to keep in mind. It would probably be the norm when associating more with Blue Order society.

The door swung open revealing Lady Elizabeth, a toothy black guard drake, wearing a spiked collar, at her side. Larger and more muscular than even Kingsley, he was not a dragon to be meddled with.

"Brutus." Sergeant extended his forelegs and lowered his head. The larger drake tapped the back of Sergeant's head with his snout.

"You know one another?" Lady Elizabeth's eyebrows rose high.

The Dragon Sage did not know everything? Was that comforting or unsettling?

Brutus glanced over Sergeant's shoulder, scanning the street behind them. "Him and Kingsley, the other drake on his team. Is Alister Salt with you?"

"And now his son has joined us, too." The tip of Sergeant's tail flicked.

Brutus rumbled something that sounded vaguely like approval.

"Then I suppose there will be no issues." Lady Elizabeth backed away from the door to admit them inside. "Brutus, will you introduce Sergeant and Kingsley to Walker and the rest of the household?"

"Yes, Lady. Come." Brutus led Sergeant off.

Anne's basket mewled. "Oh, gracious! Should I have brought out the wyrmlings for an introduction too?"

"Do not worry. The babies are too young to be expected to make proper greetings. May is quite excited for their visit. Pray come with me." Lady Elizabeth led the way to a grand marble staircase with tasteful wrought-iron railings. Odd that she was doing the service herself, rather than relegating it to a servant, but perhaps that was because of the dragons, too.

Her bearing was confident, but somehow not proud. Her gown very fine, but not the sort that made one feel the difference in one's station. She was welcoming and proper, but not familiar in an uncomfortable sort of way.

For being home to those with such a significant role in the Blue Order, Darcy House did not scream out 'dragons' the way it might. Since her own installation at Kellynch-by-the-Sea, Anne had been approached by many Blue Order artisans pushing their subtle and not-so-subtle wares. Everything from china settings with draconic images like the chocolate set she had drunk from this morning, to casegoods with drawer fronts and side panels inlaid with dragons of every sort, to yards and yards of fabrics from simple Order-blue to those bearing full-out dragon depictions.

Apparently dressing one's house with dragons was a popular choice among those in the Order, though it seemed utterly at odds with the all-important need for secrecy.

The only obvious draconic influence in Darcy House were the dragons themselves. And there did seem to be plenty of them. A pair of drakes with livery badges zipped up the wide marble stairs beside them, bearing trays of dainties. Two maids followed with a full service for tea. A dark red, almost maroon, puck trotted behind the maids, with a feather duster in her mouth. Few would tolerate servants so much in the way of the family, but it did not seem to draw notice from Lady Elizabeth. More draconic influence?

They turned off at the large first-floor landing. Halfway down the spacious wood-paneled corridor, several colorful fairy dragons zipped back and forth, chittering too quickly to decipher what they were saying, but it seemed like they were excited to have spotted Anne's arrival.

Including Corn and Wall in her basket, she had seen more than ten dragons in as many minutes. And that did not even include Nanny, little Pemberley and baby May, whom she had previously met! Gracious! Surely no other house in all of England could possibly have so great a draconic presence.

No wonder Lady Elizabeth saw no need to decorate with draconic images!

Cheery ladies' voices filtered from an open door on the street side of the corridor. Lady Elizabeth urged her inside the large plum and gold parlor where the maids and drakes were setting up for tea.

Three ladies, all appearing younger than herself, sat on dark pink upholstered chairs and a sofa, backlit by a large window, hung with very sheer white curtains no doubt to block the view from the street. A stern-looking blue-green minor drake, lean and leggy, sat on a wooden chair behind a young woman who favored Lady Elizabeth. The drake looked exactly like a strict governess.

Bookcases, filled with books, mostly bound in Order-blue, lined the wall opposite the fireplace. Painted landscapes, probably of Pemberley, and two elegant ebony bombe chests populated the wall opposite the windows. It was difficult not to wonder what a Dragon Sage might store there.

April, Lady Elizabeth's Friend, perched on a low gold-painted table between the chairs, with three more fairy dragons hovering near: one pink, one white, and a tiny black and red one. A fluffy black tatzelwurmling, May, sat back on her tail, her front thumbed paws on the table, watching the fairy dragons flitter.

How had Lady Elizabeth taught her so much control that she did not try and pounce on the fairy dragons? Surely Corn and Wall would not be so well behaved.

"Lady Wentworth, may I present my sisters, Mrs. Collins, Miss Darcy, and Miss Bennet."

Mrs. Collins seemed the anthesis of Anne's elder sister: proper, demure, with little desire to draw attention to herself. Everything about her seemed sensible, a little plain, and maybe a touch severe, except for the fluffy, pink fairy dragon who flitted to her shoulder. Probably a woman with whom Anne would have much in common.

Miss Darcy looked like Mr. Darcy in the best ways possible. Her smile was sweet, her eyes sparkling, and she looked adoringly at the brilliant white fairy dragon perched on her knee, almost blending into the white muslin of her gown.

Miss Bennet seemed very different. She resembled Lady Elizabeth, in a round, soft, youthful sort of way. All fun, frivolity, and gaiety, but perhaps little sense—

that of course remained to be seen—with a tiny black and red fairy dragon chittering from her shoulder to the somber drake behind them.

"Auntie, my sister's companion, sits behind them. You have already met April. Heather is Mrs. Collins' pink Friend, Pax quite relies upon Miss Darcy, and I should warn you of Cosette's temper. She quite resembles her brood mother, April, in temperament."

Cosette zipped toward Lady Elizabeth, but little blue April cut her off mid-flight, scolding.

Anne's basket mrowwwed. She opened the lid and two black and white furry faces appeared over the edge.

"May I introduce Corn, with the white ears and blue eyes, and Wall with the black nose and green eyes. And before you ask, Kellynch, their laird, decided upon their names."

Miss Bennet giggled.

"May, come and meet your nestmates." Lady Elizabeth crouched to beckon the wyrmlings.

Corn and Wall tumbled out of their basket and met May in the middle of the room, near the tea table. They wound around each other, sniffing and purring and mewling. A Gordian Knot of tatzelwurms.

"They are so dear!" Miss Darcy clasped her hands near her chest. "Do you think they will try and chase Pax though? May has tried a few times, and it upsets her so."

"I expect they will keep each other quite entertained." Lady Elizabeth fixed her eyes on the wyrmlings, a warning note in her voice.

All three mewed and bobbed their heads. No doubt they would obey, as long as they remembered that was what they were to do.

Lady Elizabeth gestured toward an overstuffed chair covered in pale pink roses and took a seat across the tea table from her sisters.

"You must help her learn not to be so ridiculously sensitive," April chided, landing on the tea table near Miss Darcy. "Pax is a fairy dragon, and it is fair to say that something will always be chasing us."

"Stay with me. I will protect you!" A brilliant red fairy dragon zoomed in and landed on the table near April.

"Lady Wentworth, this is Phoenix, Heather's nestmate, who is staying with us for a little while."

Phoenix puffed his chest and strutted, his bold red crest of scale-feathers flared to make him several inches taller. A male fairy dragon! So that was what the little blokes looked like!

April pounced and pecked the top of his head. "Enough of your parading. We are not your harem. You are not dominant here. I would thank you to remember that."

Cosette dove in and pecked at him. "Yes, remember that."

Phoenix squawked and zipped out; his ego probably as bruised as his head. Poor little mite.

"Pray forgive him. Male fairy dragons can be a bit, well, full of themselves, especially with so many females about. I will have another word with him." Lady Elizabeth extended her hand for April to perch on it and scratched her under her chin. April flitted to her shoulder, and Lady Elizabeth began to serve tea.

"I understand you are lately married, Lady Wentworth." Mrs. Collins took a small plate and added a small cheese sandwich and several biscuits.

"Yes, just this last November."

"And you became Keeper to Kellynch as well?"

Lady Elizabeth passed Anne a cup of tea.

"My husband and I did. Kellynch insisted he should have two Keepers. Lady Elizabeth is sponsoring our presentation as Keepers at the Dragon Keepers' Cotillion."

"She is sponsoring mine as well."

"Oh, you are Keeper to Longbourn! Forgive me for not remembering that immediately. I am still sorting out all the Keepers, estates and dragons." Hopefully she would not be the kind to take offense.

Mrs. Collins nodded, glancing at Lady Elizabeth, a little ill-ease in her look. "Yes. My husband is dragon-deaf, but the heir to the estate. He was accidentally made a deaf-speaker. Just recently, he was deemed acceptable to the Order. We will be presented at the Ball as well, though he is still at Longbourn for the moment."

A female Keeper, with a deaf-speaker husband? What did one say to such a statement? There could be no protocol for such a thing, could there?

"Lizzy is sponsoring us, too." Miss Bennet bounced on her seat. "Miss Darcy and I are coming out at the ball! I never expected I would have a ball at my come out. I am so excited I hardly have words. I must have a gown that matches Cosette. She is the prettiest little thing, is she not?"

Cosette landed on Miss Bennet's outstretched hand, warbling loudly, and a bit off key.

"I am sponsoring all of you to the Order at the Cotillion. But as to your gown, no, it will not match Cosette. The Cotillion Board—" Something in the way Lady Elizabeth said that, she did not like them, or did not approve, it was difficult to say. "—have decreed that all debutantes must wear gowns of Order-blue as has been the tradition of the Order since the first Keepers' Cotillion."

"But that is not fair!"

"I see it no different to the rules of presentation to the King. And those court gowns are utterly useless for anything else. At least these we will be able to wear at other events." Tellingly, Mrs. Collins did not look at Miss Bennet.

It seemed she and Anne had a great deal in common.

"Order-blue is a lovely color and will look so good on you, Miss Bennet." Miss Darcy cringed a little as she spoke.

"Not as pretty as red, or a lovely white gown." Miss Lydia harumphed.

Auntie grumbled under her breath.

Miss Bennet's face fell just a mite. "I suppose blue will do."

Lady Elizabeth nodded at Auntie, a tiny smile playing at her lips. "Tradition decrees that there is quite a bit of preparation to be done for the Keepers' Cotillion. Unfortunately, there are not enough hours in the day for me to be able to dress and tutor each of you individually. I wish I could, but I simply cannot."

Miss Bennet gasped and Miss Darcy looked crushed. Hopefully her own aching heart and held breath were less obvious.

"Lizzy, you promised!"

Lady Elizabeth raised an open hand. How could a woman so elegant and put together look so haggard? The unruly dragons did not seem to tax her so much as her sisters. "That is not to say I will not help you, or that you will be left unprepared, only that we will have to accomplish this rather less conventionally and more efficiently than we might otherwise have expected."

"Is there anything I might do to help?" As the eldest of those presented, it did seem the appropriate thing to say, despite having no idea what she might bring to bear. At least she could breathe again.

"I was hoping you might be of a mind to do something like that. Perhaps you and Mrs. Collins might be in charge of seeing that all of you learn the greeting protocols? I have no way of knowing which of the major dragons will be there. There are over four hundred major dragons in England alone, and it is possible that some Irish or Scottish dragons might attend as well."

"Four hundred major dragons at the Cotillion?" Miss Darcy turned as white as her gown.

"Oh, heavens no! It would not be possible. I do not think that many large dragons could tolerate the proximity of one another!" Lady Elizabeth laughed. "But with new Keepers presented, I expect there will be more than usual. The debutantes and new Keepers will be presented to Dragon Mates and expected to greet them, dragon and human. I wish I could say we will have a list of who will attend, but even if we did, dragons can be capricious. We will not be certain until the event itself. So, you will have to be prepared, knowing all the greetings and all the Dragon Mate pairs."

"How will they all fit in the courtroom?" Mrs. Collins' eyebrows knit as though she were trying to work out the puzzle herself.

"There is a protocol to the greeting line. The dragons will enter by rank and line the edges of the room with sufficient space between them to prevent—ah—misunderstandings. The debutantes will begin at the highest ranked dragon and proceed around the room. When each dragon has been greeted by all the debutantes, he or she will retire and another dragon will take their place, until all dragons have been greeted."

"Merciful heavens!" Miss Darcy fell back against the back of her seat.

"I fear that is not all. There will be minor dragons present with their Friends to whom you will be introduced, as well. Though those greetings are less formal and will happen throughout the evening as the minor dragons are apt to stay for the entire affair."

"How will we ever learn it all?" Miss Darcy whispered.

"That is why I recommend you study together. Lady Wentworth and Mrs. Collins will be able to co-ordinate your efforts. Together with Auntie and Nanny to assist as necessary, I am certain you will be able to help each other to manage the task. I will of course be ready to answer your questions and to test you on your learning so that you will be confident in your readiness."

Mrs. Collins caught Anne's gaze with a cocked eyebrow. Anne nodded slowly.

"Pray tell me there will be dancing at the ball as well. It sounds as though all we will do is curtsey to dragons." Lydia rolled her eyes.

"There will be dancing, to be sure. The ball always begins with a traditional minuet, which you must learn. "

"A minuet!" Miss Bennet's lip curled back. "But that is so old-fashioned. No one begins a ball with a minuet anymore."

"The Blue Order always has and probably always will. Mr. Darcy and I will bring in a dance master to teach you. It has been so long since I did my own minuet, I cannot be certain that I even remember it properly at this point."

"We are to have a dancing master! I have never had a proper dancing master!" Lydia squealed and bounced. "He will teach us more than a minuet, will he not?"

"I hope you will thank me when you have finished your tutelage with him. He is said to be rather exacting. But as some will be apt to judge you on your dance steps, as is the case in any society, we want to make sure you are well taught."

"You are doing so much for us, Lady Elizabeth," Anne said, "I do not know how to thank—"

"But what shall we wear?" Miss Bennet planted her chin on her fist, pouting.

Lady Elizabeth gritted her teeth and said nothing, probably counting to ten. "Aunt Gardiner will be arriving in just a few minutes to assist us with that point. In fact, I think I hear them now." Lady Elizabeth opened the door. "Yes, yes, your timing is excellent, Aunt, do come in."

A pretty, trim matron in an excellently made forest-green striped walking gown entered with three sturdy men carrying trunks and boxes. "Pray put them there, near the bookcase."

The men grunted and obeyed.

April and Pax softly sang, "Such pretty cats and little birds in this room and dogs in the hall. Lady Elizabeth has such a fondness for her many pets."

Each of the men patted the wyrmlings on their heads; two of them looked like they wondered why they were doing so.

"Go down to the kitchen when you have finished. Cook will provide refreshment for you." Lady Elizabeth waved the men toward the door.

Several minutes later, they returned with more boxes, several bolts of Order-blue trims and a dressing screen they set up near the fireplace.

"Lady Wentworth, may I present my aunt, Mrs. Gardiner?"

Anne stood and curtsied. "Pleased to make your acquaintance."

"As am I." Mrs. Gardiner curtsied in return, poise and grace in her every motion.

"Lizzy said you would help us with our gowns?" Miss Bennet jumped to her feet.

"Gardiner's warehouse has been working with the Order for years to provide garments for the Dragon Keepers' Cotillion. Many times, gowns are needed on very short notice."

Was it wrong to believe dragons seemed averse to planning?

"So, we have taken to having gowns cut and made up in preparation for the ball, so they only need to be tailored and trimmed for each debutante. Some still prefer entirely bespoke designs, but many prefer the ease our approach offers."

"What an excellent idea." Mrs. Collins glanced back at Miss Darcy and Miss Bennet, who looked just a little crestfallen.

"I agree entirely." Anne said. "Have you brought some of the gowns with you?"

Lady Elizabeth nodded and smiled at Anne as though relieved to find an ally.

"Indeed, I have. Pray help me unpack them." Mrs.

Gardiner gestured at the trunk next to her and several boxes on the floor nearby.

All the ladies set to work and soon nearly a dozen gowns were laid out on the couch and the settee, and hung from the dressing screen and the top shelves of the bookcase for viewing. Mrs. Gardiner pulled several chairs close and laid out ribbons and laces, silk flowers and bows until the room resembled a linen-draper's and modiste's shop made into one.

Each gown was different and cleverly designed to be easily modified to fit a range of figures and tastes. The fabrics were all of excellent quality. Granted, they were rather plain, without trims, but it was easy to imagine how different lace and ribbons would enhance the gowns.

"Please, look through them. I see Lizzy—ah, Lady Elizabeth—has already had a mirror brought in. You might try on whatever you like. Several of our seamstresses will be here in an hour or so and can begin the fitting process."

Miss Bennet squealed and dragged Miss Darcy up by the hand. "This one, this one! It is perfect for you." She dove for a particular gown draped in layers of gauzy Order-blue muslin.

Despite her effusive enthusiasm, Miss Lydia was correct. It would suit Miss Darcy very well.

Mrs. Collins wandered toward a demure gown, with slightly longer sleeves, a modest neckline, and several rows of ruffles along the edge of the skirt. She bit her lip.

Lady Elizabeth approached, nodding. "I thought of you specifically when I saw that one."

"It is lovely, but the estate is still paying back Longbourn for all those years of salt that were not offered him. I do not think … perhaps this is not the year to do this."

"Mary, do not worry. Please, I want you to have this and any trim that you like for it. When I had my Cotillion, Papa found me a second-hand gown which neither fit properly, nor did I like very well at all. Uncle offered to make it better, but Papa—you can imagine. I do not want you to have the same experience. You should have something that you like, that makes you feel like a proper part of the Order."

Anne was probably not meant to overhear that exchange. How lovely to have such a caring sister. It was good that someone did.

"But I cannot …"

"Darcy has already set aside the funds for each of you. I know your taste. I do not have to worry about you exceeding my budget. Lydia, I may need to have words with. But not you."

"If you are certain." Mrs. Collins blinked back the brightness in her eyes. "I would like that very much."

The door burst open. "Lizzy, Lizzy!" A little boy dashed in, hair frazzled and shirt half untucked. "Lizzy!"

"Joshua Gardiner, where are your manners!" Mrs. Gardiner trotted across the room to the boy who resembled her greatly.

"I need Lizzy. It's Phoenix. He flew off in a huff and went to the kitchen. Now the warehouse men are there, and he is hiding from them. You know he does not like them. He likes to hide behind a loose stone he found in the fireplace, but I am afraid he will get too hot there and the heat will make him sick. Pray help me get him out."

"Silly little creature! Forgive me, I will return in a

moment." Lady Elizabeth sighed and followed the boy out.

"Joshua and that fairy dragon have been inseparable since my eldest left home for school. They are alarmingly similar youngsters." Mrs. Gardiner shrugged with more good humor than Anne's sister Mary ever had about the antics of her own boys. "Mary, dear, what do you think of these trims?" She picked up some gauzy lace and two different widths of ribbon embroidered with little beaded fairy dragons and held them against the dress Mrs. Collins had been admiring.

"They are exquisite."

"Get me my pins, there in the small box. Let me show you what I have in mind." Mrs. Gardiner trimmed the sleeves, the neck and waist of the gown.

Gracious, what a difference it made! The once-plain gown became absolutely memorable. The woman was truly talented!

"Why not try this one on now, Mary?"

"I would like it very—"

A piercing cockatrice shriek filled the air, sending chills down Anne's back and a sense of dread permeating her bones. Her knees melted, and she grabbed the nearest chair for support. Feet—taloned feet—pounded up the staircase and thundered toward them. Kingsley and Sergeant burst in, with two formidable black cockatrice winging in behind them, all wearing Order insignia.

"Stay here, do not leave this room. Lady Elizabeth and the boy have been taken."

6
Chapter

January 16, 1815 London Order Offices

WENTWORTH SAT AT a wide stone-topped table beside Kellynch and across from Sir Carew Arnold, Minister of Keeps. The office, near the Blue Order courtroom on the lowest level of the Order offices, smelt of stone and burning torches. Their flickering light only added to the sense of a cold, dank medieval dungeon that lingering at the edges of his awareness. Happily, no iron chains hung from the walls lest he be entirely unable to escape the image.

Laconia sat on the edge of the limestone tabletop, black tufted ears pricked, curled and ready to spring. Kellynch had asked for his attendance, in support as it were. Despite Laconia's dislike for crowds and unfamiliar major dragons, he stood by his laird, just as a good officer did his captain.

Langham, Sir Carew's wyvern Dragon Mate, sat—no, not exactly sat, more like crouched on her two legs—how did one describe that posture?— beside her Keeper. Despite being one of the lower-ranking Blue Order officers, he enjoyed one of the largest offices, not because of prestige, but practicality. Significant space was required when one brought dragons to the table for discussion. It also explained why he was hidden away in the lowest basement—getting major dragons into the above ground levels, except perhaps for snake and wyrm-types, was hardly feasible.

Despite Sir Carew's slow steps, hunched shoulders, and thin grey hair in something of a disarray, his mind was quick and his temper rather short. Langham, a lean, even-tempered, female wyvern, her dark hide and wing leather sporting light streaks—almost stripes, a most unusual pattern—proved an excellent foil for Sir Carew. What was more, her presence seemed to soothe Kellynch's concerns that his voice would not be heard. No doubt that was her intended role in the affair.

While it resulted in a few cross words and demands from her that Kellynch himself might not have made, the whole process went rather more smoothly and with far greater satisfaction to Kellynch than Wentworth had expected.

All told, this experience was probably as beneficial for Laconia as it was for Kellynch. Respect among the Order for all manner of wyrms seemed, in his eyes, rather low and seeing Kellynch's concerns taken seriously could not but raise his esteem for the Order.

"I will make arrangements for tunnel repairs immediately." Sir Carew scrawled something in his notebook.

Laconia purred approval.

"While those are going on, Laird Kellynch, would you care to make use of a temporary lair here at the Order? With the Keepers' Cotillion coming up, I am afraid there are many dragons coming and going, so you may not have the privacy you might prefer ..." Langham cocked her mostly square head and lifted her brow ridge, looking for a moment so much like Anne that he held his breath not to laugh.

"Might introductions be arranged? After so much solitary hibernation, a bit of company might be an agreeable bit of variety." Kellynch wrinkled his long grey-green toothy snout as he spoke, as though trying to remain noncommittal.

He was lying. The tiny twitch of the tip of his tail and lift of his long mustache whiskers marked him as very intrigued indeed.

"I can arrange for that. Most who come to the Order offices are not unamenable to a bit of company." Was Langham resisting a smile?

Now this was a true Dragon Diplomat!

"I think I shall remain here for a few days, then." The fin down his back rippled, a sure sign of his good humor. "Laconia, you and their majesties will be most welcome to visit me at any time."

Sir Carew hid a chuckle behind his hand. Word of Kellynch's tatzelwurmling friends and his particular name for them had spread through the London Order with the speed of a scandal sheet.

"If you would follow me, I will show you the available lairs that might suit you. You may choose the one you best prefer." Langham strode with surprising grace toward the tunnel opening. The table quivered in time with her steps.

Kellynch slithered off behind her, every inch radiating contentment with the circumstances.

"She is very good, is she not?" A wry smile lifted the corners of Sir Carew's lips.

"I confess, I am impressed. Please convey my regards to Langham. Kellynch can be rather temperamental with regards to his comforts."

"Rather like a certain earl we know?"

"Indeed. And I am to meet with him immediately upon finishing here with you. So, I must bid you good day lest I incur the wrath of the man, his dragon, or both." Wentworth rose, bowed, and left, Laconia weaving between his feet as he walked.

They climbed the multiple flights of stairs—was it three or four—at a comfortable pace. What sense in arriving flustered and breathless? No doubt this meeting would be more challenging than simply soothing wounded dragon pride. What were the chances Sir Richard brought better news than he?

They stopped on the ground floor, at a dragon-width door inlaid with an intricate rendering of the Order's crest. Glass, stones, polished wood, even a bit of porcelain here and there created an image as clear as a painting, a masterpiece of craftsmanship.

"Mroow." Laconia reared up on his tail, sniffing the air, and batted at the door with his oversized, thumbed paws.

Wentworth grumbled low in his throat. What was wrong with giving a man a moment to gather his thoughts?

Laconia chirruped, harsh and raspy. That was one

of his warning sounds; Wentworth tensed into battle mode.

Sir Fitzwilliam—Darcy—opened the door and ushered him inside the ample room. Mirrors multiplied the light filtering in from frosted windows, providing just barely not enough light to read by. Shadows obscured the contents of the shelves at the far side of the room, lending a rather ominous air to the space.

Lord Matlock sat in his command position near the center of the room, behind his mahogany desk, which bore a masterfully painted seal of the Order. Three large chairs were arranged in front of the desk. A man with an uncanny resemblance to Lord Matlock occupied the farthest seat—Sir Richard Fitzwilliam, no doubt—a juvenile grey cockatrice perched on the back of the chair, serpentine tail snaking down to lie across his shoulder. Lacking the commanding presence of the cockatrice guard, the youngster seemed gawky and out of proportion, much like a stage all young men went through. His tail, wings and legs seemed a bit too large for his body and disheveled, ragtag feather-scales stuck out from the top of his head, bobbing as he flapped his wings and squawked.

Laconia stopped suddenly, nearly tripping Wentworth. "Roooow?"

"Laconia, Friend of Sir Frederick, may I present Earl, Friend of Sir Richard." Darcy gestured from one dragon to the other.

Laconia slither-crept forward as Earl landed on the limestone tiles just behind Darcy. They circled Darcy, Earl's wings spread, Laconia's fur and body pouffed. Lovely, this would be a prolonged dance.

Just for once, it would be nice if they could simply

bow to one another and be done with it.

Squawking and hissing as Laconia reared up on his tail to be as tall as Earl, the circling dance began anew. Earl lashed his powerful tail at Laconia, who caught it between his paws and bit it—just enough to break skin. Earl screamed and pulled away. He should not have challenged the older, more experienced dragon.

Laconia held on to Earl's tail until he touched his beak to the ground and Laconia plucked a single scruffy feather-scale from the back of his neck. Earl extended his wings and allowed Laconia to thoroughly sniff him beak to tail and back again.

"I warned you not to test him." Sir Richard extended his arm, protected in an elbow-length leather glove.

Earl hopped to his Friend's arm, head down and grumbling, the universal expression of young lads shown their place by a grown man.

Lord Matlock cleared his throat. "Perhaps now we may continue?"

Laconia jumped to Matlock's desk as Wentworth sat in the leftmost chair and edged it closer to Laconia.

"What is the news from the North?" Matlock turned to Sir Richard.

"We came by way of Birmingham, Newmarket and Cambridge." Certainly not a direct route by any means. "The blackguards are good at covering their tracks, that much I can say for certain."

"Which implies you are not certain they exist, yes?" Matlock drummed his fingers on the arm of his chair.

"Oh, they exist. What traces we found are unmistakable." Sir Richard's shoulders twitched in a barely concealed shudder.

"What did you find?" Patience was clearly not one of Matlock's assets. If he just held his peace and let Sir Richard speak—

"There was an apothecary shop near Newmarket that had a jar of wyvern scales for sale, marked as— what was it?" Sir Richard glanced at Earl.

"That is a component in a ladies' lotion, I am told," Wentworth said.

"Uppercross has a family receipt for the stuff," Laconia drummed his paws on the desk. He had always felt rather uncertain about Anne concocting the brew even after Uppercross had assured Laconia of his approval.

Earl growled. Apparently, he shared Laconia's sentiment.

Sir Richard soothed the feather-scales on the back of his neck. "There is no wyvern estate within thirty miles of Newmarket. Wyverns are not known for giving away their scales readily and certainly not to one who would sell them."

"All that tells us is some unscrupulous Keeper cleans up the lair and sells the debris. That is hardly proof of smuggling." Matlock's hands flexed in and out of fists.

Wentworth soothed Laconia's raised hackles. "We saw the same between Hungerford and Pewsey and again in Ludgershall."

"And Basingstoke." Laconia spring-hopped to Wentworth's lap.

Getting distance from Matlock? Interesting.

"That suggests something more." Darcy rubbed his chin. "It seems worth looking for a link between those apothecaries. It is possible a branch of that trade could be involved. It seems a most likely candidate of all the trades. Who else would be likely to use such articles?"

Laconia and Earl growled in tandem. Who could blame them? Cockatrice feathers and tatzelwurm claws were often cited in fairy stories' magical potions. If there was a trade in wyvern scales, no doubt buyers could be found for their claws and feathers as well.

"The Dragon Sage has connections with an apothecary, Garland, whose Friend is a minor drake, Bedlow. He specializes in potions to soothe dragon ailments. We might be able to tap him for assistance." Darcy rubbed his right knuckles into left palm.

"It might be best to see that April does not find out we also found fairy dragon enclosures at a shop in Bedford. The locks were fashioned for keys not beaks and on the outside rather than the inside." Richard covered his ears briefly as though to dodge an ear-nip.

Laconia shrieked and lashed his tail. Earl flapped and joined the chorus.

"Captive dragons?" Matlock bolted halfway up from his seat.

Darcy closed his eyes and shook his head. "Elizabeth will be—"

A soul-piercing shriek echoed down the dragon tunnel into the office.

Wentworth's ribs struggled to contain his heart as icy chills suffused his body. He barely ducked in time as a large cockatrice swooped to land on the corner of Lord Matlock's desk.

Laconia dove for the floor, growling, and coiled to pounce.

Walker.

Darcy's Friend.

"What is the meaning of this?" Matlock slammed his fist on the desk.

Walker, easily the most spectacular cockatrice Wentworth had ever seen, made himself very big and shrieked again, flapping and rearing back on his tail. "They have been taken! They have been taken!"

Laconia sprang back to the desk, keeping his head below Walker's.

"Who?" Darcy, paler than any man Wentworth had ever seen, barely forced out the word.

"Lady Elizabeth, the boy and his Friend fairy dragon! Mrs. Gardiner's men brought the fripperies for the ladies. Sergeant found two of them in the kitchen, insensible along with the staff. The other was gone. He must have played a part in taking them." Walker flapped, nearly slapping Matlock in the face.

"Gardiner's men have been vetted! They would not have been allowed in the house otherwise. How is this possible?" Darcy pressed his hands into the edge of the desk, breathing hard. "Brutus—where was he?"

"Our entire guard plus the two that Lady Wentworth brought were patrolling their stations outside the house. The house was thought secure!" Walker hopped from one foot to the other.

Wentworth stood and backed away. Close proximity to a dragon that angry was neither wise nor safe.

"I have already alerted the cockatrice squadrons. They are all on wing. Brutus leads a team of drakes in search of the rented coach that took them. Rustle has been notified, and I expect Gardiner is tracing the origins of the coach and the missing man. Sergeant and Kingsley remain guarding the ladies at Darcy House."

"Bloody hell and dragon bones." Richard pounded the desk with his fist, exactly as his father had. "Is this enough proof for you, Father?"

Matlock glowered. "How could they have been so brazen as to take the Sage? What do they hope to gain by offending all the dragons of the Order? And why would they take the boy? The Gardiners are not nearly wealthy or influential enough—"

"They might have wanted Phoenix." Darcy bounced his fist off his forehead and squeezed his eyes shut.

"Whatever for?" Matlock seemed to puff up like an agitated dragon.

"His new trick of breathing fire, do you not recall? We have no way of knowing who may have seen those two practicing that trick at the Gardiners' home."

"The creature is a fairy dragon! Who would take him seriously?"

"Darcy has a point." Sir Richard's brow knit in a faraway look. "Those who do not know dragons well would not necessarily recognize Phoenix as a mere fairy dragon."

"I have heard it said that if one squints and sees them from a distance, they look like tiny firedrakes." Wentworth edged another half-step back.

"You said that Pemberley's hatching is a widely known event." Darcy glanced at Sir Richard as though there were more to the story than was widely known. "One who has never seen a firedrake might mistake—"

"Nonsense, utter nonsense!"

"No, Father, he is right. If Phoenix was seen to actually breathe fire, even in some very small way ..."

"Mrrrrow!"

Wentworth gasped, eyes wide. "Pendragon's Bones! What a prize he could have appeared to be."

"Damn, damn, damn, damn!" Matlock's voice grew louder and deeper as he stood, fists clenched. "Of course, a worthless little flitter-bit would bring such trouble upon the Order."

"No." Darcy snapped with all the force of a physical blow. "Have you forgotten that the theft of Pemberley's egg was our first suspicion of traders in dragons? For all their faults, you cannot blame the fairy dragons for this."

Odd to hear a knight of the Order defend the lowly flutter-tufts with such vehemence.

Matlock snorted something that sounded like a surrender. "I will alert General Strickland and call in General Yates and have him recall all the Pendragon Knights. Alert your households that you will be traveling. You should take up quarters here."

Laconia's fur stood on end.

"Kellynch is staying until matters of his lair are sorted. That will leave Anne with only the tatzelwurmlings for protection. I cannot permit that." Wentworth laid a hand on Laconia's shoulders.

"Darcy House has already proven vulnerable. I will not—"

Matlock grumbled and muttered. "Very well. We will find quarters for your dependents here. We cannot have our resources spread thin protecting additional properties."

"But this is hardly a place for young ladies! Mother will—"

"Your mother is a loyal member of the Order." Matlock rounded on his son. Earl hopped to the back of Sir Richard's chair. "She will do what needs to be done. I will ask her to make sure accommodations are appropriate for a party of ladies. And with Lady Wentworth and Mrs. Collins to chaperone, there can hardly be any further objections." He turned to Darcy. "Pemberley should stay in the care of Barwines Chudleigh. She will be inconsolable when she learns of Elizabeth's absence and will need full-time supervision. We cannot have her hampering our efforts and making herself vulnerable. The last thing we need is dragons—particularly young impulsive ones—taking matters into their own talons."

"What about Longbourn?" Walker shifted his weight and resettled his wings across his back.

"What of him? He has nothing to do with this." Matlock said.

"I expect him to make an appearance here no later than afternoon tomorrow. Lady Elizabeth may no longer be his Keeper, but he will not tolerate this insult to her." Walker cocked his head at Darcy, who nodded gravely.

Matlock squeezed his eyes shut, muttering. "Since Pemberley will not be using her lair, house him at Darcy House if you must. Mrs. Collins can tend to him via the dragon tunnels as needed. Who knows, we may yet have need of a major dragon's help in these matters. It could be to our advantage to have one ready to come to our assistance."

Darcy leaned forward on the edge of the desk, voice dangerously soft and level. "Sir, I think you underestimate Elizabeth's position with the dragons. The problem will not be having one ready to come to our aid. I fear there will be far too many dragons ready to exact justice for this insult to the Order."

7
Chapter

January 16, 1815

ELIZABETH SWALLOWED BACK the bile and odd-tasting cotton wool coating her tongue. She wiped away a tear. How poignant and moving the tale told by the vibrant shade of blue that bobbed and wove next to her. So touching ... how could she bear the anguish?

She curled into a ball and sobbed; deep, gut-wrenching sobs that had not been drawn out of her since ... since ... when was that? It should be clear, memorable. How could one mislay such a memory? It had such a profound taste. When was it she had tasted this before?

There had been a dragon involved, that was certain. All her most moving memories had a dragon involved. They had been the source of everything that had touched her.

Almost everything.

There was someone else. Someones else. Someone elses? Someones elses! Why were the words not there?

Choking sobs overtook her, wracking her being until she was empty.

Better. Yes, that was better. Some of the fog washed away in her tears and in the lulling rocking that embraced her at the pace of a familiar clop-clip in the distance. Yes, that was pleasant.

Think, think!

She used to be able to do that. Regularly. With ease, perhaps? Certainly, it had not always been so muzzy ... had it?

Why were the colors singing? Make the orange-red stop singing!

There was someone, someone who smelt of sandalwood and shaving oil who could make it all stop. Yes, the memory was there.

Oh, that felt good, knowing!

And another, small and soft. She ... it was a she and the other, he!

Yes! Yes. The small one smelt of lavender and rose and dragon musk. Dragon musk?

Dragons. Images, comforting images floated in the air around her.

So many dragons—small and large; very small and very large. Where were they? They should be here.

All of them. Cold-blooded and warm-blooded.

Where was he? What was his name. Sandalwood, yes, yes, sandalwood. She screwed her eyes shut and pressed her fists into them. Wisps of an image—a face. Where was Sandalwood?

He would know what to do. He always did. He was always safe, and strong, and secure. Trust, she could trust him, always.

The dragons did.

Yes, yes, that was right. They did. And so did little Lavender-and-Rose. She trusted him, too.

But where was he? When would he come for her?

Sounds and motion. Splitting pain in her head. Sounds piercing her ears. She retched, spitting bile on something—someone?

She forced her eyes open and pinpricks of light burned into her skull, rapier sharp and hot, but they did not burn her hand as she held it in front of her face. No, the light felt cold on her skin.

"Lizzy? Lizzy?"

Something—someone shoved her roughly.

"I … I don't feel right." Sounds of retching and vomiting beside her. The voice was familiar, but not Sandalwood.

She pushed herself upright—what had she been lying upon and how did she get here? Where was here? Moving, here was moving, swaying and rocking; rhythmic clopping and crunching.

So loud, so very loud.

But the sounds were familiar. Think! Think!

A carriage. Yes, that was it! She was in a carriage, with the familiar voice. Why? When? How had she come to be in a carriage? Where was it going?

She shook her head. Bleary, watery thoughts clung like a frantic animal. The world around her spun, flinging her retching on the hard, swaying floor.

Cool; a cool breeze filtered in with the light from somewhere. She gulped in fresh air even as it drove daggers into her lungs.

The little blue one who smelt like sweet ... who? Was it ... yes ... April complained about the cold. She did not like it at all.

April! Her Friend April. Where was she?

Anne! What had happened to Anne?

Elizabeth bolted upright, eyes wide. Where was Darcy?

Space spun around her.

"Are you all right, Lizzy?" A boy, shirt stained, tears trickling down his cheeks, stared at her.

Joshua.

She grabbed his cold little hand. "Yes, I think I am now. And you?"

"Why did they take us? You and me and Phoenix? What are they going to do with us?" He pressed close to her.

"I do not know." She blinked her eyes hard, and everything faded into focus.

They sprawled on the dusty floor of a small coach with curtains drawn on all the side glass. Slivers of light danced around the curtains, brightening the space just enough to make out four, probably two pairs, of forest wyrms, one stationed in each corner.

In most respects they were typical, square-faced, shaggy brown-green forest wyrms. Snaggle-toothed fangs hung outside their closed mouths, giving them a rather fierce countenance. But their eyes were uncommonly blue. A wide stripe of a similar shade ran under their chins to their bellies. What sort of wyrms were these? No bestiary she knew described these.

She reached out toward the nearest one, the smallest of the females, fingers curled toward herself. The wyrm cocked her head and blinked, leaning a little closer.

"No!" Phoenix—where had he been hiding?—bright red and pouffed big, hovered over her hand and pecked it hard. "Do not touch them! They poisoned you!"

The wyrm jumped, and she snatched her hand back and inched away from the wyrms. "Do you know what happened?"

Phoenix chirruped and hovered before them. "The delivery men came into the kitchen where I was—I was resting from the twittery females. I hid from them. I never liked those men to start and there was a strange one among them. I think I heard his brother worked for Gardiner's. He came in his brother's place as his brother was ill. He was the one who called the wyrms in—I think the wyrms made his brother ill. Then you came to get me out of the kitchen. I do not think that was part of their plan."

She rubbed her eyes again. "I remember nothing of it."

"The wyrms came in, and you invited them for a scratch, but when you touched them, they poisoned you somehow and you fell, unable to move. They turned on everyone else in the room but the strange man. Rubbing against them until they fell over, insensible, too. I tried to escape, but the man had a net and caught me as well. He let two more men in. They had hidden in the coach we are now in. It has the number plate of a vetted carriage company, or so I heard. That's why it was permitted in the mews. Another carriage tried to enter the mews and took all the attention of the house guard, and we were carried away into a coach. Now we are here."

"Where are we? Where are you taking us?" Elizabeth addressed the wyrms.

The largest one, a male, stared at her, bobbing and weaving as though she were prey to distract.

"You know you kidnapped an Officer of the Blue Order, yes?" Joshua snapped.

"A member of the Blue Order." Elizabeth glowered at him. "Do not exaggerate."

He clapped his hand to his mouth.

The largest wyrm, with a broken fang and a scar across the side of his face, exchanged glances with a smaller female at a diagonal from him. Probably his mate, and probably the leading pair of the cluster. Wyrms nearly always traveled in pairs.

The female smacked her lips, a gobbet of spittle gathering at the side of her mouth, and flicked her forked tongue. There was a small red knob atop her head, reminiscent of a mushroom cap.

"We were not to take the boy, the woman, not anyone. Only the little dragon." The smaller male near Joshua stammered, quivering and salivating. The small spots on his underside formed a rather hypnotic pattern as he wove back and forth. "Why did they do it?"

"They must be valuable, yes? The Movers like valuables." The smallest of the wyrms, a juvenile female, whose dull, flaky hide looked close to shedding, inched toward the small male. Probably her mate.

Wyrms often mated very early, even before they matured, and their pair bonds lasted for life. Many times, the surviving wyrm did not live long after the loss of its mate.

"Perhaps means good luck. Movers will be happy for more value." The one with the red head knob nodded with her whole body.

"Azure is right. Our luck is good today." The largest wyrm lisped slightly, probably from his missing fang. "Indigo, tell your mate, tell Lapis! Listen to Prussian, trust Prussian. The boy, the woman are valuable. Will be good for us. It will make the Movers happy."

"Those are all blue pigments." Joshua whispered. "I visited the colorman with Papa, and I heard them talking about those colors. Why would they all be named that way?"

"You are right, but I have no idea." Not that it was particularly useful information right now, but it was good that he was thinking.

More important, who were these Movers?

"They want the red tasty one!" Indigo, the smaller male, smacked his lips and lurched at Phoenix, who darted behind Joshua.

Indigo and Lapis wove around each other and returned to his side of the coach, entwined.

There was a reason wyrms were not typically Dragon Friends. They preferred the company of one another to that of warm-bloods. It was an offense many found difficult to overlook, putting them below even fairy dragons in the Order's esteem. Major wyrms only fared slightly better. Right now, it was easy to see why.

"What do they want with the fairy dragon?" Elizabeth directed her question to Prussian, who was probably the most intelligent of the cluster.

"Do not try and trick me, Blue Order woman. I am not stupid. That is no fairy dragon, is a baby firedrake! It breathes fire!"

Joshua gasped and opened his mouth to speak. Elizabeth elbowed him hard and caught Phoenix in her other hand, effectively shutting his beak.

Who could possibly mistake a fairy dragon for a

baby firedrake?

How could she use such ignorance to their advantage? Was it good she had not been their target? No way to tell right now.

"So, you know him to be a baby firedrake. We did not disguise his true nature well enough. What could you possibly want with a baby firedrake? They grow large and hungry very quickly."

"What is that to us? Not for us. The Movers want it to move it elsewhere. Money will be moved, and we will gain." Azure slithered toward her mate, the red knob atop her head bobbing hypnotically, and wrapped herself around him.

"Where will the Movers take the baby?"

"Far away. There are those outside the authority of your Blue Order who think to make captives of such things." Prussian punctuated his statement with a loud clap of his jaws.

Cold shivers, like tiny, scratchy-legged spiders, coursed down her back. "Why are you in league with them?" And perhaps more importantly, who were they in league with?

Prussian flattened his body, hissing and lashing out in feinting strikes. Azure mirrored his movements.

Elizabeth pushed Joshua back to avoid the yellowed fangs. She threw her arms wide, hissing and spitting first at Prussian then Azure. They shrank back. "We are no threat to you. You have no right to threaten us."

"The Order has never served wyrms. We do not observe their law! Enough talk." Prussian made an odd keening as he wove in a deliberate pattern.

All four wyrms dove for them, rubbing their blue stripes wherever they could find bare skin. Her vision wavered and faded as her limbs turned to lead.

January 17, 1815

Strange men's voices roused her from the talking colors and sympathetic floorboards. Cold air slapped at her face, shaking away the lingering muzziness and throbbing headache.

She looked up into the painful brightness, blinking her surroundings into focus. A large, angry, very human face stared into her eyes. A man; tall and straight with glasses, a green coat, and a vague air of refinement.

"Up with you, and no tricks." His hard boot shoved her ribs.

Definitely not a gentleman.

She pulled her legs underneath her, but her hands had been tied behind her back. How exactly was one to gain her footing under such circumstances? Rough hands, belonging to two scruffy but silent men, caught her as she tripped, feet tangled in her skirt. The same hands hauled her down from the coach and dropped her, barely balanced, on the packed dirt.

Where were they?

The air tasted of salt and a gull screamed overhead. The coast—had they been unconscious that long?

The sun hung in the grey-mist sky, higher than it had been when Aunt Gardiner had arrived at Darcy House.

It had been that long.

Traveling that many hours—she knew her English geography, truly she did. If they had gone east, they would be near Dover. West would have taken them toward Portsmouth.

She glanced about. Docks nearby, warehouses at their back, with a narrow alleyway leading probably to a main street. If she ran, could she make it to the street and find help?

She shuffled her feet and tested her bonds. Her limbs barely cooperated. Such a powerful poison. If she tried, she could never make it, and there was little telling what would happen to Joshua and Phoenix if she did.

Waves lapped the rocky beach perhaps thirty yards before them. And not another soul—man nor drag-on—to be seen nor any useful signs of where they were—wait, there. On that rooftop, a weathervane in the shape of a crescent moon and eight-pointed star.

The crest of Portsmouth!

True, it made little practical difference, knowing where they were. But somehow it was comforting, grounding.

"Here's the cage. Carefully now, get this little thing in there, but mind yourself. We don't need no flam-ing!" To her left, one of the scruffy men came around the back of the coach with a boxy iron cage in his arms.

The other scruffy man, on her right, held Phoenix in a net as he shrieked and struggled. When had that happened?

"Let him go! Let him go! You have no right!" Joshua struggled in the not-gentleman's grasp, kicking at his shins and reaching for the cage.

"You will only hurt yourself if you fight, little fire-drake." She said softly, looking at Phoenix. "Both of you. Do as you are asked and do not become in-jured."

Joshua settled down and the not-gentleman set

him on the ground. "What are we going to do with them? Why did you take them? This was not to be a kidnapping."

"What is you, woman? Some kind of governess?" A fourth man climbed down from the box. Shorter than the not-gentleman, he walked with a swaggering limp—his left knee or leg had been injured. His cheeks were ruddy and weathered and his thin hair poked out in unruly wisps under his battered hat.

"I am his protector." Elizabeth looked straight at the limping man. Something about the way the others looked to him suggested he was in charge.

Prussian slithered beside her and reared up on his tail, but did not offer any information.

Interesting. The leading wyrm did not fully trust the men they were with.

"Young ones need a protector." She flashed a warning look at Joshua, who immediately pressed his lips together. For all that he was a scamp, he also seemed to have the good sense to know when to allow a bigger dragon to manage the situation.

"Which one are you protector to?" not-gentleman asked. The glasses perched on the end of his nose hinted he had some useful knowledge about dragons and perhaps even the Order. But not enough, it seemed, to know who she was.

"Both."

Phoenix stopped fighting and chirped.

The limping man stood very close. Breath like a dragon and crooked front teeth. "Then if you value their hides, I suggest you start your protecting by making sure they do as they been told. We ain't running a nursery here. The only one I know I'm gettin' paid for is the dragon. If either of you can't keep 'im in line, I ain't bothering with ya'. Yeah?"

"Understood." Elizabeth stepped closer to Joshua. No one stopped her. Surely that had to be a good thing.

"Why did you take them, Corney, and what are you going to do with them?" Not-Gentleman stepped into Corney's space.

"It were too easy to take 'em, and I have a sense for what's valuable. I be certain they's valuable."

"I am not. We need to wait on Scarlett. She knows these matters better than you. If she agrees, then we take them."

"I'm not a-waitin' on some fancy feathered female to tell me my business." Corney shoved Not-Gentleman back. "If you don't want a part in this, then get out now. Go!"

"I got you the dragon. You owe me. I want my share."

"You'll be paid when I am. That were the arrangement. You ain't gettin' paid any sooner. Now leave or come with. The tide is shiftin' and it's time to go." Corney crossed his arms and glared.

Not-Gentleman muttered something untoward and stalked toward a rowboat of some sort, pulled up on the shore.

The scruffy men roughly shoved Phoenix into the cage. Poor little mite bore the ignominy well. She cringed as the lock was set. No dragon should be kept against their will.

"Move on, move on." The limping man called and trudged through the steady breeze to the cold stony beach.

The scruffy man who smelt like sweat grabbed her elbow and urged her and her calf's-foot-jelly knees along. His slightly less sour-smelling companion did the same with Joshua.

Getting into a small boat, with the wind whipping her skirts and without the use of her hands, proved rather challenging, but at last, the boat was full: the captives, four Movers—Corney, the sweat-smelling one at the oars, Not-Gentleman and the other scruffy man at the rear. The four wyrms stationed themselves between the captives and the rower. Were they Friends of the Movers?

Instinct said no.

The fishy-smelling craft bounced and lunged on the choppy waters as the oars threw up cold droplets in a steady, unsympathetic rhythm.

"I do not feel well." Joshua's face was positively green. It was some mercy that by this time there was nothing left in his stomach to cast up.

"You will feel better after we are fed." Elizabeth looked at the presumed leader. "You do intend on feeding us, do you not? I think it has been nearly a day since we have eaten. If the baby dragon does not have food soon, he might perish."

"And I will not eat if they are not fed." Phoenix twittered. Naturally, he could not give up all expression of defiance.

"Shut yer yaps, they'll be food in good time. If you behave." The limping man glowered at her.

That was enough. Now was not the time to belabor the point.

The outline of a ship appeared in the misty distance. Had it always been there, and she just failed to notice? Two masts, square sails with a long bowsprit at the front. A figurehead hung below the bowsprit, the front half of a lion, the back half of a fish. A sea-lion. Reminiscent of a tatzelwurm or hippocampus, but patently wrong. Like everything else was. A creature, a situation that could not, should not exist.

Long and sleek and probably fast, the Sea Lion seemed the sort of vessel smugglers and privateers would probably favor.

Clearly this was not a crime of impulse or convenience. Some effort had been made in planning the affair. Certainly not a factor in their favor.

By the time they reached the Sea Lion, Joshua was not the only one feeling ill. Pray this sensation pass quickly.

Sailors lowered a rope ladder and the scruffy Mover from the back scampered up, the smaller wyrms, Indigo and Lapis, right behind him. How easily the wyrms navigated the coarse rope.

Corney pointed at her, then at the ladder. He freed her hands—how thoughtful.

The task was far more difficult than it appeared, with the boat and the rope seeming to move in opposite directions, tearing at her palms, dodging out from beneath her feet. No doubt there would be little help for her if she fell.

Not the sort of motivation she would have preferred, but it was enough.

She scrambled up over the side just as her arms and legs threatened to give way.

By comparison, Joshua made the task look easy. Not-Gentleman carried the birdcage up, his movements seeming nearly draconic.

Utterly unsettling.

Corney hauled himself over the railing. "Give the dragon here, Ayles."

Not-Gentleman handed him the cage.

"Tie 'em again?" A man with most of his face covered in burn scars asked.

"Don't bother, Nickleby."

"You sure, Corney? We don't need trouble 'ere."

"What trouble are a woman and a boy gonna be? At the first sign, throw 'em over and it be done. Put 'em all in the 'old. What do it eat?" Corney held up the cage and poked at Phoenix.

Now was a fine time for him to discover if he had appropriate food.

"Small bits of meat or fish cooked in broth would be best. He cannot eat hard tack or very much bread. And he must be fed at least three times a day. Four is better. He is tiny and cannot go without very long."

"And if I don't believe you?"

She shrugged. "Do as you will. But if you value your cargo, do as I say. I am sure a dead dragon is not worth as much as a live one."

"And if you're lying to me—" Little bits of spittle flew to punctuate Corney's threat.

They stared at each other for a long time.

Finally, Corney nodded. "Take 'em below. Tell Cooky to cook up a plate for the dragon as she says. After you see that the dragon eats, feed them." He leaned close and wagged a finger in Elizabeth's face. "No trouble, you hear? None. I got no patience for it."

She nodded.

He handed the cage to Nickleby and turned away. Nickleby and Ayles propelled them across the undulating deck, down a ladder, and into a dark chamber, a lock clicking loudly behind them.

A small grate in the ceiling allowed just enough light to filter through. The room could not have been more than ten feet across, and maybe as many feet deep, possibly less. One corner held a pile of still sweet-smelling hay. A currently empty bucket, for the necessary no doubt, occupied the opposite corner. Rough blankets, or perhaps feed sacks, lay rumpled in the center of the room.

Nothing else.

No furniture. No comforts of any kind. Almost like the cavern Netherfield—rather, Netherford— had hid her and Lydia in. At least here they had some light.

But this place moved, rocking with the waves. Definitely the worst part.

Joshua stumbled to her and grabbed her about the waist, holding her so tightly she could not breathe. Phoenix clung to the bars of his cage and keened—a poignant, soul-rending sound she had never heard a fairy dragon make.

How tempting to join him. But to what end? It would not return her to Darcy and Anne and April and Pemberley any sooner. No, for that she had to keep her wits about her and her sensibilities under control.

"Lizzy, I'm so sorry. I don't know how anyone knew about Phoenix's trick," he whispered into her side.

"Where fairy dragons are present, there are few secrets." She rubbed his back.

"What are we going to do?"

"When they open the cage to feed me, I can fly out. I can escape and seek help," Phoenix said.

Elizabeth sat down beside the cage. Gracious, it was difficult to move about with everything rocking and swaying. "You are very brave, my little friend, but without you, we are no use to them. You heard Corney. We will be thrown overboard if you escape. Our lives depend upon you not doing that."

"I do not like it." Phoenix extended his wings and pouffed out his feather-scales.

"None of us do."

"Then what shall we do, Lizzy? How shall we get home?" Joshua wrapped his arms around his knees, his voice wavering just a bit.

"I am not sure yet. But in moments like these, I have always tried to think like a dragon and act accordingly. It has worked for me in the past, and I hope it shall now."

8

Chapter

DARCY STARED INTO little Anne's face as she cuddled into his chest. The dim evening light filtering through curtained windows was just enough to make out her features. The confined nursery, tucked in an awkward gable of the Blue Order offices, was quiet, so quiet this late in the evening, though the building was usually filled with the noise of too many people and dragons. It was not home, but for now, it would have to do.

She looked so much like her mother and smelt of rose and lavender. Her eyes, her smile, her laugh, her special peace and satisfaction in the presence of dragons. She was her mother's daughter.

Emptiness opened in his chest, and he pulled her in closer. She murmured a little sigh of contentment, unaware of the storm swirling around the Order.

They would find Elizabeth. Find her and bring her home.

They would.

They had to.

"Sir Fitzwilliam?" Nanny whispered at his shoulder. Perhaps one day it would feel normal to hand his infant to a waiting, toothy drake, but even here in the Order offices, it still did not feel natural. "Perhaps I should take her to her cradle now?"

The move from Darcy House to the Blue Order offices had been difficult for Anne. It was not a building ever conceived to house an infant. Barwines Chudleigh, maternal instincts in full force, insisted on overseeing the project. In less than a day, a suitable space was identified and converted to a nursery. As astonishing feat of management as there ever was.

Unfortunately, though well away from the hustle and bustle of the Order Business on the floors below, little Anne's preternatural hearing proved exceptionally problematic—every little sound seemed to waken her from sleep. The little mite still did not sleep through the night under the best of circumstances. Hence the use of the awkward little storage room-cum-nursery that Chudleigh was embarrassed to even suggest little Anne stay in.

Chudleigh all but come out to say that, perhaps, Anne belonged in her own lair with Pemberley and her snakeling. But even Elizabeth would have taken pause at that idea. It was unlikely the baby could sleep easily with the noises of dragons coming and going.

Elizabeth had assured him Anne's issues would sort themselves out eventually. According to Mrs. Bennet's reports, Elizabeth had been a difficult infant, who rarely slept and started at the slightest noise. It was not until she was at least two years old that she was not a constant disruption to the household. Hopefully it would not take so long with Anne.

Little May's arrival had definitely improved the situation with her uncannily soothing purrs. Perhaps that was part of her appeal to Walker, who could not abide the sound of babies crying.

If only he could stay here with her. But Nanny was right.

He passed the baby to Nanny. "I will ask Georgiana to send Pax to you. April is in no condition to assist in the nursery now."

Poor creature. It had been difficult enough when Elizabeth was taken by Netherford. This was far, far worse.

For all of them.

Nanny's long blue-green nose wrinkled. "I am sure I can manage without Pax's help. There is no need to separate her from her Friend. It is quite enough to have the tatzelwurm in the nursery." Something about the way she said tatzelwurm …

"Anne's Friend's name is May, and I would enjoin you to use it." Darcy glowered and dodged around a small table, Anne's cradle, and a press to make it to the doorway. "Did not the Sage make it clear to you that family Friends were to have free access to Anne, especially the fairy dragons?"

"Yes, sir, she did, but it is most irregular. The Order does not officially support the notion that infants or children should be exposed to dragons." It seemed Nanny missed the irony of her own statement. "And I registered my protest to her, but she insists the infant can hear dragons even though none can really be sure yet. And to expose any infant to fairy dragons! The thought! They are senseless little flutter-tufts who will only—"

"Not another word against the species or our Friends." Darcy pulled his shoulders back and towered over Nanny just enough to remind her. "If you cannot lay your prejudice aside—"

Nanny blinked rapidly. "With respect, sir, it is hardly prejudice as you understand it. They and the tatzelwurm are prey. It is not natural—"

"Nor is it natural for human and dragon to live in peace. Yet we do. If you cannot abide by our standards, I will see that another suitable nurserymaid is found for our daughter. Feel free to give me your notice at any time. Until then, I will consider any repetition of this conversation, or one like it, to be your notice. Do I make myself clear?"

Nanny bared her teeth in a draconic frown, but lowered her head slightly. "Understood. Sir."

"Expect Pax to be here soon. Offer her warm tea with honey when she arrives." Nanny did not think fairy dragons had any business drinking tea or being served honey. Darcy turned on his heel and left.

Perhaps he ought to go ahead and speak to Lady Astrid about finding a new nanny in any case. If she felt so strongly about mingling with prey, her attitude was not likely to change. That was not what Anne needed to be taught, even now.

He made his way down the scantly lit, narrow staircase to the primary guest quarters on the third floor. Where Anne should have been, in a room adjoining his own. His steps echoed on the limestone tiles. Why was nothing as simple as it should have been?

Rest, he needed rest. Probably should retire for the evening.

A shadowy figure appeared before him, and Darcy stopped short.

"Darcy." Gardiner stood, several paces away, shoulders slumped, dark rings under his eyes. He had aged ten years since Darcy had last seen him. "My wife came to call on her nieces and Miss Darcy."

Lovely. No doubt Gardiner hoped for an invitation. Darcy was hardly fit for company.

"Come." Darcy plodded past Gardiner and inclined his head toward an oak door carved with a fanciful depiction of a firedrake. It looked nothing like Pemberley, not even remotely. But it served as an outward sign of the sort of accommodations that could be expected behind the guest quarters door.

The invitation was neither formal nor even polite, but Gardiner was the rare and well-appreciated sort of family who would not notice such things. Today that made him tolerable.

They entered Darcy's quarters. A low fire lit the space in a somber orange-red glow. The room was exactly as large as it should be to accommodate the four-poster bed, cabinet, dressing table, and two large chairs near the fireplace with a small table between, and no larger. Elizabeth might have described it as cozy and intimate. But without her nothing could ever seem so.

"Brandy? Port?" Darcy headed toward the decanters on the dressing table.

"Feels like the sort of situation for a great deal of cheap gin." Gardiner snorted, grim and weary.

"I suppose. But it is all have to offer now. I have not the will to head into the parts of town where cheap gin might be acquired. Will it do?"

"Very gracious of you." He took the offered glass, cradling it in his palms, and sank into the nearest chair. "How fares Pemberley?"

"Not well." Which was, of course, a firedrake-sized understatement. "She is beside herself, which is only to be expected, but dragon-sized tantrums are unpleasant, nevertheless. I have never been so grateful for Barwines Chudleigh before. No one else can manage Pemberley right now. She is entirely discontented to remain here, under the protection of the Order. Somehow, she has determined that she should be allowed to search for Elizabeth. She can fly now, after all."

"Not so very different from my children: too much ability, and too little discernment." Gardiner took a deep draw from his brandy. "Daniel would give anything to be able to assist in the search for his brother. As would I."

"Imagine explaining to Pemberley that Elizabeth's abduction could easily have been intended to bring her out where she, too, might be taken. The very suggestion only makes her even more angry. How dare warm-bloods consider such a thing?"

"I imagine an angry firedrake, even a very young one, is quite formidable."

"Doubly so when her favorite Keeper is involved." Darcy covered his face with his hands.

Gardiner hunched over his glass, head bowed. "I am so sorry, Darcy. I feel responsible for this, you know. Those men, I thought they had been properly vetted, all their connections carefully examined. I cannot believe I allowed—"

"It was not your fault. Elizabeth would tell you the

same. The men who worked for you were loyal. Even the one who sent his brother in his place. He is aghast at his brother's betrayal. It is hard to fault them either."

"I should not have allowed them to go to Darcy House—"

"How could you have foreseen such a thing? No one could have. No, this was not your fault. At the very least, we have found a few more avenues of investigation to follow." Darcy swallowed a large sip of brandy, relishing the burn down the back of his throat.

"That does not bring your wife and my son back." The words hung, threatening, dangerous, in the air.

"Not yet, but it will." It would. Darcy's fingers closed hard on his glass. Hopefully it would not shatter in his hand.

"Would that I had your certainty."

"It is all I have right now."

The crackling fireplace seemed to agree.

A fist pounded on the door.

He jumped and nearly dropped his glass.

"Sir Fitzwilliam, Sir Fitzwilliam!"

Darcy dragged himself to the door—what new crisis could possibly warrant such an assault on his ears?—and yanked it open, revealing a breathless, somewhat haggard, Blue Order footman.

"Sir, you are wanted in the lairs. Urgently."

"Pemberley?" He clenched his fist and gritted his teeth.

"No, sir, Longbourn has arrived."

Of course he had. What joy was his. "Pray excuse me. If you wish, feel free to use my quarters until your wife completes her call." Darcy followed the footman downstairs.

Mrs. Collins joined him at the first-floor landing. Hopefully she would be helpful. Elizabeth thought her sister was becoming a quite competent dragon Keeper, but with Longbourn's temper, there was no way to predict the sort of tantrum to expect.

Light and warmth faded as they reached the subterranean levels, where nearly all decoration ceased and the stairs grew narrower. Flickering torches filled the air with wan, yellow light and their own peculiar scent. Two more flights of stairs down, to the lowest level, containing the guest dragon lairs.

Several steps from the bottom, Longbourn lunged to meet him face to face. Darcy stopped short, catching Mrs. Collins just before she fell headlong down the last few steps.

"It is true?" Longbourn's booming voice echoed painfully against the stone walls.

Not a spectacular creature on the best of days, the wyvern's hide was dull and dusty and his expression grim. Longbourn's breath reeked and his talons were ragged.

"He did not look like that when I left him." Mrs. Collins whispered. "He is so particular about how his person is cared for. He barely accepts ministrations from me. Mr. Collins is not permitted to touch him."

That would have sounded like an excuse from another Dragon Keeper, but knowing Longbourn …

"We do not know where she is." Darcy sidled in front of Mrs. Collins.

"Who has taken her?" Longbourn's voice reverberated in Darcy's chest.

"We do not know that either."

"What is being done?"

"Cockatrice and drake teams are searching for her, but to little avail so far. The carriage which we thought took her has been found, but it seems that the number plates have been switched and the wrong coach was followed. That is as far as the search has taken us." Darcy braced himself for a roar.

Mrs. Collins peeked over Darcy's shoulder. "We have not given up though. The entire Order is determined to find her."

"I will help. I must help." Longbourn stomped. "What can I do?"

An excellent question that demanded, if not an excellent answer, at least some direction for something he could do.

"Gardiner's men tell us the kidnappers used poisonous wyrms to incapacitate everyone in the kitchen. That is how they took her so quietly, without notice. Do you know anything of such wyrms?"

"Dragons were involved in her taking?" Longbourn's tail lashed as he fanned his wings. If he could have belched fire, he probably would have. A drop of ochre venom gathered at the tip of his fang.

Darcy gulped and edged back a step. "It seems as though it may be possible."

"What kind of wyrms?" Longbourn growled.

"The men who saw them only said they seemed to be forest wyrms, but had a blue stripe running down their bellies."

Longbourn grumbled and growled low in his throat. A sound powerful enough to set Darcy's ribs and the hairs on the back of his neck vibrating as well. Longbourn sat back on his haunches, tail whipping.

"You are familiar with such wyrms?" Mrs. Collins asked.

"I have never met such a creature. But there are stories. Old stories, the kind that Bennet likes. Or perhaps the bookish woman—she might know something of them."

Lady Astrid! She would rejoice at something productive to do.

"There is something more, I can hear it in your voice." Mrs. Collins edged past Darcy. Perhaps it was good that she was here.

"I do not know for sure. But there are rumors."

"Tell us."

"No. No, it would not be good. There are matters which belong to dragons alone. Not to be shared." Longbourn shook his head in broad sweeps.

"If it could help us get Elizabeth back, I insist you tell us." Darcy spoke slowly. Longbourn would not respond well if he lost his own temper.

"No. Not a warm-blooded matter. I will see if the rumors are true. It might be nothing, but it is what I will do."

"There is something you should know before you go." A deep, slithery voice came from a dark corner far from the stairs.

Darcy and Mrs. Collins jumped.

"Why have you been listening in on our conversation?" Longbourn did not look toward the voice.

"You are in the public space between the lairs. This is not a place for secrets." Netherford slithered closer, his blue hide dirty and his whiskers frayed.

"What are you doing here? Richard said you remained at the Netherford estate." How long had the lindwurm been traveling alone?

"That had been our plan. But when I heard the news about the Sage, I felt compelled to offer my services."

How quickly word had traveled!

"As what?" Longbourn looked over his shoulder as Netherford approached.

"There is a great deal of unrest among the major dragons at this news."

"The warm-blooded segment of the Order is not exactly pleased either." Darcy muttered.

"I think you misunderstand me, Sir Fitzwilliam." Netherford slithered in beside Longbourn and rose up to look eye to eye with Darcy, forelegs crossed over his chest. "Word has gotten around that the Order is concerned about a possible trade in dragons and their parts and that it may be connected to the Sage's disappearance."

"Already? I had hoped for more time."

"The suggestion has been made that the Pendragon Accords are not being upheld by men and a few vocal dragons are wondering what should be done about it."

"Done about it?" Mrs. Collins clutched the banister.

"You imply the dragons are threatening to take action on Elizabeth's behalf?" Darcy said.

"I think there are many who are beholden to her and even more who are fond of and intrigued by her, who would be happy to assist in her recovery. But those are not the voices to which I refer. No, there are those who wonder if the Blue Order has outlived its purpose and if it is time for dragons to exert their will over men again, to remind them of whom they are dealing with."

Pendragon's bones! Who would have conceived? "Which dragons precisely?"

"I have a complete report to deliver to Lord Matlock. Once he has heard, I am certain he will wish to inform all of you as well. In the meantime, perhaps, Laird Longbourn, it might be wise for you to delay your journey long enough for the Order to draft a statement to the major dragons. That way you might position yourself as the bearer of the Blue Order's news and travel more freely among the dragon estates."

Longbourn snorted and stomped and pawed at the ground.

Mrs. Collins approached Longbourn, hands held up and open. "I know you do not wish to wait, but it seems like it would improve your chances of success. And if you find that your rumors of wyrms are not useful, then at least you will have done something that Lizzy would have wanted to see done. There is that."

Longbourn pushed his head toward Mrs. Collins, and she scratched behind his ears. "Very well, but I will not wait more than two days."

"That is generous of you. I am certain Matlock can be made to make a decision in that length of time. If you will excuse me." Netherford retreated through the tunnels.

January 19, 1815 London Order Offices

The mantel clock in Darcy's guest chambers chimed nine times, morning light filtering in through the frosted windows. A few hours of sleep left him rested enough to try to do something useful, but not enough to be in a good humor about any of it.

The map he studied hung over both edges of the small table, crisscrossed with cryptic scribbling by Wentworth and Richard: their routes, their contacts, the locations where they had identified traces of dragon traffic. He penciled in the path Wickham took with Pemberley's egg, as best he could reconstruct it from memory. He would have to check with Walker on some of the details, especially on the cavern locations he and Elizabeth had searched near Meryton. Netherford might be helpful with that, too.

Was he imagining it? His lines seemed to fit well with the others.

He fell back in his chair, raking his hair. How long ago that seemed. So much had happened.

How could he have lost her again? Acrid bile burned the back of his throat. He fought back the urge to be sick. Was this what it would always mean, their service as Dame and Knight of the Pendragon Order? Had he conceived such a thing could ever happen again, he would have forbidden her …

He chuckled darkly.

Forbidden Elizabeth. As if that were ever going to be successful.

One did not forbid the Dragon Sage. Reason with her, yes; request respectfully, definitely; but forbid? Absolutely not.

It was hardly proper, unwomanly even; how he loved that about her.

A woman who knew her own mind, had her own opinions and was not afraid to offer them. One who knew how to stand up to ridiculous dominance displays with her own. One who was not afraid to admit the rare occasions when she was wrong. One who expected him to do the same. A partner in every possible sense of the word.

And because of all the things he loved most about her, she was missing.

Would he ever see her again? How could he possibly raise Anne without her? Could he ever marry again?

Impossible. Simply impossible.

A loud rap at the door, not Richard's, though. He knocked like he was giving an order.

But who else would dare disturb him so early in the day? He shambled to the door and pulled it open.

Bennet.

What was he doing here? How quickly could he make the Historian leave? Now was not the time he could listen to Bennet's criticisms of Elizabeth with grace.

"May I come in?" Bennet seemed more hunched and frail than when Darcy had last seen him. A bit like Gardiner.

Perhaps …

Darcy gestured him to come inside and shut the door. He pulled two chairs closer to the fire—Elizabeth had often reminded him her father's discomfort was lessened—and his temper improved—when he was kept warm.

Bennet slowly lowered himself into the chair as though his joints were too stiff to move any faster. "It is true then?"

"I am afraid so. She, Joshua Gardiner, and Phoenix." Darcy steeled himself for the first bitter words.

"Longbourn came to visit me last night. He told me everything." Bennet wrapped his arms around his waist.

"I am surprised he was allowed at Middle Set House."

"He is not, but he came nonetheless. One cannot turn away a determined dragon."

He was right. "Did that cause problems with your wife and daughter?"

"It does not matter."

Since when?

Darcy sat up very straight. "I was given to understand that it mattered very, very much."

Bennet rocked side to side ever so slowly, gazing vacantly into the fireplace. "I have made arrangements for them. I just saw them off to stay with Jane and Bingley for a visit of indefinite duration. Several eligible fellows have moved into the neighborhood. Jane wishes to make the most of the opportunity for her sister."

"How convenient." Would that he had made the decision sooner.

"How is April?"

"Beside herself. She has been staying with Mrs. Collins and the others in the rooms the Order has assigned them."

"I want to help."

"What do you mean, help?"

Bennet winced. Apparently Darcy had not concealed the snide tone in his remark as well as he hoped. "Longbourn told me about the wyrms you mentioned, that knowing more about them might be important to finding the kidnappers."

"We do not know, but at this point, anything might be helpful."

"I cannot be certain, but I recall something in the histories about them."

"What do you remember?" Darcy resisted the urge to shake the words out of him.

"They are not common forest wyrms. I am certain of that. I think I saw reference to azure-striped forest wyrms in journals from two estates in the north. Farther north than Pemberley, I believe. I cannot recall the estates' names now, but I know I read of them here, in Lady Astrid's collections."

"I shall inform her of that possibility immediately." It was not much, but it was something. And that could qualify as help.

"That is not what I meant."

"What do you mean?"

"I did not send Mrs. Bennet and Kitty away so that I could sit and stare into my own fireplaces. I intend to go to the collections myself and begin looking for those journals. Perhaps Lady Astrid and her apprentices might wish to assist, but I will do the task myself. I have brought Drew, my secretary, to help."

"You need not trouble—"

"She is my daughter." His voice turned frail, brittle as he gripped the arms of the chair.

"And she is my wife. I will see to it everything that can be done on her behalf is done." Darcy sat straighter, expanding his chest.

"The last time I saw her, we did not part on good terms. I did not think it would be the last time that I saw her." Bennet's voice broke.

"It will not be. I am certain of it." Sometimes it was the right thing to lie.

"So, you will permit me to help?"

"I would accept a team of fairy dragons and tatzelwurms if they thought they could be of assistance."

The mantel clock struck twelve times, midnight, as Darcy stumbled into his chambers. Another day with no more answers than they had before. Granted, he now knew a great deal more about forest wyrms in general and how necessary they were in the management of estate lands. But nothing useful toward his most pressing concern.

Walker slipped through the open passage door, silent and dark as death. Had Darcy been prey, he would have been dead. Leaving the door to the dragon passages open was one of those little acts of trust that marked the decades of their Friendship.

Walker glided to the mantel, above the low fire. A little show of dominance that: being over Darcy's head. Somehow it managed to be a demonstration of dominance and not at the same time. That Darcy permitted it was a statement of his esteem for Walker.

No one ever suggested having dragon Friends was simple or uncomplicated.

"I imagine this means you have no fresh news." Darcy stalked toward the decanter of port. It was tempting to drown himself in it, but something insisted he be ready at a moment's notice, so he merely used it to knock the razor's edge off his anxiety.

"No, not of that sort." Walker hissed the word, wings half-extended. "You need to talk to April."

"I saw her just a few hours ago when I brought her a fresh jam and honey pot from Darcy House. I still do not understand why no one here deigns to provide her with sufficient sweets. It is not as though any other dragons have the penchant for them that fairy dragons do."

"That may not be the issue." Walker lifted his foot and picked at something between his toes. "Go talk to her. Now. She is with Lady Wentworth in the ladies' sitting room."

It was late, and he was tired, and hardly in the mood for company. But what sort of Friend would he be to ignore such a demand? And it might be distracting for a few moments.

He set his port aside, back and shoulders aching. Had he aged so much in the last few weeks? Gardiner and Bennet certainly had.

Darcy knocked at the ladies' door, the inlaid agate eyes of the carved drake staring back at him. Was that disapproval in its expression?

"I am so glad to see you, Sir Fitzwilliam." Lady Wentworth opened the door and ushered him in. Candlelight painted the otherwise domestic chamber in dramatic yellows and golds. "She will not tell me what is troubling her, but it is clear that something is, very much."

Vague perfume, a mix of flowers, none Elizabeth's lavender, hung in the air.

"Would it be an imposition to ask that you permit me some time alone with her?"

"I had planned on it. Corn and Wall will come with me as well. We shall be in the library if you have need of us." She slipped past him, the two wyrmlings in her wake.

The door clicked shut behind him, and he scanned the room. Signs of Elizabeth's sisters were strewn everywhere. A sewing basket, lying open on its side in the middle of the couch. Books, probably Georgiana's, sitting open on a nearby chair. A half-finished board game occupying a small table near the window. And April's fairy dragon 'cage' on the mantel to keep warm near the fireplace.

A little mass of blue huddled on the cage floor, shuddering.

Did fairy dragons cry?

It only took five steps to cross the length of the room. "April?"

She did not even lift her head.

"Are you well?"

"No. No, I am not." She tucked her beaky nose under her wing.

"Pray, come out and tell me about it." He offered his hand as a perch. "I brought the jam and honey as you requested."

She lifted her head slightly and looked at him with one eye, evaluating, considering. Her entire being drooping, she hopped to his hand.

He pulled a chair close to the low fire and sat down, holding her close to eye level. "Pray tell me, what is wrong?"

"What is wrong? What sort of fool are you? Everything is wrong and you know it. Everything is wrong!"

He stroked the back of her neck, soothing ruffled feather-scales. "Beyond the very obvious. What is wrong?"

She rocked back and forth, keening softly. Her mournful notes raking his heart like tiny talons. "What is to become of me? What is to become of me?"

"Become of you? Whatever do you mean?"

"If ... if ... something happens to her? What is to become of me?"

Of course. It was so obvious now that she voiced it. But it was a good question. He drew a breath to speak, but released it in a sigh. That was not the right thing to say.

Nor was that.

Nor that.

"What do you want? That is to say, should you not be the one to decide what is to become of you?"

She looked up at him, head turned half upside down. "Do you mean that?"

"Of course I do. You know I am not apt to say what I do not mean."

"I am to choose my own fate, my own direction?" Her eyes grew large as if surprised.

"Certainly. And in so far as I am able, I will see to it your wishes are honored. It is what Elizabeth would want." He scratched under her chin. "I hope, though, that if such a decision does become necessary, you would choose to stay with me. I know I am not your particular Friend—"

She chirped, loud and sharp, and pecked his hand. "I have never said that."

It was difficult not to drop her when she did that. "I would not presume—"

"You do not need to. You are my … Friend … like she is." She ran her cheek along his hand.

Darcy swallowed back a lump in his throat. "I am honored."

"I know. That is why you are my Friend."

He drew her close to his chest, and she leaned into him. "Somehow, my little Friend, we will all get through this, and things will be right in the world once more. I do not know how. But they will."

9
Chapter

January 19, 1815 London Order Offices

ANNE FOUGHT THE urge to pace as she awaited Lady
Matlock in the small parlor on the second-floor of the
Order offices. The lower walls were paneled in dark
wood, the upper walls painted in soft blues and the
furniture upholstered in deep gold. Wooden dragon
perches were interspersed among the chairs, sofa and
low table.

Ladies should not pace, so she sat, straight and
proper, digging her fingernails into her palms.

Afternoon sun filtered through the frosted windows with a warm and friendly glow that released a
light fragrance from a bowl of dried flowers. Perhaps
one day she would become accustomed to the odd,
muted light of the offices. Thankfully, she did not
need the same precautions at home since her walls did

not boast huge oil portraits of significant founding dragons of the Blue Order, nor were their descendants walking the halls.

The latter bit was a touch of exaggeration. Major dragons could only be found in the lower floors of the offices. Those above the ground floor generally did not have accommodations large enough for them. It seemed draconic imagery in all manner of décor took their place.

She smoothed her cream and plum striped skirts, a half-dress gown, supplied by Mrs. Gardiner just in case a meeting such as the upcoming one were necessary. She had been right; being properly garbed did help one to have the right frame of mind for such things.

In so far as it was possible.

"Lady Wentworth." Lady Matlock swept into the parlor, her own not-quite-Order-blue gown a mite more formal than might be expected for what was essentially a morning call.

Yes, this was going to be lovely. What a way to experience her introduction to the Blue Order Cotillion Board.

Mrs. Gardiner had offered no good opinion of the group. All were peeresses: two viscountesses— granted, one was a dowager— two countesses and a baroness—and they felt their rank very deeply. They enjoyed their reign as Blue Order's answer to the patronesses of Almack's. In fact, two of them were patronesses of Almack's.

Anne swallowed hard as her limbs grew cold. These women were the arbiters of Blue Order society. It was in their hands—or at least largely so— to decide whether she and Wentworth would be admitted into their good company or not.

Heavens above! She sounded like Father!

Why be so anxious? It was not as though she had cared one whit for warm-blooded society and whether she was admitted into it. Typically, such company lacked the elegance, manners, accomplishment, and understanding to be worth associating with.

Somehow, though, it seemed different for the Blue Order. Would not the good opinion of Dragon Keeping society be worth having? It surely should.

Should it not?

"Are you ready." Lady Matlock did not ask a question. "The Board has convened downstairs in the amphithere drawing room that they favor for their meetings. I will make introductions for you."

"Thank you, Lady Matlock." Anne stood and curtsied, more by reflex than intent. "I do not understand why they have insisted on my presence. Do you know the business they wish to discuss?"

Something in her posture suggested she truly did not care. "I can only imagine it is in regards to the unfortunate disappearance of your sponsor before you have been properly prepared for the Cotillion."

"Surely they are not planning to go on with the event?"

Lady Matlock's eyes bulged as though she had just said something very stupid indeed. "Whyever not? Lady Elizabeth is not part of the planning committee. Why would her situation change anything about the Cotillion?"

Anne clamped her jaws shut. No point in saying something else equally offensive.

Lady Matlock led the way out of the parlor and to the grand stairs. Wrought-iron railings with fairy dragons supported a carved banister on either side of the polished marble steps, wide enough for four to walk abreast.

"Do not think I am unsympathetic to the plight of our Dragon Sage. She is my niece by marriage, after all. I am concerned. Truly I am. But I do not think the Cotillion would be halted by anything less than a direct threat to the Order itself."

What exactly did they think the kidnapping of the Sage and of a dragon—even a fairy dragon—was? Oh, this meeting was going to be a joy.

Not surprisingly, a gaudy, brightly painted amphithere graced the drawing room door, which sat slightly ajar. Lady Matlock pushed it open and paused in the doorway. Was that to allow Anne to become oriented or to warn the grand ladies that someone inferior was about to enter their exalted company?

Expensive perfumes, several competing scents, vied for dominance in the large space. Five small couches, each bearing a single, finely dressed woman, ringed a low table holding tea and dainties. Tall windows with sheer curtains bestowed the ladies with lighting complimentary to their complexions. Was that why they liked this room?

It could hardly be because of the icy green walls, overpopulated with landscapes—probably all dragon estates—or the white-painted wrought-iron amphitheres which flanked the fireplace. Gracious, those were probably the ugliest things she had seen in the Order offices, yet.

Interesting, no minor dragons occupied the room. How strange that seemed. Laconia and the wyrmlings were always in their company or Kellynch's. The Darcy ladies' fairy dragon Friends and little May were always near their Friends. Were these ladies too good to befriend minor dragons?

Or perhaps no minor dragon would have them.

That was not the right attitude to begin this meeting on.

Each of the fine ladies, garbed in Order-blue, wore the same expression Anne had seen in the society Father most preferred. Self-important and eminently aware of their own status.

At least it was an attitude she had a great deal of experience in managing.

"Good morning," Lady Matlock dipped the barest of curtsies. "May I present Lady Wentworth, daughter of Sir Walter Elliot, baronet, wife of Sir Frederick Wentworth, baronet. His seat is Kellynch-by-the-Sea."

Anne curtsied until her knee nearly touched the floor. They nodded at her as a single unit.

"Lady Torrington, Lady Dunbrook, Lady Jersey, and Lady Cowper, I present Lady Wentworth. Lady Dalrymple, I believe you are already acquainted."

Lady Dalrymple was a member of the Cotillion Board? How could she not have known that? Would having her cousin here make things easier? Likely not. She had taken great pleasure in the gossip of Father's social demise. Surely, she would hold that against Anne.

"Pray do come in, Lady Wentworth." Dowager Lady Dalrymple, with her deceptively pleasant expression and icy blue eyes, gestured toward a chair. A plain one. Set at an awkward distance from the other ladies. "You do understand it is not our usual way to invite nonmembers into our meetings, but as you are my cousin, we thought to make an exception."

"I am honored by your invitation." Anne sat in the chair indicated.

Lady Matlock backed out and shut the door. Should it be meaningful that she did not turn her back on this group? Probably.

"We understand that you, Miss Darcy, Mrs. Collins and Miss Bennet have all taken up temporary residence here at the Order offices. I hope you find your accommodations comfortable." Lady Cowper had a youthful face and kind smile that matched her reputation as the most gracious and genuinely nice patroness at Almack's.

"Lady Matlock has been most gracious in seeing to our comfort. We deeply appreciate her efforts."

"Good, good. I am glad to hear that. Staying in a strange place can be most uncomfortable."

"Especially under such circumstances as these." Lady Jersey had that sort of long face that gave the impression that she was looking down her nose at one. If not literally true, it probably was figuratively. "These are such trying times, you know, tragic really. That our membership has been so assaulted, that one of our own has been snatched. We all quite fear for our own safety now." She pressed her hand to her chest—probably to show off her expensive gold rings—and attempted to look aghast.

"The security at the offices is quite impressive. I am certain we have nothing more to fear. And when the Sage is returned—"

"If she is," Lady Jersey cut in sharply. "There is no anticipating what that woman will do."

Well, that was telling.

Lady Dunbrook, whose very blonde, nearly white curls clustered around her face suggesting a halo, cleared her throat and glared politely. "The Sage is a revered officer, for all that she might be considered unconventional. We are given to understand that her comprehension of all matters draconic is exceptional—even if incomprehensible to most of us."

Anne pressed her lips hard. Now was not the time to contradict any of these knowledgeable ladies.

"Not that such a thing has ever happened before," Lady Torrington, who had the unfortunate distinction of looking like the dragon she kept—an ill-tempered basilisk—muttered under her breath. The question was, did her temperament match as well?

"Yes, yes," Lady Dunbrook pushed off their chatter with an open hand. "None of that comes to the point of our concern. The Cotillion is only six weeks away."

That was not a question. How was she supposed to respond?

"You and Lady Elizabeth's sisters were to have been sponsored by the Sage and without her here—"

"It is clear that you will not be ready for the Cotillion." Lady Jersey's eyes narrowed as she pulled herself up very straight.

She was enjoying this!

"It is such a shame. It must be very disappointing." Lady Cowper had the decency to appear distraught.

Lady Torrington squinted her small eyes at Lady Jersey, her lip curling back just a bit. Definitely a basilisk in temperament, too. "It is just a ball. There will be another next year. I do not see why you make such an issue of it. Just tell her our decision, and be done with it."

Lady Jersey glowered at Lady Torrington, then

turned the same expression on Anne. "Yes, as to that—despite the ramifications on the Sage's reputation, it is clear that you cannot be presented unprepared."

Anne stood and shook out her skirts. Now was the time to be large. "I appreciate your concern, ladies. Truly I do. I know you have the best intentions and greatest concern for our reputations, but I can assure you that it is unnecessary. We can go on with our presentations as planned."

"Excuse me?" Lady Dunbrook half rose in her seat, her very full bodice heaving. The look of utter shock on her face would be quite amusing under other circumstances. "What are you going on about? Our decision—"

"Is certainly appreciated, but unnecessary. We will be ready in time for the Cotillion." Anne lifted her chin. She might not like playing dominance games, but that did not mean she was unprepared for it.

"How is that possible?" Lady Jersey knocked the tea table with her knee, rattling all the china.

"Our gowns are on order from Gardiner's. They only need trimming and fitting to be ready. A dance master has already been engaged to see to our minuets—"

"I intend to introduce a quadrille to the Cotillion, just as I will introduce it at Almack's this year." Lady Jersey's cheek twitched just a mite as she spoke.

"Do stop going on about that ridiculous dance," Lady Dalrymple murmured, glancing aside, eyes rolling.

"The dance master was already made aware of your plans and has sent written confirmation that the quadrille will be included in our instruction." That was not exactly accurate, but she would make sure that it was so.

"And you already know how to appropriately greet all the Dragon Mates at the event?" Lady Dunbrook's lip curled back in a sneer.

"The Sage has prepared a detailed course of study for us on that subject. We have the matter very well in hand, I assure you. We are all most confident."

"I do not like it. It is most irregular." Lady Dalrymple never liked anything out of the ordinary under the best of circumstances. "Excuse my bluntness, cousin, but you do not come from a proper dragon Keeping family. Your father—the less said on the matter the better— he never mingled among Blue Order society. How can you be expected—"

"Your concern is most gracious. I am most indebted to you for it. Rest assured, Lady Elizabeth's sisters and I take the standards of the Blue Order most seriously. You will not be disappointed in us."

"I will not risk embarrassment on the Cotillion floor." Lady Jersey stood, face flushing an uncomplimentary shade. "How can the standards here be any less than we would hold at Almack's?" She cast a meaningful look at Lady Cowper.

"This is hardly Almack's." Anne looked directly at Lady Cowper, who actually appeared to be listening. "Are not all Keepers and future Keepers to be presented at the Cotillion? Even the hearing children of important Dragon Friends are presented. That is a very different standard to the one kept at Almack's."

Lady Torrington snickered a breathy, hissy sort of laugh. "She does have a point. If they are not presented this year, they will be admitted next."

"But the Sage's reputation!" Lady Jersey looked

like she might stomp. "How can she sponsor them if she is not here?"

"Will it not show her to great advantage to be successful even without her direct presence? I am certain it will be an asset to her standing to permit us to attend." Then again, that might be the wrong way to try to argue this point. "As members of the Order, I know that seeing our officers presented in the best light is important to you."

"But the risk of failure is no less great than the reward of success. It is too much—" Lady Dunbrook glanced around the room as though looking for an escape route. So, she did not like conflict. Interesting.

"Then test us yourselves before the Cotillion. The day before the Cotillion, examine us, with your Dragon Mates if you wish, and see if we are not acceptable. Dragons are not shy to offer their opinions. If they do not believe we are sufficiently prepared, then we will stand down with no argument."

"We cannot trouble our Dragon Mates with such trivial matters!" Lady Jersey's eyes bulged.

It did make one wonder exactly what sort of terms she was on with her Dragon Mate.

"I do not know. Torrington might just find it amusing." Lady Torrington chuckled behind her hand.

"I no longer have a Dragon Mate now that my son has inherited the estate," Lady Dalrymple sounded genuinely sad. "So my voice must be somewhat muted on this matter, but it seems like an appropriate scheme."

"But if you fail, you know the dragons will talk, and I do not think they will be kind." Lady Cowper clasped her hands in her lap. "Would you truly wish to take that chance?"

Anne looked from one lady to the next. Their gowns and feathers and jewels, all a warm-blooded display of dominance. No, she was not going to allow them to peck the back of her neck. "I am confident in the Sage's plans. We would be honored to be tested by your committee. I know we will make you proud."

A quarter of an hour later, Lady Jibbering Idiot, a dramatic, tragic princess to be sure, and Countess Claptrap dismissed her from their exalted presence, after considerable debate pitting the latter against the former, with Anne's cousin, the warm-blooded basilisk and the halo-wearing viper appearing to switch sides simply for their own amusement.

Mrs. Gardiner's estimation of them had been kind and generous! No wonder Lady Elizabeth seemed haggard at the prospect of dealing with them.

Had she done the right thing, standing up to them and insisting their presentations go on as planned? It had seemed right at the time. Allowing the Cotillion Committee to cast aside Lady Elizabeth's debutantes stank of the sort of games played in the *ton* as a whole. While the Sage was well able to manage dragons, it seemed the games of warm-bloods were more difficult for her to control. After all she had done for Kellynch, they owed her whatever assistance she could offer. Hopefully this would be looked on as assistance.

It was a risky move, though. Alienating the Cotillion Board would not be without its consequences. Such women would be masterful in their revenge. But what loyalty did she owe them?

Anne paused at the door of the suite the Sage's sisters shared: two bedrooms, each with a dressing room, and a large sitting room between. The door carving depicted a fanciful large drake with inlaid agate eyes. She closed her eyes and listened, but there was little to hear. It was difficult to know what that might mean.

Eavesdropping was probably not a good habit to acquire in any case.

Had it been a good idea to commit all four of them to this course of action without even getting their consent? The Sage's Bennet-blood sisters would likely support her choice—they seemed to have a great deal of the same stubbornness and cleverness that the Sage had. Mrs. Collins in particular seemed the steady, reliable sort who could be depended upon in a crisis.

But Miss Darcy might be an issue. Kind, mild, and even a bit hesitant, she might lack the boldness to be able to stand up to the likes of so many warm-blooded dragons and their Dragon Mates.

No, stop, this line of thinking was not at all helpful.

She pressed the door open and slipped inside.

Under other circumstances, the sitting room might be considered the perfect scene of domesticity, with an attractive chamber, comfortable furnishings, and sufficient dragons in the décor to mark it as a Blue Order establishment. Mrs. Collins looked up from her soft chair near the frosted windows and set aside her book; Miss Bennet and Miss Darcy abandoned their board game on the low tea table near the brown sofa and sprang to their feet.

"Dare we ask?" Mrs. Collins hurried toward her.

"Do not make us wait, tell us what they said!" Miss

Bennet all but ran to her side.

Four colorful fairy dragons leapt from the table to hover in the middle of the room as Corn and Wall tumbled from their basket and wove around Anne's ankles, purring loudly.

"Pray allow her to sit down, Lydia. Can you not see that she has had a trying time of it?" Mrs. Collins urged Anne to sit in a soft armchair near the fire.

"Thank you." Corn and Wall sprang into her lap, pushing their furry faces into her hands.

"Were they particularly awful?" Mrs. Collins poured her a cup of tea and sweetened it to her liking. How dear that she had paid enough attention to recall Anne's preferences.

"Nothing that I did not expect."

"But what did they say?" Miss Bennet, standing near Anne's seat, barely restrained herself from stomping, but Cosette hopping on her shoulder completed the image rather nicely.

Anne drew a deep sip of tea. "In short, Lady Jersey was rather convinced that we should not be presented due to the Sage's absence."

"This is unfortunate." Miss Darcy, who stood at a distance from the others, hung her head. But was that a note of relief in her voice? "I suppose we will have to wait until next year."

Miss Bennet whirled on Miss Darcy. "How can you say that! It is patently unfair! We have been accepted for presentation. We should be able to attend the Cotillion. Our father and our sister are officers of the Order! They cannot keep us away."

Mrs. Collins waved the others into seats. "Technically, that might be true, but without our sponsor, I am afraid they can take that step. Granted, it is only a delaying tactic and would not keep us entirely out of the Order—"

"Horrid warm-bloods." April zipped between Mrs. Collins and Anne, a bright blue blur. "Can you not see what this is?"

"I expect you will say it is a show of dominance," Anne said quietly.

"That is exactly what it is. It is what large dragons do. They wait until the dominant among them is away from their territory, then they swoop in to try to claim some of it for themselves. The Accords have made that maneuver illegal, but it seems that only applies to dragons, not men."

"That sounds precisely like what I saw happening." Anne lifted her hand, inviting April to perch.

"We must defend my Friend's territory. We cannot allow them to believe they are equal." April buzzed in dizzying circles in the middle of the room.

"But how are we to do that? It is not as if we have any recourse to their decision." Mrs. Collins poured jam into a saucer and lifted it toward April.

Thankfully she landed on the saucer and plunged her face into the jam. She had not been eating well since the abduction, and it seemed starvation did not agree with her temperament.

"I am glad to hear you say that." Anne leaned back into the chair and closed her eyes. "I spoke rather boldly on our behalf. I was afraid I might have overstepped myself."

"What did you say?" Miss Bennet bounced in her seat, sending Cosette back into the air.

Anne took another draw from her tea. Was that Earl Grey? No, it was a touch too floral, but definitely flavored with bergamot. Somehow there was strength in the warmth of that cup. "I told them about Lady Elizabeth's excellent preparations; Mrs. Gardiner's help with the gowns; the dance master hired; and all the study materials arranged. I argued that there is every reason to believe we will be able to make ready for the Cotillion whether she is here to prepare us or not."

A slow smile spread across Mrs. Collins' face.

Oh, thank heavens!

Miss Darcy gasped, and trembled as she lifted her hand to her cheek. "What did they say?"

"There was a bit of debate, to be sure, but at the end, it was agreed that we might continue our preparations for the Cotillion. They will test our readiness—much as Lady Elizabeth said she would do—before the Cotillion itself so they might be as confident in our preparations as we are."

"You are joking! How could you?" Miss Darcy covered her mouth with her hands as soon as the words tumbled forth.

"Very easily, Miss Darcy. You do understand your sister's reputation is at stake in a very real way?"

"It is not her fault this awful thing has happened."

"While that is true, it does not really matter. For whatever reason, the women of the committee do not appreciate her dominance over them and are seeking whatever means they can find to usurp it."

"That is not fair. Surely—"

April dove toward Miss Darcy, who cringed back. "No, no one will care or interfere. It is the way with dragons. The smaller and the weaker will always be overshadowed by the large and powerful. No one until Elizabeth has ever cared about the plight of us little dragons. No one else will fight the she-dragons for her sake but us."

"Then indeed, we must stand up for her." Mrs. Collins stood and moved to Anne's side. "I am with you, Lady Wentworth. We will not permit Elizabeth's territory to be lost to them."

"What about us, what can we do?" Heather, fluffy and very pink, landed on Mrs. Collins' shoulder. "There must be something we can do to help. Elizabeth has been so good to us, there must be some way we can help her."

"It is not fair! They keep us little dragons away from anything important and useful." Cosette returned to Miss Bennet's shoulder, warbling loudly. "The cockatrice guards may go search for her. They have asked for all the cockatrice in London to be alert for signs of her. The small drakes who pass for dogs and the like have been set to look for her. But we—we have been told to stay quiet and out of the way lest we get ourselves eaten by some passing cat or hawk."

"Indeed, indeed." April hovered near Cosette. "They overlook us, even now—now when our abilities might be the most useful of all."

A cold shiver slithered down Anne's back, making it difficult not to twitch in a most unladylike manner. "Pray tell, what do you mean? I have not had the pleasure of knowing any fairy dragons, so I know nothing directly of your strengths and abilities."

"Only that we are unreliable twitter-pates who have not a useful thought in our heads." Pax twittered from the back of Miss Darcy's chair.

Miss Darcy turned, slack-jawed, to stare at her Friend.

"And that we have quick tempers and nip at ears at

random." Heather mimicked ear-nipping.

"And that we are not very smart nor are our memories reliable." Cosette was adorable in her fluffy display of offense.

"And that we are forever putting people to sleep with our songs." Pax seemed desperate to add something less controversial to the conversation.

Anne leaned forward, elbows on knees. "Indeed, I have heard all those things. However, I also understand that the common opinion may very well be incorrect. So, tell me yourselves, what are your particular strengths?"

"Gossip." April flitted to the arm of Anne's chair and settled her wings back as though she were crossing her arms over her chest.

"Tell me more."

"Our kind hear everything that is going on, nearly everywhere. People speak freely before us, as do dragons. We are too small to matter, you see, so they take no care around us."

"And we are so small, they often do not even know we are about. There are no secrets where there are fairy dragons." Cosette rubbed her head against Miss Bennet's cheek.

"The cockatrice and drakes are far more obvious, and they are not adept at putting many stories together to understand a whole picture," Heather added.

"This is something I have never heard or considered." Nor had she heard anyone else consider it either.

"No one ever does. Granted, not all of us can do it well. But with experience, we become very good at putting together the things we hear and creating a complex understanding." Heather looked directly at

Mrs. Collins, who seemed more than a little surprised.

"Why have you never told me?" Mrs. Collins scratched under Heather's chin.

"It never seemed important before."

"If I am understanding you correctly, it sounds as though you wish to assist in the efforts to recover the Sage?" Was it possible? Corn and Wall purred in her lap—or was that her own blood thrumming in her ears?

"Of course we do! Why is that so difficult to conceive?" April hovered at Anne's eye level.

"You are the smallest of dragons. Is it not said that it is important to know when to allow a bigger dragon to handle matters?"

April shrieked very much like a cockatrice as she dove for Anne's ear. "Can none of you see what is right in front of your face? A fairy dragon is in the center of all this disruption to the Blue Order. A fairy dragon! The minorest of minor dragons, the worthless little flutter-tufts who some barely consider dragons to start with. Prey to nearly every other species of dragon! If we are found to be a danger to our kind, how do you think that bodes for our future? It is not inconceivable that we could be removed from the protection of the Order and left to fend for ourselves with the rest of the wild animals."

"Surely not!" Anne let her hand fall from her well-nipped ear.

"What do you think will happen if it is determined that our kind brought England to the brink of dragon war and offered nothing useful?"

"Are things that bad?" Miss Darcy whispered, cuddling Pax close.

"Far more than you know," Heather murmured.

"No one has faith in our kind."

Mrs. Collins gasped.

"Rather the same attitude most have toward young ladies in general." Lydia tossed her head.

Anne bounced her heel against the worn carpet as she chewed her lip. "I have been told that dragons value boldness, and if ever there were a time for boldness, it is now. What is more, I think our studies in preparation for the Cotillion could offer an excellent cover for our real work."

"What are you thinking, Lady Wentworth?" Mrs. Collins leaned in close, her voice soft and serious.

"If the Order intends to bring all its resources to bear to recover the Sage, then all the resources should be utilized. The risks are high, but you should be permitted to do what you are able to do. I say you should go out and seek whatever information you can find. Come back to us, and we will help keep track of it all and look for patterns. When we find something—" That was perhaps the boldest statement she had ever uttered. "—I will bring it to Wentworth and Sir Fitzwilliam. They will know how to present it to the Order so that it may be acted upon."

"I do not think I can do that." Pax trembled and cuddled into the crook of Miss Darcy's arm.

"As I recall, Sir Fitzwilliam has asked you to spend time in the nursery with Nanny and little Anne. Your presence would be missed. It will be up to you to make sure no one notices that your friends are gone on their mission. Are you up to that?"

The little white fairy dragon's brow knit as though she were thinking very deeply. "I think I could do that."

"The rest of us will have to manage our Cotillion

preparations while disguising the fairy dragons' absence and recording and coordinating the information they bring back. It will be no small effort. It will require all of us to be committed to the cause. And willing to diligently guard our secret. If you are not certain of this course, you must speak up now. Too much is riding on our effort to go forth without full agreement. Even with that, I am not sure only three fairy dragons will be enough."

"Lady Astrid will be willing to assist, I am sure. Verona is swift and smart and savvy." April bobbed up and down. "I will approach them."

"Are you all comfortable with that? What do you all say to this?"

"I am not willing to sit around all day being stupid. The littlest always miss out on all the fun and adventure. I will do my part." Miss Bennet crossed her arms over her chest and nodded firmly.

"Longbourn has already gone to seek out information on the wyrms thought to have had a part in Lizzy's abduction. We have just begun to become friends. I do not think he would forgive me if I knew there was something we could do to help Lizzy and failed to act. Heather and I are committed."

"Miss Darcy? There is no pressure. Speak up and be honest, if you cannot, then you cannot. It will do none of us any good for you to agree to something that you cannot commit to. Will you be able to do this?"

"Will I have to lie to my brother?"

"No, you will not." April flapped definitively. "If he finds out, he will see sense in the plan. It is the sort of thing my Friend would have approved of, so he will approve as well."

"Very well, then, yes, I will support this effort, too."

"What shall we do?" Wall rose up on his serpentine tail and looked up at her with big eyes.

"Yes, we want to help as well, like Laconia does." Corn mimicked Wall's posture. Two tatzelwurms begging? Merciful heavens.

"Perhaps you might distract visitors from asking questions about the fairy dragons in whatever way you see fit?" Mrs. Collins suggested. "They could carry messages as well?"

Those were not bad ideas.

They purred.

"We are resolved to begin immediately, then."

Recruiting fairy dragons and baby tatzelwurms into espionage? What had she just done?

10
Chapter

January 20, 1815 London Order Offices

"THE CHANCELLOR IS not in good spirits," Laconia muttered as he wove between Wentworth's feet on the rapid march through the dim, rather crowded corridors to Matlock's ground floor office.

Somber portraits of human and dragon alike stared down at them, as if to judge their errand. There were some who avoided these halls just for that reason.

People and dragons still stopped to stare at their peculiar little dance. A "kind soul" stopped to tell him, once, that being constantly seen in company with a tatzelwurm might not be the best for his image as a baronet. He returned the kindness by politely suggesting to Laconia that individuals with such opinions were definitely below his notice. One would think Order members who worked in the central office would know better than to insult a dragon, even a small one.

"How did you come by this information?"

"Quill Driver, Lady Astrid's assistant." Laconia growled softly. "He is reliable."

Wentworth winced. "I did not mean to question you, old Friend, merely to get a sense of what precisely 'not in good spirits' might mean."

"Perhaps the expression 'fit to be tied' might capture it better?" Laconia paused and looked up at Wentworth.

"What exactly did Quill Driver say?"

"'Not fit to be around other predators' were his exact words, but that is not something that, as I understand, makes a great deal of sense in warm-blooded terms." Laconia's serpentine tail flicked.

"True, but it is quite a turn of phrase, is it not?"

"You might be surprised at how poetical dragons can be." Laconia continued on. They turned the corner to the wider corridor containing Matlock's and several other important offices.

He was probably right. Poetry, human or draconic, was not something he had ever spent a great deal of time contemplating, despite Anne's protests that the letter he had written her was the most poetic thing she had ever read.

Those were very special circumstances.

And now look where they were. Neither of them had ever conceived of dealing with matters like these when they had agreed to take on Blue Order work. Anne was a determined and hardy soul, but this affair threatened to be beyond even her fortitude.

But she was working hard at it, dear woman. And if anyone could make a way through such circumstances, it was her. Clever, reliable, steadfast, wholly and utterly dependable. She did not always think those terms a compliment, but they were, of the highest order.

Matlock's elaborate carved door stood ajar, so he slipped inside, pausing near the door to identify which dragons might already be within, and if introductions might be required. It took a few moments for his eyes to adjust to the candlelight.

Heavens above, what a crowd!

Cownt Matlock, his blue-green hide darkened to something close to the twilight sky in the dim light, hunched uncomfortably in the corner farthest from the dragon tunnel entrance. What kind of information could require the cownt's presence in an office not really large enough to accommodate him?

Laconia pouffed, his fur standing on end. The hair on the back of Wentworth's neck did the same.

A blue lindwurm curled tightly in the opposite corner as though trying to give as much space as possible to the other occupants. His long mustache whiskers and square snout gave him a rather scholarly look. Sir Richard sat nearby with his Friend Earl perched on the back of his chair. No doubt then, the lindwurm must be Netherford.

Darcy sat near Matlock's imposing, carved desk where the Chancellor himself sat, looking impatient at best. Walker perched on an iron dragon perch just behind and to Darcy's right. An empty chair near a desk pillow suggested where Wentworth and Laconia should take their places.

"General Strickland will be here shortly, then we will begin." Matlock glanced at Wentworth as he drummed his fingers on the desk.

Walker landed on the floor near Laconia. He

spread his wings as Laconia reared up and puffed his body as large as he could. They danced in a circle three times around, hissing and chittering, slowly allowing the circle to close until they touched nose and beak in the center. Remarkable, a greeting of equals. How many of those had he ever seen?

Darcy and Sir Richard exchanged glances with each other and with Wentworth, eyebrows cocked in such a similar fashion that their resemblance to each other was made all the more obvious. Was it the presence of the two major dragons that kept the small ones from vying for dominance?

Sharp brisk steps came through the door and it shut hard. Laconia spring-hopped to the desk pillow as Walker landed on his perch.

Minister of Dragon Defense, General Strickland, stayed near the door, clearly awaiting introduction. Tall and thin as a whip, with tousled grey hair, and a large black patch covering what remained of his left eye. His face could have been an illustration for the word "severe" and his every movement echoed that. Responsible for domestic and international dragon defense concerns, he had earned the position through a long career in the 'conventional' army. There was hardly an officer, Army or Navy, who did not know his name or his reputation.

Matlock conducted the appropriate introductions and General Strickland took the remaining seat, between Darcy and Wentworth.

"Yates, Abbot and Easterly are on their way here. I expect them to arrive in the next day or two," Strickland said, extending his hand, fingers curled toward himself, to Laconia.

Yates? They were calling in the head of the

Knights of the Pendragon Order? However bad the situation had seemed, Yates being involved made it dozens of times worse.

The neat little swing-hitch in his belly turned into an ugly stopper knot.

Laconia gave Strickland a cursory smell. His hair did not stand on end. All in all, that was a good sign.

"Excellent. You are familiar with Wentworth and Fitzwilliam's reports?" Matlock pointed to them in turn.

"I have a few questions, but those can be addressed later in light of Netherford's new intelligence." Strickland looked directly at the lindwurm.

Lovely, just lovely. What else was going wrong now?

Sir Richard rose and stood near Netherford. "Netherford had not planned to attend the Cotillion this year, so he remained at the estate."

Netherford stretched a little further into the room. "But gossip reached me that was too alarming to leave lie, so I went to investigate."

"What kind of gossip? Where did you hear it from?" Strickland's words were clipped, like a man used to giving orders.

"The source is irrelevant as I have verified it all myself." Netherford gestured with his right paw as if to emphasize his point.

"I do not trust gossip." Strickland leaned back, arms crossed over his chest.

"What I bring is not gossip. I have spoken to all the original sources myself."

"What kind of source?"

"Let the dragon speak." Matlock slapped the desk.

Strickland's eyes bulged. Apparently, it was acceptable to be rude, but not have the behavior returned in kind. Telling, but not surprising.

"By your leave, General," Netherford tipped his head and waited until Strickland nodded. There was the diplomat in the room. "On the way to London, I spoke with a wyrm in the north and a wyvern between there and London who had been approached by separate major drakes, both promoting the same, rather alarming, rhetoric. They suggest that the recent kidnapping of the Sage is indicative of men losing control of the Blue Order. They are chafing against the restrictions put upon them by the Order, wondering why they should acquiesce to creatures so much less powerful than themselves."

Dragon's fire!

"They are younger dragons who have never experienced dragon war, clearly seen in how casually they put forth the notion that it might be worth the casualties for dragonkind to establish dragon dominance in England once again."

Dragon war. He said dragon war.

The knots in his stomach unraveled into a twisted, tightening tangle.

Strickland drew in a deep whistle with all the force of a string of military invectives. "You spoke to the drakes as well, I imagine?"

"No, I did not."

"How then can we be certain?"

To his credit, Netherford only blinked. "I beg your pardon, sir, but I would hardly expect such a drake to speak honestly with me, or even speak with me at all. With Sir Richard, a Knight of the Order and son of the Chancellor as my Keeper, I am hardly the sort of soul they would reveal such attitudes toward. Do you blame them? It is not difficult to imagine that I would bring such information directly here."

"What proof do you have that the wyrm and wyvern were correct? Why should we believe them? Both dragons are of low standing, all things considered. Would it not be in their interest for them to stir up trouble for their betters?"

"That is not the way dragons would handle such matters, settling our conflicts through warm-bloods."

"That is not what I understand."

Netherford's mustache twitched in time with Sir Richard's cheek.

Oh, Strickland was a gem indeed.

"Consider, if you will, what the wyrm and wyvern have to gain by spreading such a falsehood. Even should those drakes be somehow removed, they would obtain no new territory. Similarly, their charters with their Keepers remain unchanged. No material advantage would come to them by defaming the bigger dragons. And it is a dangerous game. To speak calumny against a bigger dragon is to invite retaliation, which, in case you are not aware, is specifically allowable in the Accords. Their very lives are in danger for having spoken to me."

"Then why would they?"

"Because in a Dragon War, smaller major dragons stand to lose a very great deal and it is in their best interest to stave off such an occurrence. Maintaining that which they already have, and would not likely be able to replace, is a strong motivation."

Strickland grumbled something untoward under his breath. For being a member of the Order, he seemed to have little respect or appreciation for Netherford.

Perhaps it was because Netherford was French.

Matlock cleared his throat. "It is the official position of the Order that Netherford brings us notice of a credible threat to the Order, one that must be thoroughly investigated, and dealt with if necessary."

"If I may be so bold as to suggest, the return of the Sage and appropriate punishment of the kidnappers, and the dismantling of any possible smuggling networks would go a long way to proving the men of the Order have not lost their usefulness to its dragons." Netherford's tone remained even and smooth, despite his eyebrows now twitching like his mustache. What a feat of self-control.

"Such a thought has not been overlooked." Matlock rolled his eyes as though he were fed up with talk of the abducted Sage. "Strickland, we need a coordinated approach among the army, navy and Pendragon Knights. In the meantime, Richard, you and Netherford are to conduct a thorough investigation of these allegations. Immediately. Wentworth, we have received reports from the cockatrice guard that unusual activity has been identified at the port of Dover, unfamiliar ships and cargos bound for France. Take Kellynch with you and investigate what you can there. Talk to the sea dragons and see what might be learned from them."

Laconia rose up on his tail. "You do realize, the sea dragons are not members of the Order nor have they any connection to the Sage."

"I am sure you will find a way." Matlock did not dignify them with a glance.

That was the military way of saying they would be

expected to make something from nothing.

It would not be the first time.

Wentworth called upon Kellynch first. Not because his feelings were more important than Anne's, but rather that they were less reliable. Anne would be supporting and comforting, supplying an abundance of good sense as she offered to manage whatever needed to be done. Laconia had gone ahead to alert her of their impending departure.

Who knew what to expect with Kellynch? Although his good days had been outnumbering the bad recently, with ongoing issues with the tunnels to the lair under the house, the situation seemed ripe for a tantrum.

Thankfully, today was a good day. He felt deeply the importance of being given a mission directly from the Chancellor of the Order. Wentworth left him happily mulling over the prospects of proving himself a valuable member of Blue Order dragon society and not the clever little thief that Cornwall had declared him to be.

Oh, how that little insult had stung his pride. But perhaps it was just the thing needed to remind Kellynch that cold-blooded dragon society would judge him just as much as warm-blooded society would judge his Keepers.

Wentworth plodded upstairs—when would they be done with climbing this presumptuous grand staircase?— to find Anne.

Knowing her, she would have his trunk packed

and waiting for him.

He opened the door to their quarters, carved and painted with a garish lindwurm terrorizing a horse. Thankfully, the chambers within were not nearly so alarming. Truly, who thought that an appropriate decoration for a guest chamber door?

The rooms were finely finished, but a touch plain, quite to his taste really. Just enough furniture to be functional, but not enough to clutter. More significantly, they smelt fresh and sweet; they smelt of Anne.

That made them right.

Soft light from the window bathed her as she stood by the large press, near his battered trunk, and added a neatly folded shirt to the carefully organized contents.

He swallowed hard. Did she realize how much such gestures meant to him?

"I think this should be sufficient for your trip." She smiled, a mix of sadness and resolve in her eyes. "You are to Dover in the morning? I took the liberty of informing Alister Salt of your impending travels. He will be ready for you at sunrise. He seemed quite pleased to be of service. I got the sense he and his team prefer to be on the road as much as possible." She chuckled and shut the trunk.

"It would seem. Thank you." He sat on the trunk and pulled her down beside him. "I do not know how long we will be gone."

"I understand. We will make do, though, keeping ourselves occupied preparing for the Cotillion and showing those she-dragons that they may not exert their dominance so easily."

Wentworth laughed. "How easily you have adopted the mentality of the dragons, my dear. Has the exposure to all those fairy dragons begun to tax your good nature?"

"About the fairy dragons." She had that look in her eyes.

"Why do I have a sense this is only going to make life more complicated?"

"Because you have been dealing with dragons, and you know they make everything more complicated." She leaned into his shoulder. "The Darcy contingent of fairy dragons have been very unhappy to be relegated to being decorative in the guest quarters and forbidden to do anything to assist in the Sage's recovery."

"I certainly can see her little blue Friend would be disturbed." Wentworth covered his ear.

"Apparently they are certain they can be a useful resource for information. They believe themselves to be the hearers of everything useful, and not, in the Kingdom."

"What are you telling me?" He looked deep into her very determined eyes.

Heavens, the last time she wore that expression, she was telling him she would stand with Kellynch at the Blue Order Court!

"After a long discussion with them—yes, I know, we did have a long discussion with fairy dragons! In any case, it seems prudent to have them try and seek out what information they can regarding the Sage's disappearance."

"But they are senseless flutter-tufts. Surely the Order cannot support this. You will get no useful information out of them. Just bits and bobs of gossip that is of no worth."

"Perhaps that is true. That is why the Order does not need to know about it, at least right now."

He leaned back and sighed.

"I know what you are thinking, but what if they can be helpful? Can we afford to ignore any potential resource? I have gotten a sense of the trouble that is abounding in the kingdom. Is it wise to overlook any asset we may have in this situation?"

"When you put it that way, how can I disagree? But if they discover anything, how will you—"

"All their information will filter through Mrs. Collins and me. Only that which we deem important or credible will go beyond our doors. If there is anything at all, you can be sure I will let you know. You will listen, yes? Even if it is from fairy dragons?"

How was it she made such a thing sound so reasonable, and even wise? "If your good sense deems it important, you can be certain I will listen, my dear."

January 22, 1815 Dover

Alister Salt and his team pulled away from the modest Dover Blue Order offices, the wheels crunching and clacking against the cobblestone street. Golden rays of sunrise crept down the street as though reaching out to meet them. The coach would probably arrive back in London even quicker than they had gotten him to Dover. That man and his son could change a team of horses faster than any would have believed possible. Salt and his team were at least as fast, maybe faster than the Royal Mail.

The stories he had to tell! Like listening to an old seaman, difficult to tell where the facts ended and the imagination began. But it was warm and companionable, good company around the fire at the Blue Order office last night.

Today they were both off on business once again.

Salt air, sharp breezes, sea bird calls. Familiar, oddly comforting after the bustle and confinement of London. Perhaps he could achieve what the Order demanded, after all.

Wentworth, with Laconia at his side, took out a dinghy—one with a sail— that the Order kept. He would talk to the local warm-bloods later in the day. Early morning and twilight were the best times to find sea dragons.

Morning mist, hanging low in the barely pre-dawn sky, kissed his cheeks as his limbs found the rhythm of the waves once more. Was it possible he could taste the salt in the air? Perhaps he needed the sea as much as Kellynch.

What would Anne think about purchasing a dinghy? He smiled in spite of himself. She was probably already arranging the budget for it. Dear, dear woman.

Kellynch met him in the calm, open water, far enough out that none would be able to see him rising from the surface of the ocean.

"This is entirely agreeable." Laconia put his paws on the edge of the hull, his mouth open, tasting the air with his long, forked tongue.

Wentworth brought his little boat alongside Kellynch. It was a neat, responsive little sailboat, so satisfying. "How was your journey?"

"It has been a long time since I have made such a journey. I had almost forgotten what it was like to truly be at sea."

"Have you missed it?"

"I am a marine wyrm, of course I have. More than I think I realized." Kellynch bobbed in time with the waves.

"Enough to leave the land and return?"

Laconia leaned against Wentworth's leg, purring something that was neither agreement nor dissent.

"At first, I thought so, but I suppose I have become accustomed to the ways of the land as well. I think I would miss them. So, I expect I shall be content to live at the edge of land and sea. Kellynch-by-the-Sea is right."

"Perhaps we might find a way to sail like this together at Lyme as well."

"That would be pleasing." Kellynch smiled. He smiled! A toothy, terrifying expression, but it was a smile.

It should not make Wentworth so satisfied, but it did. "Are there any local sea dragon pods?"

Kellynch looked toward the open sea. "I have encountered one, and some sea-dwelling cockatrice as well."

"Are they willing to talk with us?"

"Of that, I am not yet certain. They have agreed to meet with you, in no small part because of Laconia's reputation, but what they will say, I cannot be certain. I expect they will have noticed your arrival and will make themselves known soon."

Laconia chirruped and flicked his tail. He was used to being Wentworth's liaison to the sea dragons. Kellynch was thoughtful to recognize that. "So, I suppose now we wait."

Back on the Laconia, he had spent many an hour waiting on the sea dragons that Laconia helped him speak with. Often, waiting felt like wasted time, and sometimes it was. But often enough it proved sufficiently fruitful to make the effort worthwhile.

Lazy waves lapped at the hull as the mist gave way to a mackerel sky, golden light painting the underside of the clouds like a ceiling overhead. The sail luffed against him, resting as they waited, ready to be ordered back into service at a moment's notice. There was no calm like a sunrise over the ocean.

The sea's surface rippled in a deliberate, anticipatory way. He knew that look. Laconia chittered expectantly, fur pouffing and ears erect.

The first sea dragon broke the surface—a small serpent-whale, about the size of a typical horse, a sort he and Laconia had encountered often enough. Their bodies were long and bulbous, like whales, with flat tails and a prominent dorsal fin like a shark. A short, thick neck began just in front of two short limbs sporting webbed fingers or maybe toes at the ends. Their heads were thick, but narrower than their bodies, with long, toothy mouths, ending in a long snout maybe as big around as his thigh. Their bodies were more slick than scaly, some mottled grey and white, some more brown, a few nearly black.

The one who approached was female—she sported a small set of head fins near where it seemed ears should be. Males lacked the decoration. At least twelve more serpent-whales followed in her wake. In all likelihood, a dozen more individuals lurked in the depths, guards ready to come to the aid of the pod should anything go amiss.

The large female swam closer to Wentworth's vessel and brought her head and front flippers out of the water. Kellynch rose up, his squared head above hers, flattening his scaly body to look large. She bared her teeth and screamed an otherworldly sound. Kellynch growled and shrieked, weaving back and forth, rising higher out of the water with each pass. He dove down upon her, stopping just short of her neck, and touched the back of her head with his tongue. She fell back into the water with a commensurate splash, ceding dominance to Kellynch.

After several moments underwater, she appeared once more, with head and flippers out of the water, staring at Wentworth.

"My Keeper, Wentworth, and our Friend Laconia." Kellynch bobbed his head toward Wentworth. "The pod matriarch has a name you lack the ability to say. She has agreed to be called Dover."

"You are gracious to permit me a name that I can pronounce." Wentworth bowed from his shoulders. It had been sufficient when encountering other sea dragons. Hopefully it would be sufficient now.

"We have heard of you and your Friend. It is interesting that the stories are true. There is a land dragon that goes to sea. You two have a reputation for being worthwhile to deal with. Kellynch said you have something to ask of us." Dover's voice was high, like a fairy dragon's, but with more squeals and clicks.

"I have come to ask you for information. One of our kind was taken, and we believe has been forced on a ship that has recently traversed these waters or might well be in them."

"Why is this so important that you would seek us out?"

"The woman in question is very important to British dragons. She is known as the Dragon Sage and has offered great service to the British dragons."

"The landed dragons. Of the Blue Order?" Somehow, she did not sound as though she approved. "We have heard of the Order and of the woman you seek. Why should we tell you what we know?"

"You know something of her?" Laconia leaned a little farther over the railing, purring. The sound seemed to ease Dover's agitation.

"Why would I be here if we did not? I repeat, why should we tell you anything?"

"The Sage is very valuable. Unrest grows among the British dragons. There is growing fear that violence between men and dragons could erupt because of it. No dragon species will profit from that."

"He speaks the truth," Kellynch lowered himself to be closer to Dover.

"There has already been significant violence against my kind. It would be fitting for the warm-bloods to suffer for what they have done to us. We are harried by pirates, fishers and hunters. We have no legal recourse, treated like animals by the landed warm-bloods, ones who should understand and respect our true nature. Is not this conduct in opposition to your Pendragon Accords? Should we not have the same privileges as the landed dragons?"

"Those Accords were drawn up with the agreement of the landed dragons of Britain. According to our laws, they do not pertain to any dragons beyond our shores." If only Matlock had given him something to bargain with!

"Kellynch is covered by the Blue Order."

Damn. She was right.

"It was an illegal agreement offered by a powerful dragon who had no right to make such an agreement in the first place. The courts recently ruled to accept the agreement because it had remained unchallenged for so long, but …"

"Kellynch is a sea dragon, covered by the Pendragon accords. It does not matter to us how it happened, only that it has. If he is covered, then there is no reason why we cannot be part of them as well."

"We lack the authority to offer such relief. With the current crisis, I do not believe the Blue Order is ready to negotiate new treaties to include dragons beyond its shores."

"Then we do not know that we are ready to assist you in what you desire." She slapped the water with her front limbs.

"If you will help …" Laconia leaned over the water, extending a paw.

"No, we have no reason for trust. Give us assurances that the Order will assist us first, and we will assist you."

"Then you know where the Sage is?" Kellynch said.

"I did not say that we did. I only said we would assist you in finding her. I did not make promises as to how." In truth, that was a more valuable promise than simply knowing where she was.

"I could offer the words you seek, but the truth is I do not have the authority to make the promises you ask for. I will not give you empty words."

"Nor will we give you what you seek. Find one dominant enough to give us what we ask, and we will help you."

"We may have very little time to find her safely."

"Then I suppose you must hurry. You may contact us only if you are able to offer what we have asked. Kellynch will know how to find us, but do not attempt to unless you are ready to discuss a treaty." Dover splashed hard with her tail and dove, the rest of the pod following.

Laconia hissed, his tail lashing hard against Wentworth's leg.

How long would it take for a Blue Order messenger to get word to Matlock? More important, what would it take to convince him to offer the serpent-whales what they wanted?

Chapter 11

SOMETIME AFTER SUNDOWN, the storms began in earnest. Weathering a storm at sea proved so unlike doing so on land it was difficult to even think about them as similar events. One sheltered in a house, be it large or small, as the storm swirled around the structure, wreaking its havoc on the realm outside. But not so at sea.

Here, their sanctuary became part of the storm itself, swallowed by some ethereal dragon. Hemmed in, bound without escape. The sea roiled and tossed the sloop about like a child's shuttlecock. Howling frigid winds shoved them, shrieking with glee, driving icy rain into the dark little hold. No recourse but to cling together, their shivers blending into terrified trembling.

January 22,1815 On board the Sea Lion

On what might have been their third, fourth or even fifth morning shipboard, the winds died down and the sea settled. Poor little Joshua, despite his brave face, was pale and wan, matching Phoenix's dull and faded hide. Even the blue-striped wyrms, who now shared their dark, dank space in the hold, seemed faded and limp.

In theory, the wyrms were there to guard the captives. But snippets of conversation she heard from above suggested they had served their purpose for now and were being kept out of the way.

Did the Movers not think that the wyrms could hear them talking? Perhaps they really did not understand dragons and their capacities.

Interesting.

Heavy steps approached, the lock rattled, and the hold door swung open. Two unfamiliar men tramped in, the feeble dappled light from above painting their expressions more frightening than they probably were.

Oh, how they stank!

One strewed several pieces of hardtack on the floor near the wyrms, muttering insulting things about them under his breath. The other pressed bowls and mugs into Elizabeth's and Joshua's hands and dropped a whole fish, probably boiled, into Phoenix's cage. Without words, they left.

Joshua sipped the grog, sighing, most likely with joy that his stomach had finally settled. When they got back home, he would probably ask his mother for grog. The look on her face would be memorable.

When they got back.

If they got back.

No, when.

The wyrms dove on the hardtack like starving creatures, which probably was not far from the truth. Prussian, the scar across his face pulsating, managed to get his jaws around a piece, but his small, sharply pointed teeth were no match for the biscuit. He shook his head and the hardtack flew from his mouth, landing near Elizabeth's feet.

Prussian hissed and the others growled as they retreated and wound around each other in a writhing angry cluster.

She picked up the hardtack and dipped it in the greasy brothy soup of some form of meat and peas. Her stomach growled. It did not smell as dreadful as it looked. Darcy would be appalled at the very thought. The look on his face—how rich that would be.

What was he doing now? Was he with Anne? Did she even realize her mother was away, or perhaps Nanny and April kept her distracted so she did not yet know?

Was that a good thing?

What of Pemberley? Surely, she could not be so easily distracted. Who would comfort her, keep her from dangerous, rash choices? Chudleigh perhaps? Rosings? She dabbed her eyes with her sleeve.

The hardtack softened in the broth. She tore off a piece and threw it to Prussian. Eyes directly on her, he sniffed the hardtack, then touched it with his tongue. A moment later, he dove on it, gulping it down whole.

She tore off more and tossed pieces to the other wyrms. After gulping a large, sodden fragment, Azure tossed Elizabeth a second piece of hardtack, the red knob on her head seeming to flush. Hopefully that was a good sign. Elizabeth softened the sailor's biscuit and tossed it to the wyrm cluster.

Azure and Lapis, the females, inched toward her, their long, forked tongues tasting the air.

She fished strands of meat from her bowl and tossed them toward the females, who slithered closer still. Soon, they were within arm's reach, taking dainty bites directly from her hands.

"Have they not been feeding you properly?" she asked Prussian, clearly the leader of the little wyrm cluster, as she tossed him a bit of meat.

"There are many days the warm-bloods call banyan days, days without meat." Prussian rose up high on his tail as he hissed the words.

"Have you not told them you are predators, that you need meat?"

"Why would they listen to us?" He growled and inched closer to the females.

"Have they not had your help? Are you not as much a part of the crew as they? What was your agreed-upon share?" Elizabeth spoke very softly but kept her head above his. This sort of discussion could prove volatile.

She sipped her grog. Not awful. They had even added a mite of lime juice to the water and rum. Apparently, the Movers wanted to keep them alive, for now.

Azure twined with Prussian. Somehow it was comforting to see them behaving as normal wyrms did. "You have strange ideas, Lady Warm-blood."

Lady? Hopefully that was a good sign. "Whatever do you mean?"

"We are wyrms, the least among dragons." Prussian wrapped his square shaggy head in front of Azure's.

"Except for fairy dragons," Joshua muttered.

"Indeed, he is right." Phoenix twittered and flapped over the now bare fish bones, making sure none missed his remark.

"Perhaps. But some of you are taken as Friends, kept in warm little cages and fed all the delicacies you care to eat." Azure rose up high on her tail, sniffing and tasting the air. She hissed toward Phoenix's cage.

Who could blame her offense that Phoenix was given meat whilst they were not?

"I did not understand that wyrms often wanted Friends. I thought they were more content to live in their territories than in warm-blood dwellings." Did she know anyone at all who had a full wyrm Friend?

"We would be content to be allowed that." Lapis muttered as Indigo approached.

"I do not understand." Elizabeth held her breath and stared hard at the wyrms, skin tingling. Something important was in the air.

Indigo entwined with Lapis, her hide dry and starting to shed, and thrust his head forward of hers, yellowed and stained fangs exposed. "According to warm-bloods, we are neither appealing nor attractive. We look like the snakes you detest. We like one another more than warm-bloods. We are ill-suited to life as Friends."

Lapis bobbed her head hard, hitting Indigo under the chin. "It is not merely the warm-bloods—"

Prussian pounced, nearly landing on the twined smaller wyrms. "Do not tell her anything. She does not need to know. It will only bring us more trouble."

Elizabeth bit her lips. It would be risky, but dragons valued boldness. "I am more than you think I am. I can help."

"You are important to the Order?" Prussian growled.

"I am." She tossed out another sliver of meat.

Azure snatched it up. Prussian allowed that—perhaps she would be clutching soon.

Indigo snarled. "The Order that has betrayed us, that cares not for our trouble."

"I have heard nothing about it."

"That is proof! That is proof! The Order ignores our complaints. The Pendragon Accords say that we are part, but they lie, do nothing for us." Azure retreated behind Prussian, her red head-knob just visible behind him.

"Tell me of your complaint."

"So that you can promise more empty words? No. Do not talk to her anymore." Prussian hissed and feinted several strikes toward her.

Elizabeth withdrew. She would get no more, at least for now. She tossed out several more gobbets of meat, and they gobbled them up. At least that was a good sign.

Lapis slid a hardtack toward them with her tail. Joshua scooped it up and dusted it off on his shirt-sleeve. He broke it and offered half to Elizabeth.

No wonder the dragons could not eat it. She could barely break it with her back teeth. She dunked it in her grog as she sat on the pile of hay near Joshua and watched the wyrms.

Strange, these creatures were very strange. Not nearly as confused and addled as most of their kind, in truth, they were more talkative and personable than most wyrms. What could have happened to them to leave them so angry and suspicious?

At least, like most wyrms, they were motivated by their stomachs. Perhaps a few more shared meals would loosen their tongues.

And if it did not, at least the cluster would not starve. That was something.

Several hours, or at least what felt like several hours later, Joshua poked her shoulder and leaned close. "I think I hear the Movers talking." He pointed toward the ceiling, as though they were standing right above them.

How could she have missed that?

She glanced at the wyrms. They were woven into a tight cluster near the door, the females sleeping and the males keeping watch.

Elizabeth leaned back into the stale-smelling hay, her shoulder pressing into Joshua's as she clasped her hands in her lap and closed her eyes.

"How much has the damn weather cost us?" That voice—it was the not-gentleman—Ayles, yes, he had been called Ayles.

"Two, three days, and I 'spect there be more storms a'coming." Corney's coarse voice was much easier to identify.

"Our buyer is not going to be happy. It already took too long to get the bloody creature in the first place."

"Damn him. So, he thinks there ain't any other out there who would want a baby firedrake—a dragon fit for royalty? If he won't pay, we just take our things and find another. We might not even have to leave Bermuda to do it. I 'eard that there were another prince what would have a fire-breathing dragon for his court."

"How do you propose we find such a prince?" Ayles' feet shuffled overhead.

"The same one who lined up this affair will find 'im."

"What is the name of this man?"

A foot hit the deck hard, followed by several off-rhythm steps— Corney's limp. "You don't need to know."

The ball of wyrms jumped and several growled, staring at the grate overhead.

"If anything happens to you, there should be someone else who can find this mysterious dragon broker."

"Then you just best make sure that nothing happens to me, eh?" She could imagine Corney poking Ayles' chest.

So it was true, there was no honor among thieves, and they even acknowledged it among themselves.

"What are you going to do with the boy and the woman?" Ayles asked.

Elizabeth's heart pounded hard enough to drown out their voices. She held her breath. Joshua clutched her hand.

"Sell 'em with the dragon as handlers, trainers, what have you. If not, the boy is not too young for work. The woman looks good enough. I reckon we can get a decent price for her one way or the other."

Joshua squeaked and squeezed her hand harder.

"And if they do not want them? If they are not worth what you think?"

"I ain't worried about that none 'til we get to Bermuda and offload the dragon. I'll figure it out then."

Bermuda?

Bermuda. Did the Pendragon treaty extend to British territories like Bermuda? There was some statement about that in a recent paper the Minister of Foreign Dragon Affairs had written. Or was it a proposal?

"Are you certain we have the right dragon?"

"What d'ye mean?"

"Have you looked at that creature? He looks nothing like any of the bestiaries with fire-breathing dragons. You really think something that tiny is going to grow into a full-size dragon? Scarlett would have known for certain."

Pray that Corney believed it possible.

"Them firedrakes live hundreds of years. He gots plenty of time for growing up."

"He has done nothing to prove he's a firedrake. Nothing but fly around in that cage and eat. Oh, and sing a bit here and there. I do not think dragons sing. Who heard of a firedrake singing? You ought to make sure you got the right scaley before you see the buyer."

Dragon's blood! Why did Ayles have to be talking sense right now?

"I've 'ad enough of you questionin' me. Shut your trap and get back to navigating us a course there."

The men stomped away.

Elizabeth forced herself to breathe as she slipped her arm around Joshua's trembling shoulders. They were not prey to these men; she had to think like a predator, like a dragon.

Several minutes later, a key rattled in the lock. Corney and Ayles tromped in.

Elizabeth jumped to her feet and met them in the

middle of the room, shoulders pulled back, head high. "Where are you taking us? What is to become of us?"

"Some kind of fine lady, you are, I assume, or perhaps you used to be one." Corney slapped her with the back of his hand.

She shrieked, staggered back, and fell. How dare he!

The wyrms stared from their huddle in the corner. Had this been anywhere else, the dragons in the room would have killed him.

Perhaps she had become too accustomed to that. She dragged herself up to her knees. Perhaps now was not the time to vie for dominance.

"You ain't getting far with that act here, missy. I don't care who or what you were. All we care about is whether that—" he pointed at Phoenix. "—can breathe fire."

"Of course I can do it!" Phoenix hopped and flapped in the middle of the boxy cage.

"Then do it now." Corney crossed his arms and limped toward Phoenix.

"Just because I can do it does not mean I am able to do it on command." He tossed his head and turned his back on them.

"I think he is lying." Ayles crouched to look through the bars. "No dragon so little can do such a thing."

"I can." Phoenix turned and pouffed.

"Then do it." Ayles rattled the cage.

"Not now."

Corney grabbed Elizabeth by the shoulders and shook her until the room spun. "Is this one of your friends? You wouldn't want to see no harm come to her now, would you?"

"Do not threaten her. I will never perform if you threaten her."

"Then perhaps we just pitch you right off this here boat, yeah?" Ayles stood and lifted Phoenix's cage, shaking it hard. He hovered in the middle, trying to avoid being struck by the moving sides.

"Stop that!" Elizabeth staggered toward Phoenix. "We have been tossed about like a child's toy for days in storms. He has hardly been able to keep down the little food he has eaten. He has no energy left for making fire. It is a very taxing thing for one so small."

"You are saying the rough seas have left him unable?" Ayles snorted, lips drawing back in a sneer.

"It do make sense after a fashion, I think. Look how sick they been." Corney pointed at Joshua and Elizabeth. He wrestled the cage from Ayles. "We invested enough in this venture, I ain't ready to throw it all away yet. I'll give you some time on calm seas, but I 'spect you to spew fire soon."

"I will. You will see."

Corney pushed the cage at Elizabeth and turned toward the door. "See that he is ready to flame."

Ayles opened the door.

"The wyrms, they need meat." Elizabeth braced herself for another assault.

"What?" Corney turned on his heel and glowered.

"They cannot eat hardtack. Their teeth are not right for it. They will starve if you continue feeding them like that."

Corney stared at the wyrms, grumbling. The wyrms bared their teeth as though to prove Elizabeth's point.

"They will be of no use to you when they are too weak to stand guard."

Corney rolled his eyes and muttered something under his breath.

They left, locking the door loudly behind them.

"You will get your meat." Elizabeth whispered. "That's what he said under his breath."

Prussian licked his lips.

Lapis inched a little closer. "Can the small one really breathe fire?"

Elizabeth nodded. Thankfully Joshua and Phoenix said nothing.

Chapter 12

HOW COULD DARCY not be sentimentally fond of the Blue Order library? The main library, which took up nearly half the second floor of the building, had been the place where he had found Elizabeth while desperately searching for solutions to Pemberley's problem. He had found those answers, and so many more that day.

Would they be as fortunate today?

Bennet sat beside him at the long table, hunched over a dusty tome, mumbling under his breath. His drake secretary, Drew, jotted quick notes in the flickering light of the pewter candelabra in the middle of the table. His crest flared in and out as he wrote.

Apparently, Drew's hearing was particularly acute and allowed him to accurately perceive Bennet's muttering without asking for him to speak up. They actually seemed to work well together. Who would have imagined?

Darcy stood and stretched. Three days he had been huddled here with Bennet and Lady Astrid. Even the wonderful scent of old books could not drive away the sense of being lost amidst shelves upon shelves of volumes, none offering firm answers.

On the other side of the table, Lady Astrid, quick and sharp, pointed out several more volumes for them to search. Already covered in library dust, Quill Driver, her assistant, a muscular deep-grey drake who wore glasses that matched hers, scurried away to find them.

"I have a good feeling about these next two journals. I definitely remember references to unusual forest wyrms in those Keeper's journals." Lady Astrid removed her glasses and rubbed her bloodshot blue eyes. Though a tiny woman, her energy seemed boundless.

She had slept very little since learning there might be something she could do to help. She and Elizabeth shared a friendship of equals, a rare thing for both women.

"I realize I am likely speaking out of turn here, but perhaps it would be helpful if there were some sort of guidance for what Keepers should be keeping track of in those journals. Perhaps even insist on an index like many ladies craft for their commonplace books?" Darcy cringed as he spoke. Perhaps so much time in the dimly lit, crowded room was affecting his judgement.

Lady Astrid laughed, something she had not done in days. "Yes, you are speaking out of place, and yes, you are right. It is a pipe dream of mine to have such directives in place. But not all Dragon Keepers are like our esteemed Historian, as I am sure you have noticed. Many barely keep records. If we were to add more demands upon them, I fear nothing would be recorded at all."

Bennet looked up and nodded briefly, the corner of his lips pulling back in a brief, tiny smile.

Lady Astrid was one of the few officers in the Order who seemed to get on quite well with Bennet. Perhaps it was because their peculiarities and penchants aligned so closely.

"I am done with this volume, Drew." Bennet closed the book and pushed it away.

"I will return it to the shelves." Drew scurried away.

"I need something from that section as well. I will go with you." Astrid followed.

Bennet hung his head, eyes closed.

"Are you unwell?" Darcy sat down beside him. The hard, slightly too short chair had grown no more comfortable in the few minutes away from it.

"Who among us is well right now?" Bennet raked his thinning hair and laced his hands behind his head. "Lizzy has always been getting herself in trouble where dragons were concerned. Did she tell you the story of how she introduced herself to a basilisk? Or how she arranged to pull Dug Bedford's bad tooth herself, thus spawning a new call for dental surgeons among dragons?"

"I did not hear that latter bit of Dug Bedford's story."

"I have never really given her the credit she deserves for her service to the Order and to dragonkind." How small his voice had become.

"Why?"

"I have always intended to, eventually. At the time, though, it had seemed inadvisable to praise her uncouth methods. And then after, it always seemed too late and rather difficult to bring up." He shrugged, wincing. Was that the pain in his shoulders or his conscience?

"When she is returned, you must tell her. She would be happy to know of your approval."

"I doubt it would matter to her very much. I rarely see her now. She hardly writes. I do not think my opinion is one that matters to her at all." Bennet wrapped his arms around his waist and stared at the blank spot on the table.

"You have taken the comfortable route for a very long time. Now it sounds as though you may be having some regrets. If you have the opportunity to change that, it seems that a wise man—"

Bennet sniffed and looked aside. "How is little Anne?"

Naturally.

"Sleepless, as I understand her mother to have been at that age. But she is never happier than when in the company of dragons. Little May is at her side as much as April was … will be at Elizabeth's."

Bennet nodded, rocking slightly in his chair.

"She is in a nursery in the attics here. If you like, I will inform Nanny that you are welcome to visit at any time. I am sure Anne would enjoy your company."

"That is kind of you. It sounds like she is very much like her mother."

"I think she is."

Bennet pursed his lips into too many expressions

to clearly identify. "I had hoped Elizabeth would permit me to assist her in her duties as Sage."

Darcy bit his tongue. Now was not the time, nor here the place—

"I have found the books!" Quill Driver staggered to the table and dropped four volumes bound in Order-blue on the table, raising a small cloud of dust with an echoing thud. "Let us each take one." He shoved books at them, and one at Drew's currently empty place at the table.

Darcy rubbed his gritty, dusty eyes. What was the point of yet another volume? He needed to do something, not be stuck staring at illegible script about things no one cared anything for.

"Oh, this is interesting!" When had Drew returned?

"What, what?" Lady Astrid peered over his shoulder.

"Here, look, a reference to striped forest wyrms. The Keeper calls them Azure-Striped Forest Wyrms. It says he chased them out of his territory because of their venom. It seems touching their blue skins caused paralysis and hallucinations in the farm hands, allowing the wyrms to decimate the poultry, and even a small flock of sheep." Drew pointed at various spots on the page.

Darcy shut his volume hard and bolted up from his chair. "That aligns with the report given by Gardiner's men. I am sure they must be one and the same. What estate is that journal from?"

Quill Driver checked the frontispiece. "Nunnington Hall. All these volumes are from there."

"Excellent! Sir Fitzwilliam, hand me your journal. I just heard Longbourn has returned and wishes to speak with you." Lady Astrid reached for the thick tome.

Darcy bit his tongue. Best not tempt fate by hoping aloud for good news.

So many stairs. Five flights down, each growing darker and colder as he descended. Days like today, the entire Blue Order offices seemed like they were made up of stairs.

At the lowest level, Longbourn met him in the deep shadows at the base of the stairs, pacing. He should have waited in his guest lair. Was he impatient or controlling? Difficult to tell. It was never a good sign when Longbourn paced, though. Wings and hide layered in travel dust: another not-good sign.

He leaned in, close to Darcy. "I found something."

His voice rumbled in Darcy's chest. Nothing like being direct. "Pray tell me."

"The wryms you asked about, they are native to the north."

He probably should not mention that they had found that out themselves. "How far north?"

"Old Northumbria."

There was a lot of territory there. "Into Scotland as well?"

"Possibly, I could not trace them that far. But rumor suggests that they may be native to there, too."

"How widespread are they? Why have we not heard more of them? They are not in any of the common bestiaries."

Longbourn sat back on his haunches and folded his wings, like an old man preparing to tell children a tale. "In the days before men, the wyrms ate the vermin of the forest, but when men came, their livestock was easier prey. So, they have long been the bane of men. They tried to drive the wyrms out. When the wyrms appealed to the major dragons, as the Accords require, the major dragons sided with men and placed the wyrms under great restrictions. The wyrms have a great resentment against men, major dragons, and the Blue Order."

Dragon's blood! Another class of discontented dragons? Was the very fabric of the Order falling apart around them?

No, not now. This should be dealt with later. After. "Did you discover any specific locations where they might be found today?"

"There may be more, but Nunnington Hall and Bolton Castle were both mentioned."

"Do I understand correctly? These wyrms have currently been found at Nunnington?"

"As I understand, there is a large cluster there that are kept in check by the dragon, Nunnington. Rumor has it several of the wyrms turned up missing in the last few months."

"Nunnington is only thirty miles from the coast at Scarborough. That puts them in easy reach of smugglers. I need to get this information to Matlock. Thank you." Darcy turned to leave. Wait, no. What would Elizabeth do? "Is there anything that might be done for your comfort?"

"Send my Keeper down to me. I will be in my lair." Longbourn stood and scuffed toward the tunnel.

"I will see to it." Darcy hurried upstairs, stopping briefly to dispatch a footman to Mrs. Collins.

Everything Longbourn had reported made perfect sense. Wyrms were by their nature stupid, resentful creatures. If they had felt themselves oppressed by man and dragon, turning to work against both with smugglers was exactly the sort of thing they would do.

While the major dragons were by far the most powerful dragons, the minor ones outnumbered them. Although the Pendragon Treaty and the Accords were almost exclusively drawn up for the interests of the major dragons, the minor dragons benefited from them, too.

But not nearly so much. Should they band together and reject the Blue Order, the result could be as calamitous as another dragon war.

Dragon war.

Those words again. His belly roiled and blood roared in his hear.

They could not let it come to that.

Matlock's elaborately-carved door stood ajar, so Darcy paused only to knock, announcing his presence, and went directly in.

"What do you want?" Matlock snarled, barely looking up from his desk, strewn with cryptic documents.

Tall brass candelabras stood on either side of his desk, filling the room with reading light and the bacon-y odor of tallow. What was Matlock studying?

Darcy approached the desk. "I have information which may assist us in locating Elizabeth."

"Sit, sit and out with it. I have no time for civility."

Darcy pulled a chair near and quickly related his conclusions about the azure-striped forest wyrms.

Matlock squeezed his eyes shut, threw his head back and rolled his shoulders. "Damn. Damn. Damn and bloody hell."

"Excuse me. I do not have the pleasure of understanding you."

"You are off chasing forest wyrms while I have significant issues on my hands." Matlock slapped the nearest pile of documents.

"You do not consider the implications of a minor dragon rebellion significant? Forgive me if I must differ with you on that point."

"Wyrms are stupid and easily manipulated. A few of Gardiner's fancy dried beetles and they will agree to do anything. You have seen that for yourself. How can they measure up to what I am dealing with now?" He gestured across the piles on his desk. "General Yates arrived earlier today with more news from the north and east."

"Not good?" It seemed unlikely that the Grand Cross of the Blue Order Knights brought good tidings.

"Would you be surprised to learn that Pemberley is at the center of the latest unrest?"

"Pemberley? How is that possible? She has not even begun to take part in the regular activities of the Order." Surely this was nothing more than rumor and hearsay.

"And apparently, therein lies the problem. Do you know how long it has been since a major dragon with a territory like Pemberley's has been hatched?"

"Not precisely."

"Let us just say, then, that it is a very infrequent occurrence and several major dragons are disgruntled that the natural order of the world has been disrupted by the Accords," Uncle Matlock said.

"What do you mean?"

"The natural way of things, it seems, is that baby dragons hatch without territory and must fight for it, gaining it as they grow, or they are killed by their elders. The Accords did away with those 'natural' ways, assigning territories to each dragon and its heir in perpetuity."

"And the dragons of England agreed to the Accords. I do not understand the problem."

Uncle Matlock grumbled and huffed under his breath. "It seems there are those who object to the Accords now they are forced to see an infant major dragon's interests are protected. An estate like Pemberley, territory protected only by the Accords, is not a welcome reminder of the limits placed on major dragons."

"Are not all the major dragons served by that treaty?"

"There are those, naturally powerful and cranky, who question that Pemberley's territory should remain unchallenged when the true way of dragonkind is to take what they can get and hold it for themselves. In short, they are intimating that the Treaty, the Accords, and the Order are not to their benefit. They cite our recent decisions against Cornwall as another disruption to the natural way of things. The biggest, most powerful dragon should always prevail. To them, Cornwall should have been permitted to slit Kellynch's belly to retrieve any remaining gold."

"Pendragon's bones!" Who among the English dragons could possibly hold that such a thing would be beneficial?

"So, whilst we try to manage this nightmare, you had best give some thought to the defense of Pemberley or if it is even possible. If you have any still there who might be harmed in a hostile dragon takeover, it would be best to get them out now."

"You cannot be serious."

"Serious enough to have a meeting scheduled with Brenin Londinium."

"But he is old and lazy—"

"And mostly bored and self-absorbed. I am well aware. And Cornwall, the next in power, is utterly useless as well. That is why I will petition Londinium to make Cownt Matlock Grand Dug with full ministerial authority over the Conclave."

Darcy clutched the arm of his chair and tried not to allow his jaw to gape. "That will send Cornwall into a rage. What say the other dragons of the Council—"

"They agree to the necessity of it and will support Cownt Matlock. There are few choices. If a powerful dragon does not step up to counter this threat of rebellion, the Accords will not survive."

He was right.

"The Dragon Sage is important to this Order and to the dragons of England, but under these circumstances, I can offer no further resources toward her recovery. We must prepare for the possibility of full-scale insurrection."

A quarter of an hour later, Darcy dragged himself from Matlock's office, the weight of the news almost too much to carry. How was this possible? He made his way upstairs to the attics by the force of will alone.

Nanny welcomed him into the awkward little nursery, scented with lavender and rose. The white walls and mismatched furniture that definitely did not fit the space made for an odd bastion of peace.

A single glance at his face and Nanny offered to step out and allow him time alone with Anne. No telling what she inferred from his expression, but it was probably not far from the truth.

He gathered little Anne into his arms and settled into a large chair near the fireplace. She looked up at him, her eyes deep and intelligent, just like Elizabeth's. May wound around his feet, sniffing and purring. She could probably smell his anxiety. Tatzelwurms were peculiar that way.

Pax perched on the back of his chair, turning her head this way and that, twittering softly until he scratched under her chin.

"Where is April? Have you seen Walker today?" Darcy asked.

"No. I think Walker was flying with the guard today, looking for useful information. April might have gone back to Darcy House to see the housekeeper for more honey or jam. The kitchens here do not seem willing to provide enough for her tastes. Now does not seem to be a good time to try to change her habits." Pax twittered a soothing melody.

April needed still more honey? No, Pax must be in error.

Pax and May were lovely creatures, but they were young, and untested. They depended upon him. While he could not blame Walker or April for their absence, tonight he needed the comfort of Friends he could rely on.

It was up to him and him alone to find Elizabeth now. With so few resources to bring to bear, and orders specifically against it!

How could they refuse to protect all that was dear to him? Even Pemberley estate was in danger and they offered little. The Order was failing him. Could he just blindly allow it?

But what could he do? Richard and Netherford had already been sent off on the Order's bidding. Wentworth was in Dover. Perhaps Longbourn could be of more assistance, if he could be trusted not to make things worse. With his temper, it was always a possibility.

But he was not even Keeper to Longbourn and had no real right to ask anything of him. At least according to the strictures of the Order.

The rather useless ones.

Father would reprove him for that sentiment and Uncle Matlock declare him seditious.

Still, without April and Walker, he only had a few young fairy dragons and tatzelwurms who might be of help to him. How was he to save his Lady with such an army at his disposal?

"Elizabeth would say 'think like a dragon and act accordingly.'" He sighed and scratched under Pax's chin. "But what would a dragon do in such times? And how am I to do it?"

Pax peered down at May, who nodded a mite and purred louder. What could they possibly be thinking?

13
Chapter

January 25, 1815 London Order Offices

"FIVE, SIX, SEVEN, eight!" Mr. Dodge, the dance master, rapped the floor with his walking stick.

Anne pressed her temples with both hands. The sound echoed off the hardwood floor that had been cleared of furniture and carpet to facilitate their dance lessons in a small second-floor sitting room. With the couch, chairs, and small tables pressed up against the walls, the pale blue room was just large enough for them to form a small dance set and for Mr. Dodge to circle them and criticize—or rather critique, that was what he called his constant barrage of corrections—their steps.

He was a short man carrying a large stick, the sort of man Wentworth had little respect for. A furry mustache perched above his upper lip like a caterpillar hemmed in by his very high, very starched collar. His tousled hair was held so strongly by some sort of pomade, it would likely have broken had it been touched. Not unlike the seams of his very tightly-fitted tailored jacket that might burst if he breathed too deeply. A Rowlandson caricature if there ever had been one.

She sniffled and rubbed her nose. Chalk dust that smelt much like the stone floors throughout the offices made them all sneezy. But it did make the floor less slippery, so it was worth tolerating, even if the dance master had complained he was a teacher, not an artist the entire time he chalked the floor. Wonder that he did not burst a seam doing that.

How kind of the Cotillion Board not to object to their use of the Blue Order offices for such mundane purposes. Not that they had any authority to object, but it was not likely to stop them, in any case.

Of course, it did not hurt that Lady Jersey had pounced on Mr. Dodge as soon as he arrived to review the quadrille steps she wanted to introduce. How lovely Lady Elizabeth's efforts proved so convenient for Lady Jersey—not that it would ever be recognized.

"That will do, ladies, that will do. Enough of the quadrille." He waved them off the floor.

Thank heavens! It was not enough that her calves and feet ached, but now her head throbbed in time with the dance master's thumping.

"Your performance was not dreadful." He said that as though it were some kind of a compliment.

If it was, it would be the first to escape his lips. According to Pax, his cockatrix Dragon Friend was every bit as ill-tempered and particular as he. But that was only a rumor. A very easily believed one.

He glanced at Anne, eyebrow raised as though he was dealing with a very stupid woman.

Honestly, she could hardly be blamed right now. How could one concentrate on dance steps when waiting, hoping for news from the patrolling fairy dragons? It seemed easy enough for Miss Bennet, who did not seem to grasp the gravity of the situation, and for Miss Darcy, whose worry was relieved when Pax had been assigned to the nursery.

That probably was not fair, not entirely. They were both full young to truly grasp the gravity of what was going on. Miss Darcy was a quiet type of woman who might not show her true sensibilities easily, like her brother.

"Now for the minuet." The dance master clapped sharply and two eager, amiable, and eligible-looking young men appeared in the doorway. "For the minuet, one must have a partner to learn with and practice with. Here are partners. Mr. Fifett and Mr. Oakley."

Miss Bennet bounced on her toes and all but clapped, her broad smile far more enthusiastic than any young lady should be. Miss Darcy simply blushed. She did that a great deal.

The young men stepped forward and bowed, eyes on their prospective partners.

The names were familiar from the roster of Dragon Keepers they had been studying. Mr. Gregory Fifett, too rugged to be a dandy, but too polished not to appear to be one at first glance, was the heir of Holmewood, an estate near Bradford in West Yorkshire. Holmewood was a—what was it, surely, she knew—yes, a female wyvern, one of the younger major dragons of the Blue Order.

Mr. Allen Oakley had recently inherited his family

seat called Ambleside Hall, near Cumbria and Windermere, in the Lake District. Young Mr. Oakley, blonde and blue-eyed, seemed very young, and a mite too innocent, to be charged with Keeping an ill-tempered water wyrm (different from a marine wyrm!). Said wyrm was no doubt the reason for stories circulating of a monster that lived in Lake Windermere.

Both respectable gentlemen, with minor estate holdings and dragons who did not particularly stand out as important. The sort of gentlemen who could most benefit from connections to young ladies like Miss Bennet and Miss Darcy.

It was just possible some payment had exchanged hands in the selection of these dance partners. It was the sort of thing Father would have done for Elizabeth had the opportunity arisen.

"You may go." Mr. Dodge waved Anne and Mrs. Collins toward the door. "Married ladies have no need to show their plumage with a minuet."

"Truly? I have not heard—" Anne traded glances with Mrs. Collins. Was it married ladies in general, or those with connections to disgraced Blue Order members and the dragon-deaf? Hard to tell.

"The committee decided that years ago. It is old news. Everyone knows." He flashed his brows.

Everyone except the Sage, it seemed. Was he in collusion with the Cotillion Board? No, that did not make sense. He could not risk his students failing at the Cotillion. But, still, something did not smell right.

She glanced at Mrs. Collins, who was already frowning. Probably sharing in the same line of thinking. Over the last few days, it happened quite often.

"My sisters need a chaperone. I will stay." Mrs.

Collins folded her arms across her chest and settled into a chair near the wall.

The dance master glared at her, but she met him with a far more powerful glower of her own. He grunted and turned to the couples.

Anne headed for a chair next to Mrs. Collins, but Corn appeared in the doorway, a demanding expression on his face. With the new responsibility they bore, the wyrmlings had matured tremendously in just several days. They were much more like their sire than she had expected.

"Go, I will keep Lydia proper, somehow," Mrs. Collins whispered.

"You must come to the sitting room, now!" Corn's black and white tail lashed.

The claws on his thumbed front paws tic-tac'ed on the marble steps while the scales on his serpentine tale whispered softly behind. Anne all but ran upstairs to keep up.

No, she must walk like a lady and draw no notice to herself and Corn lest anyone suspect what was really going on. It was bad enough that the fairy dragons had been awfully conspicuous by their absence. More prying eyes she could do without.

Walker stood on a small table near the sitting room windows, wings extended, game pieces and board scattered on the floor. He shifted his weight from one foot to the other, keening softly while Wall licked at something between his feet.

Merciful heavens!

"Help. She needs help!" He opened his wings.

April lay in an awkward blue heap, blood marring her scale-feathers.

"Corn, find the Lord Physician, tell him I am

bringing April!" How to transport her without hurting her further? Yes! She dumped Mrs. Collins' work basket and made a little nest with a torn petticoat. "May I place you in the basket to take you to Sir Edward?"

"Yes, yes. It is … not so bad … only a little blood." April's tone declared her a liar.

Wall backed away and Anne cradled the broken fairy dragon in both hands.

"My wing! My wing!" Who knew fairy dragons could make such a blood-curdling sound?

Anne barely managed to nestle her into the basket without dropping her. The wing was definitely broken.

Would she ever fly again?

"I killed the hawk that had her, but not before its talons—" Walker peeked into the basket.

"She was seen! She was seen… Not east, west …" April collapsed.

Thank heavens she still breathed.

She grabbed the basket tight to her chest, and ran out, Walker winged his way ahead of her, scattering all in their path. No chance of keeping April's injuries quiet now.

He left her at Sir Edward's open door.

Sir Edward, already wearing a stained leather apron over his clothes, met her at the doorway. "What happened?"

"She has been careless since Lady Elizabeth's abduction. She got caught by a hawk whilst out today." All of that was an entirely true, if incomplete, picture of what had happened.

"This is very serious." He took the basket and strode to a brightly lit table in the middle of the room. Multiple mirrors focused light from the frosted windows and multiple candelabras on the table, throwing the rest of the room into deep shadow. The warmth intensified the herbal perfume filling the air, rather like an apothecary's shop.

With a touch far gentler than the size of his hands would have suggested, he removed April, still nestled in the petticoat, and peered at her. "Pray excuse me, but I must understand your injuries."

April groaned, nodding just a bit.

He expertly turned her over, exposing the gashes to her breast and thigh. "This—the humerus is displaced from the furcula." He pointed to her breastbone. "Hold her like this whilst I reset it. I fear this will be uncomfortable, April, but necessary."

Anne swallowed hard. What was it about this sort of injury that always seemed to find her? She held the fairy dragon firmly.

A swift move of thumb and fingers; April screamed, panted, then sighed. "Better."

Walker swooped in with Sir Fitzwilliam close behind. "What happened?"

"Lady Wentworth may be able to tell you how it came about, but I can tell you, she has a broken wing for certain. There are cuts and bruises as well. I do not know yet what sort of internal injuries are present. She is falling into a state of torpor, which is typical of injured fairy dragons. I hope it will work to our advantage, conserving her energies and allowing us time to treat her wounds."

Sir Fitzwilliam peered over Anne's shoulder. "Whatever can be done for her, do it. See that she is cared for—"

"My care has never been based on the size of the dragon, sir." Sir Edward glowered.

"She is my wife's Friend, and my own ..."

"I understand. I will do everything possible for her. Leave and permit me to do my work. Walker can stay here with her, but you, both of you, should go." He gestured toward the door with uncharacteristic energy.

They stepped out.

"Will you join me in the library, Lady Wentworth?" Sir Fitzwilliam's words had the force of an order, his expression so dark it was nearly frightening.

Anne followed him upstairs and to a corner of the library, with two hard chairs and a small table. Flanked on three sides by bookshelves and the aroma of old books, they were well away from the windows, only the mirrors stationed throughout the space provided light.

He pulled a chair for her and sat down himself. "There is something you are not telling me, Lady Wentworth, and it seems rather crucial that I know." The strain in his jaw belied the evenness in his tone.

"I suppose there is something to be said for draconic forthrightness. It does seem to save a great deal of dithering about in a conversation." Anne tried to force her features into something pleasing, but it was difficult when she was certain he could hear her racing heart.

"It does indeed. I expect, madam, we are on the same side here. We both seek to see Elizabeth and the rest returned safely as soon as may be possible."

"You are not satisfied with the steps the Order is taking towards their recovery."

Sir Fitzwilliam sighed. "There are many priorities for the Order which all compete for a finite number of resources." His lips tightened into an expression of pure frustration.

Oh, the amount he was not saying! Wentworth had intimated some of the possible priorities before he had left—none of them were good news.

"I suppose that is why your sisters, their Friends, and I have sought to devise a strategy to increase the available resources."

Did it hurt when his eyes opened that wide? "I do not understand. What resources?"

"April and the other fairy dragons expressed deep concerns that since one of their kind is at the center of this incident, it would reflect poorly on their species. Since they are at the bottom of the dominance hierarchy, they fear it could go very poorly for them in the future if something were to happen to the Sage."

"I would like to argue they are being silly twitter-pates, but I cannot. Once one begins listening to fairy dragons, what they say makes more and more sense. I believe the same is true of tatzelwurms, who are just above them in status. Rumblkins at Longbourn estate has found a way to be Friends with a woman who cannot even hear dragons. It is quite the relationship, to be certain. I know of no other dragon who has managed such a feat. It is worthy of respect, and understanding."

If anyone could be trusted, it was he. She swallowed hard. "Then I am sure you will respect the fairy dragons' insistence that they should be allowed to help in the recovery efforts. It was their belief they might be able to discover information that others could not. Their very lowness would make them privy to gossip and information others would not have."

He braced his hands on the edges of his chair and

leaned forward. "Spies? The fairy dragons decided to become spies?"

"After a fashion."

"But they are prey! The danger—"

"Obviously, you are correct. And believe me, it was discussed. But they argued, and I believe rightly so, that they deserved the right to bring their unique skills and abilities to bear to save Lady Elizabeth, and, I believe, themselves as well."

"Dragon bones! Who would have thought them willing, much less able—"

"April knew what she was risking and did so quite willingly. We are all fortunate Walker followed her out today and was there to rescue her."

"Did she say anything?"

"Very little before the torpor set in. Only that Elizabeth had been seen."

"Seen? Where? When?"

"A general direction, I think, but I do not know anything more specific."

"Damn, damn, damn, damn!" Sir Fitzwilliam slammed his fist on the table, nearly toppling it. He fumbled to keep it upright. "Pray excuse me."

"I am married to a sailor, sir. It will take far more than that to offend me. Unfortunately, all we can do now is to trust Sir Edward's ministrations and wait for April to awaken and give us her news."

"Will the other fairy dragons continue their efforts?"

"After this, I do not think they can be stopped, although I expect Walker and whomever he can recruit from among his cockatrice acquaintances will be watching over them from here on out. Unless there is anything else, I should go to your sisters and tell them what happened. I will let the other fairy dragons know as well, when they return."

"You will keep me apprised of any news?" He stood and held her chair. Was that gratitude in his eyes?

"Absolutely. Pray excuse me."

Mrs. Collins needed to be told of this first. Breaking the news to Miss Darcy would be difficult, she was so very sensitive. Miss Bennet would handle it much better. She was made of sterner stuff.

But perhaps—yes, that made sense.

First a letter.

.

14
Chapter

January 27, 1815 Dover

WENTWORTH RUBBED HIS eyes with thumb and fore-finger. The Blue Order offices in Dover provided only a single candle for his small room. Not precisely the best light for reading.

Nothing about the room was precisely the best. The bed, the chair, the press, the desk, all functional but nothing more. Not even pleasant to look at, the sort of articles that just faded into the background as they performed their purpose unremarkably.

Dover was hardly an important office, though it should have been. With access to the coast and the dragons there, and its proximity to France, it could have been an important hub of Order business.

Instead, the Regional Undersecretary for Kent was adequate to his task, visiting the Dover office precisely as often as necessary, no more. The Blue Order offices were adequate, managing the Keeps and other Blue Order business, exactly as the Accords said they should. The Dover office was adequate, providing exactly what it should, and nothing more. His room was adequate ...

Damn it all, adequate was not enough! They had little to offer and little incentive to put forth more than minimal efforts.

He stared at Anne's letter again, placed squarely in the center of the small writing desk. It smelt of her. The firm, practical loops of her handwriting managed to sound like her voice. If only she were here, too.

She was convinced there was something useful in the fairy dragons' intelligence, even if it was incomplete and sparse at best. But fairy dragons? Truly, who could take the creatures seriously? All fluff and twitter and nary a bit of sense.

Laconia bumped his hand with his black furry head. "Mrrooow."

Rather like the general opinion of tatzelwurms.

But Laconia was different. From the moment he cracked shell amidst those Gibraltar apes, he was different. He was thoughtful, serious, and sensible, not like those other tatzelwurms. Not even Corn and Wall had his clear-mindedness.

Then again, Anne's letter detailed how very practical and useful the twins had become once given a purpose. Laconia had always had a purpose at sea with him.

Maybe there was something more to tatzelwurms, and to fairy dragons, than was commonly accepted.

"You are agitated. What is in that letter?" Laconia spring-hopped to the desk and put his thumbed paw on the paper.

"I do not know what to make of it. Anne tells me the fairy dragons have been seeking information on the Sage's whereabouts."

"That is a good thing. I do not understand why it did not happen sooner." Laconia sat back on his tail and licked his paw.

"So, you support the notion?"

"No one minds their tongue around a fairy dragon any more than to a tatzelwurm or a servant." He had a good point. "What did the fairy dragons say?"

"April, the Sage's Friend, was badly injured and said little before falling into torpor. All we know is that the Sage was seen and in the west. It is very little to go on. But I have also received word from Matlock to continue our efforts here, in Dover—"

"Which is east from London." The tip of Laconia's serpentine tail flicked. He was annoyed.

"—and to interview the major dragons of Kent. It seems there is a great deal of unrest among them, and the Order needs to understand its extent."

"You intend to do that?"

Wentworth stood and stretched. "Ordinarily I would. That is what an officer does. He follows orders."

"Not when they are stupid." Laconia licked his paw and slicked it over his face.

"Yes, even when they seem stupid, my Friend. I know you know that. More than once, you questioned, we questioned, our orders, but we followed them."

"As Captain, you made many decisions on your own. Good decisions."

"It is different on land." Damn it all, everything felt different and foreign here.

"If we do not act, the Sage may be lost."

"What is there to act upon? West? That is hardly an actionable piece of information."

"Come." Laconia hopped to the floor. "We must discuss this with Kellynch." He spring-hopped for the door and slithered through.

Wentworth huffed and followed. He did not need a conference, he needed clarity, information … orders that he could follow in good conscience.

Damn.

Laconia did not look back as he led the way down the cobblestone street, to the beach, and the secluded cove where Kellynch had made a waterside lair. Wentworth fought to catch his breath, sweat trickling down the back of his neck despite the nip in the air and steady sea breeze.

Laconia was rarely in such a hurry.

Shrubs and a few small trees obscured the cliffside in the little cove, helped by the shadow of the cliff. Waves lapped on the rocky beach, giving no evidence of the extensive passageway hidden in the cliff face.

"There is news?" Kellynch slithered from the shadows, his whiskers crumpled and hide muddy. The cave there was not large enough for his comfort, but he seemed willing to endure the privation in hopes of being useful to the Order.

"After a fashion." Wentworth quickly related the contents of the letter.

"Fairy dragons? They are silly bits of fluff." Kellynch snorted. "Still, has any other information come forth?"

"Neither Anne nor Darcy has heard anything."

Kellynch exchanged a conversation of glances with Laconia. "In the absence of other information, does it not make sense to pursue this?"

Truly? The dragons agreed? "How does one pursue 'west' as information? Besides, Cornwall's territory is to the west and you cannot go there."

"That is true enough, but there is a great deal west that is not his territory." Kellynch snorted and wrinkled his snout. Cornwall would always be a very sore point with him.

"Matlock has ordered us to seek out the landed dragons in Kent, to interview them. He is concerned—"

"That there is discontent among them? I do not need to talk to them to know that is true."

"How do you know?"

Did Kellynch just roll his eyes? Who knew dragons were capable of that expression? "The small dragons of their territory, they talk and I listen."

"Why would they talk to a major dragon about such things?"

"Wyrms are the lowest among the major dragons. We are more approachable. All creatures appreciate being listened to. The minor dragons of the estates are supposed to be protected from me by their lairds, according to charter. So, it is safe to approach me to converse. I am sympathetic to their plight." Kellynch bunched his length in something that looked like a shrug.

"What have they been telling you?"

"Their lairds are angry at the loss of the Sage and are losing faith in the Order and its promises."

"Over just one woman?"

"She is not just one woman." Laconia snarled softly.

That was unusual.

"She is the Sage. She is the first human in our rec-ollection who thinks like a dragon and understands us, represents our interests properly. That the Order would not feel her loss as deeply as we do is an insult of the highest order."

A chill snaked down his back. Something in Kellynch's tone. This was deadly serious. "I had no idea. I am certain Matlock does not, either."

Laconia made a sound deep in his throat that could have passed for muttering.

"And therein lies the problem. The warm-bloods have ignored so many draconic concerns for so long, making this final insult nigh on intolerable. If the Sage is not recovered, I am not sure the Blue Order will survive."

"Forgive me, but you are so new to the Order yourself, how can you possibly know that?"

"Those in high places talk to the low, thinking that those below them can do or will do nothing with the information." Kellynch seemed to shrug again.

"So, you would suggest—"

"That you ignore Matlock and think like a drag-on," Laconia hissed through his teeth.

Is that not what the Sage was said to do? "I do not know how to think like a dragon. I am new to this world myself."

Kellynch swung his head in broad sweeps from side to side. "But I am not. I am a dragon and know how to respond. Ignore Matlock's dithering and get us to the west. Laconia and I can begin talking to the sea-faring cockatrice. Dover's pod are not the only sea dragons. Perhaps once we are out of their territo-ry, we can find some who will talk to us."

"You do realize what this means? Going against

the Blue Order's direction? Your territory can be re-moved from you. Your admission to the Order can be revoked."

"So, I will go back to the sea and make my way there. There is plenty of unoccupied territory I could claim in the ocean. I fear it is you and Anne who will suffer the most if this goes badly."

He was right. What would Anne say?

She was the one who had sent him the infor-mation.

"Laconia? You will be affected by this, too."

His tail lashed, tossing beach rocks aside. "I have told you already. You should not waste any more time."

Wentworth drew a deep breath. "We will head west as soon as I can arrange a small ship and dragon-hearing crew."

.

15
Chapter

January 27, 1815 On board the Sea Lion

HOW MANY DAYS had passed since the door locked behind them and the once-fresh bed of straw began to grow stale and musty in their shadowy, dank confines? Joshua sat near Phoenix's cage, knees drawn to his chest, watching the cluster of guarding wyrms in the far corners, fascinated. The younger pair, Indigo and Lapis, seemed to return the sentiment, frequently staring at him as though to work out what he was about.

Elizabeth stood and stretched. Too many, far too many days here. Where was "here?" Near-constant storms had beset them. How had that affected their journey toward Bermuda?

And what would they do when they got there?

Had there been any progress made toward finding them? Darcy would move heaven and earth and the

Blue Order if necessary to recover them. What was he doing now? How many dragons had come to his side to help? Perhaps this might be a rallying point that would see major dragons working together in ways they had not before?

Maybe, somehow, this would be a good thing for dragonkind…

What was she thinking? Dragons were always difficult and stubborn and often self-centered. If there were a way to make things even worse, that is what would happen.

And Darcy would have to handle it and little Anne all alone.

This was not the way it was supposed to be. They were supposed to be together, managing affairs of home and hearth and dragon side by side. He had a way of seeing, of understanding, of planning different to her own. One she needed, especially now.

Could she manage to think like him and like a dragon, too?

Darcy would want to know about Bermuda and what could be expected there. She had read something about Bermuda at one point, but what was it?

She paced the length of the hold, across the weak sunlight filtering through the grate above them. Sometime in the recent days, she had got the knack, more or less, of traversing the undulating deck.

Ground that stayed firm beneath was definitely underappreciated.

She squeezed her eyes shut and pressed her temples.

Yes! Bermuda's first local parliament sat in 1612, well after the Pendragon Treaty came into being. Self-governing, with preferential treatment toward its own citizens; that meant if any Blue Order authorities existed on the island, they would have no power to enforce the treaty. It would be difficult to find any sort of legal aid. Without identification or a male relative, a woman and a boy would likely have little standing in court. Especially with the claims that Corney would no doubt make about them.

But surely there were dragons in Bermuda. There had to be. They could be prevailed upon for aid. Surely, they would be sympathetic and helpful, would they not?

Dragons had always been so before.

A key jangled in the lock and the door groaned open. One of the two scruffy men who had transported them to Portsmouth shambled in, a tray with foodstuffs in his hands and a pail over his arm. He slipped a small fish into Phoenix's cage, handed bowls with hardtack, some sort of stew, and grog to her and Joshua, and set the pail down in the middle of the hold as he backed out and relocked the door.

Phoenix set upon his meager rations with the ferocity of a tiny, hungry cockatrice. Semi-starvation had begun to take its toll on his color and energy.

"Do you think Mama will let me have grog when we get back? I think I have developed a taste for it." Joshua took a sip and winked at her.

He was a good lad, a brave, sturdy one for certain. His mask of calm and bravado did an excellent job hiding the fear that only revealed itself when he muttered in his sleep.

Prussian slithered out of the corner shadows towards the dented rusty pail. He circled it, tasting the air around it with his long, forked tongue. Finally, he shoved it over, sending greasy meat scraps slopping across the floor. Azure, Indigo and Lapis, in that order, approached the puddle, waiting until Prussian took the first gobbet of meat. Then they fell into a feeding frenzy, just shy of a complete loss of control. Like Phoenix, their rations were inadequate, but it was better than hardtack.

In a very few minutes, Indigo and Lapis, the smaller wyrms, licked the floor clean as Prussian and Azure scoured the bucket. For all his ill-temper and scarred visage, Prussian was a reasonable leader, maintaining a dominance structure but ensuring the smaller members of his cluster received a fair share of their paltry provisions.

Did all clusters operate this way? Fairy dragon harems all functioned similar to one another, but drake communities varied widely. Which did forest wyrms resemble? This was the first opportunity she ever had to interact with them so closely.

Elizabeth fished meat chunks out of her stew and held them out. The two females slithered close, Azure, with her red head knob, leading Lapis to eat from Elizabeth's hands.

"It was your doing. You made them bring meat." Azure slipped in close against Elizabeth's skirt, careful to make sure her blue hide did not touch bare flesh.

"When you spoke, they listened. They not listen to us." Lapis slid in along Elizabeth's other side.

She could not contain a sigh of contentment. For the first time since they had been forced upon this horrid vessel, something felt right.

"What means that sound?" Prussian's missing fang left him with a peculiar lisp.

"I suppose it means I am glad to have all of you near. At home we have many house dragons, and I am used to having them close by."

"It is true," Joshua said. "There are Slate and Amber, Friends of the housekeeper and butler, and the maid's puck Friend, I cannot recall her name, and April and Pax and …"

"Why you live with so many?" Azure turned her head sideways, rather like April did when she was puzzled.

Heavens, it was difficult not to scratch her under her blue-scaled chin. "I suppose because I like them."

"No one likes wyrms." Lapis stretched toward Joshua for a scratch.

"That is not true," Joshua's attempt at an authoritative tone proved more cute than convincing. "I like you very much."

"We are only ever liked for our stripes." Indigo muttered from near the spilt pail.

"She does not need to know that." Prussian's tail lashed.

"What harm is there? She got us meat." Azure rested her head in Elizabeth's lap.

"Getting meat is not the same thing as freeing us from the dragons." Prussian hissed as though to punctuate his opinion. "It sounds like she is a Keeper, in league with the big ones."

"What dragons?" The air around the wyrms seemed to crackle with the pending revelation. Something very important; surely it was.

"The ones who kept us." Lapis pressed into her side, making herself small.

That was a fear reaction. She scanned the wyrms' faces. Each wore the mien of prey not predator. "What dragons do that? I have never heard of dragons keeping other dragons."

"The Blue Order knows. We have sent word." Prussian snarled. "Our pleas for help were ignored."

"I do not know that they were ever heard, sometimes—"

"They were heard. The cockatrice that brought them said they were dismissed by the regional undersecretary of North Umbria." Prussian held his nose up like a man looking down upon another.

"There is no office by that name. It is an old name, not often used anymore. Perhaps the cockatrice was not … accurate." She meant honest, but that would not likely facilitate the conversation. "Where are you from? What territory?" Northumbria could mean Northumberland, in Ireland, or Yorkshire, Tyne or Wear, perhaps all of them. Or even none.

"Nunnington's hold," Azure said.

Nunnington Hall! "Sir Bellingham, the baronet and deputy lieutenant for the North Riding of Yorkshire is Keeper, is he not?" Elizabeth squeezed her eyes shut. There was something about that Keep... Yes! Peter Loschy was buried in the church there as the slayer of the Loschy Dragon. That was the popular story, but it had been shaped by the Blue Order.

The grave actually belonged to Sir Walter de Teyes, the Lord of Nunnington Hall in 1300. The dragon, the ancestor of the current Nunnington, was not killed by Loschy or any other, but rather, officially agreed to a Blue Order Charter and accepted Teyes as Keeper.

The dragon slayer myth was a convenient way to explain the disappearance of the local dragon and the rise in favor Teyes appeared to enjoy.

But neither Nunnington nor the Keeper there had ever formed more than a passing acquaintance even into the current generation. They occupied separate spheres, much as men and women usually did. Which meant that it was hardly a well-managed Keep according to Blue Order standards.

"The Keeper likes his sport more than his dragon." Azure snorted and tensed.

"His dragon likes her sport, too." Indigo drew closer.

"Dragon sports? This is new to me. Pray tell me more." Elizabeth laid a hand on each of the nearby females. Their rising agitation needed some soothing presence. Hopefully they would not become too distraught and bite her inadvertently.

"She is a lazy, lonely wyrm. She wants for company and for entertainment." Azure pressed her head into Elizabeth's hand. Frightened, definitely frightened.

Those were needs the Keeper should have been attending.

"The old Keeper wanted us gone from the land, said we ate too much from his property. Nunnington took to chasing us. Even invited other big dragons to join her hunts." Lapis wailed into Elizabeth's skirts.

"They tried to eat us." Indigo shuddered.

Elizabeth gasped and pulled the wyrms in a little closer. A landed dragon was supposed to protect those in their Keep, particularly those minor dragons who had imprinted upon humans, whether or not they had Friends.

"But they did not understand our defense." Prussian rose high on his tail and flared his head, cobra-like, reveling swaths of bright blue, otherwise hidden. "Our poison works on major dragons."

"Not well." Azure curled into a knot. "When they

tried to swallow us, they had strange sensations. See-ing and feeling things. They no longer bored."

"They liked us very much for that." Lapis wrapped herself into a tight ball.

Indigo slithered closer. "We amused, they said. They collected us. Nunnington divided us among her friends. They kept us trapped in their lairs."

Prussian rose up higher, his body puffing. "She would lick our blue when she grew bored. Wanted those sensations. Then return us to the cavern."

"We were trapped; held captive!" Azure bolted away and twined around Prussian. "A heavy storm caused a mudslide that allowed the river into the cav-ern. We escaped, but there are more of us held."

Joshua gasped and extended a protective arm around Lapis.

"Pendragon's bones!" Elizabeth pressed her fist to her mouth. No wonder they had fallen in with the smugglers. "I had no idea! No dragon is ever to be held against their will except by official judicial action. This cannot continue. When I return to the Order, I will launch an investigation—you must tell me the names of all the major dragons involved. If I have to, I will go to those estates myself. I will see that the others are freed and those who held them are pun-ished."

Major dragons, like the peerage, were always wont to see how much propriety they could flout, often treating the Order's rules as flexible according to their whims. But this? This was utterly beyond the pale.

"You can do that?" Prussian leaned closer, eyes narrowed, studying.

"She can and she will do it, too." Joshua whis-pered. "She is angry now, and no one, not even dragons stand in her way when she is angry—"

"Who is Lady Warm-Blood that the Order would listen—"

The door lock rattled and they all jumped. The wyrms scattered to their corners.

Corney shambled in. Had his foot-dragging limp become more pronounced in the days since they had seen him last? Ayles, carrying himself a little less gentlemanly than before, with dirty shirt and boots, followed several steps behind. Was he angry, impatient, or simply tired? Or all three?

"Seems like you 'et all that were put in front of ye. Now that you been fed, it be time to do what you were brought to do." Corney pointed a scarred finger at Phoenix.

Phoenix huddled in the corner of the cage, trembling. His matted red feather-scales lay limp against his body, his eyes big and round.

"Time to breathe fire." Ayles lifted the cage to eye level. "We will have it now."

"Not now." Phoenix twittered, trying to sound big, but only managing frail and hollow.

"None of that nonsense now. You gots no choice." Corney balanced his fists on his hips.

"I am too weak."

Ayles shook the cage, bouncing Phoenix like a stuffed doll inside.

"Stop!" Elizabeth grabbed for the cage. "He is telling you the truth. He is too weak to even fly, can you not see! He cannot breathe fire under these circumstances."

"What circumstances exactly do you mean?" Ayles stared directly into her eyes with a cold predatory gaze.

Her breath hitched, but she forced words. "He is cold and half-starved. I was not exaggerating when I told you his kind need to eat four times a day, at least. You give him meat, but not nearly enough. He is half-starved. And he is cold! His kind hibernate in the cold. He cannot help it. He needs to be in the warmth, the sunshine."

"It don't bother them none." Corney pointed at the wyrms huddling in the corner.

"They are of a different kind, who tolerate the cold better. They are as much alike as a pigeon is to a snake."

"A dragon's a dragon! That's what Scarlett said." Ayles stood so close she could feel his fetid breath on her face.

"No, they are not. No more than a horse is a whale or a boy. They are all different to one another and need different things. The wyrms are hungry, too, but do not need as much food as a ... baby firedrake. They are from the north of England so tolerate the cold better. You cannot demand a performance if you do not take care of him properly."

Corney stared at her for a long, uneasy moment. "I do not think we understand each other, missy." He waved toward the door and Nickleby, filthy, hunched and scarred, shambled in. "Take the boy. Ayles, bring the cage." He grabbed Elizabeth's arm. "You come with me."

Joshua screamed and kicked, but Nickleby tucked him up under his arm and hauled him out.

Everything in her demanded she do the same. But to what use? In the middle of a cold, unforgiving ocean, what escape could there be? None, unless she found allies. And to do that, she needed her wits, and her strength. Struggling now would provide neither.

Corney dragged her up a ladder to the deck, wrenching her shoulder in the process. Burning brightness assaulted her eyes. How long had it been since she had seen the sun full on? Though the chill wind scoured her face, the sunbeam's warmth still penetrated.

She forced her eyes open. Sea to the horizon in every direction. Nothing else.

So very alone.

Corney forced her to the side railing, where several scraggly sailors waited. "I'm gettin' tired of waiting on your baby scaly, missy, real tired. Ain't gonna wait much longer." He turned to Phoenix. "Just so you be clear at what's what. Take her."

The sailors grabbed her arms and legs and tossed her over the railing. She landed with a thud into a small boat tied off just a few feet below the edge.

Joshua and Phoenix screamed.

"Let her down, boys. Show 'er what the ocean be like without our kind assistance." Corney's voice seemed so far away.

She scrambled to sit up as the dinghy shuddered and bumped against the hull, descending toward the lapping waves. From the corner of her eye, the garish yellow Sea Lion figurehead, horrid unnatural creature, grinned at her, as though laughing at her plight.

The dinghy smacked the water with a tooth-jarring thump. The ropes securing it to the sloop fell away and it drifted back. Only a single line, tied to the front of the dinghy, tethered it to the sloop.

So thin, so frail. If anything should happen to that line …

She held her breath against a welling scream. It

would do no good. Demonstrating they could frighten her had no benefit. Shading her eyes, she peered up at the looming ship. Ayles held Phoenix's cage up so he could see her. Joshua peeked over the railing, horror in his eyes. It seemed as though Corney were speaking, but his words were lost to the sea.

Chill winds, waves splashed, dousing her thin garments with pure cold. She huddled down as far as she could, letting the hull provide a break from the winds. How long would they leave her here? Would they cut the rope? If they did, what then?

Her teeth chattered, and she shivered, ears and nose and hands aching. A small blanket lay tucked up on one of the seats. Coarse and musty, it broke some of the chill. Perhaps there was something else…

No. No oars, no food, nothing of use.

Utterly and completely dependent on that single line to the Sea Lion. The figurehead laughed at her, mocking. So much like a dragon, but not—mythical and useless.

The boat jolted with a resounding blow against the side. She screamed and clutched the nearest seat.

A long, silvery speckled nose peeked over the side, horse-like, with large blue eyes and long lashes. A silver fin ran down its dark-streaked back like a mane. He resembled White, the Crofts hippocampus Friend.

Sea dragons!

"What are you? What are you doing here?" What an odd, watery quality to the creature's voice.

"I am an officer of the Blue Order, the Dragon Sage. I am here as a captive, against my will. Pray, will you help me and the others who are held prisoner?"

The creature bobbed with the rough waves, blinking slowly, studying her. "Why would I meddle in the affairs of sailing men? They only bring trouble to us."

"I am not a part of them. They are not a part of the Blue Order."

The hippocampus whistled a sound between a nicker and a whinny. "What is the Blue Order to me? To my pod? They are nothing to us. What authority, what importance do they have here?" It pawed the water with its glistening front hooves. "None, that is the answer, none. We are many here in the ocean, and they have ignored us. Why should we do otherwise?"

Why indeed? "I will represent your cause to the Order—"

"You are adrift in a craft you cannot even move. The water is too cold for you to swim if you could even manage such a simple task—which I must strongly doubt. How precisely will you do that? What value has any promise you make now?"

How did one answer such a challenge?

"No, we have no need of you." The creature dove, slapping a wave up over the side with its tail, catching Elizabeth in the face.

She stared into the sea, but it did not reappear.

The sea-dragon had just cut her.

That never happened.

16
Chapter

January 30, 1815 London Order Offices

THE SUN ROSE and the world was as utterly upside down as it had been when Darcy retired the night before. He tossed the sheets and counterpane aside, resenting the bed for being empty beside him, especially when it smelt of lavender and her.

How totally unreasonable to be angry at a piece of furniture, but how could a man be reasonable under such conditions? Pacing the floor, the thin carpet, scratchy underfoot, one more detail that was simply not right.

Dragon's fire.

His valet arrived to prepare him for the day, silently presenting him with a newspaper and a very strong cup of coffee. Both probably essential before he dare face polite company. Or in Matlock's case, not so polite.

Truly, how could he be expected to trundle off to Pemberley when Richard and Wentworth were sent off to do something that had the potential at least for being useful in recovering Elizabeth?

From the cracked-leather wing chair near the fireplace, he scanned the newspaper for any scrap of pertinent information. It was surprising how often dragon-related articles appeared, if one knew what to look for.

Naturally there was nothing beyond what Parliament would do about the smuggled tea and silk.

He drained his coffee and banged the cup against the small table with a satisfying thud.

If only April had been able to communicate her intelligence before losing consciousness. How long would it take for her to awaken?

Or would she at all?

His throat spasmed so hard he could not draw breath. He sprang up and staggered to the window and shoved the transom open. Cold, fresh, London-smelling air poured in. Gulping and choking, he managed to draw one breath, then another. He panted, ribs aching, leaning heavily on the windowsill.

Pray, no. No more loss, not now.

Walker swooped in through the door left open to the dragons' and servants' corridors and landed on the back of the wing chair. "She has awoken!"

"She is well?" Darcy whirled so fast the room spun.

Walker flipped his wings neatly to his back. "It seems she will recover, but she is hardly well. Her wing will not be healed for weeks and it will be some time after that before she regains the strength to fly. If she is even able to again. She still has pain from the talon wounds and the scars could be significant."

"But she will recover?" He balled his fists so hard they trembled.

"So it appears. She wants to talk to you."

Darcy dashed out. He probably should have taken leave from Walker, but he would understand. His concern for April might have been greater than Darcy's own.

He pounded down the main stairs, like a mannerless adolescent, nearly knocking over several proper folk on his way. Thankfully, Sir Edward's Pa snake carved door was open. Good, otherwise Darcy might have torn that down to get inside.

Earthy herbal scents filled his lungs as the room's quiet penetrated his anxious mantle. Somehow calming, reassuring, the promise of a healer who truly knew his craft.

Sir Edward met him just steps inside and led Darcy through the neat main room to a door beside a bookcase that carried all of Elizabeth's monographs. He restrained the impulse to take one and pore over it, just to hear Elizabeth's voice on the page.

The plain, narrow door opened to a small, warm stillroom, bundles of drying herbs hanging from the ceiling. Frosted transom windows lined the wall and lit the narrow space. Wall-mounted shelves lined the entire space, laden with bottles and boxes and equipment he did not recognize. A narrow work table occupied the center of the room, a basket surrounded by warm bricks in the center.

"April." Darcy peered into her basket, radiant warmth touching his face and hands.

A bright blue mass of scabs and ragged featherscales puddled in the center of the pale cotton-wool lining. Squinting, he could make out the outline of a beak and a face, bright eyes blinking up at him. "How are you feeling? You have been sorely missed."

April lifted her head just a mite. "Has she been found?"

"No, yours has been the only intelligence. But you collapsed before telling us more than that she had been seen. Pray, what did you find?" He smoothed her ruffled head feathers.

"A sea-faring cockatrice heard that she was seen in Portsmouth. Possibly with Cornwallis Jackson—"

That name! How many times had he seen it in various reports recently? Even in the paper today! What had that article said?

"She was taken aboard a ship, a... what was it called? Bermuda Sloop, no, that was not the name. It had a yellow creature on the front, a lion of some sort. Perhaps ... yes ... The Sea Lion. Heading toward Bermuda."

"When, do you know when?"

"How long have I slept?"

"Five days."

"Perhaps ten days ago. But ... but storms. Many storms. There were storms, strong enough to confuse the navigator and slow their progress."

"Thank you! That is excellent, excellent news! You have been so brave to accomplish this. I am proud of you and I know," he swallowed hard, "I know that she will be as well."

"Go, find her, find her now. I need to sleep." April fell back into the cotton-wool nest, snoring softly.

Sir Edward tapped his shoulder and beckoned him to follow, shutting the narrow door behind them.

"I believe she is out of danger now. She is a hardy

little soul. Not many of her kind survive a hawk." Sir Edward pushed his glasses higher up his nose. "You may send Walker back—I doubt you could keep him away. She is not strong enough for other visitors yet. I would not have called you down except she was desperate to give you her news. I trust it was worth it?"

"Indeed it was. Will she be able to fly again?"

"I cannot say, but if it is up to stubbornness, then I am sure she will. It is best to let her rest now. I will send for you when it is safe for her to have company." Sir Edward escorted him out, shutting the door behind him.

Darcy leaned against the door, letting his head fall back against it and drawing his first unencumbered breath in days.

Soft footsteps approached. "Sir Fitzwilliam? Walker came for me. He said she was awake."

Thank heavens it was Lady Wentworth and not one of the many people he would rather not see now. April's injuries had become the point of a great deal of gossip and speculation.

"She has fallen back to sleep now, but I am told she is expected to recover. I am sure Sir Edward will tell you more."

"Thank heavens!" Anne pressed her hand to her chest, leaned closer and dropped her voice. "Was she able to tell you anything?"

"Yes, yes, I am going to Matlock with that word right now."

"Pray tell me what he says." Something in her expression said there was more to be told, but it would have to wait.

He bowed and all but ran to Matlock's office, earning not a few disapproving glances along the way.

The wide door with the Order's seal was shut. He rapped politely. Once, twice, thrice.

No answer.

He pounded a satisfying tattoo with his fist.

Matlock yanked the door open. "What do you want?"

"I have word on Elizabeth."

Matlock grumbled and opened the door enough for him to enter. "Come in and tell us what you know."

Three imposing men sat around Matlock's central desk, obscuring the painted Chancellor's seal. Three candelabras behind the desk lit an array of maps and lists and notes strewn across the desktop.

General Strickland looked over his shoulder at Darcy, the dark patch over one eye even more severe in the uneven candlelight. Admiral Easterly sat beside him, his white hair ragged and unkept.

"Darcy, General Abbot, General Yates." Matlock gestured at the two men just beyond Easterly.

General Abbot, the Blue Order's Chief Army Liaison to His Majesty's Army, acknowledged Darcy with a nod. He had gone to school with Darcy's father and had once stayed at Pemberley. His manners were gentlemanly and his conversation informed. Dark-haired and blue-eyed, except for a few additional lines on his face, he was little changed from Darcy's memory of him.

General Yates wore a military-style coat in Order-blue, with the insignia of the Grand Cross of the Pendragon Order on his left shoulder. With a square jaw and pronounced shoulders, he might have been a knight's effigy carved from marble at a parish church. Not exactly the sort who seemed very conversational.

"Why are you not at Pemberley, Darcy?" Matlock snapped as he sat behind his desk. "I told you—"

"My dragon and my child are here. I have sent instructions to my steward and await his response. I have word on Elizabeth."

"Word, from where? I was not informed."

"Ten days ago she was seen in Portsmouth, forced aboard a Bermuda sloop called the Sea Lion, destined for Bermuda. She was in the company of Cornwallis Jackson, a known smuggler. His name has been bandied about in the newspapers as a known smuggler of tea and silk. He has appeared in a number of the reports you have recently received. An article in the Morning Post today confirms he has been seen both in London and Portsmouth."

"Bermuda?" Easterly drummed his fingers on the arm of his chair. "There is no telling where they hope to ship that dragon from there. My guess would be India. Jackson is known to have ties there."

Yates sneered. "The creature in question is a fairy dragon. I am quite certain there are British ladies with fairy dragons in India. It will do quite fine for itself there. I see it hardly our concern, especially in light of what is happening on British soil."

"I understand there is a crisis at hand, but with respect, sir—"

"With respect, Sir Fitzwilliam," Yates stood and glared. "You are a knight under my command. I have not asked you for advice, nor for information. It is your place to wait for my orders and act on them."

"Have you forgotten, sir, that the Dragon Sage, an officer of the Order, chosen by the dragons themselves, and my wife, has been abducted by these same blackguards?" The veins along Darcy's forehead throbbed.

"We are quite aware of that, to be sure," Abbot's tone bordered on conciliatory. "But there are bigger problems at hand. Further reports of unrest have arrived. That is a far bigger risk than the loss of a single human officer, even one dear to you."

"Once again, sir, with respect, I do not think you understand the role she plays among the dragons themselves. If she is not recovered, I fear there is nothing you can do to stop insurrection. I believe her return alone—"

"Where did you come by your information?" Strickland asked.

"Walker, and Elizabeth's Friend April—"

Yates slapped his forehead. "The fairy dragon? You expect us to take the word of a fairy dragon in these matters? I have no words, Darcy. A Knight of the Order should know better—"

"I do know better than to discount the word of a dragon!"

"Fairy dragons are hardly dragons and not worth listening to. Get out. We have actual work to do." Yates waved him to the door.

Before he could protest, Matlock grabbed him by the arm and propelled him to the doorway. "Fairy dragons? Truly, Darcy? I need you back in Derbyshire, immediately. Tend to Pemberley. Interview the major dragons in the area. I need to know how deep the discontent runs there. Leave little Pemberley here, though. She does not need to be influenced by disloyal dragons." He pushed Darcy out and slammed the door.

Ignorant, short-sighted warm-blood! Could he be

made to understand that Elizabeth's abduction was central to the looming insurrection? Probably not.

Anne paced from the Chancellor's office, past the Secretary's office, past the Minister of the Court's, and back again. Past the scrutiny of somber portraits. And again. And again.

The carved dragon holding the scales of justice on Baron Dunbrook's door, and the inlaid one on Baron Chudleigh's door that looked down upon smaller in-laid major dragons representing each county of England, stared at her judgmentally. It probably was not seemly to haunt the dimly lit halls this way, rather like eavesdropping. But how could she not?

Sir Fitzwilliam stumbled out of the Chancellor's door, and it slammed behind him. Resounding, firm and final.

Anne dashed to him. Oh, the look on his face! What had they said? "I take it that did not go well?"

"Hardly."

"Pray, sir, Longbourn is anxious to speak to you regarding April's news. May I join you, as there is … ah, something … I would like to discuss with both of you?" She bit her upper lip.

Sir Fitzwilliam dragged his hand down his face and grunted. Too tired or too frustrated to argue? It hard-ly mattered. Regardless, she would be heard.

They descended three flights of limestone stairs in silence.

Longbourn, looking as ragged as a dragon might, met them at the bottom of the stairs, in the large, open junction of the many corridors that led to guest dragon lairs. A single torch bathed the space in more shadows than light. A vaguely damp, limestone scent harkened back to the temporary lair Kellynch had used in Bath.

"What is the news? Is the flutter-tuft well?" Longbourn scratched at the limestone floor.

"She will recover, but she was severely injured." Sir Fitzwilliam went on to explain April's intelligence and Lord Matlock's response.

Disappointing, but hardly surprising. Not unlike the Cotillion Board, who seemed unable to consider anything but their own very limited viewpoints.

Lovely women all.

Longbourn leaned into Sir Fitzwilliam's face, breathing hard. "What are you going to do about it?"

"I have been ordered back to Pemberley to interview—"

"You will do no such thing." Longbourn's stomp echoed painfully against the stone walls.

Sir Fitzwilliam chuckled grimly. "I suppose not."

"You would disobey the Chancellor's orders?" Anne held her breath. Perhaps, just perhaps.

"For Elizabeth, I would disobey the king." It was probably an exaggeration, but a sentiment as lovely as Wentworth's letter to her. "My Uncle vastly underestimates Elizabeth's importance to the dragons. Her return will have a greater effect on dragon concerns than he imagines."

Longbourn flicked his tail in what seemed to be approval. "What will you do, then?"

"That is an excellent question. We are rather low on allies and resources at the moment and—"

"Forgive me for interrupting, but I have some information you might be interested in." She clasped her hands tightly before her, lest their trembling detract from her words.

"Pray go on, Lady Wentworth."

"Wentworth was ordered to interview the major dragons in Kent. But when I told him of April's initial report, he determined they needed to be at sea searching for Lady Elizabeth. The letter I received today revealed he has arranged a sloop called Cerulean, crewed by Blue Order men. He intends to set sail today from Dover, heading west toward Portsmouth."

Sir Fitzwilliam gasped. "I would join him, if there were some way to get there …"

"I believe I might help you there as well. Alister Salt and his team can carry you to Portsmouth. You can meet Wentworth's ship there and join his efforts."

"I would come, too." Even a Longbourn's whisper was hard on the ears. "There is no moon in the sky for the next several nights. I can fly to Portsmouth. Will his ship hold me?"

"Perhaps. It is not something he thought to tell me. I believe it is possible the vessel is large enough for that."

"I am for Portsmouth, then. Are you, Darcy?"

"I cannot do nearly as much for the Order by going to Derbyshire as I can by finding her. Pemberley would never forgive me if I did not go myself to try. I can be ready to leave in an hour. Just tell me where to meet Alister Salt."

"I will make the arrangements with him and send word to Wentworth." It might be the end of the Wentworths as part of Blue Order society, but without Lady Elizabeth, there might not be any Blue Order society. They would find the Sage, somehow.

17
Chapter

February 1, 1815 On board Cerulean

WENTWORTH SAT AT his desk in the Cerulean's captain's quarters and fastened the satchel on the Blue Order messenger's back. The cockatrice squawked and flew. Not nearly so impressive as the guard assigned to the London offices, but this messenger seemed as sure and steady and fast. The latter seemed the most significant right now as he disappeared from view in the early morning sky.

Dawn had broken, and Darcy was waiting for him at Portsmouth.

Wentworth made his way onto the deck, sea air catching him full in the face. Somehow, it felt like home.

It would have been simpler had Darcy—and Longbourn—not insisted on joining him. Darcy was hardly a seaman and could prove more liability than asset. Nor was Longbourn a sea dragon—could wyverns even swim?—then again, he could fly and that might well be a boon. Assuming, of course, he did not cause problems being aboard the ship.

He laced his hands behind his neck and stared at the glowing sky. What was he thinking, permitting a wyvern on his vessel?

Sailors scurried about, doing precisely what they should have been doing, under the bo'sun's watchful eyes. Not unlike dancers on a ballroom floor, ebbing and flowing with the rhythm of the vast ocean.

Thankfully, the Cerulean's crew was keen on the prospect of rescuing the Sage. At some point she had answered the navigator's letter regarding an issue with his puck Friend's hoard. Her advice had been good and he had felt the honor of her reply most exceedingly. His good opinion, apparently not easily acquired, was enough for the crew, and their judgement set. Hearing that the wyvern she once kept would join them on their mission only seemed to bolster their enthusiasm.

With a bit of luck, it would last.

Laconia hopped to the railing and head-butted his shoulder. "You are not pleased."

"Do you want Darcy thinking himself in charge of this mission?"

"He is not that kind. He is dominant on land, to be sure, but he is no fool. He will permit you dominance at sea."

"Permit me? Excuse me. I do not need his permission to be captain."

"He will not challenge your dominance. You really must bring yourself under better regulation or he will sense weakness and challenge you." Laconia huffed and bared his teeth. "You warm-bloods are no different to dragons, despite your insistence your ways are more civilized."

What point in arguing? Laconia might even be right.

They were sailing on the advice of a fairy dragon, supported by a tatzelwurm. There was little hope for them as it was. Hopefully Laconia was right on both counts.

Wentworth opened his spyglass and scanned the shore for the familiar spire with the brass crescent and star. Somehow Portsmouth's landmark soothed his disquiet. There, and yes, the green signal banner atop the Blue Order offices. Darcy was waiting at the docks.

Half an hour later, two of the Cerulean's sailors rowed Darcy to the sloop. He climbed the ladder exactly as Wentworth expected a landman to climb. Ungainly, bordering on ridiculous. At least he did not slip and plummet into the sea and drown. That would have been unfortunate.

It took a moment for Darcy to gain his footing on deck. He bowed to Wentworth. "I believe the correct phrase is 'permission to come aboard, Captain.' Greetings, Laconia."

Laconia was right.

Wentworth nodded. "Permission granted. One of my men will manage your things and show you about, but first, tell me what you know." He led Darcy towards the bow, Laconia following.

Darcy moved slowly, fighting the movement of the deck. "How long does it take for one to become accustomed to … this?"

"It depends. Some never do. But since you do not

seem to be made ill by the motion, it will probably come to you sooner rather than later." It was a good sign that Darcy would not spend the journey leaning over the railings, spilling the contents of his guts.

"Longbourn is waiting for us at a cove in the cliffs as you directed." Darcy scanned the deck as though trying to imagine the wyvern there. "You are certain his weight will not be an issue?"

"We do not carry cargo, so we are light to begin with. Even so, the Cerulean is sufficient to a wyvern. As long as he is not petulant and prone to tantrums. You are comfortable that he will be able to manage himself?"

"For the sake of rescuing Elizabeth, I am quite certain he could manage to breathe fire if asked."

"Kellynch is expecting him. He swims below us even now. He has agreed to accept Longbourn into his territory without the usual formalities, given the uniqueness of the situation."

"That is good of him. Please convey my thanks to him." Darcy sounded entirely sincere.

Wentworth waved to the bo'sun. "Have the Order flag run up." He turned back to Darcy. "He will be alert to the sign? I do not want to waste time waiting—"

"Nor do either of us. Before anything that might prevent me saying so, thank you. I am all too aware of the risks you are taking on Elizabeth's behalf—"

"I appreciate your thanks, but pray understand that this is more than a personal favor. We owe the Sage a great deal for her actions on behalf of Kellynch, and we are happy to be able to act in her service. But what is at stake is more than just her person. The Order itself and the peace it maintains with dragon-kind are at risk. I believe we both agree that protecting it is worth any price."

"Dragon ho!"

Wentworth turned his back to the rising sun. The ominous, shadowy outline of a flying wyvern approached. Primal fear, instinctive and inescapable, suffused every limb. In the days before the Pendragon Treaty, if a man saw such a thing, it would have been the last thing he saw.

"Mrooooow." Laconia drew out the vowels, like a long, awestruck whistle.

Men gathered on the deck, slack-jawed and staring. This would be a moment they would share with their children. Provided they survived what was yet to come.

"Clear the deck!" the bo'sun cried.

Men scurried aside as Longbourn circled the sloop. "Permission to enter Kellynch's territory?"

"He has granted permission." Wentworth waved him in.

Wing-wind, very different from natural wind, buffeted his face, laden heavily with dragon musk. The sloop sank slightly under the wyvern's weight as his feet thudded on the deck. Wentworth held his breath, listening, feeling through the soles of his boots, as Cerulean spoke to him. Thank heavens! She agreed to take this most unusual passenger.

Off the starboard bow, Kellynch rose up above the waves, water sheeting off his length, glistening on his green-brown scales. He pulled his head just high enough to be barely above Longbourn's. Longbourn ducked just a bit to accommodate.

"I accept you in my territory," Kellynch rumbled

in deep dominant tones.

"I recognize your territory," Longbourn boomed out matching notes.

"We will work together."

Longbourn carefully spread his wings, as men dodged out of the way, and bowed his head. "Cooperation."

"Yes." Kellynch slowly receded back into the waves.

Darcy exhaled heavily. Yes, he was right. That had gone very well. Surprising how well dragons could rally when the matter was sufficiently urgent.

Wentworth approached Longbourn. "Good day, Laird Longbourn. The First Mate will show you the place that has been made ready for you on deck. He will instruct you in how to move so as not to upset the sails or the sloop."

Longbourn nodded slowly as he carefully folded his wings. "I will listen."

"So then, Darcy, what news have you?"

"Elizabeth was seen by a sea-faring cockatrice, forced aboard a ship at Portsmouth, heading for Bermuda. We believe a smuggler by the name of Cornwallis Jackson—"

"Corney?" Laconia reared up on his tail and hissed.

"You know him?"

Damn. "I have pursued him on more than one occasion. Slippery little scoundrel. Do you know of the ship they are in?"

"I believe it was called a sloop, a Bermuda sloop perhaps. Is that significant?"

Damn and bloody hell. "Yes, we are familiar with the Sea Lion. It is a particularly fast vessel. But the recent storms would have slowed them down, giving us opportunity to catch them before they reach Bermuda's waters. It is exceedingly bold for him to try to operate out of Portsmouth, though, right under the nose of the Royal Navy. But that, too, sounds like him. Laird Longbourn, how is your long sight?"

"All flying dragons tend to be longsighted. How else would we see our prey?"

"Excellent. Will you be able to launch from the deck to look for a particular ship? I can describe the figurehead to you in some detail. There will be no mistaking it."

Longbourn paced several steps port and starboard, the deck creaking beneath him. "Yes, I will be able to do as you ask. Shall I go now?"

"First, I will have the navigator give you the general bearings you will need. But before that. You are certain you wish to participate? The Order could—"

"They could, but they will not. They will agree, when she is returned. The men of the Order may not understand, but the dragons will."

"And if she is not? There is every possibility—"

"If she is not, then there will be far greater problems for the Order to deal with than one disorderly wyvern."

18
Chapter

February 1, 1815 On board Sea Lion

ELIZABETH'S STOMACH RUMBLED as she edged into the little sliver of sun painting the rancid pile of straw in the Sea Lion's hold, nearly empty tankard of grog in hand. Any little warmth that could be found was worth pursuing for however long it lasted. Someday she would wear the merino wool shawl Darcy had given her—she might never take it off again. He would laugh at her for it ... heavens, she missed the sound of his laugh. His and Anne's.

Even through closed eyes, heat still trickled down her cheeks. She rubbed her face on her shoulders. Joshua should not see her thus. Perhaps a sip of grog would open the tightness in her throat.

Over the past few days, the Movers had acquiesced to her plea for more meat for the wyrms. Their color and disposition had improved with their change in diet. Unfortunately, their extra portions had seemed to come out of her own soup bowl. All told though, better her hunger pangs than starving wyrms sharing their quarters.

Phoenix, too, had rallied with extra fish tossed into his cage. His bright color was returning and he occasionally twittered, just a little. It was a good sign, but probably a dangerous one.

Joshua pulled the cage into the sun. Phoenix extended his wings as though trying to soak up the meager warmth while he could. The two female wyrms, Azure and Lapis, lay on Elizabeth's either side, pressed against her legs. Indigo curled at her feet. Prussian rested in relaxed alert at the edge of the sunshine, watching the door more than he watched them.

Though still somewhat wary, a full belly seemed to persuade Prussian that she and Joshua were cut of a different cloth than Nunnington's Keeper, the only other Order member they had known. Perhaps it was unwise to begin to consider a forest wyrm an ally, but in a place with so few, no possible confederate ought to be overlooked.

"How will you get the Order to listen to you when we return?" Joshua asked, carefully scratching behind Lapis' ear.

She murmured contentedly. The two had formed an odd little bond. Was it possible they were becoming Friends? Indigo did not seem to mind—he even seemed rather fond of Joshua himself; whatever happened, the two wyrms would do it as a pair. Wyrms did not separate unless one died.

"There is always a way to be heard." Oftentimes it did not make one very popular, but persistence and a strong voice generally got the task accomplished.

"We tried. They refused to hear our complaint." Prussian puffed up and flared the skin around his head. He often did that when annoyed.

"I wonder to whom it was delivered. If you sent a messenger, unfortunately, there are many ways in which its delivery could have been hampered. There are those who think they know what the Order should be troubled with and what it should not."

"Exactly as I told you. The Order will not hear us." Prussian trembled—was it purely rage or frustration as well?

"I have been working to change the situation. A new system is coming into place. The Minister of Keeps has been appointing staff to take and hear complaints specifically from minor dragons. They took their roles just recently, so they would not have been available to your messenger earlier. A rather regal and bossy cockatrix leads them. She takes her role very seriously—though I am still convincing her that fairy dragons—"

"And wyrms! We are as overlooked as they!" Azure protested, the tip of her tail flicking sharply.

"And wyrms, to be sure. I am personally working with her to be certain she understands that all petitions must be taken seriously. Yours will be a teaching case that I am certain will make her well understand my insistence."

"What means that?" Lapis leaned across Joshua and turned her head sideways.

"It means that she will see your captivity as the crime that it is and through that understand wyrms have an important voice in the Order, too."

Prussian slithered closer, still flared. "Why? You

have nothing to gain from us. We have nothing to offer you."

"I ask nothing from you. That is not the point. What has happened to you is a violation of the Pendragon Accords and of common decency. I cannot stand by whilst that is happening and do nothing."

"And the firedrakes and other big dragons will listen to you? Why?" Prussian leaned close, eyes narrow. "Why would they deny their instincts and their pleasure to listen to a warm-blood?"

"She is the Dragon Sage," Joshua said very softly.

"What is a Dragon Sage?" Indigo asked.

"Someone who knows nearly everything about dragons." Joshua stroked the back of Indigo's head. "The dragons themselves chose her."

"Why?" Prussian's question seemed halfway between a demand and a plea.

"The dragons chose me as Sage because they trust me to understand dragons and to be able to communicate it to the warm-bloods."

"You are special warm-blood, then?" Azure turned her head sideways, matching Lapis.

How many species of dragons did that?

"She is a very special warm-blood. All the dragons of the Council consult with her and listen to her." Joshua nodded with the vigor only a young boy could manage.

Elizabeth bit her lower lip. Time to take a risk. "I think it best that the Movers do not know that."

Prussian met her gaze with an expression peculiar to dragons. One that could only be described as burgeoning trust. "We will keep your secret." Prussian moved into arm's reach, and she carefully scratched his ears.

Heavy footsteps approached. The wyrms dashed to their corners in defensive coils. But something about their posture had changed.

The door creaked open, slow and ominous. Corney, dragging his bad leg a little more than before, limped in.

Ayles, hair freshly brushed with a fresh shirt too, sauntered in. "Well-fed and bright-eyed, I see." He tucked his thumbs in his lapels. So satisfied and full of himself—hateful creature. Pretending to be something he was not.

"Now's as good a time, then. Baby dragon, breathe that fire." Corney fumbled with a key. He opened the cage door and grabbled Phoenix in his clumsy, fat fist.

"Stop that, he cannot breathe! You are holding him too tight!" Joshua jumped to his feet, but Ayles pushed him back.

"I can't!" Phoenix wheezed. "Let go."

"If I think you're a gonna fly off, the boy and the woman will pay." Corney kicked Joshua's shin. Horrible, horrible creature.

Joshua yelped and clutched his leg.

"I will not." Phoenix's eyes darted from one side of the hold to the other, their last encounter with Corney no doubt fresh in his mind. What was he looking for?

"So long as we unnerstand one 'nother." Corney opened his hand and held Phoenix at eye-level. "So it be time for fire, little mite. Breathe fire."

Phoenix extended his wings and drew a deep breath.

What did he think was going to happen?

Phoenix warbled and twittered, flapped his wings, and lifted one foot, slightly off-balancing himself.

Did she see that right? That glance between the two male wyrms?

Prussian launched himself from the floor—who knew they could spring like tatzelwurms! He sailed over Corney's arm and wrapped himself around Phoenix, rendering him senseless, as they both fell to the bed of fetid straw.

"Damn fool creature!" Corney kicked Prussian squarely in the ribs.

Azure screamed.

"Thought he was trying to fly off." Prussian gasped for breath, coiling to protect his injured side.

"The poison will leave the creature useless for at least a day now." Ayles looked like he might kick Prussian too.

"Damn wyrm." Corney turned to Elizabeth, a look of new purpose spreading across his face. "I s'pose since I can't get satisfaction from the baby dragon, you will provide it to me instead. Tell him what his little show cost. Perhaps he be convinced to do otherwise on the morrow." He limped toward Elizabeth, one hand on his belt buckle.

She scrabbled back, kicking and clawing. Ayles grabbed Joshua with one arm and blocked the door.

No escape. Bile rose in her throat as her breath came in shallow pants.

Corney grabbed her wrist and forced her into the corner and down into the straw. Was that Joshua screaming and kicking? She drove her knee into something soft and scratched his face with her free hand.

He grabbed at her wrist as a brown and blue streak sailed past, grazing her wrist with razor fangs. It—Indigo—clamped down on the meaty side of Corney's hand. Indigo wrapped his body around Corney's arm, blue skin to Corney's.

"Ya damn bloody foolish thing! Let go! Ya gots me … not …'er…"

Ayles threw Joshua aside and rushed to Corney. "Release him!"

Indigo unwound and fell to the floor, slithering to the far corner.

Corney's eyes glazed and his knees buckled. He muttered nonsense syllables under his breath.

Ayles threw Corney's arm over his shoulder. "Bloody fool. I told you Scarlett was right. There would be no good come of dealing with wyrms." He tried to kick Lapis and Azure as he dragged Corney out, but they dodged just beyond reach. "This is the last straw. If you fail to produce again, we will be done with you." He called over his shoulder as he slammed the door.

Elizabeth staggered to her feet, the hold spinning around her. "Joshua, see to Phoenix. Tuck him into your coat as he recovers. Hide the cage in the straw. Maybe we can keep him out of that dreadful thing." She waved her hand vaguely in their direction.

"Are you all right, Lizzy? You are bleeding. Indigo hurt you." Joshua's voice was very small.

She held up her wrist in the meager light. Trickles of blood seeped from a scratch, which might not even be considered deep. No doubt Indigo had not been aiming at her. Was he clever or skilled enough to have scratched her simply to cover his true target? "It is nothing. Indigo was all things brave and noble." She rubbed her wrist on her filthy skirt and scurried to the corner where Prussian lay.

Indigo and Lapis skittered from the corner to

Joshua and pressed close. "Is Prussian all right?"

Azure pressed close to her mate, her head across his side where Corney's boot had landed. The brown-green skin was turning darker, as though bruised.

"May I examine him? I hope to be able to help."

Azure pulled back, keening softly, her mouth held just slightly open, tongue flicking in and out. Her posture was a defensive coil, but who could blame her after such trauma?

Elizabeth checked the color of Prussian's gums, his breathing, and felt along his somewhat caved-in side. Sir Edward had taught her those ways when treating Castordale after he had been accidently kicked by a running footman in the Blue Order office.

Prussian hissed and lashed his tail as she touched his side.

"I am sorry, I did not mean to hurt you. I think you have several broken ribs. With your permission, I would like to tie them up, to support them. I think it will make you more comfortable."

"Yes, yes, do so." Azure rubbed the side of her face along Prussian's.

He grumbled something that sounded like assent.

Fumbling with her skirts, Elizabeth found a convenient tear in her petticoat. A quick jerk removed a useable strip of linen. "I need to get this around you, but it may not be comfortable."

Prussian lifted his head just enough for her to wrap the bandage around. She tied it firmly around his side as he grunted and growled.

"Recover, yes?" Azure whispered. Poor creature could hardly sound more distraught and lost.

"I cannot say for certain, but it is a good sign he has not fallen into torpor. That suggests his wound is not very serious. Perhaps the bones are only cracked and not fully broken. Maybe even just badly bruised. I am hopeful all will be well in time. May I carry you to the straw where you might lie more comfortably?"

"Yes, Lady Sage."

Using her skirts, she lifted Prussian, surprisingly heavy for his size, and laid him in the straw next to where Joshua cradled Phoenix and the smaller wyrms. She sat down along his other side.

Azure, Indigo and Lapis slipped in around Prussian, leaning into Joshua's and Elizabeth's warmth, their cool weight strangely comforting.

Perhaps, just perhaps, she had Friends here, after all.

.

19
Chapter

February 1, 1815 On board Cerulean

DARCY PACED CERULEAN'S deck, front to back—or was that bow to stern?—unsteady as a child first in leading strings. Sunset's warm rays painted everything they touched a vaguely golden hue. How did a man ever walk firmly when the surface underneath him bobbed like a cork in a stream? Wentworth and his men seemed secure enough—blast them all. A gentleman should be master of his own knees at the very least! How those sailors scurried about so quickly, much less climbed those masts—mind boggling.

The coast raced along beside them on his right, the ocean continuing into the horizon, unending, on the left. Such a sight! How did one grow accustomed to being alone in the middle of such vastness?

"Pacing will not make him return any faster." Laconia bounded to the nearby railing and looked him in the eye, black fur ruffling in the wind. His tail wrapped around the rail and his toes spread to steady him. Those thumbs definitely seemed to assist his balance.

"There is little else I can do. There is no useful employment for me here." He was not fit for even the most menial task shipboard. Perhaps he should have gone to Pemberley.

"You are not accustomed to that."

"No, I am not."

"You might make note of the sensation and re-member it." Laconia licked his paw and slicked it over his face. "Perhaps it will help you to better under-stand what it is to be a minor dragon. I grant that it is hardly the same thing, but there are enough similari-ties that you might consider it."

What a very odd and thoughtful creature, this tat-zelwurm. Hopefully May would take after her sire. "That is the sort of thing I would expect to hear from my wife."

"But would you listen?"

"Perhaps not always, but I do now."

"Like Wentworth listens to Anne, now. That is a good thing. It is a good thing to have a mate who is sensible. The hatchlings are far better for it. Yours will be a suitable Friend for our wyrmling."

Darcy chuckled. Draconic bluntness did take get-ting used to.

"There, see!" Laconia pointed just left of the glow-ing sun barely touching the horizon.

A dark form hung in the sky, flapping slowly, growing larger.

What a sight! How many had ever had the privi-lege of seeing a major dragon in full flight—and lived to tell?

A frisson of primal terror tickled at the back of his head. Should he not be running for cover?

"And there." Laconia pointed right of the sunset. A distinct squared head rose in silhouette just above the sea. "I will fetch Wentworth." He spring-hopped away.

Pray that Longbourn had seen something! Surely he had—he must!

He paced the length of the ship once, twice, three, four times.

Just how long could it take the dragons to arrive? Perhaps it really was as they said, distances at sea were deceiving. And irritating. Very, very irritating.

Wentworth appeared and beckoned him to stand watch with him, the minutes crawling by as the sun dipped farther and farther below the horizon. At least Wentworth was not one to require mindless chatter to fill those idle moments. Such men seemed quite rare.

Longbourn's wing-wind preceded him, making him felt throughout the vessel. Sailors scattered as the boatswain directed him where to land. No small amount of thought had gone into accommodating a wyvern shipboard.

Though Longbourn obviously tried to land softly, a creature that size could only accomplish so much. He folded his wings and sat on his haunches, making himself as small as possible as the ship shifted and groaned around him.

Along Cerulean's left side—was that port or starboard, what had Wentworth called it?—Kellynch appeared at the railings, seawater still dripping from his long whiskers. How well his grey-brown-green blended with the colors of the sea.

The two dragons acknowledged one another with nods. Longbourn touched his chin to the deck.

Kellynch rose up just slightly higher and flicked his tongue in Longbourn's direction, but not quite reaching the back of his neck.

"I acknowledge your territory." Longbourn lifted his head slowly.

How kind of them to forgo the usual displays in deference to Cerulean's rather precarious situation.

"Pray tell me you have good news," Darcy said.

Longbourn grumbled low, a sound more felt than heard. "I saw nothing. Not yet."

"Nor I," Kellynch added, "but there have been many storms to hamper their progress. It is too soon to lose hope now. We have only just begun the search."

Darcy ground his teeth. Patience, it was right to have patience, even now.

"I fear the sea dragons have not changed their position, though." Kellynch bared his fangs in a deep frown.

"What position? What do you mean? I tried to speak to them, but they would not talk to me at all." Longbourn fluttered his wings just slightly, narrowly avoiding a collision with the sails.

"I had hoped that once we were out of Dover's territory, we would find other sea dragons more amenable." Wentworth turned to Darcy. "We asked for their help near Dover, but they refused."

"Refused? Forgive me, but I do not understand. Dragons do not refuse to help my wife. The rest of us, certainly they do, with glee on occasion, but none has ever refused my wife." A vague fluttering of something very much like panic hovered nearby. How could this place be so utterly different to all he had known?

"It seems that Cornwall has had a great deal to say about her—not complimentary—near Land's End, and the word has spread." Kellynch muttered something untoward under his breath.

Damn that bloody lizard!

"Matlock and the rest of the Council will know of this insult." Longbourn growled, barely constraining his tail-lashing to flicking the tip of his tail hard enough to be felt on the deck under Darcy's feet.

Hopefully Matlock would be made Grand Dug and be able to deal with the matter properly.

"But Cornwall is not a sea dragon. I am sure his calumny would be mitigated if we could offer the local pod what they want." Wentworth said.

"What they want? What do you mean?" Why had they not mentioned this sooner?

Wentworth sighed and rubbed the back of his neck. "I assume the local pod has the same demands as Dover's?"

"That is what I have gathered. Many were asking me how I became affiliated with the Blue Order." Kellynch snorted as though he were tired of the questions.

"The sea dragons want recognition by the Order?" Of course they would, and use Elizabeth's peril to achieve it. Darcy's shoulders knotted. Why would they not?

"Recognition, and protection. Gossip travels as fast in the dragon world as it does in the human— perhaps faster as it has wings. Kellynch's admission into the Order has convinced the major sea dragons as well as many pods of minor ones that they should have the rights, protections, and privileges of the Accords applied to them," Wentworth said.

"Are they prepared for the responsibilities as well?" Darcy clasped his hands behind his back.

"If granted the one, I am certain they would accept the other. In truth, sea dragons are not so different from their terrestrial cousins. Until now, Laconia and I have found them very dependable allies."

Laconia sprang to the railing near Kellynch. "This was the first time you could not provide what they wanted in a negotiation."

"I have not the authority to negotiate on behalf of the Order. I am merely an operative, not an officer." Wentworth's expression suggested he did not appreciate helplessness any more than Darcy did.

Darcy looked at Longbourn, whose broad scaly forehead creased. He slowly nodded. Good. "You might not have the authority, but it could be argued that I do."

"You are not an officer. How?"

"My wife." Darcy lifted his hand. "Make no mistake, I do not presume to usurp her position. However, she would hear the sea dragons, promise to bring their petition to Council and ensure that it is acted upon. I have no doubt that if I make that promise on her behalf, then, upon her return, she will act accordingly."

Was it possible to see the hair on the back of Wentworth's neck bristling? "And if something untoward happens to her?"

Longbourn grumbled deep in his throat.

"Then she will be unable to do as promised." Kellynch bobbed his head, approving. "Giving them all the more reason to see her safely back to the Order."

"Do you truly believe they will accept what you offer?" Wentworth asked.

"Given the alternatives, I will take my chances with the dragons. I think them likely to be far more honorable than the smugglers. Laird Kellynch, can you get us in touch with these sea dragons?"

20
Chapter

ANNE PEEKED INTO April's basket near the fire in the ladies' sitting room. Sir Edward had insisted April needed a soft place to rest for several months to come and that, as nice as her 'cage' might be, it was not appropriate for her convalescence. That did not please her, but she forgave him when he promised he would see to it himself that she would be provided with as much sweet as she wanted for the duration of her indisposition.

It said much about April's character that she insisted upon sharing her abundance with Heather, Pax, Cosette, and even Lady Astrid's friend Verona. Poor little mites returned every evening exhausted and, for the most part, discouraged. April's news had been so exciting and encouraging. Now, the waiting and hoping for more sapped their souls. An extra measure of

sweet helped them in the face of their disappointments.

Mrs. Collins returned several small pillows to the
couch, where they belonged, and returned a board
game to its box. Miss Bennet and Miss Darcy somehow never managed to finish the games they started.
The two misses were enjoying tea in one of the sitting
rooms with their minuet partners, Auntie acting as
chaperone. Both seemed to like their partners rather
well—too well in Mrs. Collins' estimation.

She was probably right, but in the face of all that
was happening, it was difficult to care.

"You are well, April?" Mrs. Collins—Mary, they
considered themselves bosom friends now— peered
over Anne's shoulder and checked the temperature of
the bricks under the basket.

"As well as might be expected." April fussed with
the flannel surrounding her. She must be tired, not
reiterating her litany of—justifiable—complaints as
she usually did. "I wish we knew what was happening!"

"Longbourn is attending to matters himself. You
know how stubborn and determined he can be. Along
with Darcy, I am quite certain whatever can be done
is being done." Mary straightened and smoothed
April's nest.

Corn and Wall rubbed up against Anne's ankle and
pointed toward the door. Given the tilt of their heads,
those were not footsteps they knew.

Probably not a good sign, all told.

Mary sighed and sat down beside April's basket.
Anne followed Wall to the door, arriving just as a soft
rap sounded. That was a woman's knock, but not Lady Astrid's.

Oh, this could not be good.

She opened the door. "Lady Dalrymple, what a pleasant surprise. Pray come in." Wall looked up at her, green eyes wide. Even he could tell she was lying.

Lady Dalrymple swept in, adorned in pomp, circumstance and expensive calico unsuited to their modest sitting room. Did she expect to hold court here as she did in her own home? She would be sorely disappointed.

"May I introduce Mrs. Collins, Keeper to Longbourn?" Anne gestured toward Mary, who quickly stood, her features arranged into a suitable look of politeness.

Lady Dalrymple acknowledged her with the barest of nods.

Lovely.

"To what do we owe the honor of your call?" Anne gestured toward the grandest, though not most comfortable chair in the room.

Lady Dalrymple sat down very slowly, as though she expected an attentive audience for the act. "You have no fairy dragons with you?" She scanned the room.

"April is here." Mary pointed to the basket. April snored, a sweet little trilling sound.

"The injured one, yes? And the rest are off and about, are they?"

"We do not keep them as prisoners or as pets in a cage. They are as free to come and go as we are." Mary practically bristled as she spoke.

Anne picked up Corn and Wall and placed them in their basket, whispering, "Stay here quietly."

They ducked under the edge of the basket and twined around each other. Clearly, they did not like

Lady Dalrymple.

Who could blame them?

"That is what I am here to talk with you about. Lady Jersey and Lady Cowper have sent me."

Anne's jaw tightened, pulling her face into a painful grimace that usually passed as a smile to those who did not know her well. "How are the countesses? Are they in good health?"

"They are not pleased, Lady Wentworth, not pleased at all." Lady Dalrymple's fine eyebrow raised in a distinct arch.

"I am sorry to hear that. Is there something that might be done to ease their displeasure?"

Lady Dalrymple paused, eyes flickering back and forth from Mary to Anne, considering, ruminating. "After a fashion, I suppose there is."

"How might we be of service?" Anne asked.

"The Sage's fairy dragon was left in your care, was she not?"

"April was left in no one's care, madam." Mary leaned closer to April's basket as though ready to swoop her away from such disagreeable company. "She is entirely capable of taking care of herself. Her Friendship with my sister and her husband in no way suggests she is dependent upon them."

Lady Dalrymple wrinkled her nose and sniffed in a porcine sort of way. Come to think of it, a great deal about her looks was rather porcine—fat cheeks, squinty eyes, and inclination toward stoutness. "Perhaps I should say it was incumbent upon you to see to her well-being."

Still inaccurate, and now insulting. "To what end is this questioning?"

"It has come to our attention that the Sage's fairy

dragon—"

"Her Friend," Mary all but hissed.

"Her Friend fairy dragon," Lady Dalrymple glowered, "was recently injured, rather severely."

"She is recovering well. Sir Edward is convinced that she will be making a full recovery." Anne gestured toward the basket.

April snored again as though to prove the point. Was she actually asleep or just playing along for the sake of learning what she could? Was there really any question?

"There is some concern among the Cotillion Board that the fairy dragon was injured under your watch." Lady Dalrymple lifted both eyebrows as though to imply Anne should understand what she was not saying.

"Then the Board should be informed of the inaccuracy of their assumptions."

"I do not think you understand, Cousin. It does not reflect well upon you or the Sage's sisters that a dragon was injured while under your care."

Mary cleared her throat neither softly nor subtly. "She was not under our care."

"It is a matter of semantics, that is all. A dragon, albeit a very small one, was injured and the fault lies at your feet, all of you. It is a matter that the Order cannot regard too lightly."

Really? It was amazing that they considered it at all. "What are you saying?"

Lady Dalrymple pressed a chubby hand to her chest. "All members swear to protect dragon life. That you have failed to suggests that perhaps you are not ready to be officially presented to the Order."

"Pray forgive my boldness, but what do you think

you are threatening us with? You are aware that Mrs. Collins and I are both Keepers. We are already full members of the Order." Anne hid her clenched, trembling fist under her skirts.

"Certainly, nothing can change that." Something about her expression suggested she might wish that were different. "But you have proven yourselves, and the young ladies, insufficient to the standards of polite Dragon-Keeping society. You will not be presented at the Cotillion … this year."

Or probably ever, if the warm-blooded she-dragons had their way.

"Perhaps next year, we can find a sponsor willing to take on Miss Darcy and Miss Bennet and able to properly prepare them. As for you both—you are Keepers, you are married. You hardly need presentation at the Cotillion."

"Except that it is considered the entry into good Blue Order society," Mary muttered.

"Are you suggesting, cousin," Anne allowed the word to take on a cold edge, "that we are being cut from good society?"

"I might not put it that way. In time, with good suppers and large parties, there will doubtless be those who do not find your company disagreeable." Lady Dalrymple stood and waited, but neither Anne nor Mary rose. "You will express this to Miss Darcy and Miss Bennet, no?" She strode to the door and waited again. "Perhaps I should let you know that the Cotillion Board are not the only ones who have noticed this incident. I will not stoop to naming names, but shall we say, there are others concerned about what sort of Blue Order members you might be and what, if of course anything, needs to be done about it." She let herself out.

Anne and Mary sprang to their feet simultaneously.

April poked her head above the edge of the basket. "Awful, hateful, pompous warm-blood cockatrix!"

"Did that sound like a threat to you?" Mrs. Collins wrapped her arms around her waist.

"I would say so. Do you think they know about Longbourn and Kellynch, what Wentworth and Sir Fitzwilliam are about?"

"They do not consort with fairy dragons—they are above such company." April flapped weakly. "So, it is not likely. But it will hardly remain a secret when …"

"If." Mary stared at the floor.

"When," April and Anne said simultaneously.

Mary sighed. "When Elizabeth comes back, it will all be known: they went against Lord Matlock's Orders; they took matters into their own hands. There will be a price to be paid, no doubt."

"What do you think they will do?"

"Truly, I have no idea."

21
Chapter

February 2, 1815 On board Cerulean

WENTWORTH DESCENDED THE rope ladder and dropped softly into the worn dinghy beside Cerulean. Storm clouds hung over the horizon; the waves tossed the little craft in anticipation of the excitement that would soon be theirs.

He stared into the sky. Heavy ceiling of dark, roiling clouds, curtains of rain in the distance. Winds that tasted of a particular brand of storm. It was not going to be a good day.

What would it be like, weathering a storm with the wyvern on deck? It was a topic he had never heard discussed, nor considered himself. Why would anyone have? Darcy would tell him that he would need to write a monograph on the subject when they returned to London. That was, of course, if the Blue Order did not summarily pitch both of them out on their arses for having ignored orders.

Now was not the time to consider such things.

Darcy clutched the gunnels, his face drawn in the expression of vague terror that most wore their first time exposed to the sea as it prepared to vent its fury. Pale, his face drawn, he did not give voice to his true feelings. He was made of sterner stuff. There was a reason he had earned Wentworth's respect.

Laconia slithered down the rope and dropped in beside him. How many times had they done this very thing on the Laconia? Was it wrong to enjoy the familiarity of the moment?

He signaled to the oarsman and released the ropes. Like a baby cut free from its mother at birth, they were independent now.

Kellynch waited with Dover's pod, not far off. Odd that they should be so far out of their territory. It would have been better if they had been willing to come closer and allow Longbourn to join in the discussion. However, at some point, wyverns had preyed upon small serpent-whales and the distant memory was too much for them to ignore.

Darcy chewed his upper lip, probably rehearsing his speech for the sea dragons. A good way to pass the time, all told, even if there was little chance he would actually have an opportunity to give his speech.

The oarsman stopped three or four yards from Kellynch.

Laconia leaned out across the bow. "We bring the Sage's representative to talk with you."

Kellynch sank below the waves in a move that felt so much like abandonment it was difficult not to call out. Darcy felt it too, given the way his fists clenched.

Angry waves lapped and splashed over the hull.

Pray this conversation did not take too long. The dinghy would not weather the blow that threatened.

"Mrow." Laconia pointed with his thumbed paw.

Not far from where Kellynch had been, dark forms rose toward the surface.

Dover and her pod. And more? Two large females, matriarchs of other pods perhaps? More appeared in the distance. How many lurked beneath?

Dragon's bones! They were surrounded by enough serpent-whales to take down Cerulean, the dinghy and all hands with nary a trace remaining. Perhaps Longbourn would survive, if he could fly all the way back to shore.

This was negotiating on a whole new scale.

A large male, easily half again the size of the females, surfaced in the middle of the matriarchs. The largest serpent-whale he had ever encountered.

Kellynch broke the surface, water sheeting off his square face and dripping off his whiskers. Though far larger than the serpent-whales, they drastically outnumbered him and could easily best him if they set upon him like a pack of wolves. Which they would if provoked, making his dominance tenuous at best.

Sweat beaded on Wentworth's forehead and trickled down the side of his face. Darcy had lost all color. Good, he understood the stakes.

Kellynch bugled softly. "Patriarch of this coast, Delphinus, Matriarch Dover, Matriarch Memoriae, Matriarch Legatum, I present my Keeper Wentworth; Laconia, one of my Keep; and Sir Fitzwilliam, representative of the Blue Order's Sage."

The serpent-whales squealed and clicked. Wentworth and Darcy bowed from the shoulders. Hardly the proper form of greeting, but the water was far too cold to perform a marine greeting, not to mention Darcy could not swim.

On the whole, sea dragons tended to be quite tolerant of the limitations of the land-dwellers. Hopefully the dragons would be patient today.

Delphinus rose up, front appendages above the water. "Greetings to the representative of the Blue Order Sage."

"I bring you greetings from the Blue Order." Darcy leaned slightly over the water.

"Matriarch Dover has told me of her conversation with the seafarer."

Dover's head fins twitched. That was not a good sign.

"I would hear what you have to say for myself. Begin with the request you made to her." Delphinus slapped the water.

He was not pleased.

Damn and bloody hell.

"The Dragon Sage of the Blue Order has been taken. She was seen forced aboard a sloop that took a course to Bermuda. We ask your help in locating her." Darcy's voice boomed out over the wind and waves.

"You are mate to the Sage?"

"I am."

"Your kind mates for life?"

That was not the expected question.

"We do."

"She is a Matriarch among your kind?"

To his credit, Darcy hardly blinked. "Yes, the Sage is one of our Matriarchs."

Delphinus glanced at the females around him. "Matriarchs are sometimes lost to bigger dragons. It is the way of things. Who stands to replace her?"

Darcy's jaw dropped, and he stammered.

"There is none among the Order who could replace her." Kellynch rose up a little higher. "She is unique among her kind."

"Our daughter, who is but an infant, will likely carry her legacy, but it will be years before that can be possible."

"You are foolish to have one who cannot be replaced." Legatum's squeal carried a derisive note.

Laconia hopped up on the gunnel and stretched out over the water. "She is of a kind that has not been seen before. That is why it is so important that she is returned."

"Are you willing to help us?" Darcy asked.

"How have she or the Blue Order helped us?"

"She was critical to the admission of Kellynch to the Blue Order." Technically, Wentworth was not supposed to be a part of these talks, but those plans had already dissolved.

"Neither the landed dragons nor the Blue Order are quick to change. But now that a marine dragon has become part of us, there is a precedent for more," Darcy added.

"Do you offer us membership in the Order?"

"I cannot do that. It must be approved by a vote in the Council. But I can, I will bring your petition to them and plead the case with them. Kellynch will represent your cause to them as well."

"And you know how they will decide?"

"One can never truly know such things. However—"

"So, your promises are worth very little."

"Can you predict what your Matriarchs will decide under each and every circumstance?" Kellynch snarled and snorted.

Delphinus slapped the water with both appendages. "I trust them to make good decisions for their pods."

"As I trust the Council to make good decisions—"

"For the Order. Not for us." Delphinus clicked and squeaked. Was that a form of dragon-tongue? "I will consider what you have said. We will discuss this among ourselves and contact you when we have made a decision."

"Forgive me, but the longer we wait, the less likely it is that we recover her." Darcy clutched the railing.

"The Blue Order has waited all this time to contact us, and you expect us to hurry for you now? I think not. You will have my answer in due time. If you are in that much of a hurry, there are several marine wyrms like Kellynch that are known to hunt in the depths here, in places we cannot reach. Perhaps they might be sympathetic to one of their kind and hurry on his behalf. But then again, they might feel the wrongs he has suffered at the hands of the Order rather deeply." Delphinus slapped his tail, splashing the dinghy, and dove, the pod disappearing as though they had never been there.

Darcy crumpled, cradling his face in his hands.

"She could not have convinced them either." Laconia said softly, nudging Darcy's hands with his nose.

"I know. Unfortunately, they do have a point, one that I have very little room to argue with."

Wentworth signaled to the oarsman. The winds had picked up. Being caught away from Cerulean in the storm would not make things any better.

22
Chapter

February 2, 1815 On board Sea Lion

ONLY THE MEAGEREST of sunbeams greeted them this morning. Was it a good thing that she had become accustomed to seeing through the gloom?

The taste in the air alone spoke of storms, and not the passing kind, but the sort that lingered all day, tossing them about like a shuttlecock in the wind. Such a delight of anticipation. Perhaps the Movers would forget about them for the time being.

A heavy sigh seemed in order, but it would hardly improve their lot.

"How are you feeling today?" Elizabeth sat up, the ghastly pile of straw slipping and sliding beneath her, and scratched Prussian behind the ears. "That was a very brave thing you did for me, and I shall not forget it."

If—no, when—they ever got out of this hold, she

would never have another straw-filled mattress in the house. Not even the lowest servant would sleep in this stuff.

He leaned into her fingers, a content little sound in the back of his throat. "Hurts. Cannot move fast, but I can move. The band helps."

Azure, still twined around him, extended her neck for a scratch, too. "You great help."

Beside them, Joshua carefully scratched Lapis and Indigo.

Phoenix peeked out from under his collar. "My ribs do not hurt so much either."

She held out her finger for him to perch upon and brought him very close. His color had returned and his eyes were bright, if shadowed with a dread only prey knew. "You do look much better this morning."

"What will you do when they return?" Lapis pushed her head into Joshua's hand.

"That, I fear, is a very good question."

"Think like a dragon?" Joshua seemed so hopeful, though he clearly had no idea what it actually meant.

"It has served me well so far. Why should I turn away from that now?"

"How do you know how to think like a dragon?" Phoenix flittered back to Joshua's shoulder.

The wyrms turned to her with great interest. Somehow it felt like a great deal rested on her answer.

"I think that dragons and men are really not so different, at least in many cases. The biggest difference is men pretend an air of civility to cover up what is truly going on underneath. Dragons do not. If they are vying for dominance, they claim it for what it is. If they are fighting for territory, there is no doubt what is going on. Perhaps that is why I would generally prefer to deal with dragons." Hardly the sort of confession she would make among men, but hopefully the honest answer was also the right one.

"I think I would, too," Joshua muttered.

"Dragons are not always so nice." Indigo prodded Joshua to rub his ears. "The big ones will have their way no matter what we do."

"I will see something done about that." If—no, when—heavens, she was thinking that a great deal today; probably not a good sign—they got out of this hold and returned to Blue Order territories, she would go straight to Langham and Sir Carew with the matter.

Oh, the state of the Dragon State! Worse than the Order even suspected. How much was happening that she and the rest of the Order were unaware of—

Heavy feet, familiar feet, pounded beyond the door and a key rattled in the lock. Why now? Did they not have a storm to prepare for?

Phoenix burrowed under Joshua's grimy shirt. The wyrms stationed themselves around the foul haystack—but somehow it felt protective this time.

Elizabeth's eyes pricked and she blinked hard. Dear little Friends!

The door flung open, bouncing hard off the wall as it struck.

A cockatrix resembling a brilliant red parrot swooped in, Ayles and Corney behind her.

The cockatrix landed, her long tail-feathers spread out on the grimy floor. She looked over her shoulder, staring at the floor, contempt in her eyes. It was the sort of expression Cait would have worn had she ever deigned to enter such a situation.

The wyrms slithered back towards Elizabeth and

Joshua and closer to each other, hissing. Baring their fangs, they bobbed and wove, moves used to confuse a predator.

This was not the first time they had encountered this cockatrix.

Beads of cold sweat gathered on Elizabeth's upper lip.

"There is no firedrake here." The cockatrix's voice was like the caw of a seabird, raw and grating. "You fool! Why did you not wait for me on shore like I told you to?" She whirled on Corney.

Another dragon accomplice?

What did this cockatrix have against the Blue Order? Had she been trafficked as an exotic bird and not offered assistance? That was not unlikely; no cockatrix species native to England sported such colors. Perhaps she, too, had been denied protection by the Order since she was a foreign dragon.

Interesting.

Telling.

Dangerous.

A trickle of cold sweat trailed down the back of her neck.

"I told you we should not have rushed into this. We had Scarlett working with us for a reason, same as those wyrms." Ayles flung his hands into the air, nearly striking Corney.

"How'de you know, missy smart-bird?" Was Corney trying to have his eyes gouged out? Not that he did not deserve it at this point, but it would hardly help their situation.

Scarlett whirled on him and pecked at his feet. Corney skittered back, awkward and clumsy with his bad leg. He just dodged her sharp beak, but nearly fell in the process.

"Just what do you think a baby firedrake looks like?" Scarlett extended magnificent orange-red wings.

A cockatrix vying for dominance was never a good thing. Prevailing over Cait had been one thing—Elizabeth had been prepared, and met her in open ground, with witnesses who would hold Cait accountable to honorable behavior. But here and now, under these conditions, Elizabeth would never be able to repeat that victory.

"Like a lizard with wings, o'course. 'Bout this big." Corney held out cupped hands.

"Idiot." Scarlett flapped, sending bits of mildewing straw scattering. "A firedrake's egg is bigger than I; it would take a barrel to hold it. They are the size of a small child when they hatch. There's no hiding a creature that size in this hold. Whatever might be hiding in that boy's coat is no firedrake."

Joshua covered the spot where Phoenix hid with his hands, pale and trembling.

"You lied to us!" Ayles grabbed Elizabeth by the arm and yanked her to her feet.

She fell into his chest, fighting for balance. Thankfully he had not dislocated her shoulder.

The wyrms rose up on their tails, hissing and growling.

"You made the error entirely on your own." Elizabeth pulled back her shoulders. This was a time to be big. "I simply failed to correct you."

"You said he breathed fire, you miserable bitch." Ayles raise a hand to strike.

"I wouldn't do that if I were you." Scarlett hopped between them. She really was quite lovely. "If she is who I think she is, you've got much bigger problems than kidnapping the wrong dragon."

"What d'you mean by that?" Corney stepped closer.

Only one step, no more. So, he was afraid of Scarlett ...

"She belongs to the Blue Order."

"Nearly all the dragon-talkers do. So what?" Corney sneered.

He really did want his eyes clawed out.

"Word has been going around that an officer was taken. A female officer. An important officer. The Dragon Sage. The one who the dragons selected themselves." Scarlett looked Elizabeth up and down, then nodded vigorously. "Yes, that is her. You idiots have taken the Dragon Sage herself."

"So's we 'ave a valuable hostage, what be the trouble in that? Means she could prove worth her feed, after all."

Ayles turned on Corney. "Imbecile! These are dragons we are dealing with, not men! They will not pay ransom."

"Then we will kill her. The loss is theirs." Corney reached for his belt, probably for a knife.

Elizabeth scrambled back. Azure and Indigo slipped in front of her.

"No!" Scarlett dove for his hand and ripped open a gash, nearly from wrist to elbow, with her beak. "Perhaps that might work with any other warm-blood in the Order. But not with her. She is special to the Order Dragons."

"Then what do smarty-bird suggest?"

Scarlett shrieked a blood-curdling, terror-inducing scream that Walker himself would have been proud of. "There is only one answer for such an insult to a major dragon, much less every major dragon in England. They will kill you. Without question, without quarter, without mercy. They might even entertain themselves by making it a slow spectacle in front of the entire Conclave. No warm-blood in this world will be able to stop them. This entire ship is a death trap."

Both men turned ashen as they looked at one another, eyes wide, jaws agape.

"You have only one hope."

"And what would that be?" Ayles' usually confident voice was more that of a small boy.

"Get rid of her, of all of them, now and get away from them as fast as you can. Hope the dragons find them and are satisfied. If they die, their deaths must not be on your hands. Hopefully that will be enough. If you survive this, do not contact me again. I want nothing more to do with dullards who think themselves equal to dragons." Scarlett leapt into the air and shot through the door.

"Bloody hell! I warned you! I warned you!" Ayles jerked Joshua to his feet and headed for the door.

Corney tried to block him. "Stop. We worked 'ard enough to get 'em, I ain't throwing profit away."

With his free hand, Ayles grabbed the front of Corney's shirt. "Did you not listen? We have to get rid of them and do it quickly. That is our only chance."

"You really think they's gonna find us? They ain't magic, they got no second sight. We be far and away from any o' them."

"Scarlett knows where we are. Where do you think she is headed now? How better to spare her own hide?"

Corney's eyes widened, and he grunted. Ayles

dragged Joshua to the door. Corney followed with Elizabeth. The wyrms trailed behind, twining together in an anxious knot.

Hauled up the ladder and dropped on the slick deck, sharp wind and icy sea spray buffeted her face. Even filtered through swirling storm clouds, the sunlight burned and blinded. After so many days in the dark hold, would she ever be able to see properly again?

"Just pitch 'em over and be done. The cold water will make quick work of 'em and the fish don't leave nothing to find. They'll never know we hads 'em."

"If you kill them, the dragons will know." The whispery-slithery voice—no voices, there were two—rasped against her skull, tearing at her thoughts, her mind. "They will know. The dragons will know."

"Set them adrift. Listen to Scarlett." Another, high-pitched, voice scraped through her ears.

"Angry dragons kill for revenge, slowly, painfully." This voice had authority.

Ayles rubbed his temples, blinking hard and stared narrowly at the wyrms gathered in a loose ring around them. The wyrms tasted the air, bobbing and weaving.

"Do what Scarlett said. They will die one way or the other, no one is here to rescue them. Keep their blood off us." Ayles waved toward the back of the ship.

"No point in wastin' a perfectly good dinghy on 'em—"

Ayles grabbed Corney by the shoulders and lifted him off the deck. "Do as I say or I will pitch you over!"

Corney scrabbled back, with a string of invectives fit to impress Cornwall himself.

Joshua clung to her, shuddering. If only she could offer him some comfort.

Ayles seized each of them by an elbow and propelled them to the back of the sloop, not pausing even as they lost footing on the slick deck. Two familiar scruffy men stood by ropes that hung over the side.

Ayles snatched Joshua under the arms and threw him over the side. A solid thud and a yelp. "Now you, Dragon Lady."

Before she could react, she landed in the suspended dinghy beside Joshua.

"Release it!"

Ropes creaked and the small boat swung against the sloop's hull as it dropped toward the roiling sea.

"They won't last in this storm." Corney peered over the side, laughing. "Good riddance. To you as well." He slung something long and writhing over the side.

Prussian yowled as he caught the edge of the dinghy with his single fang. Joshua grabbed him by the scruff of the neck—wait, they had scruffs?—and hauled him in beside Elizabeth.

Azure screamed and threw herself over, nearly falling across Elizabeth's back. Indigo and Lapis followed, with slightly better aim. Joshua pulled them close as they landed.

"Good riddance to you and all the scalies!"

The dinghy hit the water with a bone-jarring thud. Who ever thought the water could be so hard?

Vengeful waves caught the little craft, tossing it like a paper boat in a rain-swelled stream, dividing them from the sloop. Elizabeth and Joshua clung to the sides, keeping the wyrms between them. Screaming wind swept over them seeking to pitch them into the sea.

Huddling low in the gathering pool at the bottom of the boat, they sheltered from the winds.

At last, a wan sunbeam poked through the clouds.

Elizabeth peeked up. The Sea Lion a speck against the dark sky. How had the sloop gone so far so fast?

There was nothing but ocean in all directions.

Merciful heavens!

Nothing.

As though they were the only creatures left in the world.

Alone.

A wave bearing a grudge of its own caught her in the face. She sputtered and pushed frigid seawater away. Perhaps it would have been better to have been thrown to the waters—it would have been mercifully fast.

What was she thinking? Anne and Darcy were still out there. She would not abandon them. She had not even said goodbye to them.

There had to be options, there had to be something to do.

Phoenix crawled out of Joshua's shirt, onto his shoulder, flapping against the sea spray.

"It is best you stay warm, close to him." Elizabeth dabbed water from his face with her sleeve. "These waves could toss you out—"

"No." Phoenix stamped his foot on Joshua's shoulder. "Do not tell me what to do. This is all my fault. I cannot live with that. Now that I am out of that cage, I mean to do something about this."

"Do something? What can be done?" Joshua tried to cover him with his hand, but Phoenix hopped into the air and hovered between them.

"I am free to fly now. I will get help."

"Here, in the middle of the ocean?" Joshua shouted over the rising wind. "How do you mean to find anyone? There is no one. And this storm? How do you think you can fly in this storm? You are so small—"

"What has that to do with anything? I am a dragon. I will fulfill my commitment to protect the Order and its people as much as if I were a firedrake."

The wyrms raised their heads and rumbled something that sounded like praise.

"He is right." Elizabeth held up her finger as a perch. "He is completely right. A small dragon is fully a dragon."

"But look at him, he cannot—"

"No, he should, he must be allowed this dignity to shape his own fate." She held him close to her face and looked into his bright, determined eyes. Though tiny, stubborn resolve ran through his every ounce. "You know what is at stake. You know what you are up against. If you believe you are up to the challenge, then go."

Phoenix bobbed his head, twittered and took off. Buffeted to and fro, like a feather in the wind, the dark clouds swallowed up his brilliant red, and he was gone.

"I'm never going to see him again," Joshua choked out the words, holding Lapis and Indigo carefully close.

"He has been called a firedrake so many times recently, perhaps he believes it is true." Azure shivered and pressed close to Elizabeth's leg.

"Fairy dragons have always wanted to be taken seriously. None can doubt their fortitude now." Elizabeth inched closer to Joshua, clutching tight to the side against the fresh onslaught of wind and waves.

23
Chapter

PELTING, STINGING RAIN renewed its assault. Joshua huddled close, keeping the wyrms between them, lest they be flung out into the maelstrom, as the dinghy bucked and heaved in the waves.

Another crash. A frigid deluge descended. Was that her own voice, screaming, as she fought the water's pull overboard? How much water sloshed around her? How much more could the little craft take?

"Lizzy, look out!"

Another wave rammed into the dinghy's side, nearly capsizing it. More water gushed over the hull, dropping them low in the water.

"I will find help, too!" Indigo sprang up and dove over the side.

Joshua jumped, but Indigo had already disappeared into the waters. Brave, impetuous little creature would never survive.

Lapis huddled into Joshua in despair. "He's not …
we're not water wyrms…"

He wrapped his arms tight around the keening
wyrm.

"Help me bail." Elizabeth splashed seawater over
the side. "We are not going to give up."

"But Lizzy …"

"Now! Phoenix did not give up. Indigo did not
give up. We shall not give up."

Darcy braced against Longbourn's side as Cerulean
rocked and plunged in the roiling seas. While the
winds resembled bad storms at Pemberley, these
tempests were something entirely unique. Perhaps it
was the vast expanse of sea that allowed them to run
wild. Nothing at home had ever compared to this fury, unrelenting from all sides.

"Get below, Darcy," Wentworth bellowed as he
fought his way toward them. "I can't have you getting
swept over."

Longbourn raised his head slightly and trumpeted.
"Look! Look!"

A red blur—a cockatrix?— broke through the
clouds and dove directly toward them. Wentworth
jumped back as it raced between them.

"Remember me!" Something fell from its grasp
and it disappeared back into the storm.

More by instinct than intent, Darcy stared at the
deck. A matted splotch of red.

Red?

Feather-scales?

Phoenix!

Dropping to his knees, he seized the sodden red mass.

"What do you have?" Wentworth skidded in close and peered into Darcy's hands. "Dragon's blood! Is that...? It is...? Phoenix!"

A weak cheep filtered through the shrieking winds.

"Get him below! To my cabin, now!" Wentworth shoved Darcy in the right direction. "Warm him, get him to talk!"

Darcy stumbled and staggered—it was easier to walk drunk than in this storm—nearly falling down the ladder, but finally made it to Wentworth's cabin.

Quiet, so quiet out of the winds. Dark. Only slivers of light sneaking through. No candles; too dangerous.

He pressed his back to the wall and slowly sank down. Cold, his hands, so cold they attempted to refuse his orders. But, no, he would not relent. Peeling them apart, he stared. Pray that sodden red mass be who he thought it was.

It cheeped and peered up at him, shivering too hard to speak.

Phoenix.

Darcy yanked off his cravat and dried sopping feather-scales, then tucked Phoenix into his shirt, under his coat, pressing him close with both hands. The sooner he was warm, the sooner he could talk.

"Darcy?" How had such a weak voice survived the storm unprotected?

Did that mean—dare he hope?

"Did I hear Longbourn, too?"

"Yes, yes, he is above, on deck. Where are Elizabeth and Joshua? Are they alive?"

"They were."

"Were?" Darcy's hands shook, his throat nearly too tight to speak. "What do you mean, were?"

"When I left them, they were. Now, I do not know. So cold. Could not fly in the wind; thrown into the sea. Scarlett rescued me. Thought she would eat me, but she brought me here."

"Where are they? On the Sea Lion?"

"No, Scarlett told them not to kill her ... they put us in a dinghy."

"In this storm?" Darcy clambered to his feet—faster, why could he not move faster?— and staggered from the cabin, to the ladder, to the deck, falling over himself like a gin-addled beggar.

Longbourn and Wentworth met him as he emerged into the gale.

"What does the flutter-bit know?" Longbourn pressed his face so close he all but knocked Darcy off his feet.

Wentworth grabbed his elbow.

"They are adrift, in a dinghy."

The grimace on Wentworth's face said too much.

"I will tell Kellynch. We will find them." Longbourn backed up three steps and launched into the storm.

"He will fare better than I. He is so big," Phoenix whispered, his beaky nose scratching Darcy's collarbone.

Wentworth laid a hand on Darcy's shoulder. "You realize, the chances of a small craft being found in good weather are poor. In this..."

It was difficult not to hate him right now. "Hope is all I have. I cannot—I will not—relinquish that, not yet."

"I don't think this is working!" Joshua flung out a handful of water as another defiant wave plunged over the side, nearly tossing the weary dinghy on its side.

"We have nothing else we can do. Keep going!" She heaved a mighty splash over the hull with both hands.

The ocean swelled beneath them, rising higher, higher, higher than they had been before, then disappeared from under them. The boat fell faster than they. They landed, crashing hips, knees and elbows, throwing them both to the side.

Groaning as loud as the screaming winds, the little craft listed toward the water, slowly, as though it were a game.

They threw themselves to the other side, but it seemed determined to dip below the surface this time.

Thump!

Thud! Jolting impact resonated throughout the hull.

The boat inched back into balance.

No wave had accomplished that.

What was it? From where had it come?

A gust sloshed more dark water over the hull. The dinghy sank lower, almost level with the roiling ocean.

"We're going to sink, Lizzy! We're going to sink. I'm so sorry. I never thought Phoenix's little trick—"

"This is much bigger than you or Phoenix. It is good that it has all been exposed. You are not to blame, either of you." He was right, though, just another inch and they—

Thud!

She bounced. Something had struck the bottom of the boat.

"Look!" Joshua pointed at a dark form leaping through the waves toward them.

Was that leaping, or had it been thrown?

Indigo splashed into Joshua. "Help here."

"There! There!" Joshua pointed as the dinghy rose slightly.

Through the pelting rain, several dark, oblong shapes rose out of the water.

Dragons? Perhaps, but who? What sort?

Indigo raised his head weakly as Lapis twined around him. "They help."

Two forms drew closer. Serpent-whales? Yes, they were certainly the sort of serpent-whales she had seen in the old bestiaries.

The larger of the two lifted its front appendages out of the water and whistled. "The land-wyrm said you are the missing warm-bloods."

"You did it, Indigo, you did it!" Joshua half-sobbed and pulled the pair close. "I am so proud of you!"

She grabbed the hull and leaned out as far as she dared. "Yes, yes, we are. Can you, will you help us?"

"You do not swim?"

"No, and the cold…"

"Not terribly useful, are you?" The second, smaller one—an adolescent—they were both adolescents, that unfinished look was too clear—bobbed so close she could have touched it.

Its large, intelligent, seawater-blue eyes registered concern.

"We are not of the sea. Will you help?"

"Our patriarch has not decided." The larger one

glanced at the smaller.

"Told the Matriarchs they should stay away."

No! Not like the hippocampus! Her chest clenched so hard dizziness threatened.

"Said he would decide when he decided. Could be a long time." The larger one clicked and whistled as though speaking privately to the other.

"We will not survive that long." What should she do? Was this a moment to be dominant? Companionable? Vulnerable? A Matriarch? How did these sea dragons perceive the situation?

"Matriarch said it is no benefit to us if you die, but she must obey the Patriarch." What was the smaller one implying?

"The wyrm nearly drowned to find us." The larger one pointed to Indigo.

So they had saved him!

"Says he trusts you. Says you will take their case to the Order." The larger one bobbed as a wave crashed over … him?

"Yes, yes, I have given them my word."

"The wyrm believes you." The smaller one rose a little higher in the water.

"You would take our case to the Order?" The larger one's voice dropped into something low and serious.

Case? The sea dragons had a case? What could they possibly want? "Of course I will. That is what the Dragon Sage does."

"You cannot do that if you are dead."

"No, I cannot." She held her breath as the two adolescents conversed in looks, postures and sounds she could not understand.

"I will tell Memoriae." The smaller one disappeared into the waves.

The larger one backed away and stared at her, as though deciding what to do.

Phoenix snored against Darcy's chest. He had tried to remain awake, watchful for Longbourn's and Kellynch's return, but exhaustion overtook him. At least he had warmed enough next to Darcy's skin to be out of danger.

Cerulean heaved and plunged like an unbroken horse. Darcy pressed harder against the cabin wall. Wentworth had declared the storm bad. Not the worst he had weathered, but bad. How could he have survived worse than this?

What sort of men were these sailors to manage such monstrous gales? An angry firedrake must be less dangerous. He had faced one down and lived to tell, but this?

Longbourn was not a sea dragon. He barely flew at all over land. How would he manage against the raging winds and rain? Would he be lost too on top of … of …

No, no, he must not go there. Must not think that. Not yet. There was so much at stake. He could not lose her, not now. Not like this.

They had not even said goodbye—

The cabin door flung open.

"Longbourn approaches." Wentworth helped him stand.

One hand pressing Phoenix to his chest, he lurched to keep up with Wentworth's ridiculous sure-footedness.

A gust of wind sent him sliding into Wentworth. How had the deck become so absurdly slick?

Sailors scattered to make room for Longbourn, who landed on the deck in an ugly scrabbling-for-purchase heap. The deck lurched and bucked—was it the dragon or the waves? Pray he had not injured himself.

Darcy pushed sheets of rain from his face and fought his way across the heaving deck toward Longbourn.

"Nothing!" He snorted, ocher venom dripping from his fangs. "But a hippocampus told me he saw the ship southwest from here. Tell Kellynch." He flapped and snorted.

Darcy dodged back, barely out of the way of Longbourn's relaunch. How did he know what was southwest in these conditions?

Wentworth shook his head. "Go below, I will inform Kellynch if he returns empty-handed."

"He headed east, did he not?"

"I am afraid so. The storm is not letting up, you need to go below." He gripped Darcy's arm. "I am sorry to say this, but you need to prepare yourself. A small craft with landsmen has little chance ..."

"I do not need to hear that."

"Yes, I think you do. I am sorry. More than you can know. I am sorry. But to ignore what is in front of you ..."

"I cannot afford to give up yet. None of us can. If, and I do mean if, she is lost, the implications are too great to consider. Not just for me and my daughter, but for the Order, for all of England. If we lose her in this way, the dragons will be proved right. The Order will have failed them. If they lose faith in men, in the

Treaty and the Accords, the darkness to come is truly inconceivable."

"How could so much come to depend on a single officer?"

"Hope is a powerful thing, Wentworth. More powerful than we give it credit for. She gave— gives—the dragons hope that things could change, that things would improve. If that hope is shattered …"

"Then whatever happens, we must work to ensure that hope no longer rests on her shoulders alone. She cannot remain as the single voice to represent their interests. By all means, hope if you must, but hold on to purpose now, too. She would demand that of you."

Damnation.

Wentworth was right.

Cold. Winter in Derbyshire was not this cold. Would she ever be warm again?

Would the world ever stop moving around her?

Winds, rain. So much rain. Had there ever been a time without it?

Joshua had stopped bailing and lay huddled around all four wyrms, who were falling into torpor with the cold. The edge of the hull, nearly level with the ocean, hardly kept back the cold blackness licking at its edges.

What matter if it did or did not flood them, when the waves kept coming and coming and coming. Beating, crashing, pouring in against them.

The sea swelled, lifting them, tossing the boat. Was it possible it laughed as it did so? Ready to make its final claim.

If only she could hold Anne once more, speak to April, Pemberley, tell Darcy—

Airborne! A monstrous wave threw them aloft above the little dinghy, above the water. Was this how it felt to fly?

Without wings, she plummeted into the frothing jaws of the black ocean, swallowed whole.

Sharp, numbing cold enveloped, wrapping tendrils around her limbs, an irresistible grasp. Darkness, complete and compelling.

Suffocating.

Alone.

No—what? Something smooth and hard beneath, propelling her up through the dark, breaking through.

Air.

She choked and sputtered and gulped air. To breathe! Yes, to breathe.

Bleary, so bleary, everything around her. What, there? A small boat, their boat, on its side, sinking.

A pale grey serpent-whale? How many were there? So many surrounding them.

A deformed one, a growth on its back. No, no, a boy! Yes, a boy! Joshua! Another serpent-whale swam alongside, nudging him as he slipped from his precarious resting place.

A hard nose nudged her. How had she come to be on the back of a serpent-whale?

Cold. Aching. Every inch convulsing in shivers that came from her deepest core, trying to force her from her perch just above the water.

Another nudge, but the wind ... nearly slipping into the water again.

Chittering squeals and another nudge from the

opposite side.

Yes, it was right; she was clumsy and stupid—and so very, very cold. If only she could close her eyes. Yes, that would certainly help.

Too hard to keep them open. Just a little sleep. Darcy and Anne, even Pemberley, April would understand.

Wait, what was that against the clouds?

A dragon? In flight?

Not possible. Looks like Longbourn.

So good to see him one last time.

24
Chapter

WHAT DID IT say about one when the best thing one could offer was to remain out of the way? Certainly, it was no compliment.

Darcy had tried to use a chair in Wentworth's cabin, but somehow, sitting on the floor, firmly braced against the wall, felt much more secure. Huddling like a scared child—that was what it felt like; probably looked like as well. Did the land—or perhaps the *ton*—feel as threatening to Wentworth?

Probably unkind to hope that it did.

Phoenix snored softly against his chest.

What did that cockatrix mean when she screamed 'remember me' when she dropped him at their feet? Hopefully he would be able to tell the story once he awakened.

But what if he was the only one left to tell the story?

Darcy clenched his fists, whole body trembling.

Could he live without her? How?

Loneliness had once been familiar, tolerable, even comfortable at times. But easy to give up, once Elizabeth became part of him. How did one return to that state?

How could he?

Anne. Little Pemberley. April. Walker. The estate.

He was needed. What choice was there?

But being needed was not the same as being loved.

Loyalty and duty. They would make it easier. But not the same.

"Dragons sighted!" A fist pounded at the cabin door.

No! Not knowing and hoping was better than knowing for certain.

He pushed himself up, jelly-knees faltering with the pitching deck. What choice was there but to face the awful truth?

So much more difficult this time, climbing the ladder and crossing the deck to Wentworth. Laconia spring-hopped beside him as though to keep him from a drunken stagger through the pelting rain.

When they reached land again, he would have to get very, very drunk.

"Look, Darcy!" Wentworth handed over his spyglass, pointing to a dark form, barely distinguishable from the dark clouds.

Hands shaking, he raised it and tried to find the object Wentworth had pointed to. Damn, it was difficult to find a precise point. Who would have thought … wait … there!

Longbourn, no doubt. How many other wyverns would be flying in the middle of the ocean, in the midst of a gale? But wait, what was that?

His flight was off, labored, even ponderous. Was the distant storm that bad?

What had happened to his foot? Had he been injured? It seemed deformed ...

The glass tumbled out of his hand.

Wentworth caught it so expertly it seemed he had expected that to happen. "You see it. It seems he is carrying something, someone perhaps?"

"Sir, another!" A sailor pointed at the sea in Longbourn's direction.

Wentworth peered through his glass. "Pendragon's bones! Kellynch! With something on his back! Get the men ready to collect something from him! Quickly! Quickly!"

The sailor scurried away, as surefooted as a crab in the sand.

"What did you see?" Darcy barely forced the words out.

"I cannot be sure, but it might have been a person, a small one, carried above the water. I cannot fathom how he is able to swim that way!" Wentworth turned aside. "Clear the decks for the wyvern. It does not look like it will be a neat landing!"

Laconia leaned into him hard. "You should go below. It may be some time before they arrive."

"I cannot." His feet were rooted in place as surely as the oaks of Pemberley.

"Then step back from the railings. There, you can lean against that bulkhead and hold on to the ropes. No sense risking being swept over. Go." Laconia shoved him along.

Lightning flashed and thunder clapped, lighting the two approaching dragons for a split second. Yes, they were indeed carrying ... something ... what else would they be carrying? It had to be Elizabeth and Joshua. Nothing else, no one else made sense.

Did it?

If only he could pace, move about, release some of the electric urge to run toward them. Laconia pressed him back against the bulkhead.

The tatzelwurm was still there, like a child-minder keeping watch! A grown man did not need ... then again, perhaps he did.

Tension spiraled, too much to bear, as the dragons grew larger on the horizon.

"Move bloody faster!" No, the shout would not accomplish anything, but it did keep his heart from bursting. "Faster, damn it, faster!"

Laconia pressed him back a little harder as his legs twitched to move. Perceptive little creature.

Phoenix stirred and poked his head barely out of Darcy's shirt. "What is happening?"

"Longbourn and Kellynch return."

"Good. Then we can leave this awful place." Phoenix yawned and ducked back under the sodden muslin.

He was right, the seawater was awful. Never, never, never would he sail again, sea bathing, too—that would be out. He had had enough seawater for a lifetime.

"Look! Look!" Laconia pointed his thumbed paw at the sky. "He carries someone!"

Yes, there in Longbourn's grasp, a limp form, female.

Elizabeth.

Laconia braced his knees to keep him upright.

She was not moving, just dangling, like a princess sacrificed to a medieval monster.

Pray, no! Breathe, she must breathe!

Especially since he could not.

Larger and larger, faster now. Longbourn came into focus, Elizabeth dangling lifeless in his grasp.

No! She could not be!

Closer, overshadowing the Cerulean now, its deck dodging away like a sick game of buffy gruffy.

Back-winging rain into all who watched, Longbourn hovered, sailors assembled below, catching, gathering Elizabeth from his talons and rushing her toward Darcy.

Laconia ended his vigil, stepping aside just as Darcy could bear no more stillness. He met the sailors as they laid her on deck.

He grabbed her hand. Cold, so very, very cold. She did not move.

No! No!

His bones melted, and he fell against her, head to her chest, some primal sound wrenched from his throat.

Wait! There, wait…

Was it possible?

Movement?

He held up his hand in a universal bid for silence. The sailors obeyed, the winds did not.

Pressing his ear against her chest, he held his breath. A flutter, a tiny rise in her chest!

He bucked up, gasping, gulping rain and air. "She lives! Get her below!"

Someone slapped his back—probably Wentworth— and yanked him to his feet. "Go with her. Kellynch has the boy. I will tend them and hope for more good news."

Laconia leaned into him as he staggered for the

ladder. He probably could not have made it without the support.

The sailors laid her on blankets on the cabin floor, a pile of dry blankets heaped beside her.

"Get her dry and warm," one of them declared as they poured out, probably to help above deck.

Darcy knelt beside her. In the dark, he could just make out Laconia's black form as he began sniffing her from the toes up. If she were injured, tatzelwurm spittle was the best medicine, especially since there was no surgeon.

He pulled her sodden garments away, wrapped her in blankets and pulled her close. "Elizabeth."

Was it his imagination or did she nestle just a little closer?

The door flew open, feeble rays of light staggered in ahead of Wentworth, who stumbled in with a boy—Joshua— in his arms. A sailor followed with a bundle wrapped in what must have been the boy's coat.

Whatever would he have brought with him?

"Over there." Wentworth pointed and the sailor set down the coat near the far wall.

"Be careful." Joshua's voice was weak, but clear. "Lizzy?"

"She breathes!" Darcy reached into his shirt. "And Phoenix!" He scrabbled across to Joshua and Wentworth and placed Phoenix on Joshua's shoulder.

The boy sobbed, clutching the fairy dragon close. "I never thought we'd see you again!"

"I told you I would get help. I sent Longbourn and Kellynch." Phoenix muttered sleepily.

Granted, that was not the complete story, but no need to bring that up now.

"I am so proud of you. The others, our Friends, how are they?" Joshua pointed to his sopping coat.

Wentworth opened the bundle and wyrms tumbled out. Two, no, how many? Yes, two twined pairs in the shadows. Did they have blue belly stripes?

Darcy glowered. "Why? Did they not—"

A cold hand touched his arm. "They helped us. Take care of them."

"Are you sure?"

"She's right," Joshua crawled toward them. "We're safe now. All of us. No one will take advantage of you again." He pulled the smaller pair close.

Wentworth glanced at Darcy and shrugged. "I will send more blankets and see to Kellynch and Longbourn."

Darcy helped Joshua out of his wet clothes and wrapped him with blankets.

"Wrap the wyrms, but do not touch their blue skin. Please, bring them here." Joshua reached for them.

Darcy placed the wyrms in Joshua's care and returned to cradle Elizabeth.

"Is it true? Not some dream?" she whispered, cuddling close. "I smell sandalwood."

"It is no dream, though I can hardly understand how all of you have returned to me."

"I am so sorry. I never said goodbye." Tears coursed down her cheeks.

"We knew the danger. You should have been better protected."

"Things are worse among the Blue Order than you know." Her voice hitched.

"I am aware, though I fear the wyrms' tale will only complicate matters further."

"They have been wronged, but they risked everything to help us. I think some of them will stay with Joshua now, his Friends."

"I can only imagine what your aunt will say to that." He smoothed bits of wet hair back from her face.

"Anne? April? Pemberley? May? Our sisters?"

"They are all well, safely within the walls of the Order offices."

She pressed her face into his shoulder, sobs wrenching through her in waves mirroring the storms outside. "I still cannot believe you came for me. How … how did you find us?"

"April was the one who first brought us information. Wentworth tried to engage help from the sea dragons, but they refused—"

"No, they did help. A group, young males I think, came to us. They might have been defying their matriarch or patriarch, I am not clear… kept us above water until Longbourn and Kellynch came."

"We thought them a lost cause." He pressed his face into her wet hair. "Wentworth and I defied the Order, seeking the sea dragons' help to find you."

The door swung open, revealing a nimble sailor with a tray of food. "Just cold porridge and grog, I'm afraid. And a joint of cold salt pork for the dragons."

Darcy took tankards and bowls as the sailor placed the tray on the floor near Joshua and the wyrms. In just a few moments, the wyrms peeked out of the wraps Joshua held close, and Phoenix flittered to the tray.

"That is for you. Mind Phoenix, though. There will be plenty now. You do not have to gorge." Joshua helped the largest wyrm, with a single fang and a tied linen bandage around his middle, out of the blankets and toward the food.

He tasted the air and scanned the dim room, eyes locking on Elizabeth.

"This is my mate. He will see you are safe." She gazed up at Darcy with a look he remembered so well.

Yes, this was real!

The other wyrms moved out cautiously and set upon the joint, careful not to catch Phoenix in their frenzy.

Elizabeth sipped the grog.

"When we can have a fire again, I will see that you have tea."

She chuckled, weak and faint, but it was there. "I fear I might have developed a taste for grog. I may just serve it at our next dinner."

He sat close and wrapped his arm around her shoulder, laughing until tears ran down his cheeks.

The smallest wyrms licked the bones one more time, then slithered to Joshua, bellies distended, a funny purry sort of rumble in their throats. Joshua arranged fresh blankets into a nest beside him and the four twined into a content cluster and slept. Phoenix nestled against his neck, just under his jaw, asleep as soon as he settled. Joshua snored a moment later.

Elizabeth watched them for a few minutes, but drifted off as well.

Breathe, he must remember to breathe. The wondrous reality around him would not disappear if he breathed.

Was it just his imagination? Had the sea calmed? Cerulean seemed to have lulled into a far more restful rhythm.

The door creaked open and Wentworth peeked in. Nodding, he beckoned to Darcy.

Had he any idea how difficult it was to leave Elizabeth, even sleeping safely in a nest of warm blankets?

Then again, Wentworth had never been frivolous. This must be important.

Careful not to disturb her, Darcy made his way out and shut the door.

"Mrow." Something about the way Laconia's tail flicked.

Very serious indeed.

"Come, the dragons are returning." Wentworth led him toward the ladder.

Yes, it was easier to walk now. It was not his imagination. "Returning? Did they not already return?"

"And they left after delivering their passengers." What was that, heaviness, finality in Wentworth's voice?

Wind and rain buffeted him as they emerged on deck, but not with the same furor as before. Grey, not black, clouds curtained the sky. Perhaps, just perhaps, there might be sunshine once more. Someday.

"There." Wentworth pointed into the distance.

Longbourn and Kellynch approached, something dangling from Longbourn's foot. "What is that?"

Wentworth shook his head. "Clear the deck for dragons!"

Laconia pressed Darcy back to safety as Longbourn hovered above and dropped something large, heavy and yellow on the deck. Cerulean groaned as his feet touched down.

Kellynch pulled alongside and looked over the railing. "It is done."

"With witnesses." Longbourn rumbled.

"The serpent-whales knew the vessel. It seems the Sea Lion had tried to capture one of their young. You may find them more open to the Order now."

Wentworth approached Longbourn. Darcy followed. On the deck between them lay a battered wooden figurehead with the head of a lion and the tail of a fish.

The Sea Lion.

"Lost with all hands," Wentworth said more than asked.

"Record it so. You may tell the Order what really happened if you like. Or not. I do not care. There is no dragon in the Kingdom who will fault us." Longbourn settled his wings across his back.

"I am sure you are right." Wentworth clasped his hands behind his back.

What had they done? A chill raced from his scalp to his shoulders.

Dragon justice. That is what they had done. Justice.

Kellynch coughed an odd sound and spewed out a box, a modest-sized sea chest, covered in slime. "I do not know what is in that, but it seemed it might be worth retaining."

Wentworth brushed away the slime from the name plate. "It is a gentleman's trunk. Bartholomew Ayles. There may be something useful. Thank you. You and you, take that below."

Darcy approached Longbourn.

"If you disapprove, I do not need to know." He snorted hard.

"I do not know if she will approve."

"She may not, but she will understand. That is what makes her different. She will see that this was the only way forward, the only hope to stave off what has begun among the Order."

"I do not know that the Order will thank us for any of this. It is not what they ordered."

"But it is what was needed."

25
Chapter

February 6, 1815 Portsmouth

A SLIGHTLY SCRUFFY young cockatrice messenger landed on the windowsill and knocked on the glass of Anne's room at the Portsmouth Blue Order office, the second nicest accommodation the office had to offer. Since it was also Admiral Easterly's primary office as Naval Liaison, the facilities were far more comfortable than some of the other extension offices.

It seemed the whole of dragon-hearing Portsmouth had fallen into a dither with the news that the Sage would be visiting the offices! The entire building had been cleaned, stem to stern as Wentworth would say, with nearly every local Dragon Mate turning out to participate in some way. Some sent members of their dragon-hearing household staff to help, some offered objects of furniture or art to decorate or dishes upon which to serve the planned meals, kitchens promised food—the sudden sense of community and cooperation was noteworthy.

The Order's regional undersecretary of Hampshire had also taken the liberty of scheduling several salons and talks for the Sage to lead, because after all, that was what she was known for. She certainly would not want to miss the opportunity to grace Portsmouth with her wisdom.

No, of course not. Her recovery from her trials could hardly be a consideration, could it? Hopefully Lady Elizabeth would not resent the intrusion too much.

Anne sighed as she opened the window for the messenger.

A lean and leggy cockatrice hopped to the dressing table near the window, careful not to mar the marquetry work with his talons. That, along with the rest of the furniture in the suite, were lovely, but hardly dragon-friendly, which seemed ironic all told, considering it was designed to host Blue Order dignitaries who would likely have minor dragons in their company.

At least the room was not also fitted out in Orderblue. That honor was reserved for the Darcys' suite. There was nothing wrong with the color, precisely, but it did get tiresome. The warm wood paneling and white walls of these lesser chambers suited her very well.

Sea air and dragon musk wafted in with the chill breeze. The latter far more pronounced now that local dragons were gathering in hopes of meeting with Lady Elizabeth.

"Cerulean is in the harbor, Lady Wentworth." The messenger extended his wings, emphasizing the importance of his news. "The coachman awaits you downstairs."

"Excellent, pray tell the Gardiners that I will wait for them in the coach."

The messenger bobbed his head and flapped away.

For her sake alone, it would have been far too much trouble to take the coach for such a short distance. But Alister Salt insisted that it would be best to protect Lady Elizabeth and the boy from the attention they would surely draw if they walked to the offices from the docks.

No doubt, the local bands of she-dragons would be tempted to find fault with the Sage for her less-than-fashionable appearance after her travails at sea. As if any woman could be a fashion plate after such trials! It was the sort of thing her father would say. Certainly not the way anyone would wish to be greeted on their arrival.

Moreover, it would not hurt to give the Gardiners a little privacy as well. Calm in the face of adversity they might have been, but keeping their composure when their son was returned would be too much to ask of any parent. The carriage really was the best choice.

Anne shrugged on her navy-blue wool pelisse and headed downstairs. Could it be so simple? The return of the Sage would suddenly solve all the dragon tensions in the kingdom?

Would that it might be, but nothing, nothing was ever so simple, especially where dragons were concerned.

The Gardiners perched on the plush coach seat across from her. A faint light in their eyes helped lift their weary faces. Not surprisingly, their focus fixed on the dock in the distance as they held hands, lips pressed together tight, as though speaking of the coming reunion might somehow make it disappear. Who could blame them?

Her own anticipation of seeing Wentworth and yes, Laconia and even Kellynch, seemed insensitive to remark upon. She had not the same grief and anxiety fueling her expectations. So, they rode in relative silence, unlike the journey to Portsmouth, which had been filled by reading and rereading the tale of the rescue, in Darcy's own hand, carried by Longbourn directly to the Gardiners. A similar missive from Wentworth in which he shared a few details Darcy had not included in his, remained private.

Kingsley and Sergeant ran beside the coach, persuading the dragon-deaf they were the fiercest German boarhounds ever seen in Portsmouth, effectively discouraging even the dragon-hearing from following. They had claimed a share of responsibility in the Sage's abduction and had not been themselves since her disappearance. Now they ran with joyful draconic abandon as they chased away unwanted attention from the coach. It did not hurt that Alister Salt felt the honor of conveying the Sage to the office, then later back to London, very deeply.

Anne pressed her cheek to the side glass, just able to make out the end of the dock in the morning mist. Calm waters lapped around it, a fitting foil to the storms Wentworth had described. A small boat had already tied off and shadowy figures were debarking, Laconia's the easiest to recognize.

The carriage rolled to a stop, and Alister let down the steps. Anne deferred to the Gardiners. Nothing should stand between them and their boy now. They took off running the moment their feet touched ground. That was as it should be.

Alister, his trademark rag-tag appearance now so familiar, and even a little dear, handed her down. "Kingsley and Sergeant will keep the gawkers at bay, but don't be dawdling. Quite a crowd is likely comin' if ye wait too long."

"Thank you, Mr. Salt. I am certain the Darcys will not wish to linger." She straightened her skirts and headed toward the reunions already in progress.

Thank heavens! There was Wentworth, nearly obscured by the mist, the last one off the dinghy. Yes, it was silly to worry about him now, but she did and probably always would.

"Sir Fitzwilliam, Lady Elizabeth!" Gracious! It was definitely better that the Sage not be seen in this condition. Weariness hung over her like a wet, ratty cloak, her garments worn to rags, and only Laconia in her presence. When were there ever so few dragons with her? "Mr. Salt awaits us to take you back to the offices."

"Thank you." Sir Fitzwilliam bowed from his shoulders, dark circles under his eyes and little color in his face. The shadows had lifted from his countenance, though, replaced by weariness too deep for words. "Longbourn made it back to London, then?"

"Indeed, sir. He spread the news of Lady Elizabeth's recovery as far and wide as he could on the way. There is more, but it should wait until we are at the offices."

"Of course." He bowed again and ushered Lady Elizabeth toward the coach.

She cast a grateful look at Anne, which said everything it should have and more.

Laconia wound around her ankles. Anne crouched to scratch under his chin. "Thank you for taking care of them. I know you were invaluable."

"How did I know you would have seen to everything?" Wentworth approached and helped her to her feet. The look on his face—oh~—the one she would never have enough of.

"Once Longbourn arrived with the good news, what else was there for me to do?" She laughed.

He pulled her close, tucking her head under his chin. Yes, it was improper and impulsive, and all things wonderful. "I have never wanted to be back on land so much as I do now."

"And I have never anticipated a homecoming as much as this one."

Several hours later, Anne knocked on the Darcys' door, tea tray in hand. Yes, it was a task more rightfully performed by a maid, but Lady Elizabeth certainly did not need gawkers, and that was what every servant in the building had suddenly become. The Order needed her to be strong and sure, ready with the answers at the inconsiderate events they would force upon her. Right now, she was all too human, too vulnerable to be the Sage. For just a few hours at least, she needed to be just a woman.

"Pray not now."

"It is Anne, Lady Elizabeth."

"Oh, yes. Come in."

Anne slipped inside and shut the door behind her.

"Thank you so much for bringing a trunk of my things. I cannot remember a time when my favorite soap and a fresh gown were so very welcome." Lady

Elizabeth did not rise from the leather armchair near the fire, looking a mite unwell, but it could have been the reflection of Order-blue, which dominated every corner of the chambers.

Walls, curtains, linens—only the mahogany furniture and matching leather upholstery had the audacity not to represent the Order's signature color. It was made up for by draconic carvings occupying every available segment of the wood: talon and ball feet, dragon-scale patterns, artistic drakes and wyrms climbing legs and along the edges of tables.

If there was a room designed to be the antithesis of Darcy House, this was it.

"I cannot take credit. It was your sister, Mary, who packed it. She hoped you would find it comforting." Anne set the tea tray down on a small table, with a ring of marquetry fairy dragons inlaid in the tabletop, and poured a cup of tea.

"She has always been so practical and considerate. I am very grateful to you both." Lady Elizabeth sipped her cup. "Oh, gracious. That is a delight, though I fear I may yet find myself missing the taste of grog."

Anne chuckled, lowering her voice to a conspiratorial whisper. "Tell no one, but occasionally it is served at Kellynch-by-the-Sea for the same reason."

Lady Elizabeth laughed until tears ran down her cheeks. "Pray excuse me. I dearly love to laugh, and there have been far too few opportunities to do so recently. Thank you. I must ask, Lady Wentworth—pray, call me Elizabeth now, and may I call you Anne?—"

"I would be honored."

"What do I need to know of the happenings since

I have been—inconvenienced? Darcy has informed me of that which he thought was important, but I am sure you will have a very different, but equally valuable, perspective on what has transpired. Please, have some tea with me."

Anne pulled a chair—upholstered in a dragon-wing pattern— close and sat down. "Most immediately important, I think, is that all of Portsmouth anticipates your stay. Salons, talks, and now two teas—oh yes, and a dinner yet tonight—have been arranged. I tried to dissuade them all, but—"

Elizabeth rubbed her temples. "No, I understand. Perhaps now more than ever, these will be important if we are ever to right what is wrong with the Order. I know, they will not be sufficient in and of themselves, but they will help reassure the dragons that the Order has not lost its value. At the very least, it is a good place to begin."

"Happily, they are spread out over several days. I intend to insist that you are permitted to rest when not on display. Kingsley and Sergeant will assist in seeing you are not disturbed."

Was that a sigh of relief? "That would be most appreciated."

"Alister Salt will convey us back to London when we are finished here. I am told that at least one Blue Order office and two estates along the way have requested that you grace them with your presence as well. More requests may arrive yet. The journey back to London will take several days. Days I hope you will be able to take some rest as well."

"Grace them with my presence, you say?" Elizabeth's laugh rang from the depths of her soul, as though to make up for the missed time. "I hardly have any presence with which to grace anyone. I have barely been able to keep my eyes open since we set foot in this room. I fell asleep twice in my bath, as it is, even before I lay down! Mattresses and blankets are highly underrated, you know."

"I came to a similar conclusion myself whilst traveling non-stop with Mr. Salt and his team. A moving coach is a poor substitute for a proper bed. That will be one advantage to being forced to make stops on the way back to London."

"An excellent point indeed. I shall choose to count the blessings."

"I hope you and Sir Fitzwilliam approve of the plan for him to travel north to Pemberley to gather the information the Order sought whilst spreading word of your recovery. It was Longbourn and Kellynch's idea."

"I cannot say he is happy to be sent away, but the dragons had an excellent plan. I cannot help but imagine you might have had something to do with it as well, no? At least in arranging the services of young Mr. Salt?" Elizabeth sipped her tea and raised an eyebrow.

Anne looked aside and poured herself a cup of tea. If only her hands would not tremble! "Both our husbands have been rather at odds with the Order's demands recently. They both opted to—I believe you would say—think like dragons, and, shall we say, procrastinate in acquiescing to the Orders' directives."

It had been bad enough that Father had been disgraced and lost all good connections as the result of his transgressions toward the Order. If she and Wentworth met the same fate—even if it was for the right choices. What then?

Elizabeth stared at her for a long moment and pressed her lips hard. She trembled, then laughed until she had to set her teacup aside to double over, holding her belly. "Forgive me, please. I know it is most unbecoming. But the image of my … our husbands thinking like dragons is really very dear, and a touch amusing, considering how much trouble I have found for doing just that."

"Not at all, I am just relieved that you are not put out with me for trying to mitigate the Order's ire."

"I am glad someone is attempting to do so on my behalf, for I shall surely incur more in the days ahead. I am only going to bring them more problems that they do not want to deal with. In all seriousness, thank you for what you did for April and the other fairy dragons. If it had not been for her information, I … we …" She blinked her eyes hard and sucked in a deep breath. "Perhaps now they might be taken seriously, finally."

"April's injuries were taken quite seriously, to be sure. You may as well know that the Cotillion Board declared us all to be unfit Dragon Mates because April was injured on our watch. We are not to be presented at the Cotillion this year. Moreover, Mary and I, well, it was not said precisely, but the implication was that we would never be presented at all." Anne chewed her lip and avoided eye contact.

All levity left Elizabeth's face and her expression changed to something utterly draconic and predatory. "Is that their game? Miserable warm-blooded cockatrix pretending to vie for dominance! They will regret this little game."

"But will it not be easier on you, not having to deal with the affair this year?"

"Easier perhaps, but with dragons, taking the easier route often declares that you recognize you are prey, looking for the quickest route to flee." She sat up a little straighter, a little of her characteristic determination returning to her tone. "I am not prey. Nor are you and my sisters."

"What do you intend to do?"

"Honestly, I am not certain yet. I will let you know when it comes to me. Pray tell me, you and my sisters will be ready for the Cotillion?"

"Absolutely."

After a large dinner hosted by the Order for the local Dragon Mates—one that Lady Elizabeth had every right and reason to decline, but did not—Wentworth and Anne tramped upstairs, candle in hand, while the last few attendees continued to ply Lady Elizabeth with questions.

It was high time he had a little time to spend alone with his wife, regardless of what polite society might say. "Truly, I do not know how she manages. She has the stamina of a dragon and the patience of a saint. How many times was she asked the same questions tonight, asked to recount the same story?"

"Those jealous cockatrix should see what she endures before they start casting judgments upon her." Anne paused at the top of the stairs, drooping as though a weight had suddenly landed on her shoulders.

Wentworth led the way to their chambers, through a door not carved with some sort of dragon. Should it be a breath of fresh air to encounter a plain door?

"You did not mention it in your letter, but it is obvious something has transpired. What happed with the Cotillion Board?" He set the candle on the mantel and pulled her down with him into the large wingchair near the cold fireplace.

Finally, things felt right once more.

She cuddled into him, hiding her face in his shoulder. "I did not like being away from you."

He arranged his arms around her warm softness. "Nor I you. It has been far too easy to become accustomed to being home, every night, with you." Far easier than ever he imagined it could be.

"I would like to become accustomed to that." Her whispers gave the impression of a difficult confession.

"Do you not want to continue to work with the Order?" He intertwined his fingers in hers.

"Honestly, I do not know. At this point, I just do not know." Pain, that was pain in her voice.

"What did those women do? I will understand if you cannot bear working for the Order, but this, this is not like you. Pray tell me, what happened?"

"It is silly and stupid and should not matter at all." She shut her eyes and shook her head.

That only made it worse. "Anne, please."

"We, Elizabeth's sisters and I, have been cut from the Cotillion as inadequate Dragon Mates because of April's injury. Miss Bennet and Miss Darcy may recover and be presented next year. Mary and I, though, will not. We will not be presented, not be invited, and by extension, not welcome in any good Dragon Keeping society. As I said, silly and stupid."

"You looked forward to that society?"

She nodded into his shoulder as though embarrassed to speak the words.

"You never did have your proper share in society, with your father always pushing your sister Elizabeth forward. It seems patently unfair to be denied it now, I suppose." He stroked her back. She was trembling. "Longbourn and Kellynch did not fault you for what happened. They were impressed with what the fairy dragons accomplished. Though there will always be detractors, I think the Order will begin looking at their smallest members rather differently now. Thanks to you and Mrs. Collins."

She sniffled and swallowed hard. "The thought is rather appealing."

"And far more significant than any society a ball could grant us."

"Are you suggesting I should be indifferent to their cut?" A cold note penetrated her voice.

"No, no. Their cut should be viewed in light of their contributions to the Order."

"I am not sure I take your meaning."

"Those women, they have title, wealth, connections. But what have they actually done for the Order? I can hardly put introducing the quadrille into the Keeper's Cotillion on the same level as changing the way Blue Order society views fairy dragons. Can you?"

"I suppose not. But they are countesses and…" She tipped up her chin to look at him.

He placed a finger under her chin. "Did not you yourself decry the shallowness of that sort of company? My dear, I know that is the kind of company you were brought up to admire as worthy and important, but the world is changing before our eyes. The ability to do things, to contribute, to change, and grow in the world is more significant than it ever has been. I believe it will continue to be even more so. Maybe those of grand estates and great titles will not choose to associate with us. But they are not the only Blue Order society to mix with. Consider the crowd tonight. How many of them were high-born or titled? Influential or wealthy?"

"There were far more Dragon Friends than Dragon Keepers in attendance."

"The Darcys and ourselves were the only titles in the room. When it becomes more widely known what you and Lady Elizabeth's sisters did with the fairy dragons, I expect you will be something of a hero to the Friends of small dragons."

"There are those who could consider that being damned with faint praise." Anne chuckled.

At last, the sound he wanted, needed, to hear!

"I know those harpies have hurt you, and I am sorry for that. I will never feel that as deeply as do you, but that does not mean I am insensitive to it. I ask you again, do you wish to continue our work for the Order? You know the problems we uncovered will not suddenly resolve with the Sage's return. Things are going to be challenging for some time to come and a great deal of work will need to be done. It would be foolish to think things will become easier anytime soon if we continue."

"But that will be true whether we work with the Order or not. Keeping Kellynch, we cannot remain insulated against the disruptions in the Order." She was right. "You enjoyed being at sea again."

"I will not lie to you, I did. So did Kellynch."

"I expect the Order will need you both to begin talks with the sea dragons."

"You have not answered my question."

She stood and began to pace along the fireplace. Her shadow in the single candle's light, thin and stark. "I have not answered because I do not know. I do not like being left behind to wait, left to the clutches of the she-dragons. It was … empowering … to work with the fairy dragons and feel like we might contribute something useful."

"Lady Elizabeth and Lady Astrid are exceedingly useful to the Order. There is no reason why Lady Wentworth should not be as well." He rose and walked to her, taking her hands in his. "I think Kellynch himself would be quite pleased with the distinction of having you classed with such esteemed company."

"Of course he would. He enjoys distinctions of any sort. But I am more concerned about your opinion."

He pulled her a step closer. "You do not tolerate idleness any more than I being landlocked. If we are to serve the Order, your role must be more than waiting for me to return, embroidering cushions of little use and no beauty. Assuming, of course, the Order will have us at all. After what Darcy and I have done—"

"You do not believe going back to Dover now to interview the dragons there will be enough to allay the Earl's displeasure?"

"There is no way to know. Disobeying orders is no small thing in the military."

"The Order is not military."

"No, it is not. But what is done is done. There is no point in worrying about that now. I must be off for Dover in the morning. I would rather make better use of our hours together."

"Like this?" She rose up on tiptoes and kissed him.

26
Chapter

"WILL YOU BE all right at home alone, Lizzy?" Uncle Gardiner asked as Alister Salt's luxurious coach trundled toward Cheapside with Kingsley and Sergeant escorting on each side.

Nearly a week spent in leisurely travel, in an exceptionally fine coach, under Anne's zealous care that kept her undisturbed those hours she was not required to be present for Blue Order duties, had mostly restored Elizabeth's equanimity and sense of humor. How pleasant it was to laugh only at things that were truly amusing now, not simply at everything that stirred a reaction. That had been a mite embarrassing. Thankfully Anne and Aunt Gardiner were the souls of grace and discretion.

Leaving Anne at Thames House had proved a bit more moving than she expected. So clearly, the exhaustion had not yet passed—a little disappointing, but good to know. Was it possible to be tired of resting?

"I will hardly be alone at Darcy House. Little Anne, Mary, Lydia, and Georgiana are all there, with April and Walker. Brutus remains assigned to us, along with Nanny and Auntie. And there's the entire staff, human and dragon. I will be well attended."

"We would stay with you if you want. We can guard." Prussian peeked up over the edge of the large basket the wyrms occupied on the coach floor.

His color and strength had improved with good food and safe environments. The entire cluster's tempers had improved as well, charming the Gardiners on multiple occasions. It seemed at least Lapis and Indigo would be residing in Cheapside for the foreseeable future. They might be the first wyrm Friends in London. How would Blue Order society react?

She leaned across the coach to scratch Prussian's cheeks. "I know you would, but with so many dragons already in the house, the introductions might be a bit fraught. And since the Darcy House dragons do not yet understand the circumstances that led you to be associated with Corney and his men, there may be misunderstandings."

"That is an excellent point. You recall how reluctant Rustle was to accept the acquaintance when he met us on the road last night." Aunt Gardiner straightened the blanket covering the cluster. "Convincing a house full of dragons will be quite a challenge."

"You think we be not accepted by the Order?" Azure peeked out, her red head knob brighter than ever.

"When the full truth is known, I am confident it

will be well. But until then, we should be cautious. I think the outrage over Nunnington's actions will win you no little support. But pray, be patient whilst that is first verified, then made known," Elizabeth said.

"In the meantime, you will be welcome to stay with us. We will always welcome our children's Friends." Aunt scratched Azure's cheek.

"We have so many Friends, now!" Joshua grinned at Phoenix on his shoulder. "With six in the house, there will be one for every person! There will always be enough scratches for everyone."

Phoenix twittered happily. Once they got past the predator-prey issues, he and the wryms had become quite comfortable, even friendly, with one another.

"Do I need to ask you to stay with us instead, Phoenix?" Elizabeth pulled her shoulders back to remind him she was big.

"I have learned." He hung his head. "Fairy dragons do not breathe fire, nor should they, nor will they ever."

Joshua scratched under his chin. "And I will not encourage him to learn new tricks. At least not ones that I have not asked you about first, Lizzy."

She sighed and rubbed her upper arms briskly. "I hope that will be enough for the Order. They will no doubt be meeting with you in the coming days."

If only he knew how complicated things could become. Then again, it might be best neither he nor his parents did, at least for now.

The coach rolled to a stop in the mews behind Darcy House. Chills coursed down her arms. Home. Not so long ago, a place she might never have seen again ...

Uncle clasped her hand. "Do not hesitate to send

for us if there is anything you need. Absolutely any-thing."

"I am sure all will be well, but you have my word. Truly, I promise. No doubt the fairy dragons will hold me to that and go for you themselves should they feel the need."

They chuckled, avoiding the world-bending change she implied.

Alister Salt dropped the steps and opened the door. "You ready, Lady?"

She allowed him to hand her down, Kingsley and Sergeant standing guard before and behind the car-riage.

"We will be with Lady Wentworth should you need our services. Do not hesitate to send for us." Alister Salt bowed. Apparently, his hearing was acute even for the dragon-hearing. The drakes dropped their chins to the ground, their tails flicking.

"I am honored by your assistance."

The back door flung open. Mary, Georgiana and Lydia flew out, fairy dragons not far behind. May led a second wave, including the housekeeper, Slate and Amber, and the butler.

"Lizzy!" Mary threw her arms around her. "I hard-ly believed it when Longbourn told us the news. I am so relieved!" Tears trickled down her cheeks.

Was this staid, sensible Mary?

Her own eyes burned and her vision blurred. She wiped her cheeks on her shoulder. She definitely needed more rest.

"You must tell us everything, Lizzy! We want to hear the whole story." Lydia clapped and bounced, but shadows lined her face.

Poor thing. Though she would never admit it, this

trial had changed her, too.

"Do allow her to rest a bit, Miss Bennet. Can you not see she is exhausted?" Georgiana hung back slightly, Pax hovering near her shoulder.

"I will have your things taken inside." The housekeeper waved two footmen into motion. "Will you wish for a hot bath or a tray to be sent up?"

"Both, I think, but after I have seen Anne."

The staff bowed, curtsied, and scurried away.

"How was your journey?" Georgiana wrung her hands.

"Very long, with a great many meetings. Perhaps we can talk over dinner?"

"Of course," Georgiana looped her arm in Lydia's and pulled her toward the house.

Was it possible the two of them had become friends? It was not an unpleasant thought; they could do each other good.

"How is April?" Elizabeth peered toward the open door, hoping.

Mary put Elizabeth's arm in hers. "She is improved. Sir Edward says she looks much worse off than she is. Her wing was broken but the dislocation has not reoccurred. The talon wounds are still rather off-putting, but they are healing well. May checks her wounds daily, insisting on the privilege of attending to her hero."

Oh, that image!

Elizabeth gulped for breath, her throat tightening. "Thank you, for all you have done. We would not be here but for—"

"Would it be awful of me to say it was nice to be able to be the one to help you for a change?" Mary did not look at her.

"I still cannot believe all that has transpired."

"I think that feeling will remain for some time." She patted Elizabeth's arm. "You will be satisfied to know Longbourn is quite pleased with himself, for what he did for you and what he has done since he returned. Little Pemberley has had her equanimity restored after he visited her and promised you would see her soon."

"I am certain Barwines Chudleigh has been quite busy with Pemberley and her own snakeling to tend."

"Her snakeling is charming, by the way. He is called Haldon, for the woods near her estate. An entirely suitable playmate for Pemberley. You will find him delightful."

Elizabeth caught her eye, studying her. "I know that look on your face. What are you not mentioning?"

"Household matters, nothing so important."

"Mary, if it is significant enough to trouble you, I need to know."

"Very well." Mary huffed a heavy breath, shoulders sagging slightly. "Nanny has been quite put out with the fairy dragons since April's injury. It has been rather tense around her. She does not like them visiting Anne, despite Mr. Darcy's insistence that they should be given free access to the nursery. She keeps May away whenever she can as well."

"Oh, merciful heavens! I warned her those attitudes were not acceptable. I do not want Anne raised around such beliefs! But with all that has been going on, and all I expect to come, I cannot be without a nurse." It was tempting to mutter a few draconic epithets under her breath, but Mary would be scandalized.

"Perhaps I might be able to assist? I could keep Anne for you until you are able to find another nursery maid."

"I cannot impose upon you like that."

"It might be good practice …"

Elizabeth stopped and took Mary's shoulders in her hands. "Oh, Mary! Truly? That is wonderful news! I am so happy for you. Does Mr. Collins know?"

"I have only found out for certain in the last few days. The baby just quickened and Heather tells me she can hear—him, she believes it is a boy but I am not so certain—him kicking and stretching. I was going to tell Mr. Collins when he came to town for the Cotillion." Mary's smile faded slightly.

"Anne told me what happened."

"I do not mind. I think I am rather relieved, truth be told."

"Nonetheless, do ask Mr. Collins to come to town. We shall have a large celebration of our own in honor of your news."

Mary gasped. "You cannot be serious, in light of everything that is happening? Do you think it wise?"

"Absolutely! If we wait to celebrate until it is convenient, then it will never happen. Besides, planning a party will help Georgiana and Lydia forget their disappointments."

But she would hardly forget the insult to herself. Dragons did not easily overlook such things.

Elizabeth peeked into the attic nursery, snug and neat, decorated with treasures from the Darcy family past. A low fire and pair of candles on the mantel lit the room in a soft, friendly glow. Anne slept in her crib; Nanny silently read *A Young Dragon's Primer,* sitting in a chair nearby. Quite the scene of domesticity, even without the little dragons who should have been present.

Little Anne slept so poorly. It would be cruel to wake her now. Waiting another hour for their reunion would be better. Elizabeth wiped her eyes on her sleeve. Better Anne's convenience than hers, though.

She swallowed hard and forced herself to her dressing room. According to Mary, April was there. Elizabeth steeled herself for the reunion. Knowing April had been injured on her behalf was almost too much to bear, and facing the reality …

A low fire warmed the dressing room, likely for April's comfort. An extravagant expenditure to heat the room for a single occupant who could have enjoyed a fire in another room, but one that April deserved.

Save April's recovery basket, woven of sea reeds and lined with lambswool, nothing in her chambers had changed. Bold rose and vine paper hangings in pinks and yellows, with tiny blue butterflies, lent a garden feel to the space that April liked even more than she did. The furniture, chosen by Lady Anne Darcy, crafted of mahogany, with clean, elegant lines, suited her very well, despite Darcy's generous insistence that new could be bought if she desired. He was so very considerate. An overstuffed, faded floral armchair near the fireplace proved very comfortable. How lovely it would be to feel its embrace once more.

The perfume of dried lavender hung in the air. The housekeeper must have added some new sprigs to the mix in the bowl on her dressing table. She drew in another deep breath. So much better than the dank, cold smells of the Sea Lion. She rubbed her shoulders to dispel a building shudder.

Perhaps they would avoid the seaside for some time.

"I am cold." April twittered and poked her head over the side of her basket.

That was an interesting sort of greeting.

She climbed out, slowly, awkwardly, and landed on the mantel, scars along her chest and leg stark against her blue feather-scales. Her entire posture seemed faded and a little limp.

"Your wing! It is no longer bandaged?" Elizabeth hurried to her.

April carefully extended her wing, wincing slightly. "Castordale's Keeper removed the wraps a day or two ago. He said the bones were knit, but that I ought not try to fly yet. Flap and stretch, but not fly. I do not know when I shall be allowed to."

Allowed to? April had never before concerned herself with what she was or was not allowed to do.

"It must be very difficult not to fly." Elizabeth offered her finger as a perch.

"I do not like it. I do not like walking. It is a stupid way to move." She rubbed her cheek against Elizabeth's thumb. "But you have returned. It was worth it."

The lump in her throat was nearly too big to swallow back. "How can I thank you for all you have done?"

"You rescued my egg before I hatched. We are Friends."

"Yes, we are." Elizabeth curled into the large armchair.

"I am cold. Do you not think it is cold?" April huddled into her palm.

"We can move nearer the fire if you like. There is warm water on the hob. Shall I pour some for your bath?"

"I will only be cold again when I get out. I would rather have tea." April fluffed her feather-scales as best she could. It only made the scabs and scars more obvious.

"Very well, I shall make you tea. Why do you not climb up on my shoulder under my shawl while it steeps."

April crawled under the soft, mustard-gold wool. She must truly be uncomfortable, or exhausted, to do as she was asked without argument.

"Now I am back, you can be here with me as much as you like. Or you might consider hibernating. All the local fairy dragon harems have tucked in for the winter and will not emerge until the weather warms."

April poked her head out from under the shawl. "You have only just returned and are bored with me already. You just want me to be gone!"

Elizabeth stared at her. "Excuse me? What did you say?"

"You heard me."

"What makes you think you are unwanted?" She wrapped April in her shawl and held her up to look eye to eye with her.

"I am cold."

"You got cold at Longbourn and never complained of being unwanted there."

"It is colder here."

"I can assign someone to make sure you have fresh warm bricks—"

"I do not want warm bricks!" April freed herself

from the shawl. "I want you!" She pecked at Elizabeth's hand.

"Me? Whatever do you mean?"

April hopped to Elizabeth's hand and bobbed from one foot to the other. Should it be so heartening to see her acting a little more like herself again?

Elizabeth scanned the room for a jam or honey pot. Yes, there on the tea tray on the table near the window. She retrieved it and held it close to April. Fairy dragons were always cranky when hungry.

April turned her back and harumphed.

Gracious! Never, never had she refused jam!

She set the jam aside and pressed April close to her chest. "You are my oldest, dearest Friend. Pray tell me what is wrong. I truly do not understand, but I very much want to."

April looked over her shoulder into Elizabeth's eyes. "Very well, though I doubt you shall even care."

That was a very serious accusation.

"Do you not like Darcy House? Has anyone here mistreated you?"

"It is a strange place. But the gardens are very nice. The staff can all hear me." April resettled her stiff wing along her back.

"But do they listen?"

"Yes, they do." She twitched her head and flicked her tail as though that did not make her particularly happy.

"And the staff dragons? Have any of the household dragons been unkind to you?" It was a leading question, yes, but she needed to hear it in April's own words.

"There are so many of them!"

She was right. Few households could count so

many under their care. Oh! "You are jealous?"

April twittered and covered her face with her wings. "You have so many to take care of now—especially the hatchling."

"Little Anne? You are jealous of my daughter?"

"That nanny dragon the Order sent—she is rude and high-handed. She tells me to keep out of the jam and honey."

Finally! "I had intended to speak to her about her attitudes—"

April pecked her hand hard enough to draw blood. "How could you allow that crusty old drake to speak to me that way? Did you know that since you have been gone, she keeps me from the nursery and any other room she might encounter me in?"

That was new information.

"Phoenix lives in the nursery with the Gardiner children. Why do you encourage that but not permit me—" April pouffed up, full and fluffy. She was unfortunately cute when angry. "What harm do you think I will bring to your hatchling? You seemed happy enough to have me there to soothe you when she hatched—"

"Born. Human babies are born, not hatched."

"Do not change the subject!" April stomped, toes scratching Elizabeth's hand. "Since her hatching, I have been all but banished from the household."

Surely that was an exaggeration.

Something in the way April scowled …

Then again, perhaps not.

"Nanny forbids me from the nursery, from your chamber when she can—you have no idea how hard she fought against my basket being here and having a fire to keep me warm!— even the parlor is off limits when the hatchling is brought out. She only allows the staff dragons in to perform their tasks and then leave as quickly as possible. But at least they are allowed in. But me? She hates me. Heather, Pax, and Cosette are afraid of her."

Afraid. The fairy dragons should never fear in the household. She stroked April's ruffled feather-scales. Nothing in her posture or tone suggested she inflated the issue.

Why though? What could trigger such behavior? Nanny was the largest of the household dragons—

Dominance.

It was always dominance with dragons!

"I think I understand now. I have been away, and in my absence, she has been trying to become the dominant dragon."

April warbled and lifted her head, her eyes forlorn. "She did the same whilst you were so busy."

"The audacity! She is staff. You are my Friend. She should not believe she is dominant over you. A governess is generally above the lower staff, but not above the family. You, my dear, are family."

April's voice turned very soft. "I have wondered."

"I am sorry and appalled I did not see it sooner. You shall spend as much time with Anne as you like. Nanny has no right to keep you from my daughter nor any room in the house. I will not have such a dragon in my house."

"I can help your hatchling."

Junior Keeper. But now was not the time to insist on that.

"I can help her to sleep with my song."

"That would be welcome indeed."

"And I will help her learn to hear fairy dragon

voices and—"

"Of course you will, and you should. I am your Friend. I want Anne to be your Friend, too."

April cuddled into her hand, tension leaving her posture.

"Now, allow me to make you some tea to enjoy with your jam, and I shall pay a visit to the nursery." No staff dragon would ever claim dominance over her Friend again.

Putting on her cloak before confronting Nanny had been a good idea. Sometimes it was necessary to be bigger in order to get the point across.

Who knew all—absolutely every one of the family and staff dragons—would turn up to see the spectacle, though? Unfortunately, that only spoke to the degree of disorder that had come to plague the household in her absence. Perhaps she should not have placed so much trust in the Order's choice of her personal staff.

Nanny's ego was so bruised, she tendered her resignation immediately and quit Darcy House minutes later. It was difficult to repine her departure, considering it was far easier than sacking her. The Order would probably not be pleased, though.

She needed to tell Mary again just how welcome her assistance with little Anne would be. Tomorrow they would sort out how best she could be accommodated near the nursery.

For tonight, though, Anne's cradle and the rocking chair that Lady Anne Darcy had loved would be in Elizabeth's chamber.

Little Anne snuggled into the crook of her arm as

April sang sweetly from her basket. Elizabeth sank into the rocking chair amidst the lavender fragrance and flowered paper hangings. Only Darcy's presence could have made this any better.

Was it possible? Did Anne seem more at peace now than before? Could she have sensed Nanny's dominance struggle and have been responding to it? Could that have been causing some of her sleeplessness?

Tomorrow was soon enough to ponder that.

Tonight was for gazing into her daughter's face in wonder. How close had she been to losing that opportunity forever? She swallowed hard and blinked hard. That must not happen again.

It was tempting to simply give up serving the Order to accomplish that. Tempting, but short-sighted and wrong. Whether or not she worked with the Order, the state of the Dragon State was frayed and threadbare. Whether she wanted it or not, her life was inextricably locked with dragons.

Quitting would not change any of that. The best chance for Anne to have a peaceful future with dragons was for her to continue doing what she did.

Perhaps with some modifications.

But that, too, was for tomorrow—

A soft rap at her door. "Lady Elizabeth, a caller."

Who would be calling now?

The door swung open and a cane thumped softly on the carpet.

Papa? What was he doing here?

Mary peeked in over his shoulder and nodded. Mary? Why? She knew …

"I trust your journey back from Portsmouth was not unpleasant." Papa shuffled in, hunched and awkward in ways she had not recalled him being.

"You will forgive me for not rising. Anne is asleep. April is in the basket on the mantel."

He nodded and continued his slow shuffle toward her. "May I sit down?" He pointed to the floral arm-chair, the only chair in the room with arms solid enough for him to push against to stand again.

"Please do."

Anne stirred as though she might awaken, but she sighed and settled down.

He inched his way down into the chair and stared into the fireplace. "Kitty and your Mother are at the Bingleys' now. Jane has made an introduction for your sister. Their latest letters suggest the new ac-quaintance may have some promise. At the very least, Kitty is quite content in her new situation."

"I am happy for her."

"They will be gone for some time, I believe."

"It must be a relief for you not to have to worry about them in London company." The edge in her voice—hiding her true feelings was not her long suit.

"I do not blame you for being bitter. I should have sent them to stay at the Bingleys' for Twelfth Night and after."

"I am not bitter."

"As you say. But you are angry."

Yes, she was, and she had every right, every reason to be, and if he thought he was going to shame her out of it ... "What did you come for, Papa? You can see: I am here, and I am well. Anne is well. April is healing admirably. Darcy was well when he left with Leander Salt for Pemberley, and I have received daily intelligence that he continues to be so. He told me of your assistance in researching the forest wyrms, and I am grateful. If you wish to interview them, they are staying with the Gardiners. I am certain they would be happy to speak with you." Pray that would satisfy him.

He stared into the fire for a long time, expression unchanged. "All I wanted was to see you."

"Why?"

"I suppose I deserve that. I understand why you would say that."

She bit her lip. The urge to contradict, to argue was so strong. "What do you understand?"

"I never told you how proud I was of you when you were appointed as the Dragon Sage. I should have told you."

She shrugged carefully, not to disturb Anne. It would have been nice, but it hardly mattered now.

"I was wrong not to appreciate all that you are, to ignore your unique bond with dragons, no matter how inconvenient it might have been for me."

"I know I have been a great inconvenience to you." Those words sounded bitter.

They were bitter.

"But you should not have been … I should never have seen you as inconvenient. It was foolish, short-sighted, narrow-minded of me to try to force you to be like other dragon-hearing girls."

"It is good of you to say that now." It was, truly it was. But why was he saying that now? What did he want from her? She had already promised him access to the wyrms.

"It is not just words. I do mean it. I am sorry."

Had he ever spoken those words before? Did he even know what they meant? "I hardly know what to say."

"Most women would be happy for the apology and accept it without question." He chuckled. "But most women are not you. Dragons are cautious with apologies under the best of circumstances. And they are not apt to be content with mere words. I understand."

Such an unusual admission from him.

"I cannot give back those things you have lost because of me. Your Cotillion, the chance to have truly come out and mix in good Blue Order Society, to make certain choices for yourself ... so many things."

Had he any idea how many there were?

"You have done quite well without them, though, so there is that, I suppose."

Of course, it was all perfectly justified by the outcome. Why was he bothering ...

"But it is not much, to be sure." He turned and caught her eyes.

Were those tears on his cheeks?

Merciful heavens!

"I hope, perhaps, that you and I might be able ... that you would be willing ... perhaps, to work together with me ... perhaps on some writing?"

"The Order assigned Drew as your scribe. I cannot—"

"That's not what I mean. Not for you to write for me, but with me. A monograph, written together?"

She looked him directly in the eye. There was a hope, an earnestness there, new and unfamiliar. Was it worth the risk?

She had missed him.

After everything that had happened, Longbourn had become her friend again. Perhaps he was not the only one who could change.

"What do you know about Nunnington? There are some forest wryms who have a very interesting story to tell."

27
Chapter

CHEERFUL MORNING SUN forced Darcy's eyes open. He was in his own room—filled with the familiar lingering scents of sandalwood and lavender. His own bed! How long it had been since he had awoken there! He reached to the other side of the bed.

Empty!

No, that was not possible. Could all of that have been a dream? His heartbeat grew loud, deafening in his ears.

"Good morning. You have been quite the layabed have you not? It is nearly seven o'clock."

Elizabeth!

Thank heavens!

He propped himself on his elbow, breathing once more, and looked in the direction of her voice. His favorite voice.

The one he had thought he might never hear again.

Sunbeams bathed her as she sat near the window, in Mother's rocking chair, little Anne in her arms. "How very well Anne slept last night. She only woke once."

Wrapping his dressing gown around himself, he padded toward them. The carpet soft under his feet and the polished paneling on the walls gentle on his eyes. Was it possible everything could feel so utterly right?

Elizabeth smiled up at him, hair mussed, night-dress and dressing gown rumpled. In short, all things perfectly lovely. Little Anne grasped the edge of Elizabeth's sleeve in her chubby fist, eyes twinkling. How she looked like her mother.

A flawless tableau.

"She seems absolutely content this morning." Darcy knelt beside them, offering his finger for Anne to clutch.

She grabbed it, and his heart along with it, giggling.

"Perhaps I am assuming too much, but it seems she is happier now that Nanny is out of the house." Elizabeth shrugged.

"I am not sorry to learn she is gone. She and I had words while … while Anne stayed at the Blue Order. I am not surprised she would have, again, forgotten her place in the dominance hierarchy."

Elizabeth laughed, softly at first, then blooming into a deep, soulful melody. "I wonder how many homes in England consider the dominance hierarchy as part of household management?"

It was hardly a ridiculous question. "It is a little

odd, I suppose, but perhaps there are those which would run more smoothly if they did."

"Pray, do not suggest I write a monograph on that, too! No matter how excellent an idea it is—actually, it is a very good one. But have you any idea—the list I have of monographs I need to write!"

"You said it, not I. But you are right, it is an excellent notion. We should see Lady Astrid about finding you a secretary very soon. I am sure it would help you to get to all the writing you want to accomplish. Drew has helped your father—"

"About Papa."

Darcy pulled a nearby footstool close and sat. "What happened?" Pray the man had not done anything stupid!

"He came to the house just after I returned."

"And? Do not keep me in suspense. I have had enough of that during the last few weeks to last a lifetime."

"I do not quite know what to make of it." She leaned down to kiss the top of Anne's head. "He apologized."

"Ordinarily, that is considered a good thing. Is it not? Or has it gone out of fashion since I was last informed?" Pray let Bennet not have utterly stuffed it up.

"I suppose, but it is just so very unexpected. I am not quite sure if I can trust it. Or do you think I am judging him too harshly?"

"I will not try to tell you what to do, but when he came to me and apprised me that he had sent your mother and sister away so that he might do what he could to help in your recovery, his actions spoke louder than his words."

"He did not tell me why he had sent them off. I had no idea. I thought it was merely to assist in seeing Kitty married off."

"I heard the words straight from him. I think he came directly to the Order after sending them off. Understand, I am not telling you this to convince you of anything. It just seems you should know the full story."

"There is that, I suppose." She lifted her chin and stared out the window. "It is just …"

"A very great deal of unpleasantness has come and gone and it is not easy to believe it is at an end?"

She pressed her lips hard, nodding. Were those tears in her eyes? "He asked that we might write something together."

"Together? That is new, is it not?"

"Quite. At first it sounded as a means to have me work for him, but I think it was genuine. I suggested that a report on the situation at Nunnington might be a useful endeavor."

A truly draconic suggestion. She was nothing if not true to herself. "So controversial a situation? When the wyrms' tale becomes known, you know the stir it will create."

"Who better to help pen those documents then, than a revered historian with a reputation of avoiding controversy? Will that not lend credence to the tale?"

"That could put you two at odds once more. Are you certain that is what you want?"

"I do not want to be at odds with him. You are right. But neither do I wish to waste time writing pretty memoires and genealogies that obscure the truth." She shifted uneasily. "I have been sorely reminded of how uncertain the future is. Dragon Keeping is difficult, dragons are difficult, and to pretend otherwise has not served the Order well. It will not survive if we do not change. That is more important to me than Papa's feelings, or I suppose even my own."

Such a world little Anne was heir to. "I hope to find the Council in agreement with you."

"Those dragons are wise and sensible. I am certain they will."

"I meant the men, not the dragons." He chuckled despite her glower. "I hope that Cownt Matlock has been granted status as Grand Dug. So many things would be improved by his direct oversight."

"Grand Dug? He means to be made Grand Dug?" Her face colored and she nearly jumped to her feet, pausing only when Anne threatened to fuss. "Who came up with such a plan? It must have been Lord Matlock, no doubt. Did they actually give any thought to the complexities of such a maneuver? Even if Cownt Matlock is the most dominant dragon after Londinium and Cornwall, some will take offense that he could be given even a form of dominance over Cornwall."

"Led by Cornwall himself, I would expect." He laid his hand on her shoulder.

She shuddered just a little. How few knew what the encounters with that particular angry dragon had actually cost her. Cornwall would probably never forgive the insult she dealt him. Such unforgiveness was a bitter pill to her whom all dragons loved.

"This is not a good plan. Cornwall is not happy with the Order as it is. To further press him this way seems foolhardy."

"I fear there are a great many who are discontent right now. With the Order, with its members, and with me."

"It is not as though you did not go to Pemberley and interview the dragons there as you were asked."

"Perhaps. But even their ire toward me pales in comparison to Longbourn and Kellynch taking matters into their own talons and exacting justice on the smugglers."

"The dragons will understand ..."

"But the men might not."

"Remember, it happened beyond the pale of the Blue Order. The Order refused to negotiate with the sea dragons; by their actions, they declared it was not Blue Order territory."

"It is difficult to see how that makes a difference."

"It makes all the difference." She passed Anne to him and stood, the air around her virtually crackling. "Next to dominance, territory is of paramount importance to major dragons. The rules that govern a territory must be obeyed or the dragon holding the territory has rights of enforcement. The sea has no such regulations. Kellynch and Longbourn did not violate any Blue Order laws."

"I believe you, but the Council might be more difficult to convince."

In the deepest basement of the Order offices, Cownt Matlock, Barwines Chudleigh ,and Barwin Dunbrook sat beside Uncle Matlock, Lord Chudleigh, Lord Dunbrook, and Lord Torrington, amidst a hastily arranged collection of chairs and tables. They stared across the cavernous main courtroom at Darcy, Wentworth, Longbourn, and Kellynch, somber and subdued as only major dragons could be.

Usually, the courtroom configurations were

planned carefully, weeks in advance and reviewed by a special team, headed by Baron and Barwines Chudleigh. Typically, plans had to be adjusted multiple times before all human and dragon sensibilities could be accommodated.

No such preparations had been laid for this meeting.

Perhaps that was why Vicontes Torrington had declined to attend, as was often her wont. All told, it was just as well. Basilisks' temperaments did not lend them to be well disposed to large meetings, no matter how carefully arranged.

The courtroom was far too large for this proceeding, but no other room in the offices could accommodate a firedrake, an amphithere, a major drake, a wyvern and a marine wyrm. So many wings and tails!

Still, though, it felt strange, even oppressive for the echoing chamber on the lowest level of the Order and the levels of galleries above it, to be so empty. Only a fraction of the usual number of torches lit the space, creating odd, flickering shadows and swaths of darkness, haunting and even a little threatening.

A long stone table, bearing the Sea Lion's figurehead, separated the council from their … interviewees. That was the polite term they used.

Neither Longbourn nor Kellynch seemed to find it appropriate.

"Darcy," Uncle Matlock cleared his throat, a sound quickly lost in the vast darkness of the soaring ceiling. "Which one of you sent the dragons back to find the Sea Lion?"

Longbourn rose to his feet and spread his wings, snorting and scratching the floor with his talons. "I take umbrage at the implication that either of us would be taking orders to be sent here or there by anyone, much less by a man not my Keeper."

Kellynch rose up, his head level with Longbourn's. "It is insulting to believe that you think us some sort of minions."

Barwines Chudleigh slithered forward, her head above Kellynch's, spectacular feathered wings spread. No winged dragon sported wings as stunning as an amphithere's. "There wassss no intention to insult. The question was poorly phrased." She turned back to glower at Uncle Matlock. "You both worked to-gether on the task?"

"No, we did not." Kellynch glanced at Longbourn, who planted his foot hard as though to punctuate the statement.

What?

Wentworth started and looked from the dragons to Darcy, forehead knit. So Kellynch had told him nothing, either.

What was it about courtrooms and dragons that always inspired some form of drama?

"Then which one of you was responsible for sink-ing the Sea Lion?" Lord Torrington, wrinkled and scowling, his deep-set beady eyes glittering with sharp intelligence, leveled a derisive stare. How like his Dragon Mate he was. Coincidence or contagion, it was difficult to tell.

"Neither." Longbourn bugled. The sound rever-berated painfully from one side of the courtroom to the other. Was he enjoying taunting the council? It was a dangerous game at best.

"How was the ship sunk?" Barwin Dunbrook growled, stopping just short of a snarl.

"Sea dragons," Longbourn said.

"A marine wyrm, a pod of hippocampus and some number of serpent-whales. I lost count. Together they tore a rather substantial hole in the hull. They left then and allowed the natural course of events to take place." Kellynch tossed his head in a noncommittal sort of way.

"And you did nothing to protect the crew from the draconic assault?" Matlock pounded the table with his fist. "Your oath to the Blue Order demands—"

"The oath only applies to Blue Order territory. You refused to open talks with the sea dragons, which clearly means that the oceans are not Blue Order territory." Kellynch clapped his jaws hard.

"Technically, we were trespassing in their territory." Longbourn stepped forward, a bold and dangerous move in the presence of dominant dragons. "It was gracious of them to grant us passage. We had neither right nor authority to intervene in their actions."

Nor the desire, it seemed. But it would not help to mention that.

Uncle Matlock turned an unhealthy shade of red, then puce. "How many other vessels are in danger now that they have the notion to openly attack—"

"Kidnappers and smugglers who have been harrying them and trying to capture them for quite some time. It was high time they defended themselves." Longbourn shifted his weight from side to side and growled.

"Consider it, if you will, a demonstration of good will from those who would be affiliated with us?" The tip of Kellynch's tail flicked. Was that a good sign or not? Wyrm-type posture language was a little difficult to understand.

"Affiliated?" Baron Dunbrook's gunfire voice ricocheted through the courtroom. "They have violated the primary tenets of the Pendragon treaty, and now they seem to want to be affiliated with it, with us? That is simply not possible. They are a danger to everything we stand for. Actions must be taken—"

"Silence." Cownt Matlock rose and thundered around the table, approaching Kellynch and Longbourn, threateningly close, looming as only a firedrake could. "If what they say is true …" He stepped in front of Kellynch and Longbourn, gazing down upon them, looking in their eyes, sniffing like tatzelwurms often did. "And I believe it is, the sea dragons have come together to obey a draconic principle older than the Pendragon accords."

"What are you talking about? I have heard of no such thing." Uncle Matlock stammered.

Governing principles older than the Order? There were no such things.

Cownt Matlock, Barwines Chudleigh and Barwin Dunbrook exchanged a conversation in glances, wing postures and tail twitches. Elizabeth could probably have made sense of it.

"It is something that has never been part of the Blue Order documents, not a thing that men ever needed to know," Matlock thundered.

"I am still not certain that they do." Dunbrook pawed the floor, his deep-grey hide blending with the grey stone walls and shadows, lending him a strange, ethereal sort of look.

"Humansss are too fragile for them not to know." Chudleigh wove from side to side in a mesmerizing dance.

"What are you talking about?" Uncle Matlock looked like he might climb over the table.

Matlock snorted and flapped, swinging his head to and fro, thinking. He smacked his jaws several times and huffed. Resigned? "There are occasionally dragons hatched who have rare understanding, insight or wisdom. There is not an equivalent warm-blooded word. A significant sort of knowing. Not always a large dragon either. Their insight is sufficient to permit them a special kind of dominance and value among us. It is an unspoken agreement among all dragons that those rare creatures are protected and allowed liberties among us that others are not. The dragon who crafted the Pendragon accords with Uther was one such dragon. The Dragon Sage is another."

"But she is a warm-blood, not a dragon." Baron Dunbrook nearly jumped from his seat, eyes bulging.

"It does not matter. She is one of those special ones to us. What the sea dragons did was an act of honor toward the dragons of the Order, not an act of war. We must begin discussions with them soon. Kellynch, you and your Keeper—"

"Keepers, Cownt Matlock. I have two Keepers." Kellynch glanced at Wentworth, who stood.

Interesting. Was Lady Wentworth taking cues from Elizabeth?

What would that mean to the Order?

"I would be honored to accept the charge." Wentworth bowed from his shoulders.

"At the next Conclave, Longbourn and Kellynch,

you both will be recognized for your efforts on behalf of the Sage." Matlock rose up on his back legs, towering above them all.

"None of their actions were sanctioned!" Torrington sprang to his feet. He looked like he might jump to the table as he had seen Elizabeth once do. It probably would not go well for him. "To recognize such actions…"

"Will do much to quell the current discontent. Dragons should be honored for acting like dragons, not warm-bloods. It is time the Order recognized this. Perhaps the Sage can help you understand. We are finished here." Cownt Matlock turned his back and thundered toward the tunnels, Chudleigh and Dunbrook just behind.

An hour later, a footman found Darcy in the reading room, comfortably hiding among those humans and dragons bent on losing themselves in a book. The sort of company in which he felt most at home. A vague tension hung in the room, more from the dragons than the human occupants, almost as though they could sense something important had been happening in the courtroom below.

Among the bookcases and curiosity cabinets that lined every wall, a shelf there had been dedicated to Elizabeth's monographs. He thumbed through the volume on hoarding hunger. Her voice was so very clear in those pages. An absolute pleasure to read in comparison to most Blue Order tomes, of which "ponderous" was a compliment.

He replaced the monograph on the shelf and followed the footman to Uncle Matlock's office. It was not as though he did not know the way, but it was an official summons, after all, and protocols had to be followed.

A human form of dominance?

Probably.

The footman opened the great carved door bearing the Order's seal and Darcy stepped inside. Only sunlight through the frosted windows lit the room, sufficient for now, assuming no one was going to do any heavy reading.

Uncle Matlock looked up from his paper-strewn desk and pointed to a chair clearly set in place for Darcy's use. Somehow Uncle was still able to draw up that small-boy-in-trouble feeling out of the distant past and make it entirely fresh and new.

And tiresome.

"Pray congratulate Matlock on his new status as Grand Dug." Darcy sat down. A risky play, making that declaration, but baring one's teeth early was sometimes effective.

Heavens, that was a draconic strategy.

And it made sense.

Uncle grunted. "Do not speak of that. We would just as soon not have too much attention placed on that change. It was just a legal formality to continue the practice as it has been done for quite some time. I am rather surprised that you noticed his new status so quickly. It must be Elizabeth's influence."

Interesting.

"Are my reports from Derbyshire satisfactory?"

"They will do." Uncle pushed a pile of papers aside and looked at him. "You do understand the meaning of the word 'immediately,' do you not?"

"Yes, sir, I do."

"And yet you chose—"

"I chose to think like a dragon and act accordingly."

Matlock jumped from his seat snarling. "I take that from your wife, as a fellow officer of the Order, but from you, I do not."

So Cownt Matlock's set-down had affected him as badly as Darcy had feared.

"What, precisely, am I to understand from that?" Darcy slowly stood.

"When you are given a directive from me, you are to follow it."

"I gave you the reports you asked for. And arguably, no later than you would otherwise have had them, thanks to young Leander Salt and his team. He learned well from his father."

"Something which you could not have known would be available to you when you went off on your ill-advised quest."

"Ill-advised?" Oh, how he wanted to slam his fist on the desk. "My wife, the boy and the dragon have all been returned safely. We are on the way to establishing a maritime extension the Order never thought possible. I hardly consider that ill-advised."

"You flew off on the advice of a fairy dragon."

"Would you have considered it less ill-advised if the information had come from perhaps, Walker? Or mayhap one of the cockatrice guard?"

"Cockatrice are noble, respectable dragons."

"But fairy dragons are not?" Darcy crossed his arms over his chest and stood a little straighter.

"Dammit, Darcy, I did not bring you in to discuss fairy dragons."

"What, sir, did you call me here for?"

Uncle Matlock dropped back into this seat. "Were

you paying attention to what was said in the court room?"

"I would like to believe so, but there were a great many things said. To which are you referring?" Darcy returned to his chair.

Uncle Matlock snarled again. "Your wife, Darcy, your wife."

"I admit the dragon's remarks caught me rather by surprise." That was putting it mildly.

"Do you understand the implications of what was said?"

Did Matlock think he was an idiot? "Perhaps it would be best if you were to tell me what you heard. Clearly, you are most alarmed."

"Alarmed does not begin to describe it. What happened in there threatens to disrupt the Order and perhaps dragon-human relations as we know them."

"Disrupt the Order? I am not certain that is what I heard. Perhaps you misunderstand?"

"I hardly think so. Cownt, or rather Grand Dug, Matlock essentially declared your wife a dragon, claimed her as one of their own."

"It seems that would be a good thing, would it not?" So, he had married a warm-blooded dragon. That was a concept to wrap his mind around, was it not? What did that mean for Anne?

"Perhaps. If it were anyone else but her."

Darcy's thoughts crashed into one another like sheep crammed together in a pen, coming to a complete, chaotic stop. "Excuse me?"

"Your wife is impulsive, unpredictable, and rash. It is impossible to know what she is going to do next and even more impossible to control her."

"How is that so very different from anyone else?"

"Because not everyone has the ear of the dragons and claims to speak for them. You have seen as well as I how she plunges into situations in which she has no business. How easily she could be perceived to speak for us when she has no authority to do so."

"She would never do such a thing."

"What of those forest wyrms to whom she has promised justice—"

"She is doing what any member of the Order should do. Those wyrms are the victims of a serious violation of the law. Sir."

"They are very minor dragons, dragons without Friends. Essentially wild—"

"No, sir, they are not. Since they have become Friends with Joshua Gardiner, it is clear that they were not wild hatched. Thus, they are fully protected by the Accords. That makes Nunnington a criminal. Full stop." No, he could not be implying …

"Nunnington is a major dragon. Do you know how many cases there are of major dragons prosecuted for such a transgression, particularly involving minor dragons without a Friend at the time?"

"Are you implying that major dragons do not have to abide by the rules of peaceful coexistence as outlined in the Accords?"

"Do you think prosecuting Nunnington is going to improve the attitudes of the major dragons toward the Order? I can tell you with certainty, it will not. Show them one more place where their supremacy is challenged, and we may have a complete breakdown of the Accords. The risk is immense."

"Have you considered the risk of the minor dragons giving up on the Accords if they believe they are not protected? They may not be as powerful as major dragons, but they are far more numerous. Do you think we would be able to stop a rebellion from them?"

"Nonsense—" Uncle Matlock paused and grimaced. Good, he was thinking. For all his bluster, he would think on the matter for quite some time. That was hopeful. "There is still a network of smugglers dealing in all things draconic. Neither major nor minor dragon is safe from that."

"That is to say, the Order is beset from all sides."

"Precisely. And now we have a single member for whom any threat to her wellbeing could utterly destabilize the system, possibly destroying the possibility of restoring any sort of balance to the Order! Have you any idea how dangerous that is?" Uncle Matlock had turned that unhealthy color again.

"Who but the dragons will know that of her?"

"That does not mean she is safe, you know. Your forest wyrms have already proven that dragons can ally themselves with their enemies. Consider, Cornwall has a grudge against her."

"He would not …" The words caught in his suddenly constricted throat.

"I wish I could be certain. You have no idea how much I would like that." Uncle Matlock thumbed several papers on his desk.

"You have read my reports. Attitudes have improved with the assurance she has been returned."

"Indeed. But there are those who will need to see her for themselves. She will have to travel, and travel is dangerous."

"But little Anne—"

Uncle Matlock raised his hand. "It is unfortunate. But the Sage has brought this on herself. It seems only her reassurances will satisfy the dragons. She must travel and you must accompany her for her protection. What you do with the baby is entirely at your discretion."

"She is my wife. Of course I will protect her." A wave of dizziness assaulted him. What would this mean?

"Not only from those against the Blue Order, you know. You must somehow protect her from herself. She must be brought under better regulation, for her own protection and the good of the Order. You are the only one who can do it. I do not envy you the task."

Epilogue

PEMBERLEY, HER BRIGHT red hide shining from a fresh oiling, trumpeted as Elizabeth emerged from the dragon tunnels. "Come in, come in. I show you!"

She waddled toward Elizabeth from the far side of the guest dragon lair, the largest the Order offices had to offer. It would be some time before she lost her baby ungainliness despite having learned, from Rosings and Matlock, to spit—not breathe!—fire and, from Chudleigh, to fly —well, more like flap and glide, but she had managed to become airborne and that was all that counted in her mind.

Large enough for a high-ranking firedrake, the more or less round room boasted rough-hewn walls and a mostly smooth limestone floor. Not impressive to warm-bloods but pleasing to large dragons. Wall torches lit the space, their distinct smoky-oily scent hanging in the slightly stale air. Several candelabras stood among the torches, probably for the human guests, who usually found them more aesthetically pleasing than torches. Bedding and other articles of comfort specific to the guest dragon were absent, leaving a great deal of somewhat awkward open space.

Pemberley ran back and forth, from Elizabeth, and April who was napping under the collar of her spencer, to Lady Wentworth to Barwines Chudleigh and Cowntess Rosings. The latter had only recently arrived in London in anticipation of the Cotillion.

Technically, the guest lair had been assigned to Rosings, not Pemberley. How gracious she had been to permit her offspring to use the space to host her event.

Uncommonly gracious.

Undraconicly gracious.

And that look Rosings and Chudleigh just shared? It was more than an acknowledgement formal greetings were not currently required. No. There was something more. Was Rosings' red hide just a touch brighter than usual, and freshly oiled? Chudleigh's wings shone as though freshly preened for the event.

Odd, very odd.

An exceptionally large, yellow-painted tea table with matching chairs had been brought in and set up in the middle of the lair. Stylized blue Eastern dragons flew around the circumference of the tabletop. How very strange it looked amidst the unfinished stone walls and floors. Between the torches and candles, one might just be able to do needlework in so much light. Certainly not an arrangement the dragons would have crafted without a purpose.

"Next time, little Keeper will come, too?" Pemberley shuffled up, flapping excitedly.

"It was kind of you to invite her, but perhaps she needs to be out of leading strings before she can attend a tea party." She scratched under Pemberley's ever-itchy chin.

"Nanny-dragon really gone now?" Pemberley's dark eyes widened as though with hope.

"Why did you not tell me you did not like her?" Elizabeth crouched, taking Pemberley's face in her hands.

"Thought you liked her."

"You must always tell me when you think something is wrong. And especially if there is someone, man or dragon, in your territory that you do not like."

"I will." Pemberley hung her head, just a little.

Elizabeth kissed the top of her head ridge.

"Look! Look!" Pemberley bounced toward the tunnel where two maids and a footman were bringing in the elements of an elaborate tea service. A silver urn for water; Blue Order china, white with a blue rendition of the Order's seal in the center, edged with a gold stripe; platters of delicacies made mostly for human tastes; but wait, no, the pile of roasted goose and turkey legs was clearly for the dragons.

"What are those?" Anne nodded her head toward the maid carrying a tray with several exceptionally large tankards made of the same Blue Order china with pewter lids.

"Despite looking like they belong in a pub, those are dragon tea cups, of Castordale's design." Elizabeth winked. "They are very clever really. Since he is a snake-type without any sort of appendage to grasp with, they are modified to be used that way. Now that I think of it, I was with him the first time I had tea with a major dragon. April of course likes tea with honey, so I would have it with her before then, but it is a different experience with a major dragon."

Such a peculiar look on Anne's face. She giggled, then covered her face with her hands and laughed. "Pray forgive me. That just gave me the most amusing thought! Growing up with Lady Russell—I had tea with a dragon many times and never even knew. Of course, she was able to manage the use of a standard teacup with the odd little fingers at the end of her wings. But still …"

"Entertaining dragons unawares, indeed." Elizabeth chuckled. How good it was to laugh again.

"You happy!" Pemberley bounded up, almost going airborne as she flapped. "I make happy you?"

"I am always happy to be with you." She caught Pemberley in a brief hug.

An improper show of emotion, to be sure, but if the dragons did not object, and certainly Anne did not, then why deny Pemberley and herself the pleasure?

"Come, come," Rosings lumbered up behind Pemberley—it was difficult for a dragon her size to walk gracefully in such a relatively confined space.

"Yes, do come and ssssit down, it is time for tea." Chudleigh extended her wings full length around the tea table. Resplendent, multicolored feathers glinted in the torchlight. Stunning, utterly stunning.

Anne gasped.

"An amphithere in her full glory is spectacular, is she not?" Elizabeth whispered.

"I suppose for a snake-type, she is," Rosings sniffed and ushered them toward the table. How truly charitable of her to allow a compliment to a less-dominant dragon in her presence.

What had come over them?

And why were there seven chairs at the tea table?

A quick glance at Anne revealed she had no idea either.

"Ssssit here," Chudleigh indicated the two chairs closest to her, oddly separated from the others.

Pemberley plodded after them and sat on the floor beside Elizabeth. She was big enough now that she could quite comfortably reach the dragon cup set before her.

Pemberley was drinking tea now? When had that happened, and why did she not know? Had she been neglecting the drakling?

Perhaps she was spending too much time away. That would have to be remedied.

A footman appeared at the mouth of the tunnels, waiting, at attention, to be recognized.

Rosings ignored him in the way dragons ignored irritating creatures.

How long would she keep him waiting? Usually a count of ten was enough to establish Rosings' disdain.

What did a count of twenty mean?

Chudleigh pointed her wing at the footman.

He cleared his throat, "The Cotillion Board has arrived." He stepped aside.

No wonder he seemed so uncomfortable. What a very strange way to announce them. ... Wait, what? The Cotillion Board?

Anne's face lost a little color as she slipped her chair back a mite and stood.

Rosings pulled herself up to her full height and glowered. Five ladies stepped out of the tunnel and stared back stupidly.

Who had they expected to see at a dragon's tea party if not dragons?

"Perhaps you are unaware of how to properly greet a Cowntess. Lady Elizabeth, Lady Wentworth, might you be so good as to demonstrate the proper etiquette?" Rosings grumbled with disdain.

Elizabeth bit her tongue, hard, and sidled between the table and Chudleigh to join the warm-blooded she-dragons—no, she should not think of them thus! Anne followed.

They stepped together in front of the … others …, gathered their skirts and curtsied, knee to floor, bowing their heads until they almost touched the other knee.

Rosings stepped closer and sniffed them both and touched the backs of their necks with her tongue. "Welcome, Lady Sage, Lady Wentworth." She looked expectantly at the she-dragons.

The well-dressed and bejeweled Lady Jersey's and Lady Cowper's eyes bulged, and they blanched. Though they attempted to curtsey, they offered a curtsey to the king, not to dragon ranks. The differences were subtle, but significant. Did they ever greet their Dragon Mates?

Baroness Dunbrook, with her halo of nearly white curls, and Viscountess Torrington, with her glasses perched on the end of her nose, magnifying her expression of distaste, followed suit, slightly more practiced but not happier to be recognizing Rosings' dominance.

"Pray forgive me, Cowntess," the rather porcine Dowager Viscountess Dalrymple curtsied halfway down. "My knees no longer permit—"

"I care nothing for your knees." Rosings growled.

Anne nodded at Elizabeth, and they went to Lady Dalrymple's sides.

"You cannot be serious, she cannot demand …"

"Yes, she can. It will not do to insult her. We will help you up." Anne gently took Lady Dalrymple's elbow.

Grimacing and grunting, she dropped her knee to the ground and bowed her head sufficiently for Rosings.

With both Anne and Elizabeth lifting under her arms, the dowager made it back to her feet, barely.

"You have not greeted Barwines Chudleigh." What was Rosings about?

Elizabeth and Anne curtsied knees to floor and covered their heads with their arms. Best not wait to be asked to demonstrate. Rosings was in quite a temper.

"I cannot do that! I will not." Lady Dalrymple sputtered and stomped back down the tunnel, past the footman, who seemed to be holding his breath, given the color of his face.

"That wassss very rude." Chudleigh hissed, fangs bared. Amphithere fangs, while rarely seen, were most impressive.

The other four mimicked Elizabeth's greeting, missing all the subtlety in the gesture. But they tried.

Chudleigh slithered forth and examined the women, sighing.

How long was she going to make them wait?

A long time.

Chudleigh tapped the back of each lady's neck with the tip of her tail. "You may rise. I will, today, recognize you. Do not appear before me again if you cannot properly perform a ssssimple greeting."

Pemberley seemed to glance at Rosings for permission. After a brief nod, she waddled toward the four ladies. "You come tea now. Sit, sit."

Lady Jersey and Lady Cowper shared startled and slightly offended looks.

"It is an honor to be invited to the Vicontes' first social engagement." Anne curtsied to Pemberley and headed for the table. Hopefully the she-dragons were intelligent enough to follow her lead.

With some hesitation, they curtsied and followed Anne to the table.

Pemberley pressed close to Elizabeth, whispering, "Help me serve tea?"

"Of course. You are doing splendidly. Barwines Chudleigh will be very proud of you." She laid her hand on Pemberley's shoulder as they took their places at the table.

"You like tea?" Pemberley stood up on her hind legs and grasped the teapot with her forepaws.

Lady Jersey gulped. "Ah, yes?"

Pemberley poured the first cup of tea from a rather larger than average teapot, sloshing only a little. "You take?"

Elizabeth took the cup and walked it to Lady Jersey, who looked as though she might refuse it altogether.

It was probably a good thing that the dragon tea-tankards arrived already filled. How large a teapot would be required otherwise?

After the ladies were served, Pemberley took her own draconic cup and sipped with a slight slurp.

A drakling drinking tea should not be so adorable.

What a shame the she-dragons did not appear to appreciate the sight as much.

Rosings lifted her own cup, taking a deep draw of her pungent tea—it smelt much like the blend Castordale preferred—without slurping.

Such manners! Had no one taught the countesses not to stare?

Rosings placed her tea-tankard on the table and lifted her head above Chudleigh's. "The Barwines and I are pleased to announce that Pemberley is sufficiently prepared and will be presented at the Cotillion next month."

What? That was not what had been decided. Rosings would not do this capriciously, though. There must be good reason.

Lady Jersey choked on her tea, while Lady Cowper nearly dropped her cup. But—was it possible?—Lady Torrington smirked?

Why?

Elizabeth patted Pemberley's back between her wings. "I am so proud of you, Pemberley! I know you will do splendidly at your presentation. The rest of the Order will be happy to officially make your acquaintance."

Pemberley bounced from one foot to the other. "I so happy!"

"Pray … pray excuse me, Cowntess, but did I hear you correctly? Pemb…Vicontes Pemberley is to be presented? We have not—that is to say, she is not among the presentations we have planned for." Lady Jersey looked around at the other board members, perhaps looking for support.

Rosings snorted. "Change the plans. What problem is that?"

"But … but … we have been planning for months, we cannot possibly add another—"

"Nonsense!" Rosings stomped hard enough to rattle the table. "You seem to perceive this as a request. It was not. Pemberley, my offspring, will be presented at the Cotillion."

"And I want presented with *her* sisters." Pemberley wound her neck around Elizabeth's waist.

Anne gasped as she locked her gaze with Elizabeth's.

"That should not be sssso difficult, should it?" Chudleigh slithered toward the she-dragons.

"That will not be possible." Was Lady Cowper usually that pale? "They are not ... that is, those the Sage is sponsoring have not demonstrated themselves prepared to be presented."

"That is not what Vicontesssss Torrington told me." Chudleigh brought her wings forward across her chest. "You must be mistaken."

Lady Torrington pressed her lips hard and turned her face aside—trying not to laugh?

Lady Jersey and Lady Cowper turned to Lady Torrington, glowering.

"Do not look at me that way. Torrington does as she will. She decided it would be amusing to test their preparation for herself when she heard of your decisions—"

"To what decision is she referring?" Rosings spread her wings slightly, her voice booming off the walls.

"Presentation to the major dragons is no small thing. We do not want any young lady to risk embarrassment ..." Lady Jersey tried so hard to appear composed.

Did Rosings just roll her eyes? "Torrington has declared that is not an issue. Am I to understand that there was some ... confusion ... as to the Sage's sisters and Lady Wentworth's presentation? Surely they are among the most important debutantes to be presented this year."

"Yes, yes, of course, Cowntess." Lady Cowper bobbed her head so hard it might have fallen off.

"I have request, too. I want *her* to dance at the ball." Pemberley looked up at Elizabeth.

"Of course I will dance at the ball, dearling."

"A minuet? You will dance minuet?" Pemberley's eyes twinkled. Was this part of Rosings' plans?

"What do you know of the minuet?"

"It is a special dance. Important dance. Barwines Chudleigh say most important lady opens the ball with minuet. You open ball."

"Pemberley is right. It would only be appropriate to celebrate your return by having you and Ssssir Fitzwilliam open the ball with your minuet," Chudleigh declared.

Elizabeth gasped and blinked back the burning in her eyes. How did Pemberley know—no, it was Chudleigh. She remembered Elizabeth's only Cotillion. Few knew or remembered she had not even been permitted a minuet. "No, there is no need for that. It would be far too disruptive to the Board's plans."

"Yes, yes," Lady Jersey stammered. "Pray listen to Lady Elizabeth. The order for the minuet has already been established."

"Indeed—" Lady Cowper leaned slightly toward Rosings.

Elizabeth winced. Had she any understanding of the challenge she just offered a far bigger dragon?

Rosings growled until Lady Cowper shrank back,

and still longer after.

"Perhaps we can rearrange the schedule." Lady Dunbrook looked expectantly from Lady Jersey to Lady Cowper and back again, a pleading note in her voice.

Elizabeth swallowed hard. "Truly, it is not—"

"Yes, it is. As needful as Pemberley's presentation." Rosings' tone was more warning than anything else.

Pendragon's bones!

This was not about the Cotillion at all, but about making a statement; a statement about Pemberley, about herself, the Sage, about the state of the Dragon State. Only her exhaustion could explain how she missed such a thing! "Of course, the Cowntess and Barwines are correct. I should be honored to dance—"

"With Keeper, yes?" Pemberley pleaded.

"Of course with Keeper." Elizabeth stroked Pemberley's head as she beamed.

Had the she-dragons ever seen a dragon smile before? Pemberley had the most amazing, genuine smile.

"Very good, very good." Rosings folded her wings across her back. "I look forward, then, to a most memorable Cotillion."

For more dragon lore check out:
JaneAustensDragons.com

Acknowledgments

So many people have helped me along the journey
taking this from an idea to a reality.
Debbie, Diane and, Ruth you are amazing in everying.
Linda, Catherine, Patricia, and Marureen your eagle
eyes are incredible. Your help is worth your weight in
gold!
My dear friend Cathy, my biggest cheerleader, you
have kept me from chickening out more than once!
And my sweet sister Gerri who believed in even those
first attempts that now live in the file drawer!
Thank you!

Other Books by Maria Grace

Jane Austen's Dragons Series:
Pemberley: Mr. Darcy's Dragon
Longbourn: Dragon Entail
Netherfield:Rogue Dragon
A Proper Introduction to Dragons
The Dragons of Kellynch
Kellynch:Dragon Persuasion
Dragons Beyond the Pale

Remember the Past
The Darcy Brothers
Fine Eyes and Pert Opinions

A Jane Austen Regency Life Series:
A Jane Austen Christmas: Regency Christmas Traditions
Courtship and Marriage in Jane Austen's World
How Jane Austen Kept her Cool: An A to Z History of
Georgian Ice Cream

The Queen of Rosings Park Series:
Mistaking Her Character
The Trouble to Check Her
A Less Agreeable Man

Sweet Tea Stories:
A Spot of Sweet Tea: Hopes and Beginnings
Snowbound at Hartfield
A Most Affecionate Mother
Inspriation

Darcy Family Christmas Series:
Darcy and Elizabeth: Christmas 1811
The Darcy's First Christmas
From Admiration to Love
Unexpected Gifts

Given Good Principles Series:
Darcy's Decision
The Future Mrs. Darcy
All the Appearance of Goodness
Twelfth Night at Longbourn

**Behind the Scene Anthologies
(with Austen Variations):**
Pride and Prejudice: Behind the Scenes
Persuasion: Behind the Scenes

Non-fiction Anthologies
Castles, Customs, and Kings Vol. 1
Castles, Customs, and Kings Vol. 2
Putting the Science in Fiction

Available in e-book, audiobook and paperback

Available in paperback, e-book, and audiobook format at
all online bookstores.

❧About the Author

Six-time BRAG Medallion Honoree, #1 Best-selling Historical Fantasy author Maria Grace has her PhD in Educational Psychology and is a 16-year veteran of the university classroom where she taught courses in human growth and development, learning, test development and counseling. None of which have anything to do with her undergraduate studies in economics/sociology/managerial studies/behavior sciences. She pretends to be a mild-mannered writer/cat-lady, but most of her vacations require helmets and waivers or historical costumes, usually not at the same time.

She writes Gaslamp fantasy, historical romance and non-fiction to help justify her research addiction.

She can be contacted at:

author.MariaGrace@gmail.com

Facebook:
http://facebook.com/AuthorMariaGrace

On Amazon.com:
http://amazon.com/author/mariagrace

Random Bits of Fascination
(http://RandomBitsofFascination.com)

Austen Variations (http://AustenVariations.com)

White Soup Press (http://whitesouppress.com/)

On Twitter @WriteMariaGrace

On Pinterest: http://pinterest.com/mariagrace423/